Ann Swinfen spent her childhood partly on the east coast of America and partly in England. She read Classics and Mathematics at Oxford, where she married a fellow undergraduate. While bringing up t   or an MSc in Mathematics and  ad a variety of jobs, including t   ance journalist and software de   as a manager in the computer   e job to concentrate on her writing.   ast of Scotland with her husband, vice-principal of Dundee University.

Her previous publications include many academic and technical articles, and one book of literary criticism, *In Defence of Fantasy*. Her previous novels, *The Anniversary* and *The Travellers*, are available in Arrow paperback.

Praise for *The Anniversary*:

'not easy to set down' Rosamunde Pilcher

'a poignant tapestry of loves, losses, confrontations and family relationships in this warm, penetrating portrait of an era' *Woman's Realm*

'A gem of a book' *Good Book Guide*

Praise for *The Travellers*:

'an original and compelling novel from the author of the highly praised *The Anniversary*' *Publishing News*

'I enjoyed this serious, scrupulous novel . . . a novel of character . . . [and] a suspense story in which present and past mysteries are gradually explained' Jessica Mann, *Sunday Telegraph*

'I very much admired the pace of the story, the changes of place and time, and the echoes and repetitions – things lost and found, and meetings and partings' Penelope Fitzgerald

Also by Ann Swinfen

The Anniversary
The Travellers

A RUNNING TIDE

Ann Swinfen

ARROW

Published by Arrow Books in 1998

1 3 5 7 9 10 8 6 4 2

First published in the United Kingdom in 1998 by Century

Arrow Books Limited
20 Vauxhall Bridge Road, London SW1V 2SA

Random House Australia (Pty) Limited
20 Alfred Street, Milsons Point, Sydney,
New South Wales 2061, Australia

Random House New Zealand Limited
18 Poland Road, Glenfield
Auckland 10, New Zealand

Random House South Africa (Pty) Limited
Endulini, 5a Jubilee Road, Parktown 2193, South Africa

Random House UK Limited Reg. No. 954009

A CIP catalogue record for this book is available from the British Library

ISBN 0 09 922752 5

Typeset by SX Composing, DTP, Rayleigh, Essex
Printed in Great Britain by Cox & Wyman Ltd, Reading, Berks.

For my sister
Marilyn Pettit
with love

Remembering Maine

Acknowledgements

Many people have sustained me during the writing of this book. Tracking down research materials was made easier by the following people: Sheena Alexander, Gordon Dow, Marilyn Pettit, Tanya Swinfen-Wilkes, Pamela Tulloch and Mark Wilkes. Cindy and Graham Forbes checked the MS with the benefit of their own expertise – Cindy as a New Englander and Graham as a farmer. My husband, David, philosophically endured gloom, enthusiasm and scratch meals. My editor, Mary Loring, encouraged and cajoled; my publisher, Kate Parkin, despite her intimidating schedule, gave generously of her time; her assistant, Kate Elton, skilfully gathered up all the pieces and Beth Humphries copy-edited with speed and panache. Working with my cover artist, Sarah Perkins, and my designer, Juliet Rowley, is always a delight. In particular, I feel a great sense of gratitude to my agent, Anthony Goff.

Although I did not know Maine in Tirza's time, it shaped me in childhood, and I have carried the place and the people with me ever since. And ever since have felt uneasy out of sight of the sea.

Everything an Indian does is in a circle, and that is because the Power of the World always works in circles . . . all our power came to us from the sacred hoop of the nation and so long as the hoop was unbroken the people flourished. The flowering tree was the living centre of the hoop, and the circle of the four quarters nourished it. The east gave peace and light, the south gave warmth, the west gave rain, and the north with its cold and mighty wind gave strength and endurance . . . Everying the Power of the World does is done in a circle. The Sky is round and I have heard that the earth is round like a ball and so are all the stars. The Wind, in its greatest power, whirls. Birds make their nests in circles, for theirs is the same religion as ours. The sun comes forth and goes down again in a circle. The moon does the same, and both are round. Even the seasons form a great circle in their changing and always come back again to where they were. The life of a man is a circle from childhood to childhood and so it is in everything where power moves.

Hehakah Sapa (Black Elk)

The air is sharp
The rocks many
The grass little
The winter cold
The summer hot
The gnats in summer biting
And the wolves at midnight howling

Written by an early woman settler in New England

Chapter 1

Prelude
Scotland: Winter 1980

TIRZA LIBBY'S LIFE had rolled her, unexpectedly, into this remote corner of north-west Scotland, and she had grounded here like a sea-washed stone come finally to rest. The very blood in her veins had thickened and slowed. Her island lay a quarter of a mile offshore – west and slightly to the south of the mainland village of Caillard. No more than a few rocky acres thrust up from the sea, it supported a thin layer of salty turf, some gaunt bushes of thorn and whin and broom, and a small central hillock almost bare of vegetation. Once, generations ago, some desperate family had tried to farm here, though it could have supported no more than a handful of sheep, and no crops. The Atlantic gales whipped across its surface, scraping like pumice stone.

Birds, though, felt at home here. The short stretch of cliffs facing the sea rang in the nesting season to the raucous cries of black-headed and herring gulls, and in the small pockets of turf above them puffins made their burrows. Sandpipers swarmed at the tide line. In a corner of level ground at the foot of the hillock, where a meadow might have grown in a kinder place, there were other birds – curlews, thrushes, blackbirds, pied wagtails – so that the seeming desolation was always full of bird cries and the flight of wings across cool, forbidding skies.

The island was nameless, yet its terrain was strong, spare and confident. It had withstood the batterings of wind and tide, of erosion and time. It carried no soft flesh, but its bones were good.

This coast is looped and fretted like some elaborate piece of antique lace – pleated and scoured and pounded into its final form. Fragments of it have broken away and lie strewn for miles offshore: large islands and small, old worn boulders smoothed into submission and jagged rocks around which the tides rip and fling passing ships carelessly. When Tirza first encountered this place it was with a sense of recognition and kinship. The curious nature of the ocean currents brings a climate surprisingly kind for a place so far north, but in winter, when the winds howl down from the polar icecap, even their influence cannot entirely vanquish the cold, and the winter darkness settles over the soul.

It was barely light when the letters arrived, though it was past nine. Tirza sat at her solitary kitchen table drinking a third cup of strong coffee amongst the watery reflections cast into her cottage by the long arm of the sea loch. She knew she drank too much coffee, but since she had given up smoking it provided the impetus to her mornings, which began sluggishly. It was hard to recall childhood when she had sprung from bed eager for the day. Or those times, later, when she had barely slept, alert even in half-sleep for sounds which might threaten danger.

The pile of envelopes landed on the doormat with a heavy thud. More than one letter, then, but probably nothing of interest. Most of her correspondence related to business. She was in no hurry to read it. Angus Maclean, the postman who came over by boat, passed the window and raised a hand to her. Though they had barely exchanged a word for days, he always waved. She could hear the crunch of his boots in the snow as he headed back to the landing stage to take his boat round the headland south of Caillard to the crofts lying on its further shore – easier to reach by boat than over the frost-broken track. Tirza shivered and turned up the collar of her sweatshirt. Cold as the winters were here, and the days pitifully short, she had known much more bitter times in her childhood, and accepted them philosophically.

The letter – lurking amongst several bills, a leaflet on double-glazing, and an envelope bearing the address of her agent in London – was postmarked Edinburgh.

The owner of a gallery in George Street was proposing an

exhibition of her work. A retrospective. Tirza did not think herself quite ripe for a retrospective, but Colin Tennant was persuasive:

I have long been an admirer of your work, from the early days of your photo-journalism during the Vietnam war. The power of your vision remains with me to this day. Your work in Africa and the Indian sub-continent, portraying both traditional life and the disasters of flood and famine, marked another phase in your career. Now that you are living in Scotland and have turned to photographing the dramatic landscape of the Highlands, we seem to be witnessing yet another stage. I would like to propose a two-month exhibition, with a large private view to launch it, major media coverage, and various spin-offs – books, prints and so on.

Damn, she thought. What is Max Prescott thinking of, giving away my private address? She ripped open her agent's letter. As usual it was brief and to the point:

Colin is a very old friend and will do us proud. I've taken the liberty of giving him your address so he can contact you directly. There isn't much time if we are to organise things for an April opening. Frankly, Tirza, you need the publicity. Since you buried yourself up there and started photographing wet sheep, commissions have dried up. You have to earn enough to eat, whatever else you may be up to.

Angrily, Tirza pushed back her chair so that it squealed on the flagstones, and grabbed the telephone from the wall.

'This is *not* the kind of thing I can do with just now, Max,' she shouted into the phone. At the other end of the line she could imagine him holding the receiver away from his ear and raising his elegant eyebrows at his secretary.

'Tirza,' he said, 'I don't see your problem. This will mean a good boost to your income in return for practically no effort on your part. You know you need the money. You'd be a fool to turn this down.' For Max he sounded momentarily almost cross. 'You *would* buy that God-forsaken island and bury yourself up there, but you can't run away from life. Or from your own reputation. Accept graciously and let me look after things.'

3

Tirza bit furiously on her thumbnail.

'What would I have to do?'

'Well, of course, Colin would like you to select the pictures for the exhibition yourself. I've a fair collection in your files here, but you must have hundreds more stored away. He'd like you to be involved in setting things up, if you are willing – deciding whether the display should be chronological or thematic, for example. He'd quite like some of your juvenilia, if you've kept any. You know, family shots...'

Suddenly aware that he was treading on forbidden ground, he hastened on.

'You'd have to attend the private view. And give one or two interviews – national press, radio, TV.'

'I am not,' said Tirza between her teeth, 'going on any TV chat show.'

'OK, OK,' he said soothingly. 'Nothing like that. But the interviews and the launch needn't use more than a week of your time, then you can go back to taking snaps of the wee stag at bay amongst the braw heather.'

This was an area of conflict for them, but Max would not learn to leave it alone.

'Promise you'll think about it at least, eh?'

'Oh, all right,' she said grudgingly. 'I'll think about it. But I'm promising *nothing*.'

She had been planning to take her boat out to the rocky islet just offshore in the bay of her island, as soon as the light was suitable. When she had woken this morning it had seemed the perfect day for it; the sea was relatively calm, the wind light, the sky, filling with dawn light, as clear as it ever would be in winter. There were empty nests on the islet from last summer, and she had an image in her head of how she would shoot them – huge, abandoned, daubed with white bird droppings, but hanging on doggedly to the rough cluster of rocks amongst the breakers. From one angle she could set them off against the light-reflecting sea, from another she would photograph them from slightly below, with the staggering rocks rising up behind. Max declared himself aghast at what she had been doing for the last eighteen months, but she was steadily putting together a collection. It might make a book, but she was still keeping that idea

4

to herself.

A bad case of malaria and dysentery had brought her back two years ago from Bangladesh to recuperate in London, her long-time base. In the past she had never spent more than a few weeks there. Busy developing and printing her films, meeting editors, arranging future commissions with Max, she had never had time to notice the cramped and dingy surroundings of her small flat. Three months of convalescence there, confined, claustrophobic and boring, had determined her to move out of London, and on a whim she had driven up to the west coast of Scotland, urged on by a compulsion to see the Atlantic again and to fill her lungs with its winds.

Fate or coincidence landed her at a small dour-looking hotel at Caillard on the mainland, overlooking a cluster of islands spattered along the mouth of the sea loch. In the bar that night she discovered that the only habitable one, with a house, a dock, a water supply, a telephone line and electricity, was for sale. Had been for two years. Bought by a German brewery owner in pursuit of some romantic dream, it had been provided with these luxuries to make the primitive life tolerable for a man accustomed to the comforts of his Bonn apartment and his Bavarian country house. He had endured his dream for two bitter weeks in spring; by the end of the month the island had been put on the market. After her one visit in May 1978, Tirza bought the island, and moved in two months later.

She untied her boat from the mooring post at the end of the short pier and stepped firmly down amidships. The weight of her cameras, one resting against her hip, the other on her breastbone, always obscurely comforted her. On the rare occasions when she did not carry them, she felt undressed. She dropped the oars into the rowlocks and pulled steadily towards the small island, no more than a lump of broken rock poking up from the waters of the bay. For the short journey across to the mainland she had recently bought a small outboard motor, but she preferred to row whenever she made her way coastwise around her island.

The air was icy, and her hands turned blue despite the rowing. She began to wish she had brought the fingerless gloves she sometimes used for winter work, but it was not worth going

5

back now. She would lose the light, which was so fugitive on these brief February days. The wind was getting up, too. The Atlantic swell was broken by the Outer Hebrides before it penetrated to this narrow neck of the waters – the entrance to a long sea loch reaching miles into the uninhabited mountains up behind the coast. But the ocean swell always lurked, treacherously hidden, as a powerful undertow. When the wind drove on shore, as it was doing today, it gave the waves an extra lift, so they regained some of their diminished strength, heaving and foaming about the dangerous rocks and half-submerged islets which dotted Tirza's bay.

She landed on the bird island and made fast the painter around a spur of rock. It was difficult to find a footing amongst the slippery boulders, but she made her way cautiously, changing between cameras – one loaded with black and white film, one with colour. She worked quickly. War experience had taught her that. You shot your pictures fast or you were dead. She hadn't learned the art of slowing down, of lingering over focus and exposure. She went in fast and trusted her eye.

Even so, it was nearly three o'clock by the time she pushed the boat off again and headed back to the landing stage. Ragged bands of orange lay smeared across the horizon and were flooding upwards, tinting the undersides of the cumulus. She was hungry and aching with the cold, but satisfied with what she had achieved today. Out on the water, amongst the lonely rocks, she was filled with new strength. Tomorrow she'd spend shooting along the mainland cliffs and the next day developing the films.

The letter from the Edinburgh gallery lay accusingly on the kitchen table where she had thrown it down that morning. She tried to ignore it as she opened a tin of soup and made herself a cheese sandwich, but it obtruded itself on her vision, the logo in the letterhead – a stylised Viking ship – staring up at her like an eye. It was an irritation and one which couldn't be ignored, like a stone in her shoe. She was still too tired, too discouraged, to make the effort of an exhibition. Ever since her illness it took more energy to get through a single day than it would once have taken to trek upcountry through the jungle, crossing and recrossing enemy lines. The excitement of those days, the ever-present threat of death, had seemed to empower her. Now, she would leave dirty dishes piled on the draining board for days until she ran out of clean ones, too weary in spirit, more than in body, to fill the sink with hot water.

She pushed the letter away, but it continued to glare at her, naggingly. Max was right. She did need the cash. It had been a crazy extravagance, buying the island. It had used all the money from the sale of the remaining ten years' lease of her London flat, and most of her savings as well. Since moving to Scotland she had had almost no income, apart from an occasional fee for one or other of her more famous pictures. And before that she hadn't worked for nearly six months, although the income from the Bangladesh piece had tided her over. Now she was living off capital, and it was running out fast.

With a sigh, Tirza poured herself a small shot of whisky. She was still feeling cold, and it would be colder still in her photographic store. The white-washed outbuilding, with its massive stone walls, stood separate from the cottage and had probably once been a small barn. The German brewer had made it over into a wine-store, freshly painted and fitted out with shelves and shelves of wine racks. Tirza could not imagine how he had supposed he was going to consume so many bottles out here on this remote coast, in a cottage which would barely hold three people. She had torn out the wine racks but retained the shelving. It now held rows of box files – the harvest of her life's work.

She switched on the light, closed the door against the darkness and the wind, and set her glass down on the shelf just inside the door. Conditions were ideal here for the storage of her prints. The small building was cool and dry, although she had taken the precaution of packing sachets of silica gel amongst the files. She did not keep her negatives here. They were stored in controlled conditions on the premises of a major London photographer. She had known Jimmy and Edna Kelansky for years. They had facilities she did not, and kept her negatives in store for a reasonable annual fee. She took photographs for them occasionally too, when they were overrun with assignments. As they were mainly society photographers, the work did not much appeal to her, but she amused herself by thinking of the empty-faced girls and overweight young men as prey, and stalked them at Ascot and Henley, at charity concerts and hunt balls, as if she were back in the jungle. As well as the irreproachable photographs she presented to Jimmy and Edna, she had a separate portfolio of comic and slightly compromising shots she kept to herself. Should she put these on show?

Tirza shook her head irritably. She was already thinking of the exhibition as an accepted fact instead of a proposition. She need not be bullied into this.

The kitchen sink might be a mess, but her photographic store was meticulously neat, each file labelled with date, place and general subject matter, the shelves arranged chronologically. Inside every file a typed sheet gave detailed information about each of the numbered photographs, with exposure, shutter speed and light conditions whenever she had had the opportunity to make a note of them. She walked round the shelves, trailing her fingers over the files. This was her whole life, bottled up. She had no husband or lover, no children, no intimate friends. Everything she had felt and experienced in her life was captured here, like so many insects trapped on glass slides.

Calcutta streets, January 1977
Colombia, December 1975
Nigeria (rural), October 1973
Cambodia, May-June 1970
Mekong Delta, burnt-out villages, June 1964
Alaska, March-July 1958
She walked backwards through her life.

At the far end in a shadowy corner were the earliest years. And earliest of all, not a file, but a shoe-box of faded grey cardboard, unmarked except for a peeling label which depicted a pair of child's ankle-strap sandals. The very cardboard felt fragile as she ran her finger along the edge of the lid, as though it were so friable that lifting it would cause it to collapse into a heap of dust. She thought of fossil creatures, surviving only through the impressions their bodies had made on the gathering limestone of the sea-bed. And of the people of Pompeii, vainly trying to flee the eruption of Vesuvius, preserved for the voyeurs of today by hollows – life-casts of their bodies lying within the shrouding dust and lava. This box contained a hollow cast of herself.

Tirza pondered the question of her own professional integrity. If she consented to a true retrospective of her work,

8

then this box ought to be included. Like an artist's childish sketches, the box held her own first essays in her art. But could she face public exposure of what lay there? Not her inexpert fumblings with her first camera, but the photographs themselves. The people looking out of her past. This box had travelled with her, from one temporary dwelling place to another, but she had not opened it for more years than she could remember. Not since she had made up her mind to leave Maine, forsake her past, make a different world elsewhere.

Reluctantly she lifted the box. It felt unpleasant against her fingertips, as though the porous cardboard was somehow impregnated with sticky dust, a viscous residue of the life briefly glimpsed inside. On her way out of the door, she picked up her glass with her other hand and drained it. The whisky burned down into her stomach, warming, giving her the illusion of courage.

Switching on lights as she walked through the cottage, she went into the sitting room. Mostly, during the winter, she lived in the kitchen for warmth, but she would never examine photographs where there might be traces of food. The fire was laid and she set a match to it. Gradually the pungent odour of peat seeped into the room. The window overlooking the sea was a cold square of darkness, and she jerked the curtains across it, suddenly conscious of loneliness. How different might her life have been, without the events glimpsed in the photographs contained in that dull grey box? Would she now be alone? Would she be living like an exile so far from the country of her birth?

As if to contradict her, Grace followed her into the room and sat down in front of the fire. Striped grey and white, and of uncertain ancestry, the cat had adopted Tirza during the week she had spent at the Prince Returning, the hotel in Caillard, arranging the move into her island house. No one knew where the stray had come from. She had never been seen before in the streets of the small town, but had arrived at the same time as Tirza and with her had moved to the island. Not a young cat, but still energetic, she bore the scars of a hard life.

When Grace had first found Tirza, sitting on the wharf-end, staring across at the island and wondering whether she had made the most expensive financial mistake of her life, the cat had looked like a scrap of fur-fabric loosely folded over a wire coat hanger. Now, with feeding and care, she had filled out and appeared to be an altogether larger animal. Tirza had not wanted to adopt her. It was not her practice to allow herself to become involved with any creature, human or animal. But – when she found that the stray had stowed away amongst her baggage in the open boat – she had been too tired, that first evening, to row back again. Grace had vanished into the night and wisely kept out of sight for the next two days. On the third she allowed herself to be fed a few tinned sardines; with dignity she had left a few scraps uneaten, indicating that she was not starving and not dependent on Tirza. By the sixth day she had permitted one brief caress of her matted pelt, and that evening ventured into the cottage. When Tirza rowed over to the town to fetch supplies at the end of her first week, Grace guarded the cottage from a chair beside the stove.

Tirza sat looking at the shoe-box, reluctant to open it. Then the telephone bell rang, startling her and making her jump. Just before seven o'clock.

'Yes?' she said cautiously into the receiver.

'Tirza? Max here.' He sounded apologetic. 'Look, I'm sorry. I think I came on a bit strong this morning. I was having rather a bad day. I'd no right to take it out on you. This exhibition – if you're not feeling well enough yet, there's no rush. I'll phone Colin, if you like.'

'I'm still thinking about it. I don't know...' She gazed at the shoe-box, sitting innocuously there on the table like Pandora's casket, inviting her to open it. 'I need a few days. There are things I have to decide. And I am still feeling a bit tired. Can I call you Monday?'

'Of course. No need to do anything before then.' He paused. 'Are you all right? You sound a bit down.'

'I'm fine.'

'That's what you always say. Would you like me...' He paused again, momentously. 'Would you like me to come up and see you?'

Tirza laughed. The thought of Max in these surroundings was bizarre.

'No. Great of you to suggest it. But I'll be OK. I'll call you

Monday.'

Even so, she felt bereft when he rang off, and the cottage seemed emptier and more desolate than before.

Unlike the files, the shoe-box was not arranged and catalogued. The photographs – all black and white, with wide borders and deckled edges – lay in a heap at haphazard angles, the corner of a face peeping from under a pile of lobster pots, the hotel on Todd's Neck (photographed somewhat askew) nestling against a dark shot, overexposed, of balsam firs, through which the ocean could be glimpsed.

She remembered taking that photograph. Her grandmother had said, 'Look at the spaces in between the trees. They have their own shapes, their own identity.' And suddenly she had seen it for herself and tried to photograph it.

Between her fingers the photograph felt unexpectedly thick. At the Portland store where her first films had finally been developed, they must have used a good quality photographic paper. Better than you would get nowadays. They were still there, the shapes between the trunks of the towering firs, caught through the lens of her grandmother's vision.

Slowly she began to lift the pictures from the box and lay them out on the table. A feeling half of excitement, half of dread, churned in her stomach. The lobsterboats loaded with pots. Some of the feral cats on the farm, lying in a hot patch of dust outside the cow barn. More lobster pots. Charlie Flett posing self-consciously, with 'Flett's General Stores and Post Office' on the painted board above his head and someone's foot sticking out from a rocker on the store porch. She peered at it. A big, heavy boot, much worn and mended. Maybe old Mr Swanson. Inexplicably she blew her nose. Why should she care about Charlie Flett and Bert Swanson? The beach, with the ledges behind and Simon doing something where the sea and sand met the rocks. Digging for clams, that was it. And the beach again, with her cousin Martha lovely in a two-piece swimsuit which had seemed impossibly daring at the time. Aunt Harriet had chided her, declaring the soldiers would think her fast.

Then the other pictures. The ones she didn't want to remember. Martha was in some of them, but not all. There was one – a young man, laughing, with his arm carelessly thrown round the mast of Tirza's catboat as he balanced, a little unsteadily, on a thwart. The end of his sticks could just be seen above the coaming. How could he look so young?

Tirza glanced up and caught Grace's eye. The cat was regarding her steadily, as though she were trying to read Tirza's thoughts.

'I don't want to do this exhibition,' said Tirza. 'It will be too painful. Why should I? Isn't this just what I've been trying to avoid?'

Something in her voice brought the cat to her feet. She leapt on to the table, neatly avoiding the photographs as she landed and then stepped delicately among them. Cat and woman eyed each other. Then the cat climbed down on to Tirza's lap and curled up. It was a moment of trust, of comfort even, for the cat usually kept her independent distance. Tirza laid one hand on her, caressing the neat dome of her head, free now of burrs and silky with grooming. With the other hand she began to sort out the photographs. Although she was not ready to admit it to herself, she had made her decision.

Chapter 2

Maine: Winter 1942

THE NEW YEAR following Pearl Harbor had come to Maine in a deluge of bitterly cold air. January storms had blocked roads and by February most of the inland farms were cut off. Libbys' farm, near the sea, never suffered quite as badly. The coastal path to Flamboro usually stayed clear, so Harriet Libby could walk to Flett's for supplies, or send Simon to fetch groceries after school. Not that they would have starved even if they had been snowbound, for Harriet had grown up on a distant farm under the edge of the northern Maine forest, and she always laid up food for the winter like a siege. The treacherous night of bombing and death far away in the Pacific had reached out remotely to Flamboro through the tight voices of the newsreaders on the radio, and later in blurred images in the newspapers, but it was only during the last few weeks, as young men like Pete Flett left their homes, that the first ripples of war had truly begun to touch this remote corner.

Tobias Libby whistled up the cows as he let them out for a short spell into the pasture. Along one side, under the scented lee of the pine wood, there was a strip of grass kept clear of snow by the overhanging boughs. It was thin grazing and only served as a supplement to the winter hay, but he liked to see the beasts outside getting air and exercise and not cooped up in the barn. He always swore this increased his milk yield, a matter of long but amiable dispute with young Swanson, who had not long since taken over his uncle Bert's place just inland from Libbys'. Hector Swanson had come in with his fancy college ideas, and believed you could run a farm like a factory. He didn't like getting his hands dirty, and he thought of his cows as machines for producing milk. Couldn't see that the creatures were like any womenfolk, subject to moods and fancies. Tobias's milkers always perked up if they spent some time outside on winter days, barring blizzards.

Tobias turned his back on his cows and surveyed the farm critically. Every morning he would pause like this, however many chores lay waiting. If a man never lifted his nose from the furrow or the muck heap, how could he get a feeling for how the farm was doing? The rhythm of the farm moved in his blood, and failure of crops or sickness amongst the beasts infected his very sense of himself.

The buildings formed three sides of a square around the yard – the house with its deep porch facing west to catch the evening sun when the day's work was over, the cow barn and tie-up with the milk room in a lean-to building beyond, the grain shed, the horse barn with half of it partitioned off as a coach house. At any rate it had been a coach house in his father's and grand-father's and great-grandfather's time. Now, as well as the hayrack and other farm machinery, it held the Ford pickup and the tractor. Between the horse barn and the farmhouse was the chicken shed for Harriet's hens and the sty where he would fatten a pig during the summer. Beyond the house itself, well away from the slurry, were the ice-pond and ice-house and further still, fenced in and sinister, the lime-pit.

The silver-grey shingles of the house walls were dusted with frost which caught the low-lying morning sun. And the snow weighing down the roof bulged out over the eaves – like the ample flesh of a man's white-shirted beer belly sagging over his work pants. It was nearly four years since Tobias had given the cow barn its last coat of rusty red paint, and it was faded – drab, almost. The sad look of it offended him. He would need to get on with that after the spring planting.

'That's the yard done, Dad.' Simon came over to the rail fence, hefting his shovel. His boots were mired to the ankle with manure-stained slush.

'Done the barn?'

'Not yet, but Mom just blew the breakfast horn. Didn't you hear it?'

'No. Too much wind, and this darn hat!'

Tobias pulled it off and they both laughed. At Christmas Tobias's mother Abigail had presented him with this swanky leather hat from L. L. Bean's mail order catalogue. It was the latest headgear for city-dwelling hunters, made of cowhide and lined with a woollen fabric in a bright yellow tartan pattern. There were earflaps which could be fastened on top of the head or let down and tied under the chin. Tobias compromised by letting the flaps hang loose. He reckoned he looked fool enough without a bow under his chin. Secretly, though, he found the hat warm, and proof against the north-east wind which regularly gave him the earache.

Simon leaned his shovel against the back doorstep and they both prised off their boots before padding into the kitchen in their grey hand-knitted socks. The air seethed with the smell of bread proving and bacon and sausages frying.

'Better day today,' said Harriet cheerfully, piling up their plates and pouring cups of strong milky coffee.

'Ayuh,' said Tobias, spearing a sausage like a man who hadn't eaten for a week. 'Wind's not as bad as yesterday and sky's clear. It'll stay fine today, but there'll be bitter frost tonight.'

'Can I have more bread?' asked Simon, shovelling food in as fast as his father.

Tobias grinned. The boy had started eating like a man lately, and was growing to match it.

Harriet cut more slices. 'What are you going to do today after your chores? Have you finished your homework for Monday?'

'Sure.' Simon chewed. 'I don't know. Might go down into Flamboro.'

The door flew open, caught by the wind, and Sam Rolands, the hired man, came in, followed by Tirza. Patches, the three-coloured money cat, slipped in behind them. One of the feral barn cats, she had wormed her way first into Tirza's affections and then into Harriet's. Her presence in the house was tolerated by Tobias, though he made a point of reminding them that the farm cats were working animals and not pets.

Sam washed his hands silently in the wash-house which led off the kitchen and sat down in front of his plate. Tirza grabbed a chair, powdery blue with soft old paint, swung it round back to front and straddled it with her arms resting on the back rail. Her cheeks were red from the cold, and melting snow slithered from the folds of her dungarees. She reached down and rubbed Patches behind the ears.

'You're up here early,' said Harriet, passing Tirza a cup of coffee.

'I thought we could go skating.' Tirza looked pointedly at Simon.

'What's so great about that? We've been skating on the ice-pond for a month.'

'Not the ice-pond, stupid. Gooseneck Lake is frozen hard enough to bear. A whole crowd of folks are going up today. They're taking picnics and making a campfire.'

Simon looked enquiringly at his father. 'You don't need me once I clean the cow barn, do you, Dad?'

'Ask your mother.'

'Your room?'

'It's OK, Mom, it's OK. I made my bed.'

Tobias looked across at his wife. Her eyes were sparkling and she raised her eyebrows questioningly. He gazed at the ceiling.

'Well, I've been calculating to fix that manger in Lady's stall. Just waiting till we had a good enough day to turn the horses out with the cattle. Think I'll spend the rest of the day fixing that.'

'Tobias Libby, don't be so provoking! You and me, we're going skating too. If there's going to be a skating party we're not going to miss it.'

'Now, Harriet, just because you were a neat thing on skates when you were a girl! That was a long time ago now.'

'Land sakes, you fix your old manger if you want. I'm going skating with the rest of the folks from Flamboro.'

Tirza winked at Simon. She had reckoned on Aunt Harriet coming along. That was why she had ridden her bike over first thing to the farm. If Aunt Harriet came, they would have a feast, not a mug-up of wieners half charred on the end of a stick. She wasn't fooled by the talk of fixing the manger. Her uncle had been going to fix that manger for two years now.

'I'll help you get the food ready,' she suggested hopefully, 'while Simon cleans the cow barn.'

Simon laughed derisively.

'Since when did you take up cooking?'

She made a face at him.

'Leave your cousin be,' said Harriet comfortably. 'She'll take an interest in woman's work soon enough, now that she's growing on. Time she stopped running wild, crewing for her dad on the *Louisa Mary* and heaving lobster pots like a young lad.'

'I like crewing for Dad,' Tirza contradicted, regretting her offer to help in the kitchen. 'I'm as good a crewman as any in Flamboro, and I can bait a crab line faster than most anybody.'

Tobias got up from the table, wiping his mouth on a big spotted handkerchief.

'Well, if we're going off to spend a day on tomfoolery, I've chores to do first.'

He went out the back door, followed silently by Sam, who always hunched his shoulders and ducked going through doors, for fear of banging his head.

'You could help me in the barn first,' said Simon cunningly. 'Then we could both pack the food for Mom. What do you say?'

'Ayuh,' said Tirza. She was still smarting from the suggestion that she might soon be transformed into a woman, interested only in boring female chores. 'Mind, you'd better help me next Saturday with the net-mending. *If* you're capable.'

'Sure,' said Simon equably. They both knew Tirza would show him up, mending fast and neat while he tangled himself in a cat's cradle of twine, but they took turn about to help with each other's chores, as they'd done since they were old enough to make their way alone between Tobias's farm and his younger brother Nathan's mooring and lobsterboat.

The cow barn was lofty as a young church, but instead of a clerestory it had the hayloft, sweet with the trapped scent of summer grasses. Motes of golden dust danced in the slanting light that lanced in from a slatted window high on the south side, and the mounds of manure spattered amongst the straw still steamed gently into the sharp winter air. Without the cows' warm bodies it was chilly in here, and Tirza and Simon worked fast, shovelling the manure into a wheelbarrow and carting it out to the manure heap behind the barn. They hosed down and scrubbed the whitewashed walls and the floor, then Simon forked fresh straw from one end of the loft and Tirza spread it efficiently, making a clean carpet of bedding for the night.

When they came back to the kitchen the breakfast was cleared and washed up and Harriet was packing a big wicker hamper.

'I really shouldn't go off like this, with the house chores only half done,' she said guiltily.

'We'll help with redding-up the house,' Tirza hastened to reassure her. 'Both of us.'

Patience Warren, the hired girl, did not work weekends. If her aunt started to worry about the state of her house and its tidiness ready for Sunday morning, they would never get away in time to join the party before it left for Gooseneck Lake. Tirza grabbed a couple of dusters, a broom and a mop, and pushed Simon ahead of her out of the kitchen. She reckoned they could give the place a flick round before her uncle finished in the yard. It might just pass muster if she could hurry her aunt through her inspection quickly enough.

Like all farm wives, Harriet spent her life battling with dirt. Although boots were always shed at the back door and fouled overalls were never allowed further than the kitchen and wash-house, the thin but persistent Maine soil worked its way indoors. In the dry periods of summer it swirled in on the air, a fine grey dust filtering through screen windows and doors, sloughing from the bodies of everyone who lived on the farm. In winter, minute scraps of hay and straw from the barns clung to clothes, drifted down on to carpets and lodged in the folds of loose covers and bedding. Yet determination – or Yankee cussedness – drove Harriet and the other women to demand immaculate standards of their own and their neighbours' houses, just as it drove their husbands to struggle with the harsh climate and the unforgiving land.

———◈◈◈———

They left the farm at eight o'clock, the four of them. Sam had shaken his head when invited to join the expedition. He smiled at Tirza.

'Ain't never skated since I was a boy. Ain't got no skates, nor any wish to break my neck neither.'

He went back to a quiet pipe in his room over the horse barn, promising to start the evening milking on his own if they weren't back in time.

'Lord,' said Tobias, 'I'm not fixing on spending that long.'

'Long way to Gooseneck Lake. Evenin' settin' in early. Don't you worry, Mr Libby. I kin take my time and milk the whole herd if need be.'

Tobias had looped a string round the neck of a flagon of cider to make it easier to hold. Tirza wheeled her bicycle while Simon steadied the hamper on top of the saddle to save carrying it; she had tied her skates to the handlebars, and the rest of them wore theirs slung round their necks. The two cousins owned modern skates, screwed on to lace-up skating boots, but Harriet and Tobias still used old-fashioned runners with high, curved fronts, which had to be strapped on over their ordinary boots.

From the bedrooms of the farmhouse the ocean could be seen, though not the beach, but down here at ground level everything was hidden by the land until they reached the far end of the second field. In the snow-covered meadow to the right the cows moved slowly along the strip of clear grass against the dark curtain of the pine wood. One or two looked up as they walked past, and the warm breath flowed up from their nostrils and hung about their heads. The early morning wind had dropped altogether now, and if they stopped walking they could feel the harder frost setting in through the bones of their legs. Sam had turned out the two tough little plough-horses as well. Dancer and Lady cropped the thin winter grass without enthusiasm. They would be back in their barn by early afternoon – more tender creatures than cows, unable to stand so much cold. Both of them were in foal, due in a month or so.

'Good thing we kept the horses, wasn't it?' said Harriet. 'Now there's a gasoline shortage, with the war.'

Tobias grunted. It had taken him years to save up for the John Deere tractor, which cost a frightening amount of money, and he had been like a boy with a new model train set when it arrived. He had wanted to get rid of the plough-horses, sell them on to some farmer who was stuck in the old ways and could not see how farming was going to change. But Harriet had disagreed, and she could be stubborn as a mule when she got an idea in her head.

'What if the tractor breaks down in the middle of the

ploughing season or during harvest?' she had demanded. 'A good horse doesn't break down, so long as you look after it right. You have enough trouble with the Ford truck.'

He was no mechanic, Tobias knew that. It was this recollection that persuaded him to keep the horses, not the sentimental point that Harriet used to clinch her argument: 'Dancer and Lady have given us years of good service. And we're due at least one more foal from each of them. I'll not see them go to someone who'll drive them too hard and then send them to the knacker's yard. When this terrible war is over, we can retire them. We've land enough to give them a decent old age.'

Lot of women's nonsense. But he had to admit now that he was glad he had kept the horses. Since Pearl Harbor and the warnings about wartime shortages, he worried constantly whether he would have enough fuel, so he spared the tractor when he could. And it was true there was nothing quite like the thrill when a mare dropped a foal.

As they walked up the rise in the track at the far end of the second field, their boots crunching on last night's new fall of snow, the ocean came into sight. It was the dark blue of slate, looking nearly black because of the low-lying sun in their eyes and the white dazzle of the snow-covered fields in front. Lines of breakers rolled in across its surface. From here they looked small, harmless. But if a lobsterman caught one of those great seas wrong, with all the weight of three thousand miles of running tide behind it, his boat could founder and sink in minutes.

To their right, a mile to the south, the straggling length of Todd's Neck reached outwards. Narrow as a causeway where it joined the mainland, it bulged into a rounded end like a head where cliffs dropped sheer into the ocean. Its Abenaki name meant Head of the White Crane Bird, but it was called now after some seventeenth-century settler who had farmed part of the land and fished the seas there. His descendants had built ever grander houses until the last one, finished a hundred years ago, had beggared them, and they had moved south to the softer living of Massachusetts. The house was now a hotel patronised by wealthy financiers from New York and merchant families from Boston. Or had been until the grim years of the Depression, when it had been forced to lower its prices and accept a slightly more humble clientele – doctors, professors, lawyers. Flamboro had thought the Mansion House would be forced by the war to close its doors, at least in winter, but it was still functioning, and that meant work for girls of the village as chambermaids and waitresses, and jobs as bellhops or gardeners for sons who turned their backs on their fathers' work of harvesting land or sea. There were young men in Flamboro who believed that a job at the Mansion House might start them on a road out of this isolated place, and lead to the wonders of Fifth Avenue and the Empire State Building. As far as Tobias knew, only one son of Flamboro had come near this goal. He was now running a diner for truck drivers somewhere on the freeway in New Jersey.

When the farm track reached the rock ledges sloping down to the beach, one branch turned right and followed the low shore south round the bay to Todd's Neck, keeping to a ridge of solid ground above the marshes which filled the dip between the broken rocks and the pine woods. In the opposite direction the track turned north and climbed round the steep cliffs before dropping down to Flamboro in the next bay.

Beyond the neat stone wall that marked the northern boundary of the Libby farm lay an unkempt stretch of woodland. Not natural woodland, this. The woods on the next property had once been maintained, planted with specimen trees two centuries earlier and managed carefully – pruned and thinned and cleared to create a beautiful prospect from the great house and a pleasant retreat for ladies with wide skirts strolling there out of the sun.

The Tremayne place had been built the year after the English capture of Quebec had brought peace to these parts following the long devastation of the French and Indian wars, and the grounds had been laid out in the style of the latest English country houses of the time. The Tremaynes had been powerful people in Flamboro and the surrounding country, although they spent only the summer months down Maine. Even in Tobias's youth they had still pretty well run things. But one summer's day in 1930 there had been a great stir of automobiles and the Tremayne family, father, mother, aunts, six children and lapdogs, had departed with their suitcases and their servants. The great gates, a mile and a half along the driveway which led inland to the Portland road, had been bound together with three chains, each secured by a padlock, and no one from the family had returned since. For a few years the Tremaynes' manager had hired local women to spring-clean the house every May as if the family would be coming from Boston the way they had in the past. That practice had stopped seven or eight years ago, and the rumour was that he had not been paid a penny since the family left. Now the great house looked out blindly towards the ocean with its windows blanked by shades. The gardens had filled with wild briars and honeysuckle, and the fruit trees in the orchards threw out leaders like uncombed hair.

Tirza halted her bicycle just opposite the house and looked across the climbing layers of snow-filled terraces to the sweep of stone steps.

'The Haunted House looks like a wedding cake today.'

Harriet made an impatient movement. All the children called it that, but it always made her uneasy.

'Perhaps the Tremaynes will come back,' she said. 'I heard tell the eldest son is something to do with armaments now. The war might make them rich again.'

Tobias shook his head.

'Never,' he said firmly. 'Nobody wants a place like that now. Mr and Mrs Tremayne might have come back, but now that he's dead and she's a poor bedfast creature, I doubt the next generation will ever use it.'

As they walked on, past the far end of the estate and down the steep ground to Flamboro harbour, Simon said under his breath to Tirza, 'I know a way into the house.'

'You don't.'

'I do so. I'll take you if you want. If you aren't scared. It's full of stuff, you know. Furniture with sheets over it like shrouds, and bags hanging from the ceilings, and creaking floorboards, and dark portraits leaning out at you watching from the walls.'

Tirza knew he was only trying to scare her.

'OK, we'll go. Maybe when it's some warmer, though. It'd be perishing now.'

Outside Tirza's house on the waterfront a group was gathering.

Twenty or thirty people, adults and children, were milling about with baskets of food. They wore layers of warm clothing and thick boots. Five-year-old Joey Harris, who lived next door to Tirza, was so padded with sweaters and snowsuit that his arms stuck straight out from his sides. Her grandmother Abigail came down the steps and handed a chip basket covered with a red and white checked cloth to Nathan Libby.

'There's plenty of food in here, son,' she said, eyeing Harriet's basket sideways. 'No need for you and Tirza to share your brother's dinner.' She turned to Harriet as if noticing her for the first time. 'Good day to you, Harriet. You're never going skating?' She sounded faintly scandalised.

'Good day, Mother Libby,' said Harriet calmly. 'Ayuh, I'm going to keep an eye on things and make sure no foolish child skates on thin ice. And I'll see that everyone keeps warm and well fed.'

Abigail, outflanked, retreated backwards up the three steps, which gave her the advantage of height over the rest of them.

'Well, Tobias,' she said reprovingly, 'I never thought to see you neglecting the farm for this sort of nonsense.'

Tobias looked aside and muttered something about what was the use of having a hired man?

Nathan took charge.

'Come along now, folks. If we stand gossiping all day we'll not get to Gooseneck Lake in time to do any skating. We'll be back by nightfall, Mother.'

With that he ushered the party ahead of him along Shore Road, the main street of Flamboro, past Flett's Stores. They turned left along Schoolhouse Lane, which led uphill and inland over a shoulder of Mount Manenticus where a track branched off through the pine woods above the town. Gooseneck Lake lay within the woods, a five-mile walk ahead of them.

By the time they reached the lake the sun was well up. They had been walking for more than an hour through the woods. Even in the sharp winter cold the scent of spruce and balsam firs hung in the air, a whisper of the heady perfume of hot midsummer days. Beneath the shelter of the trees and walking briskly they felt almost warm. This was old woodland. A strip of snow lay along the open ground of the path, splitting the wood like a white ribbon, but many of them walked alongside under the edges of the densely packed trees where no snow lay. Their feet made no sound in the centuries-deep fall of pine needles.

Coming out from the trees they stood at one end of the lake, which stretched out in a long curve, lying westwards and then disappearing behind the woods to the north-west. As far away as they could see, the lake was hard frozen, and the ice gave back a deep ring as Charlie Flett pounded it with a heavy branch. A mile away, though, where the lake curved north, the water became suddenly deep, plunging down into a vast hole that was said to be bottomless. In summer there was the menacing spiral of a whirlpool here in the elbow of the lake. This was where the ice might be half-formed and dangerous.

Mary Flett and Harriet began clearing a place under the edge of the trees and unpacking food while some of the men gathered fallen branches for a fire.

'Heard any news of your Martha lately? Has Will been posted overseas yet?' asked Mary, spreading a gingham cloth and laying out butter and cranberry loaf from her basket.

'We had a letter this week. They're back in married housing just outside Washington again, but she doesn't know how long they'll be there. Will has been moved three times in the last three months. I don't know how she can live like that, after growing up on the farm and always knowing where she was.'

'I don't suppose,' said Mary carefully, 'that Will knows whether he'll be sent overseas? Our Pete doesn't have any idea where his ship will have to go.'

Harriet laid out knives and forks in precise lines and did not look up.

'Well, I reckon most of the airmen will be sent to Europe,' she said, 'or more likely out to the Pacific, won't they? That's where they're needed. The Japs seem to be spreading out every-where, just wiping out our boys on all those queer-sounding islands.'

Mary pressed her fingers against her lips.

'I've told Martha,' said Harriet, 'if Will has to go overseas she should come back with Billy and live with us. It's best to be with your own family in times like these.'

'Will she come?'

'I reckon so. She probably wouldn't have, if they'd still been in their first married housing. That was a better neighbourhood and she made plenty of friends there. But now all the service families are scattered and she doesn't like this apartment they've been given. Six floors up and nowhere for Billy to play. And when the hot weather comes she'll want to get out of Washington anyhow, with the polio they have there every summer.'

Harriet sighed.

'Of course we hope that Will won't have to go overseas, but it's almost certain, isn't it?'

'At least Simon is too young to be drafted,' said Mary. 'That's one bit of good luck.'

Peter was her only child, engaged to the new young school-teacher. Charlie had hoped to take him into partnership in the store now he had finished his business course in Augusta.

Harriet knew she was lucky.

'I'm sure Pete will be all right,' she said awkwardly, not look-ing at Mary. 'These new warships – they're almost as big as a small town. It's not like going to sea in a lobsterboat or a trawler.'

Involuntarily her eyes turned to her brother-in-law. Nathan might just be young enough to be drafted, if the war lasted any time at all. But fishermen would be draft exempt, like farmers, surely? And him with that child to bring up on his own. Abigail might live with them and keep house, but Tirza needed her father. Even if he did treat her more like a son than a daughter.

Tirza sat apart from the others on a tussock of rough grass by the edge of the lake. In the summer her feet would have dan-gled into the water here, but now they were stretched out in front of her, the heels of her skate blades resting on the ice. From this low angle of sight she could see patterns of colour wavering across the ice, glints of blue and sparks of orange. Grabbing hold of the long grass in each hand and drawing her legs under her, she pushed off, shooting straight away from the shore and rising to her feet as she moved. She loved to skate. It was the one thing that made the long bitter months of winter endurable. In sum-mer the days never seemed to last long enough, when she helped her father with his lobster traps, or tended her own crab-lines, or sailed her catboat, or roamed the pine woods with Simon, or helped on her uncle's farm. But the snow-bound Maine winters meant hours of boredom indoors. The days of winter frustration seemed to choke Tirza until she became irritable and rude, defying Abigail and sometimes feeling her father's belt across her backside. Abigail didn't hold with anyone reading books or playing solitaire, however long and empty the snow-laden winter evenings. People discovered lounging around with a book or cards in their hands had better be given something useful to do pretty quick, whether it was scouring pans or knitting bait bags for the lobster pots.

As soon as the freezing weather had set in, Tirza and Simon had started skating on the ice-pond at the farm. During the coming weeks, before the thaw began, Tobias and Sam would finish cutting the ice into blocks a foot square and storing them in the underground ice-house, packed around with sawdust. All through the warm weather the ice would keep the ice-boxes cold at the farm and at Nathan's house on the harbour. Tobias also sold ice to a few of the other Flamboro families, any he could spare. Every other evening he or Sam would drive the Ford truck, loaded with blocks of ice, down the farm track to the county road opposite Swansons' gate, then round Tremaynes' place and along to Flamboro. Simon and Tirza sometimes went for the ride. They sat at the back with their legs dangling over the lowered tailboard, enjoying the bounce and bang of the pickup over the rough road and the cool rush of air after the heat of the day.

Last fall, Simon had discovered he was strong enough to lift the heavy blocks of ice with the ice-tongs – like a huge pair of scissors with claw ends. He was a year older than Tirza, thirteen just a couple of months ago, but until last year they had been much the same size. Then Simon had begun to pull ahead and now he was three or four inches taller. Tirza had struggled with the ice-tongs, but although she could just raise a block of ice from the ground she could not hold it. She had tried again and again, resentful at being beaten by Simon at anything, but she had given up at last when she dropped one of the blocks on the end of her foot and went about limping for the rest of the week.

Perhaps she would be strong enough this year.

Tirza swooped round in a circle and looked back to the end of the lake. She had already come further than she realised. The figures of the other skaters were small and distant against the dark woods. The fire was roaring now and she could see the column of smoke rising straight up in the frosty air. She was too far away to smell the burning wood, but the scent of the trees hung about the lake, and the ice had its own smell – sharp and slightly metallic. She supposed she shouldn't go any further. The deep hole in the lake bottom was not far from here and she knew how dangerous it was. But she was reluctant to go back to the others. There were times when she craved solitude, especially after being cooped up with her father and grandmother in the small house during winter. At such times she did not even want Simon's company.

She swung round again and began to skate slowly backwards in the direction of the shore. This way she could watch the dark distances of the lake retreating from her, instead of the human figures drawing near. She was a strong skater. She could feel the muscles of her legs and abdomen tightening and thrusting, and the balance of her arms swinging in rhythm with the stroke. Her back was arched slightly as she leaned backwards into her own movement. The co-ordination of her whole body, she suddenly saw, was something wonderful, everything working together without any real thought on her part. A great sense of her own power flooded through her, heating her blood and sending it throbbing into her cheeks. It ran like an electric shock through her stomach and down her legs, where she could watch the exquisite thrust and lift of her feet as if they belonged to someone else.

'Just in time,' said Charlie Flett as she staggered on to shore with her skates still on. 'Get yourself a bowl for your aunt's soup.'

He had a skillet balanced on stones at one side of the fire and was turning pork chops in the spitting fat. The smell of food made Tirza suddenly dizzy.

'Here.' Simon thrust a bowl of soup at her and squatted down on the ground near Charlie. 'Thought you weren't coming back to eat.' He pulled a big hunk of bread from the front of his windcheater jacket and tore a piece off for her. She crouched down beside him and began spooning up the soup, which was thick with onions and cubes of browned potato and flecks of herb.

'I'm *starving*,' she said. 'I didn't realise I'd gone so far.'

'Want to watch you don't skate off the end into the mushy ice.'

'I *know*,' she said crossly, wiping up the last of the soup with her bread. 'Gosh, that was good. Do you think there's any more? I wish Grandma would make soup like Aunt Harriet's. It's always some thin kind of stuff that people like the Tremaynes would eat. You know, Boston Society.'

She crooked her little finger in the air and pretended to sip soup daintily with a look of exaggerated rapture on her face. Simon laughed and pushed her over into the heaped pine needles.

'Quit fooling about, the both of you,' said Tobias. 'Or don't you want more soup?'

Replete with soup and bread and chops and corn pickle, Tirza and Simon made off with their mugs of cider and slabs of cake to a cluster of rocks away from the rest of the party. Tirza was still hobbling on her skates.

'Why don't you take those off?' said Simon.

'I'm going to skate again in a minute.'

'I can't move. I feel as tight in my skin as Joey in his snow-suit.'

'Mmm.' Tirza licked chocolate icing off her fingers and washed it down with cider. Tobias's cider was unfermented, but it was very concentrated. You felt you could chew on it.

'Is Martha really coming home?' she said.

'What?'

'I heard your mother telling Mary Flett that she and Billy might be coming home.'

'Only if Will goes overseas.'

'We don't want that drip Billy underfoot. When they stayed last summer he was whining round us everywhere.'

'Yeah. Well, we'll just dodge him. It'll be OK.'

Tirza didn't much like Martha either, but felt she couldn't say so to Simon. In many small, insidious ways Martha had made her life unpleasant in the past. She had never bullied Tirza physically, although she pinched her a lot, on the sly. What hurt was the sneer on her face whenever she looked at Tirza or spoke to her. Tirza was skinny as a rabbit, with short-cropped dull brown hair, and she knew she was nothing to look at, but most of the time she forgot about it. When Martha was around, however, she became self-conscious and clumsy, banging into furniture and knocking ornaments over.

Martha was a beauty. Even in her baby photographs it was there. Her bones were slender, but perfect, not like Tirza with her chicken-wing elbows. Her skin had a translucent glow, and her fair hair fell to her shoulders in heavy waves. Last time she had come to Maine from Washington she had rolled the hair on top of her head into large sausages, in the style the movie stars were wearing now. Tirza wasn't sure that she liked it, but it made Martha look very sophisticated. She had also taken to smoking with a long cigarette holder, which showed off her white hands. Remembering this, Tirza looked down at her own hands, brown and callused, and criss-crossed with tiny scratches and scars from farm work and mending Dad's nets. She frowned. The thought of Martha back at the farm for more than just a short vacation depressed her.

'Come on,' she said, wiping her sticky fingers on the seat of her dungarees and pulling her wool hat down over her ears. 'I'll race you to the big pine on that point over there.'

As she shot away over the ice, she could hear Simon shouting after her.

'Not fair! I haven't got my skates back on yet.'

They stayed at the lake until the sun crept down behind the woods. Nathan had managed to teach Joey to balance on his double-bladed skates, and he was skating solemnly round and round in a small circle near the shore. His mother had warned him so many times about the dangers of falling through the ice that he had been paralysed with fear until Nathan took him in hand. Even now he watched the other skaters apprehensively as they swooped and shouted out in the middle of the lake.

Her cooking done, Harriet donned her old-fashioned runners and took to the ice. For the first few minutes she moved a little uncertainly, but soon she was manoeuvring Tobias through the steps of a skaters' waltz. Thirty years ago Harriet had won prizes and ribbons for skating, even had her picture in the paper. The others gathered at the side of the lake to watch her, but this made Tobias more clumsy than ever and at last she let him go, laughing.

'Come here, Tirza,' she called. 'Let's show them how it's really done.'

Putting on a show for their audience, they skated, linking hands, turning together with a flourish in a shower of ice particles, cutting across the first reflections of evening stars in the darkening ice.

'Land sakes,' said Harriet at last, gliding up to the shore beside the dying fire and gasping. 'Look at the time! Tobias, Mary, Charlie, Walter – we'd best be on our way. I can't think what got into me!'

'Don't fret, Harriet,' said Mary. 'The food's all packed. We just need to dowse the fire and we're ready to go. At least it's downhill all the way back.'

Tirza took off her skates and slung them round her neck. Her face was burnt with the cold and her calf muscles throbbed, but she felt exhilarated even in her tiredness. Lingering after the others started off down the path through the woods, she laid a hand on a balsam fir and took one last look across the lake, glinting silver-black and mysterious and alone under the rising moon. Later, she would remember herself listening to the silence, breath suspended, as if to catch the first whisper of all that was to fall across her path in the months to come.

<hr />

There was a hard frost that night, laying silence and stillness over the farmland and the harbour town. The only sounds Tirza could hear, waking cold in the middle of the night, were the howl of the towering blocks of ice grating against the shore and a distant groan from the woods, where the sap was freezing in the trees and the timber writhed. Overhead the brown rafters of the open roof space leaned above her in the dim moonlight reflected off the snow. The inside of her window was thick with ice in patterns like the Persian carpet that lived in the front parlour of the house occupied by the Penhaligon sisters. Their father, one of the last of the great Maine sea captains, had brought it back from one of his voyages some time in the last century. No one had ever been allowed to walk upon this carpet, which was protected by an archipelago of hooked and braided rugs, and shrouded from the morning sun by heavy drapes at the window.

Tirza turned over and huddled her arms around herself, trying to get warm. Her pink and white patchwork quilt, a gift from Miss Molly Penhaligon when she was seven, crackled as she moved, where the moisture of her breath had frozen into a thin layer of ice on the cotton. She could not stop shaking with the cold. At last she leapt from the bed, ran across the bare boards like a cat across the top of a stove, and grabbed a sweater and a pair of thick socks from her chest of drawers. Jumping into bed again, she pulled them on over her pyjamas and prised the sheet of ice off the quilt. It smashed on the floor with a satisfying sound. Tirza pulled the bedclothes right over her head and hugged one of her pillows to her for warmth. Gradually she stopped shaking. It had been a good day up at Gooseneck Lake, but the news that Martha and Billy might come back to the farm had marred it some. Still, she thought, warm and drifting, it might never happen.

On Sunday mornings, barring atrocious weather or absence at sea, almost the entire population of Flamboro and the neighbouring farms attended service at the white clapboard church which had been built two centuries before and not much changed since. It lay on rising ground at the north end of the village, past the turn to the school, where the coast curved round at the far side of the bay. It thus faced Nathan Libby's house, across the top of the lobster smacks and trawlers moored along the two wharves built on either arm of the harbour. Deceptive at a distance and well proportioned, it looked much larger than it really was. It had the classic simplicity and symmetry of eighteenth-century New England churches; its porch was supported by four wooden Doric pillars, and above the roof a slender spire soared against the dark firs and bayberry bushes behind. Its white paint was renewed every second year, and it served as a clear marker for fishermen making their way home in bad weather.

On a bright day the gilded weathervane, shaped like a clipper in full sail, glinted and flashed, somewhat to the embarrassment of the conservative population of Flamboro, who thought it gaudy and somewhat unseemly for the house of the Lord. It had been presented to the church half a century before by Mr Oliver Tremayne during one of his summers down from Boston, and the selectmen, in the face of this dilemma, had been too polite to refuse it. They had supposed that the weathervane was brass and its glitter would tone down with salt air and tarnish. It was only after some years that they learned the thing was gilded with real gold – an extravagance which made the gift even more of a frippery – but by then it was too late. It would have been insulting to return the gift to Mr Oliver's son.

Tirza liked the weathervane, sailing up there over the church, defying the storms and somehow promising a careful watch over the men at sea. She always looked out at it from her bedroom window in the morning, after studying the ocean, the instinctive first action of the day for everyone from a fishing family. The morning after the skating party she scraped the ice off the inside of her window and saw a world transformed from the glitter of the day before. She could just make out the pale gleam of the church through the beginnings of a winter fog rolling in off the ocean. Overhead the sky sagged down, heavy with cloud. The first flakes of another snowfall drifted past outside the glass.

By the time Walter Pelham, trawlerman and church sidesman, rang the bell for service, it was snowing heavily and relentlessly. The wind blew from the north-east and the weather was coming straight from the Arctic. The townspeople fought their way into church, with the Libbys and Swansons from the two nearest farms, but no one from further away. Despite the two stoves, the church was bitterly cold and the minister, a practical and kindly man, cut his sermon short and sent his congregation off to their Sunday dinners before frostbite set in. He stood beside the porch pillars, shaking hands briskly, as they struggled out into the driving snow, turning up their collars and winding mufflers more tightly.

'Fine sermon, Reverend Bridges,' said Nathan, with a grin. 'One of your best. Every point clearly made.'

'Well, Mr Libby,' said the minister without rancour, 'to everything there is a season, and today is not the season for a long disquisition. I will save that,' he added gravely, 'for another occasion.'

Miss Molly Penhaligon, coming out of church on the heels of the Libby family, exclaimed, 'Why, Harriet Libby, I never thought you would get through today.'

Harriet, in decent Sunday navy blue, with a severe felt hat of ample proportions pinned over her grey curls, smiled comfortably.

'Nothing we couldn't manage with good boots and a little care, Miss Molly. Besides, Nathan and Mother Libby invited us to Sunday dinner today. I couldn't miss the chance to sit down to a meal cooked by someone else.'

Miss Molly turned to Simon and Tirza, stamping their feet against the cold and waiting for the grown-ups to come along.

'Well, now,' she said, 'talking of visiting... We haven't seen the two of you round for tea, not for weeks. Would you like to come this afternoon? About four?'

'Thank you, Miss Molly,' said Tirza without waiting for Simon to speak. 'That would be great.'

'Thanks,' said Simon, beaming. Sunday afternoons after one of these big family meals were the most boring times in their lives. Abigail did not approve of any frivolous activities on the Sabbath, but tea with the Penhaligon sisters was permitted, and would be a lot more lively than sitting around stuffed into the small parlour of Nathan's house.

Tirza, catching sight of Miss Catherine coming out of church alone, asked, 'How is Miss Susanna?'

'She's just fine,' said Miss Molly reassuringly. 'But we thought she was best not out in this weather. She's minding the roast lamb and keeping warm. We'll see you about four, then.'

The two sisters walked off together to the big old house built by the sea captain. Tirza and Simon knew Miss Susanna had some mysterious illness, but such things were not discussed in front of them. She was, in fact, the only true Miss Penhaligon. Miss Molly had married a doctor and gone off to live in Boston, and two years later Miss Catherine had married a businessman from the same city, but when they were widowed within six months of each other ten years ago, they had moved back to Flamboro to share the family house with their youngest sister. Miss Susanna Penhaligon had never married, giving up (it was said) a romance with an English sailor to stay at home and nurse her increasingly cantankerous father until he died at the age of ninety-two, shortly before the other two sisters came home. Collectively, the three sisters were known in Flamboro as 'the Boston ladies', though Miss Susanna had visited Boston only once, twenty-five years ago.

Abigail gathered the Libby clan about her and set off at a brisk pace, down the stone steps from the church gate to Shore Road and along the harbour to home. The snow was driving so hard now that the ends of the harbour walls were hidden. Along the street each house loomed into view like a solitary iceberg. Even breathing was difficult, and although the wind blew from the north-east it howled and wheeled about the buildings so that, whichever way you faced, it hit you square between the eyes. Breastplates of snow built up on their coats, and drifts slithered down the narrow gaps between mufflers and collars. At last they stumbled up the steps and across the narrow porch of Nathan's house, into the warm smell of roast pork. Nathan slammed the door behind them and leaned against it with relief.

'Lord help us,' he said. 'I'll be thankful all my days that I'm not a whaler like Great-uncle Henry was!'

Chapter 3

Maine: Winter 1942

SIMON WATCHED HIS parents, his uncle and his grandmother eating their way through their Sunday dinner and he felt as though he was drowning. The air in the room was thick with greasy smells – fatty meat, a whiff of fumes and hot metal seeping from the Franklin stove built into the fireplace, the camphor odour of clothes brought out only for Sundays. It was like swimming through the farm pond on a sullen August day, when the water was so sluggish it dragged at your limbs, gelatinous, clinging. His elders moved in slow motion, their mouths opening and shutting like sea creatures, wallowing slowly through the depths of this torpid pond. He felt his lungs struggling for air. He wanted to shoot to the surface and gasp.

He couldn't work out what was the matter with him. He never used to feel like this. Despite his love for his family, why was it that he suddenly felt so suffocated by them? Even by Tirza. A nerve in his eyelid began to twitch, a maddening uncontrollable movement which was new and alien to him. It afflicted him sometimes in school, too, when he would lean his head on his hand, pretending to concentrate, in a desperate effort to hide this weird disfigurement from his classmates. Now his legs were twitching. Was this what his mother meant when she talked about growing pains? He drove his fists on to his knees under the table, forcing his legs down so that the heels of his boots would not start drumming on the floor. He felt sick.

Tirza was sitting opposite, but showed no sign of noticing anything peculiar about him. She was gazing vacantly off into space, an irritating habit she had when she wanted to detach herself from her surroundings.

A couple of months ago he had asked her, 'What do you *do* when you look like that?'

She had seemed confused. 'I don't know. I sort of go away inside my head. Don't you ever do that?'

'No.'

'You just float off, till everything around you is small and far away, and people's voices go faint. Then you can be private.'

He had shaken his head, not understanding what she meant then, any more than he did now. The nearest he ever came to this detachment from the surrounding world was when he was reading a Zane Grey. Then sometimes he really didn't hear his father calling him to do his chores. But he couldn't just escape at will, the way Tirza did. She could be infuriating sometimes.

'More dessert, Simon?' Abigail said, the big serving spoon poised over the remains of a steamed pudding thick with suet and syrup. Abigail's mother had come from Lancashire, and Abigail took pride in keeping up her culinary traditions. The roof of Simon's mouth was still thick with the residue of his first helping. He shook his head.

'No, thank you, Grandma.'

Only Nathan accepted a second helping, pouring a generous ribbon of yellow cream over the top. Even in winter Tobias's cows produced this rich cream. In summer you could almost stand a spoon up in it.

Simon's right leg began to twitch again, and he eased himself round cautiously in his chair, but his grandmother was too sharp-eyed for him.

'Sakes, what's the matter with the boy? Sit still, will you, Simon.'

'Cramp,' said Simon tersely. 'Could I please leave the table, Grandma? I've got cramp real bad in my leg.'

'Really badly. Oh, very well, then.' Abigail glanced along the table. 'Harriet?'

'Oh surely. Let them both go off. Then we can all have a good visit with our coffee.'

Simon caught Tirza's eye. Wherever it was that she had been, she'd come back again and was inhabiting the space behind her eyes. They got up hastily and escaped from the long room, which was kitchen at one end and dining room at the other.

'Gosh,' said Simon, looking at the pendulum clock on the wall at the foot of the stairs, next to the barometer, 'I thought we'd be there all day. It's near time to go to the Boston ladies' house.'

'Another half an hour. Come and see *Stormy Petrel*.'

The catboat was the great passion of Tirza's life. She had saved every penny she earned for three years to buy the *Stormy Petrel* – her allowance, money for baby-sitting with Joey next door, all her earnings from her crab-fishing and the occasional pay Tobias gave them both for special tasks like strawberry picking. Simon had to allow she deserved credit for it. He had never been able to save for longer than a few weeks, in the anxious penurious times before Christmas. During the months while she was saving, Tirza had somewhere come across the information that stormy petrels stay out over the ocean for months at a time, even sleeping on the wing, so she had christened her boat thus outlandishly instead of giving her a regular Maine name like *Fair Weather* or *Linda Sue*.

The boat shed was built on to the side of the house and they could reach it without going outside. A door opened from the dark back hall straight into the shed and they stepped down to the shed floor as Tirza switched on the dim electric light. The shadowy space felt like Tobias's ice-house when it had just been filled with the freshly cut blocks of ice – their frosty breath hung thick around them. Nathan kept his lobsterboat, the *Louisa Mary*, in the water until the harbour iced over, then winched her on to the wharf. He brought her into the boat shed just before spring for her annual overhaul. From the big doors at the front of the boat shed a slipway ran straight across the road and into the harbour, down which she could be launched when the ice broke. But at the moment there was no room for the lobsterboat in the shed. Two dories – Nathan's large one, once used on a whaling ship, and the small one belonging to Tirza – were upturned on trestles at the far side. They had been sanded down and repainted. In the centre of the shed *Stormy Petrel* was lovingly cradled on canvas-covered supports curved to fit her. Tirza had already scraped the bottom and put on three layers of worm-resistant paint. Now the boat was right way up and had been painted with undercoat. The spars were laid out separately and Simon ran his hand along the mast. It had been rubbed down with finer and finer sandpaper until it felt as silky as a thoroughbred horse.

'Great,' he said. 'Must have taken hours.'

'Yeah. But I really like doing it, you know. It's real satisfying, getting it so smooth. Not much more to do now. I just need to put a couple of top coats on the outside of the hull, and give the cockpit and spars three coats of marine varnish, and I'll be finished.'

'Sail OK?'

'Sure. Except I have to shape a new batten to replace the one you cracked when you stepped on it last fall.'

'I said I was sorry.'

'I don't think you're cut out for boats.'

'I guess my feet just got too big.'

'I wish Grandma would let me work on the boat on Sundays,' said Tirza. 'It's freezing in here evenings after school; my hands go stiff after half an hour. And there are so many chores on Saturdays.'

Simon gestured round at the lobster pots which were piled up in the half-loft and on every available foot of floor space, and at the nets slung in tar-scented festoons from the roof.

'Is there much work to do on your father's gear?'

'The pots aren't too bad this year, but there's one big rip in the net that you're going to help me mend next weekend.'

'OK, I remember. Come on, I'm turning into a block of ice. Let's go and visit with the Boston ladies.'

The snowstorm had slackened a little as they made their way back round the harbour in the direction of the church, then turned off up the steep path leading to the Penhaligons' house. The path wound between box hedges clipped in the European style, topped now with a layer of snow like cake frosting. The house itself had a French look, with its mansard roof. But the deep porch running along the whole length of the front was New England, and the roof supported a stumpy turret crowned with a wrought-iron waist-high balustrade. A widow's walk, where a wife could climb up to watch for her husband's ship returning from the ocean, sighting the distant sail with joy or searching the grey charnel house of the waves until hope perished.

Simon kicked up gouts of snow as they walked towards the house. The Boston ladies expected folks to come to the front door, even their younger visitors.

'Sometimes I can't wait to get out of this place.'

Tirza stopped and looked at him in surprise.

'What do you mean?'

'Out of Flamboro. Away from the farm.'

She looked baffled.

'But it will be yours some day. When your dad retires.'

'I don't know as I want it. I don't think I want to be a farmer.'

Tirza walked on again towards the house, but she pulled off her mitten and began to bite her thumbnail.

'What would you do instead?'

'I don't know. I don't know what I want to do. Do you know what you want to do when you're grown? Do you want to stay here all the rest of your life?'

She stopped again and looked down the sloping garden towards the wharf, where she could just make out the *Louisa Mary* through the swirling snow. The lobsterboat was heavy with ice, every surface coated, the rigging turned into tubes of glass. Like every winter, this one had locked in the harbour with ice, putting a stop to fishing until it thawed. The ice was piled up in irregular masses, fastened on to the wharves and the rocks with a grip that nothing would loosen until spring. Then they would begin their agonised break-up, crashing together like trains colliding head-on. Even when it seemed to be at rest, the ice twisted and tore at the land, dragging huge boulders from the shoreline and wrenching the oak legs of wharves from the sea-bed like a fistful of kindling.

The water was a sullen grey beyond the ice, dull as old pewter, giving back no light today but towering into menacing seas which burst upwards into spumes of spray above hidden reefs. The ocean disappeared into the snow and no line could be seen between sky and sea. Even the lights on the far ends of the two harbour walls were shrouded. The heavy blocks of ice in the harbour groaned and scraped as the sea sucked at them.

This was a cruel country, but Tirza could not imagine any

other. And she thought of summer days, under-running a trawl in her dory, or sailing *Stormy Petrel* along the coast to Todd's Neck with the sun beating down on her back. And she thought of the sweet smell of the cows in their barn, and the fierce jet of the milk into the pail at milking time. And haymaking. And blueberry harvest.

'Of course I want to stay here,' she said angrily. 'Why not? Where else would be as good as here?'

'What will you do?' He kept picking at it, like a crusted and itching scab. 'You can't take over your dad's lobsterboat. Whoever heard of a lobster*woman*? They'd never let you have a licence.'

He was jeering at her now, trying to shake her out of her old certainties. She opened her mouth to answer him, but at that moment Miss Molly appeared at the door beckoning to them.

'My heart alive, come in the both of you! Why are you standing out there in the blizzard?'

Captain Penhaligon had been a much travelled and a cultured man, and when he had built this house for his wife and daughters more than seventy years ago he had provided for every need. There was a library lined with panelling, where books rose to the ceiling on all four walls, with barely room for the fireplace and the two long windows. The house had a drawing room as well as the front parlour. One end of the drawing room served as a music room, housing a Steinway grand piano and a small Irish harp brought back from Cork, which no one in Flamboro could play. The three sisters lived mostly in the front parlour, with its precious Persian carpet. There were display cabinets around the walls holding the captain's curiosities from a lifetime at sea – squat stone goddesses from islands of the Pacific and ivory fans from India, child-sized embroidered shoes worn by Chinese ladies and a narwhal tusk, once believed to be the horn of the fabulous unicorn. The floor between the chairs was dotted with various worktables and sewing baskets from which current projects overflowed. A round oak table on a single pedestal leg was laid this afternoon with an embroidered cloth and a fragile Royal Crown Derby tea service.

Despite appearances Flamboro knew that – though the Boston ladies were not poor – they found the times hard. The captain had left no capital for maintaining the house, and his pension from the shipping line had died with him. Miss Molly's husband, the doctor, had been a man dedicated to serving the immigrant community in Boston's poorer districts. Miss Catherine's husband, the businessman, had lost everything in the Wall Street crash. He had struggled on for a time, working in humble positions for other men, but after falling ill he had turned his back on life. Yet the sisters' financial difficulties were partly of their own making. They would have considered it unpardonable to have sold any of the captain's possessions in order to make their lives easier. So they lived off the minute investments given to each of them in their youth, eating bread and cheese with Georgian silver from Royal Worcester plates, and drinking water from priceless colonial ale glasses.

Mrs Penhaligon, the captain's wife, remembered still by a few of the older inhabitants of Flamboro, had been a formidable woman, who believed that waste and idleness were signs of the devil's work. All her daughters had been reared to spend every moment not otherwise filled with domestic duties on useful plain needlework. But the sisters had all inherited, perhaps from the captain, an artistic eye and creative talent. Miss Molly made the best patchwork quilts in the State of Maine, turning good scraps from worn-out clothes into works of art. Miss Catherine embroidered. And Miss Susanna was the rug-maker. She always had both a braided rug and a hooked rug in the making.

'One for work and one for pleasure,' said Miss Susanna, who regarded braiding rugs as useful but uninspiring. Her hooked rugs were famous for their intricate patterns and rich colours.

It was never acknowledged publicly that the Penhaligon sisters sold any of their work – unthinkable even to suppose it. But Mrs Larrabee, who ran the fancy goods and gift store in Flamboro, open only from June to August, would occasionally drop a hint to one of the more favoured summer people that she might be able to arrange something privately. The best of the sisters' work, however, adorned their home and those of their friends.

An invitation to tea with the Boston ladies was an invitation to explore the delights of the house, which always seemed to offer up something new, and to discuss the latest piece of needlework. Today Simon and Tirza were instructed to lift the round table close to the fire, and the five of them sat down to a dainty tea of bread and butter with blueberry jam, followed by one of Miss Catherine's lemon cakes which were so light on the plate they seemed to weigh nothing at all.

Tirza was still thinking about Simon's words as she finished her cake, and she began to chew her thumbnail again.

'Tirza,' said Miss Molly, 'a lady does not put her fingers into her mouth.'

'Sorry, Miss Molly.' Tirza sat on her hands to stop herself.

'How was the skating yesterday?' said Miss Catherine. 'I hear you all went up to Gooseneck Lake.'

'It was great,' said Tirza. 'We had a big campfire and cooked over it.'

'Do you remember,' said Miss Susanna, 'the winter of '87? Father hired an orchestra from Portland, and we had pitch torches all round the lake, shining like huge lightning bugs in the dark. They played waltzes and polkas, and the party went on past midnight.'

She laughed softly.

'Remember the sleighs, coming to fetch us home? The horses cantering out across the ice, with their hooves ringing – black silhouettes against the torch flames... the moonlight glinting on the harness and the bells chiming. They were wild and skittish with the frosty air. We raced each other back through the woods. Oh, we had some high old time!'

'Give me a hand to lift the table away to the corner, Simon,' said Miss Catherine. 'Yes, I remember that winter. Everard Tremayne was sweet on you, and wouldn't let another young man near. He even came down Maine to spend the winter.'

Miss Susanna smiled. 'Ah well, he was a fine-looking man. But it came to nothing.'

'Susanna was the prettiest of us all,' said Miss Molly. 'Kitty and I used to be so jealous of her curls.'

'You've nothing to be jealous of now.' Miss Susanna laughed again, touching the grey hair which still held a trace of those curls. Her skin was very pale, and her face had grown thinner than ever this winter, but her blue eyes still glinted with mischief.

'Now, I want your opinion on my new rug.' She started to rise from her chair by the fire, but Miss Catherine moved quickly to forestall her and carried over the inlaid work cabinet in which she kept her rug-making tools and scraps. Miss Molly lifted the lid of a window-seat and brought the burlap backing for the new rug to spread out beside the fireplace. The pattern was marked out in thick ink which would be hidden by the close pile of hooked strips when the rug was finished. It showed an oak tree, detailed and precise. The border was a garland of oak leaves, studded with acorns. Under the tree a squirrel sat up eating an acorn and the head of another peered through the branches. Around the base of the tree were clusters of native Maine flowers.

Miss Susanna laid pieces of woollen fabric across the shawl which was tucked around her legs. Moss green and lime, coppery brown and gold and tawny. They were pieces from her neighbours' old skirts and jackets, but in her hands they would be blended as an artist blends his paints.

'What do you think, Tirza? These two together – do you think they will be right for the squirrels?'

⁕

Monday meant school again. Although the snow had stopped falling, the children from the inland farms did not arrive. Simon came late, but Miss Julia Bennett, the new assistant teacher, did not give him a bad conduct mark, making allowances for the weather. Tirza knew he could have arrived on time, because the coastal track from the farm always scoured clean of snow when the wind was blowing from the north-east. But Simon had seemed so peculiar yesterday, talking about leaving home and not wanting the farm, that she held her tongue when he sat down across the aisle from her in the desk he shared with Wayne Pelham.

Simon and Tirza were in the same class, despite there being nearly a year's difference between them. At three years old Tirza had started to read, and devoured anything she came across from that moment on – the Sears and Roebuck catalogue, Tobias's farming magazine, Abigail's church circular. To keep her occupied when he was lobstering, and out from under his mother's feet, Nathan had sent her to school a year early, before she was even five, and she had gone up through the years with the boys and girls a year older than she was. There were sixteen of them, nine girls and seven boys, which meant that one boy and one girl had to share a desk. Until this year, eighth grade, Tirza and Simon had shared. She had never really thought of him as a *boy*, he was just Simon, but when school had started last September, he had avoided the girls and taken the seat next to Wayne. Dismayed, Tirza had looked around for a partner. She didn't want to share with any of the other boys. But then Eileen Potts, who was sweet on Johnny Flett, Charlie Flett's nephew, had invited him with a look to join her. The others sorted themselves out and Tirza found herself paired with Wilma Potts, Eileen's cousin, who sniffed all the time and carried around with her a smell of musty rooms, mouldy food and her father's pigsty.

Wilma was one of those absent today, so Tirza could sprawl across their shared tip-up bench and spread out her elbows on the desk when she was writing. She hoped the weather would keep Wilma snow-bound for days. It was much more comfortable to have a desk to herself. Miss Bennett was enumerating the exports of South American countries in that bright voice which was supposed to make you interested. Tirza's eyes strayed to the window. Unlike most nineteenth-century schools, Flamboro's had not been designed with the windows too high for idle pupils to gaze through, so Tirza could see the houses opposite the school and to the side of them a corner of the sea. The sun was out today and the wind had dropped again. Everything glistened under yesterday's fresh coat of snow. During the night, frost had crystallised the soft surface, and the sun flashed from every fragment, so bright it was almost painful to look at.

The day dragged on. Tirza had found long ago that she could do her school work while attending with only half her mind. The answers seemed to come out of her mouth without any effort on her part, and they were right often enough for her to avoid exerting herself. During the algebra lesson she copied down the equations from the board and finished solving them while the pens around her were still squeaking laboriously. She could see Simon crossing out and starting again. When they had shared a desk they had sometimes helped each other, but, she thought with satisfaction, Wayne would not be much help with

Simon's algebra. She spent the rest of the lesson drawing *Stormy Petrel* from different angles on the cover of her workbook.

At last Johnny Flett, as bell monitor for this week, was sent out to ring the bell for the end of school. Simon waited for Tirza at the gate, but she turned away from the harbour.

'Aren't you going home?' he asked.

She shook her head. 'I'm going to see Girna this afternoon. Do you want to come?'

Simon dragged his boots through the snow, looking shame-faced.

'Nope. I don't think so. Got to get home to help with the milking.'

She had known he would say that, but had given him the chance to come.

'OK.' She shrugged. 'Suit yourself.'

She brushed the snow off the top of a boulder beside the school gate and sat down to strap on her snowshoes. Boots were adequate for walking around Flamboro or along the coast path to the farm, but she would need snowshoes to negotiate the deep drifts which built up in the hollows and corners of the forest.

To reach the woods she set out over an unmarked blanket of white beyond the schoolhouse which in summertime was a stretch of rough ground, marshy at the lower end where it dipped down towards the sea and thin and rocky at the top where it curved round behind the burying ground on the knoll up behind the church. In the late summer there were cranber-ries on the lower ground and blueberries higher up. From earliest childhood Tirza had known which were the best bushes. Now, however, not even the tops of the bushes showed above the snow, and she made the crossing to the woods across a blank white mound, swinging her feet wide in their snowshoes and leaving a double track like some monster bird.

It was quiet in the woods. The snow-laden trees muffled the sound of the breakers rolling in, so that they seemed far distant. If there were any birds or creatures about, they were hidden away taking shelter from the bitter cold. Tirza's breath hung about her face like a frozen veil in the still air.

The trees here were wider spaced than in the woods round

Gooseneck Lake. The people of Flamboro gathered fallen branches for firewood, which kept the ground between the trees clear. A network of small paths criss-crossed the forest. Tirza could see the tracks of deer and foxes and racoons, and a regular stitchery of bird-tracks. After climbing for a way, she turned and headed down a steep slope where glimpses of the sea showed beyond the trees.

⋘⋙

Christina O'Neill, heaving up a bucket of water from her well, caught sight of Tirza's red knitted muffler above her in the forest. She rested the bucket on the ground and waited for her daughter's daughter to swing down the last few yards of the snow-covered path to her house. The water in the bucket swayed and slowed, islands of ice tinkling against the galvanised metal. The surface of the well water had been frozen, even deep below the ground where it lay, but the ice was thin enough to be broken by the weight of the bucket dropping on to it. Hard ice only formed in the well during the worst winters. Christina could remember just three years when she had been obliged to melt snow.

The cabin in the woods was an oddity – not quite an Abenaki lodge, not quite a European house. Christina had built it herself thirteen years ago when her daughter Louisa had married Nathan Libby and set up house with him on the harbour front in Flamboro. Until then she had lived in a small rented house at the back of the town, out of sight of the sea, where she had moved after the death of her husband when her daughter was seven. Tom O'Neill had been the town schoolteacher – the only teacher in those days, although Christina had sometimes assisted him – and while he lived the O'Neills had occupied the teacher's half of the schoolhouse. After she was widowed, Christina rented the cramped, dark house, which was all that she could afford. Tom had died when he was barely past thirty, and other women, whose husbands had been lost along with their boats and all their gear, often pointed out to Christina that she was fortunate to receive any pension at all. But she had come to hate the mean rooms, the lack of air and light.

This forest north of Flamboro, however, belonged to Christina. Her father, Bruce Macpherson, a fur trader from

Scotland who had worked the northern woods since he was fifteen, had bought it honestly from the Nation back in 1880 when he married her Abenaki mother, and it had passed to Christina as their only child. When Tom died, the selectmen of Flamboro had made Christina a fair offer for the forest, thinking the lumber would make the town a tidy profit and the cleared land would provide building space if the town needed to expand. The selling price for the forest would be enough for Christina to invest for a decent income, they said, instead of the few dollars she had to scrape by on.

'No,' said Christina, politely but immovably. 'The forest is mine only in trust. It is the only heritage left of the Nation now that they have all been driven out of these parts. I may be only half-blood, but I do not intend to betray the trust. The forest will remain as it is. Louisa and I will manage on Tom's pension.'

Once her daughter was married and settled, Christina's thoughts had turned again to the forest. She began to build the house on the site of one of the old Abenaki summer settlements which had existed for centuries before the first English colonies in the area. In her childhood she had visited her mother's people from time to time in the reservation further north, and the memory of their dwellings had stayed clear in her mind. But she had given her house a sturdy wooden floor raised up on a foundation of logs, to keep it warmer in winter, and the doors and windows were made of conventional trimmed wood and glass, instead of being closed with the Abenakis' traditional hangings of animal skins.

Nathan had tried to dissuade her. Louisa had offered her mother a home with them. Nathan had said that if she wanted to live independently, he would pay the rent on the small house in Flamboro, but Christina had been adamant.

'I shall feel at home in the forest. And I'll be less than half an hour's walk from the village. This is better for me.'

When he saw that he could not persuade her to change her mind, Nathan had helped with the building, although Christina had designed everything and done most of the work herself. Nathan had set in the windows, and insisted on sealing them well with builders' putty, not the mud Christina wanted to use. And he had built her a huge fieldstone chimney, housing a wide fireplace and tapering gracefully towards the top. Now, after thirteen years, splashes of orange and sage-green lichen had begun to spread in intricate patterns over the stones of the chimney, the timbers had weathered to a silver grey, and the house looked like part of the forest.

'Good afternoon, Tirza.'

'Hi, Girna. Shall I carry the bucket inside for you?'

Indoors, the wooden cabin was warm from the fire of pine logs. Nathan had also installed a pot-bellied stove, and the walls were hung in wintertime with heavy hand-woven blankets which had once been part of Christina's mother's marriage goods. In the soft light from the kerosene lamp they looked rich and strange, like the hangings in an oriental palace. But by sunlight they were old, frayed at the edges and darned in places.

'Simon and I had tea with the Boston ladies yesterday,' said Tirza, tipping the bucket into the water storage tank.

'How is Susanna?'

'OK, I guess, but she was sitting down mostly. She showed us the new rug she's making.' Tirza hesitated. 'Girna...?'

'Yes?'

'What's the matter with Miss Susanna?' Tirza coloured, aware that she was venturing on to a forbidden topic.

Christina took up her paring knife and began peeling potatoes for supper. The child couldn't be protected for ever. Abigail treated her as though she was still six years old, and she was twice that.

'She has cancer.'

'Do you die of it?'

'Most people do, yes. Eventually. Susanna's got a fighting spirit, so she'll last longer than most of us would.'

Tirza unwound her muffler and took off her windcheater slowly. She knew of cancer only as some dark adult secret, whispered about when children were not supposed to hear. She did not look at her grandmother as she laid her jacket over the arm of a chair and put her boots and socks near the hearth to dry out.

'Does it hurt a lot?'

'It can be very painful, yes. And makes you terribly tired.'

'I wish the doctors could do something. She doesn't deserve to die. She's so kind. And she's spent all her life looking after

48

other people and not having any fun.'

Christina dropped the potatoes into a pan of water and put it on top of the stove.

'I think you would find that she doesn't think her life has been wasted. And she gets a lot of pleasure out of making her beautiful rugs. Go and see her as much as you can, you and Simon. I'm sure that cheers her up.'

Tirza turned her steaming socks and wandered off to the rough bookshelves that took up one wall of the main room in the cabin.

'Simon is acting really weird. He says he doesn't want the farm.' She knew it was safe to talk about this to Christina, who would not repeat it to the Libby adults.

'Does he not?' Christina stood with a spoon in her hand and her head on one side. 'Getting restless, is he? Well, some of the Libbys have always gone to sea instead of staying in Flamboro.'

Tirza laughed. 'Simon won't go to sea. He throws up even if I take him out in *Stormy Petrel*. He hates the sea.'

'Well, maybe he'll get over it. Are you staying to supper?'

'No, I'll have to get back. I brought you some things from Grandma.'

She rummaged in the burlap satchel that held her school books and brought out a Mason jar of plums and a heavy fruit cake. Christina took them with a sardonic look.

'Well, I call that very kind of Abigail. I might starve for company, but she won't let me starve for food. 'Twould be bad for the Libby name.'

Tirza, uncomfortable, looked away. The Libbys, strait-laced, upright members of the Flamboro community, felt that Christina's decision to live in the forest had somehow been intended to shame them. Why she should revert to the pagan ways of her ancestors, when she ought to live like the decent Christian she had been reared, was something unfathomable and a constant irritant in the family. Abigail hinted darkly that going away and getting educated at Vassar had turned Christina's head. Even though she'd had the sense to come back afterwards and marry her childhood sweetheart, she'd gallivanted about training as one of the first women lawyers in New England, and that had not been the act of a sane woman who knew her place in the scheme of things.

'What shall we read tonight?' said Tirza.

'I've been rereading Thoreau's *Walden*.' Christina picked the book up from the candle table beside her chair and sat down. 'Whose turn is it to read?'

'Yours.'

Tirza curled up on the floor at her grandmother's feet with her back against the wall, warm with its covering of Abenaki blanket. The burning logs glowed behind the bars of the stove and the fire in the open hearth cast flickering shadows on the walls as Christina began to read.

Near the end of March, 1845, I borrowed an axe and went down to the woods by Walden Pond, nearest to where I intended to build my house, and began to cut down some tall, arrowy white pines, still in their youth, for timber. It is difficult to begin without borrowing, but perhaps it is the most generous course thus to permit your fellow-men to have an interest in your enterprise. The owner of the axe, as he released his hold on it, said that it was the apple of his eye; but I returned it sharper than I received it. It was a pleasant hillside where I worked, covered with pine woods, through which I looked out on the pond, and a small open field in the woods where pines and hickories were springing up. The ice in the pond was not yet dissolved, though there were some open spaces, and it was all dark-colored and saturated with water. There were some slight flurries of snow during the days when I worked there; but for the most part when I came out on to the railroad, on my way home, its yellow sand-heap stretched away gleaming in the hazy atmosphere, and the rails shone in the spring sun, and I heard the lark and pewee and other birds already come to commence another year with us. They were pleasant spring days, in which the winter of man's discontent was thawing as well as the earth, and the life that had lain torpid began to stretch itself.

'Girna?' said Tirza, interrupting. They were allowed to interrupt each other, if there was something worth saying. 'How could it have been spring as early as that – only the end of March?'

'Walden Pond is near Concord, in Massachusetts. A fair way

south of here. Spring comes earlier there.'

'How old was Thoreau, when he was building his house in the woods?'

'About twenty-seven or twenty-eight, I believe. Why?'

'Well...' Tirza looked a little embarrassed. 'I was thinking... How did you manage to build your own house? I mean, you must have been pretty old.'

Christina threw back her head and laughed heartily. 'Yes, I suppose from your point of view, I was. Let me see. Your mother was married the previous fall, and like Thoreau I started to build this house in the spring. You were born that fall, 1929, so I must have been forty.'

Tirza shook her head. 'I don't see how you could do it.'

'Child, we can mostly do the things we set our hearts on. And you will find, when you reach forty, that it is not such a great age after all.'

'Why had you set your heart on it?'

Christina closed the book over her finger and gazed towards the black square of window, where the first light of the morning would show the sun sparking off the ocean just below the cabin.

'I suppose it was partly instinct and partly reason. Something in the blood, do you think?' She grinned down at Tirza. 'Something speaking to me from my ancestors who had lived here for so many centuries. One day, you may feel it yourself, for you are the only one left hereabouts with Abenaki blood in your veins. But it was more than that. I had begun to feel, like Thoreau, that we do not need all the ornaments and appurtenances of modern "civilised" society. The necessities of life are very few: food, shelter, clothing, fuel, as he names them. If we can clear away the clutter in our lives, it is easier for us to understand what the real meaning of life is – why we are here on this earth at all.'

She looked around and smiled ruefully.

'Not that I have kept to Thoreau's strict regime.'

She gestured towards the books on the shelves and lying around in tottering piles, the paintings and artist's materials strewn about, and the botanical specimens – some neatly labelled and mounted, others awaiting attention – all of which gave the cabin its distinctive and somewhat crowded air.

'Of course he only lived at Walden for two years. I've been here nearly thirteen, and I suspect he would have accumulated his magpie interests about him as I have. Shall I go on reading?'

'Just one more thing. What does he mean by the winter of man's discontent?'

'It's a quotation from Shakespeare:

> *Now is the winter of our discontent*
> *Made glorious summer by this sun of York.*

The opening words of *Richard III*. We must read that together – it's almost the only Shakespeare we haven't read, apart from *Lear*. Perhaps after *Walden*. And I want to introduce you to one of our own modern poets, Robert Frost.'

Christina opened the book again and found the place.

> *One day, when my axe had come off and I had cut a green hickory for a wedge, driving it with a stone, and had placed the whole to soak in a pond-hole in order to swell the wood, I saw a striped snake run into the water, and he lay on the bottom, apparently without incon-venience, as long as I stayed there, or more than a quarter of an hour; perhaps because he had not yet fairly come out of the torpid state. It appeared to me that for a like reason men remain in their present low and primitive condition; but if they should feel the influence of the spring of springs arousing them, they would of necessity rise to a higher and more ethereal life.*

Tirza laughed softly. 'I like the snake,' she said.

<><><>

Despite a portable kerosene stove brought in for the net mend-ing, it was bitter in Nathan Libby's boat shed. First thing in the morning the following Saturday Nathan and Tirza between them had carried the two dories out of the big front doors of the shed and down to the wharf. They rested there now, upturned on cinder blocks near the *Louisa Mary*, waiting for the end of winter. They had moved *Stormy Petrel* to the side of the shed where the dories had been, and leaned the spars up against the wall. Although Tirza had worked at the varnishing every night after school that week, the mast and the cockpit still needed one more coat. In the meantime work on the catboat had to be put aside while the nets were mended and the lobster pots inspected for damage.

When they went back into the house, stamping their feet against the cold, Abigail put down steaming bowls of porridge in front of them. Tirza wrinkled her nose. She disliked porridge, but knew better than to complain.

'I've got chilblains on all my toes,' she said, ladling sugar on the porridge to disguise the taste, and topping up with milk. She began to drag canals through the sticky grey mass for the milk to run along.

'You've been putting your feet too near the fire,' said Abigail briskly. 'I don't know how many times I've told you not to do it when you come in from the snow with your feet cold and wet.'

'Better ask Christina,' said Nathan incautiously. 'She'll probably have a poultice for them.'

Abigail gave him a steely look and clasped her hands under her aproned bosom.

'Don't give the child foolish ideas, son. Those messes of hot leaves and dead flowers never did anyone any good.'

'Oh, I don't know,' Nathan began, seeing the trap he had dug for himself. 'Sometimes those old Indian remedies...'

'Anybody home?' Ben Flett, Charlie's younger brother, walked into the kitchen from the front entry carrying his satchel of netting tools. 'Mornin' to you, Mrs Libby.'

'Good morning, Ben. I'll thank you not to smoke that smelly pipe in my house.'

'Beg your pardon.'

Ben knocked out his pipe in the sink, where the smouldering dottle hit a pool of water and sent a gout of smoke and steam into the air. Nathan winked at Tirza and poured Ben a cup of coffee.

'I'm mighty glad of your help, Ben. Tirza and Simon can mend, though the boy's a mite cack-handed, but it needs two men to set all up.'

'That nephew of yours is gettin' to be almost a man,' said Ben, blowing on his coffee. 'Saw him in church last Sunday. He's taller than his Ma now, and not far short of his Pa.'

'Shot up like a weed. But not much shoulder and back to him yet. He hasn't got a man's strength. As I say, I'm grateful. I'll give you a hand next week.'

'Great.'

'I will too,' said Tirza. 'With your nets – and your pots too, if you want.'

'Be glad of it.'

They started work without Simon, who arrived eventually, after they had laid out the big net over trestles in the centre of the shed. Tirza and Ben had started from opposite ends of the long tear and were working towards each other. Simon was set to mend a small hole, where his inexpert knotting could do least damage. Nathan was sorting his pots into three piles: sound, slightly damaged, and past hope.

'How did you tear the net like that, Uncle Nathan?' asked Simon, pulling down his repair, which had begun to unravel. It always took him a while to master the knot again.

'I don't rightly know. Last trip of the season, net caught on something heavy, on the bottom. Must have been metal, I guess, to do that much damage. There's no wrecks and no sunkers where I was.'

'Likely some new wreckage,' said Ben, nodding to himself. 'There's been stuff washed up further down the shore from a German submarine.'

Tirza stopped knotting and gaped at him.

'But the Germans are thousands of miles away. Over in Europe.'

'Not that far away, Tirza. They shadow the British convoys right across the North Atlantic and torpedo them anywheres. They were doin' that even before we got into the war. Now they'll be comin' right up to our shores.'

'Could they come here?' asked Simon. He seemed more excited than worried. 'I mean, could they come right into Flamboro harbour?'

'Don't see why not. Not as they'd want to. Nothin' for them here. No big naval ships to attack.'

'Ayuh,' said Nathan, dismantling a broken lobster pot to use for spares. 'But they might try to land men anywhere along this coast. That's what they do – bring the submarines close inshore at night, then surface and send out their spies and saboteurs in rubber dinghies. They could do it easily along that stretch of Libby's Beach below your dad's farm, Simon. Can't even see the beach from your bedroom windows, hidden below the ledges. And with nobody at the Tremayne place, the coast would be clear for them right from here to Todd's Neck. Easy.'

Tirza wondered why they sounded so chipper about it. She thought of German soldiers – dressed in black they would be – hauling their rubber dinghies up the pure silver sand of the beach under a small moon. They would let the air out of the boats and hide them in the marsh behind the ledges and then they would just melt into the countryside. They could walk straight into this house, if it came to that. Nobody ever locked a door in Flamboro. Her skin crawled.

'What's the matter, Tirza?' Simon teased. 'Scared of a few Krauts? I wouldn't be. I'd just get my hunting rifle...'

'That's enough, Simon,' said Nathan sharply. 'The war isn't some boys' game. It's real, and men are getting killed.'

Simon flushed an ugly red and bent over his netting needle. Tirza felt sorry for him.

'I don't think Simon meant it was a game, Dad. I think he'd be as brave as anyone if he had to be.'

'Oh, forget it,' said Simon. 'It doesn't matter.'

Chapter 4

Maine: Winter 1942

HARRIET LIBBY LEANED her cheek against the rounded side of the cow and pulled rhythmically at the teats. Snowball was a temperamental milker. She would allow herself to be milked by Tobias or Simon or Sam, but she merely tolerated them – her legs tensed, and the yield poor. She loved Harriet with the simple, unquestioning love of an orphan who has been hand-reared and has never since questioned where her loyalty lay. She turned her head as far as the halter rope would allow and blew affectionately in Harriet's direction.

'Good girl,' said Harriet. Her hands were raw with chilblains and split with broken skin across the knuckles. No amount of cold cream soothed them, and there was never time for them to heal during the hard months of the Maine winter. She hunkered down on the old three-legged milking stool which had been here in the tie-up in Tobias's father's day, and his father's before that. There was a dusting of snow on the shoulders of her threadbare navy woollen coat, which had once been her Sunday best but which, by degrees, had dwindled to her town visiting coat and now to her working coat. Underneath it she wore thick underwear, a flannelette blouse, a tweed skirt and an old sweater of Tobias's with the sleeves turned up, but she was still cold. The winter penetrated her to the bones and she knew she would not feel warm again until May. The warmth of the cow's belly against her cheek made a small point of contact between them. She crooned to Snowball and the cow sighed and relaxed, and the milk came down easily into the bucket.

If only, thought Harriet, the children were as easy to deal

with as the animals. Simon had been jumpy and difficult all winter, but he was evasive about what was troubling him. He said so little these days. Usually he was a talker, needing to be prodded to get on with his chores or his homework, or to set off to school on time. It wasn't that he was surly now. Just shut in. For a time she thought he'd fallen out with Tirza, but that didn't seem to be the problem. Only this morning she had tackled Tobias.

'Have you and Simon quarrelled?' she asked.

Tobias looked baffled.

'Me? I thought you'd been laying down the rules to him. Seems a mite moody.'

Harriet shook her head.

'I've hardly spoken to him this last month. Moment he's home from school he's shut away in his room. And you know he doesn't listen to the radio with us in the evening any more.'

'Ayuh. Maybe he's just getting bored with our company. That age, they start getting restless. Don't fret.'

Harriet carried the bucket over to the end of the cow barn into the milk room, and poured the milk through the strainer into the can. Then she swabbed down Snowball's teats and gave her an affectionate pat on the rump. The cow twitched her tail and lowered her head to the hay in her manger.

Then there was Martha. Two days ago she had telephoned to say that Will was going to be sent abroad soon, probably at the end of the month.

'I can't decide whether or not to come down Maine,' Martha said crossly.

Harriet could understand her hesitation. Martha had always been ambitious, had wanted the bright lights and the big city from the time she was just a little girl. With her pretty face and her lively, outspoken manner she had seemed destined to leave them young. Harriet hadn't been surprised when she announced her engagement, but she *had* been surprised that Martha had fixed on Will Halstead. The Halsteads were regular summer people, who had been coming to Flamboro for years, staying at the Mansion House out on Todd's Neck. Will's father was a distinguished specialist in some branch of medicine Harriet did not altogether understand, and Will seemed a stolid quiet boy, not at all Martha's type. They got acquainted at local dances during the summers of their teens. Then he had joined the air force, instead of following his father into medicine, and had turned up in Flamboro the summer Martha was eighteen, resplendent in uniform.

'It was the uniform that did it,' Harriet informed the next cow in the row, a placid reddish beast called Rosie. She washed down the udder and began to milk Rosie, who never gave anyone any trouble.

'Suddenly Will seemed desirable, and Martha saw herself as a glamorous officer's wife. Travel, excitement. Nobody thought in those days that there would be a war.'

Martha had sounded peevish and patronising on the telephone.

'I don't know whether I want to come, Mother. I don't think I could endure that dreary old hole. And it would be so bad for Billy. He's used to playing with intelligent boys and girls. He goes to the kindergarten for officers' children, and he has his handicraft classes and his Little League. There is nothing to stimulate a child in Flamboro. And I'd be so bored. There's nothing to do on the farm.'

'There's plenty to do on the farm,' Harriet said mildly. 'I could do with some help.'

'Oh, *Mother*, you know what I mean.'

Harriet sighed. She knew exactly what Martha meant. Martha would create a lot of extra work in the house. And if last summer was anything to go by, Billy would be spoiled and difficult, throwing tantrums whenever he didn't get his own way and alternately clinging to his mother and driving them all demented by running off to all the things from which he was banned – the farm machinery, the lime pit, the cliffs near the Tremayne place. Once, she had looked forward to being a grandmother, but it was difficult to hold her tongue and watch Martha making such mistakes with the child. She was just laying up a burden for her own back by neither disciplining him nor paying him any real attention. Harriet was fond of children, but she was clear-eyed too. The eldest of seven herself, she knew what monsters they could be if they weren't kept reasonably in hand.

In the village store that afternoon she confided some of her worries to Mary Flett.

'It might just do young Billy the world of good, coming here,' said Mary consolingly. 'If he has to mix with ordinary children instead of officers' kids who think themselves king of the castle. Bring him down a peg or two.'

She finished counting the eggs from Harriet's basket into the wooden crate on the counter.

'That's four and a half dozen, Harriet. Will you have it in goods or cash?'

'Oh, goods, I think. I need coffee and sugar and I'll take six of those oranges for a treat.'

Mary weighed out the coffee beans in the brass scales, then poured them into the coffee grinder and began to crank the handle.

'Our good Maine air will set the child up too, I shouldn't wonder. I don't know how any child can thrive in the city. It isn't natural. No wonder Billy was fractious last summer – he was only here three weeks, wasn't he? He didn't have time to get over the poor living in the city.'

She folded a sheet of brown paper swiftly into a bag and poured the ground coffee into it from the drawer in the bottom of the grinder.

'I always think the smell of exhaust fumes in the big cities is enough to turn a person's brains, and it must be real hurtful to a child growing up there. And the food! I stayed with my cousin in Chicago once, and you should have seen the vegetables! Potatoes turning green, carrots withered and as limp as a wet wash-cloth, and as for the cabbages, you had to throw away the half of them before you got into a few leaves in the middle that were fit to eat. My cousin got mad at me, throwing so much away, because they cost an arm and a leg, but I said, "Maisie," I said, "I will not be a party to putting food on the table I wouldn't give to the pig at home." Very snooty she was about it too.'

Mary slapped down the sugar bag on the counter to emphasise her point, and then placed six oranges tenderly into Harriet's basket.

'You're probably right,' said Harriet, tucking the coffee and sugar amongst the oranges and feeling slightly comforted. 'Billy will be old enough for school in the fall, so if Martha decides to stay on he'll have to learn to get along with the other children.'

'Mark my words,' said Mary wisely, 'you tell Martha to get herself a job if she stays at home. That will keep her out of mischief and stop her getting bored. She won't want to stay around on the farm with you all day, not after the life she's been living.'

'That's true enough, but I don't know what kind of job she could get in Flamboro. And Portland is too far away to travel every day.'

'There's the Mansion House.'

Harriet looked dubious. 'I don't think Martha would want to be a waitress, not after being an officer's wife.'

'I wasn't thinking of that. Maybe something in the office?'

'Hmm. Maybe. Do I owe you anything?'

'I'll check your account and tell you next time. It may be I owe *you* something.'

Walking back along the coast path past the Tremayne place, Harriet saw that some of the snow on the roof had started to melt in the brief period of sun the previous day, and had then frozen into great icicles which hung like three-foot swords from the eaves. The house looked more desolate and sinister than ever, yet it had been a fine place once, full of lights and laughter during the early twenties, when the Tremaynes invited half Boston society down here to evening balls and garden parties with tennis and picnics and bathing sessions on the beach. By rights, the beach belonged to the Libbys, since the Tremayne land ended in rocky shore with no sand below, but Tobias and Harriet had never liked to complain about the invasion of their property by these wealthy interlopers. Nowadays the summer people found their way over from their lodgings in Flamboro, and some of the guests at the Mansion House discovered that the wide, mile-long stretch of sand on Libby's Beach was far better than the small cove over on the south side of Todd's Neck. But these people were mostly well-behaved families or elderly couples and they gave no trouble. On the whole, she wasn't sorry that the Tremaynes no longer came, but the empty house always made her feel uneasy.

'There goes your mom,' said Tirza.

She was in a large bedroom on the second floor of the Tremayne house, peering round the edge of a sunshade brittle with age.

'Where?' Simon came to join her.

'Going home from Flett's, it looks like.'

They watched Harriet speeding up a little as she went past the end of the snow-covered lawn. She disappeared behind the neglected wood, reappeared briefly in a gap between the trees, walking more slowly as she reached the Libby property, then disappeared again.

Tirza had agreed at last to visit the house with Simon. That was yesterday, after school, when it had been a little warmer all day. Today, Saturday, it was bitter again, and their breath made frosty clouds around them in the abandoned and forlorn house. Finding herself inside it at last, Tirza did not think it was frightening so much as sad. Simon's way into the house was through the cellars. The hinges on one of the sloping cellar doors had rusted right through so that, although the doors were still held firmly together by a padlock in the middle, at the right-hand side the rusty hinges could be prised apart and the door lifted enough for them to squeeze through.

Tirza had brought her pocket flashlight, but the batteries were low and she was reluctant to use them up, being short of funds to replace them. But Simon had a packet of white candles, which Harriet kept in copious supplies all over the house for the many occasions when the Kohler system gave trouble and the electricity failed. In the small circle of light cast by one of these candles they explored the cellars, ignored by Simon on his first visit. These did seem sinister to Tirza. It was partly the smell, an ancient, musty, earthy smell, but not the clean smell of a newly turned furrow. It had something of the charnel house about it, though it was probably no more than the underground situation of the cellars, combined with the thousands and thousands of earthenware flowerpots that filled one of the three main rooms. Everywhere cobwebs were looped as thick as fishing nets, furred over with dust.

She had never seen anywhere like this. There were two big stone sinks in the first cellar, each with a cold faucet and wooden draining boards on each side. Alone of the rooms, this one had

61

windows – two narrow slots, nine inches high and two feet wide, on either side of the cellar door – which let in a little light through their grimy glass. In the middle of the floor was a long table of rough wood, on which a few rusty garden tools lay. And every inch of wall space was covered with racks built from unfinished two-by-fours, on which flowerpots were carefully arranged in long interlocking rows like stiffly articulated snakes. Each rack held a different size of pot. On the floor stood huge monsters, three feet across. On the lowest rack the pots were about fifteen inches in diameter, diminishing as the racks climbed to the ceiling until the highest ones were miniatures, no more than an inch and a half wide. The old whitewash from the ceiling was flaking away, settling over everything in a fine dust, like sugar on top of a cake.

The second cellar felt less earthy. There was very faintly in the air a warm smell which made them think of Christmas. Simon held up the candle in its tin holder and looked around.

'I know what it is,' he said. 'This is the wine cellar.'

In amazement they looked around. On principle neither Tobias nor Nathan believed in taking strong drink, and the women in their family would have been appalled at the suggestion that any should pass their own lips except for an occasional sip of communion wine. At Christmas, however, both Abigail and Harriet unbent so far as to lace their festive cakes and puddings with alcohol, and one small bottle of ruby wine was purchased from Flett's for each of the households. Now here in front of their astonished eyes Tirza and Simon saw rows of bottles lying on their sides on racks stretching away into the dimness beyond the circle of candlelight. Simon carried the candle closer and examined the bottles first on one side of the cellar and then on the other.

'It looks like white wine on the left and red wine on the right,' he announced in awe-struck tones. There was something else in his voice too. A kind of longing. Tirza felt sick. Abigail had lectured her on the dangers of drink. There was a certain small tavern, the Schooner Bar, on the other side of Flamboro harbour from their house, that she was warned never to approach. When the fishing boats came in, a few of what Abigail called 'the undesirables' were known to consort there and take strong drink, which made them dangerous to decent folk, and was rotting away their brains and livers so that any day now they would drop down dead in the street. Tirza had no reason to doubt the truth of this, though she sometimes chafed at Abigail's other strictures. She tugged at Simon's coat sleeve.

'Come out of there. It's horrible.'

She led the way into the next cellar. Simon followed her, muttering, 'They must be worth hundreds of dollars. Hundreds.'

The third cellar proved to contain nothing more interesting than bunkers of coal, logs and kindling. As their candle lit up the room there was a brief frantic scuffling from the kindling bunker.

'Rats,' said Tirza with distaste. She was not exactly afraid of rats, not on the farm where they sometimes rustled amongst the hay and were hunted down by the wild barn cats. And in fact she had a certain fondness for field mice. But she didn't want to meet rats here in this confined space with its unpleasant, grave-yard smells.

They retreated to the cellar stairs and Simon pointed out that the door up into the kitchens had no lock on it. From there they were free to wander at will all over the house. The downstairs rooms were as he had described them to Tirza. The furniture was all covered with yellowing dust-sheets. Lifting them up they could see uncomfortable-looking couches and chairs with gilded wood and silky damask upholstery, fragile and splitting with age. They recognised a harp in one corner under its cover, much larger than the Irish harp in the Penhaligons' drawing room. They climbed on top of the dining-room table to inspect one of the peculiar bags hanging from the ceiling and found that it enclosed a fancy chandelier – looped strings of faceted glass like diamond necklaces for a giantess. Touched, the chandelier tinkled with a cold sweet sound.

Generations of disapproving Tremaynes stared down at them from the walls as they poked and pried. They were a handsome lot, but arrogant looking with their high noses and magnificent old-fashioned clothes. Near the top of the row hanging on the wall up the side of the stairs there was one face which seemed much more friendly. It was a young man with a pair of gun dogs

63

at his heels and a hat perched at a cocky angle on his curly hair. Tirza took the candle from Simon and peered at the brass plate fixed to the bottom of the frame.

'Everard Tremayne 1890,' she read. 'Say, Simon, that must be Miss Susanna's young man, the one who was sweet on her when they went on the skating party.'

They looked at the painting with respect. It was history, that painting, thought Tirza. The past. But Miss Susanna had known him. And he looked like somebody you could know even now, despite his old-fashioned clothes.

Simon had not come upstairs when he had found his way into the house before, so they were exploring new territory now. The bedrooms were in some ways more intriguing than the downstairs rooms, because things had been left lying about. In the main bedroom that faced towards the ocean they found a book on the night-stand beside the bed, a pair of yellowed lace gloves and some tarnished silver-backed brushes on a dressing table inside one of the windows. There were folding wooden shutters as well as sunshades blocking the windows. Both of them pulling together, they managed to fold the shutters back, ripping apart the sticky cobwebs which were netted across the cracks. The hinges squealed, startling them for a moment, but there was no one to hear. The shade fell inwards away from the window glass with a sigh. The shades were designed to be used in summer, pulled down to keep the rooms cool and protect the furniture from the sun. The shutters were for winter warmth. For some reason the Tremaynes' manager had pulled down the shades and then closed the shutters, trapping the shades behind them.

It was then that Tirza, pulling the shade to one side, saw her aunt walking home along the coast path with her chip basket over her arm. Inside this abandoned house she felt like the ghost of one of the ancient Tremaynes looking out on the sunshine of a winter's day of some other century. The sounds of Simon moving about the room faded, but the sight of the snowy ter-races cascading down from the house to the cliff-edged lawn brightened sharply. She sensed, but did not see, other people moving about that winter garden, caught an echo of laughter from the direction of the stables. The image of the house and its interlocked life of family and servants burned for a moment on her inner eye as fierce and cold as the air over the ice on Gooseneck Lake. The sensation of herself as a someone else gripped her, then spun away, leaving her dizzy. She turned from the window to see that Simon was pulling out drawers and opening cupboards.

'Do you think we ought to do that?' she asked doubtfully. Somehow their presence seemed more of an intrusion up here in this bedroom than it had in the cellars or the downstairs rooms.

Simon looked at her in surprise.

'Why not? They've been gone for years – soon after we were born. If they wanted any of this stuff they'd have come back for it, wouldn't they? Or sent for it?'

He sounded reasonable, but Tirza felt a ripple of discomfort as he took a pearl-handled pocket knife out of a desk drawer and carried it over to the window to examine. She turned to look at the bed. It was an old four-poster, carved and ornamented, with brittle curtains looped back and tied with heavy cords to the posts at the head. There was a frilled canopy above, from which a length of braid dangled down, swaying slightly in a current of air. She realised with a shock that they must be creating the movement in the air themselves, and before they had intruded the air in the room had been quite still for years, since she was a small child. She touched the elegant frilled bedcover cautiously with a single fingertip, as though it might fall apart. It reminded her of Miss Havisham's house in *Great Expectations*, which she and Christina had read together the previous fall. Except that this room seemed prettier, less depressing than she had imagined Miss Havisham's house. And since they had opened the shutters the room was filled with a diffused sunlight, bright from the reflections off the snow.

Tirza picked up the book from the night-stand. *The Poems of Robert Frost*. A faded green ribbon was marking a place, and she let the book fall open at the page. 'The Road Not Taken'. She read the poem, standing there in the elegant empty room, and wondered who had left the marker but never come back for the book.

'Will you please stay back after class, Tirza Libby,' said Miss Bennett. It was an order, not a request. 'I want to talk to you.'

Wilma Potts rolled her eyes at Tirza. She spent most of her time in school either crouched over their shared desk half asleep or balking at supposed threats from every corner. She drew away from Tirza now as though she were contagious, taking her sour unwashed smell with her. Tirza did not like Wilma, but she felt sorry for her. When they changed into their heavy cotton slips for gymnastics, she had seen the red weals across Wilma's back, the marks of far harsher beatings than she ever received herself.

Her own minor misdemeanours were punished by Abigail, who wielded a thin whippy switch, cutting a few swift stripes across the back of Tirza's bare legs. Occasionally, if she was really angry, she insisted that Nathan give Tirza the belt – something he would rarely do on his own account. Humiliated and furious after a belting, Tirza would seek consolation by sailing *Stormy Petrel* far out to sea, until Flamboro diminished to a blur on the shoreline. In winter, when flight over the waves was impossible, she usually escaped to Christina's cabin.

In the lower grades, she had barely had occasion to speak to Wilma. She hadn't given much thought to that heavily marked back. But now that they shared a desk she was more aware of it, especially on Mondays when Wilma was particularly apt to wince if Tirza bumped against her accidentally.

She grinned at Wilma reassuringly now.

'Can't be anything too bad. Maybe she wants me to be ink monitor next week.'

Wilma gave her a feeble smile. Tirza was never ink monitor. She was too impatient. Instead of filling the china ink-wells in each desk neatly from the long-spouted ink can, she would pour too fast, splashing the ink about and overfilling the wells so that ink seeped through the well holes, trickling down and ruining the papers and books stored inside.

As the rest of the class gathered their belongings and filed out to the corridor to put on their outdoor clothes, Tirza reviewed her conduct over the last week. She could think of nothing meriting punishment. She'd even been given an A minus for her theme on the subject of 'Liberty'. She had quite enjoyed writing it. As the work on *Stormy Petrel* was finished and all Nathan's gear was mended and refurbished, she had not been pining to get her homework over with as soon as possible each evening. She hoped Miss Bennett would be quick, because she had promised to visit Christina. The snow was beginning to soften, and she would have to wade through it in boots, which dragged out the time of the walk.

Miss Bennett closed the door and came back to her desk. She looked strained about the eyes, although she smiled at Tirza. Her fiancé Pete Flett had been at sea for a month now, and was believed to be on convoy duty in the North Atlantic, though no one knew for sure.

'Now, Tirza,' said Miss Bennett, beckoning to her, 'I won't keep you long. I was very pleased with the theme you wrote this week.'

'Thank you, ma'am.'

'I've been meaning to speak to you for some while, but it was your theme that made me sure it was time.'

Tirza waited, with a politely enquiring look on her face.

Miss Bennett twisted a pencil between her fingers, and did not seem to know how to go on.

'Yes, ma'am?' said Tirza encouragingly.

'You see, you have a very good mind, Tirza. But most of the time you don't use it. You and I both know that. You do just enough to get by, and not a jot or tittle more. I watch you in class. You whip through your math in no time, then you just sit daydreaming. You've read more books than anyone else in class, I know that from some of the answers you come out with.'

'My grandmother and I read things together,' said Tirza gruffly, not sure where all this was leading.

'Mrs Libby?' said Miss Bennett in surprise.

'No, my other grandmother. Mrs O'Neill.'

'Oh.' Miss Bennett looked even more surprised. 'The – er – lady who lives in a cabin in the forest?'

'She graduated from Vassar *summa cum laude*,' said Tirza coldly.

'Really? I'd no idea. Ah, perhaps that accounts for it.'

Miss Bennett tapped her teeth with her pencil.

'You see, Tirza, I think you could be a really good scholar. Perhaps you could go to college like your grandmother, and become a lawyer, or a doctor. Do something fine with your life. I think you have it in you. But not if you go on wasting your time, not making any effort with your studies. What do you say?'

'I'm sorry,' Tirza mumbled. 'I don't understand what you are asking.'

'You'll be going to high school in Portland next fall. You have a few more months before the end of this school year. I want you to try really hard, to work at your studies, so you'll be put into one of the top classes when you go there, one that will prepare you for college boards in four years' time. Will you do that? Will you do that for me?'

Tirza shuffled her feet uncomfortably.

'I'll try, ma'am.'

'Good. Good.' Miss Bennett looked relieved to have finished her speech. 'Off you go then.'

Outside Tirza sprang up the hill towards the path through the forest as fast as the soggy snow would let her. Study harder? Go to college? She laughed out loud. Not likely. She had better things to do with her time.

<><><>

Winter was slackening its grip on the land. Snow began to slide off roofs in the warmth of midday, but at night the frost bit as hard as ever. The slipping, slithering snow — caught distorted on houses and barns, on fish sheds and fir branches — froze overnight into grotesque shapes. Tobias and Sam finished cutting the foot-square blocks from the ice-pond. Tirza stood on the ice pushing the blocks along the channel of clear water with a pole, while Tobias and Simon hoisted them on to the ice sled. The plough-horse Lady towed the sled, without anyone to lead her, down to the ice-house, a half-subterranean structure under a dark corner of the woods which never caught the sun, even in midsummer. There Sam tipped the blocks off the sled and stacked them up, piling sawdust around them for insulation. The others joined him there when each load had been shifted and they worked together, packing everything tightly till no corner of ice showed. It was serious work. Well insulated, the ice would keep until the cold winds began again in fall. Poorly cobbled together, the store of ice would turn into slush and sink away during the heat of July and August, just when it was needed to keep the ice-boxes cold for meat and fish. Even more urgently, it was needed to cool down the milk cans after milking. Tobias felt about his supply of ice for the summer just as Harriet felt about the stores of bottled and canned food she laid by for winter. When the work was finished and the ice-house filled, he sighed in satisfaction.

'That's a good job done, then. This will be one summer we won't run short.'

He shook his head with an exasperated laugh.

'You two won't remember, but when Martha was ten we had a real scorcher of a summer. Martha started inviting all her friends over. We didn't guess what they were up to, though I kept finding the ice-house door open at the end of the long summer afternoons, when I came to load the pickup. Blamed old Sam for it, didn't I?'

'Ayuh.' Sam snorted. 'I knew I ain't done it, but I guessed who had. Hung around behind that clump of trees one day, and kept my eyes peeled.'

'It was Martha?' Tirza asked hopefully.

'Ayuh. Showed her pals inside with almighty airs and graces. Let them take bits of ice to suck and put on their heads to keep cool in the heat. Charged them a nickel a time.'

Tobias grunted. 'Lost a lot of the ice with the door being left open. There was barely enough to see August out, and none at all for September, which was near as hot that year.'

'So that's why you've always said you'll tan my backside if I go in the ice-house,' said Simon.

'Wasn't ever going to run that risk again,' said Tobias.

<><><>

Two weeks after the last of the ice had been cut and the ice-house finally filled, Dancer's foal was born, in the middle of a night loud with sleet-laden gales.

It was a long and difficult birth, and Simon stayed up all night with his father and Sam in the horse barn, helping as much as he could. Harriet spent the time carrying out rags and buckets of hot water from the kitchen, and making them sandwiches and coffee. They struggled with the labouring mare, her eyes staring till the whites showed. Simon's nostrils were filled with the bitter smell of man sweat and the sweet smell of horse sweat, and the sweeter, sticky smell of blood. At last the foal, a colt, lay motionless on the straw, its coat wet and streaked with blood. It looked dead.

It wasn't the first time Simon had helped with a birth. But that night every detail seemed to burn into his mind. He felt the mare's pain and fear, and his shirt stuck to his skin with sweat. The loose box throbbed with some feeling which was new to him. A revulsion against farming, against the passion and the suffering and the ruthlessness of it all rose up in his throat, choking him. He wanted to escape, out into the clean night air, away from the tentacles of the farm which bound him like chains. But instead he knelt by Dancer's head, caressing her gently behind the ears, while she drew long shuddering breaths. Her legs were trembling, and convulsive ripples ran over the skin of her side like water in a lake under a strong breeze. Lady, whose foal was due in another couple of weeks, leaned her head over the partition between the stalls and whickered anxiously.

Feeling the coarse hair of Dancer's mane soaked with sweat under his hand, Simon began to rub her neck dry with a handful of straw while Tobias and Sam worked on the foal with an old rough towel. Usually Tobias whistled tunelessly between his teeth when he had just delivered a foal or a calf, but he was silent now, and Simon feared for the colt.

'Easy now, old girl,' he crooned to Dancer, using a rag to swab away the sticky foam which had dried in gouts around her mouth. He felt twisted up with pity for her. He wondered for the first time what it must be like to be a mare or a woman. To have to go through that agony to give birth. And it might all be for nothing. He reached up above his head and patted Lady's soft nose where it was poked over the partition.

'It's OK, Lady. She's all right now.'

But Dancer shut her eyes and let her head drop back on to his lap.

'Come on, none of that,' he said bracingly in his mother's tones. 'Back on your feet with you.' But Dancer looked so tired, and so old, too. There were hollows around her eyes and jaw that he had never noticed before, and angles of bone that stood out sharply, casting dark shadows in the light from the lamp which hung from the rafters. He ran his hand down her neck and shoulder. She was trembling less now. The mares were both older than he was and were as much a part of his life as his mother and father. He was suddenly afraid for her.

He looked round at his father.

'Is the foal dead?' he asked.

Tobias shook his head.

'Its heart's beating and it's breathing, but it's feeble.'

He lifted the foal gently and set it down near Dancer's nose. Her nostrils twitched and her eyes flew open, then she began to struggle with her back legs, trying to get them under her. Tobias lifted the foal out of the way, and they all three stood clear as the mare heaved herself wearily to her feet. She shook her head, scattering bits of straw from her mane, and a last shiver ran over her back, then she poked her head forward and sniffed again at the foal. She licked its face. The foal lay still in Tobias's arms at first, then it moved a little, lifting its heavy head, swaying, on the thin neck. Carefully Tobias put the foal down in the straw beside the mare, trying to set it on its feet. It collapsed, all four legs bending and sprawling in an uncoordinated heap. Tobias stood it up again, and Dancer turned her head to it, blowing softly and licking. Lady, watching still over the partition, whickered again. As Tobias took his supporting hands away, the foal staggered, but remained upright. It shook its head, leaned towards its mother and nuzzled her.

Tobias began to blow through his front teeth, emitting a few faint sounds. Sam gathered up the rags and buckets, and raked the bloody straw out of the stall.

'Look, Dad,' said Simon at last, with a sigh of relief, 'he's sucking.'

It was a miracle, every time. The stubby tail, brown with a streak of white showing in it now that the hair was dry, began to jerk, marking time. Dancer echoed Simon's sigh and nosed about in her manger, finding some scraps of the bran mash they had given her during the night.

Tobias gripped Simon's arm briefly. 'He'll do, son. He'll do.' As he stepped out of the stall he trumpeted into his handkerchief. 'Straw dust in my nose,' he explained to Sam. 'Heck, it's past five. Time we got on with the chores.'

Simon walked away from them, out of the barn, across the pasture and into the edge of the pine wood. He began to beat his forehead rhythmically against the rough resinous bark of an old balsam fir while the cold dawn wind dried his cheeks.

More than a week later, the afternoon after Lady's foal was born – cleanly and without difficulty – Tirza had come up to help with the evening milking because Tobias had driven into Portland to fetch a spare part for the tractor. While they were sitting in the kitchen afterwards, the telephone rang. Tobias had one of the six telephones in Flamboro, along with Flett's Stores, Hector Swanson, the Penhaligons and two other houses in the township. Nathan had declared that he saw no need for the instrument. On the rare occasions he needed to make a call, he used the public phone at the store.

Harriet lifted the Bakelite earpiece from its cradle and strained upwards to speak into the mouthpiece. The varnished mahogany box with its crank handle had been mounted on the wall inside the back door at the right height for Tobias. Harriet, who took most of the calls, always had to stand on tiptoe to make herself heard.

'Hello? Helen?... Yes... Yes, I'm sure they can... I'll call you back tonight.'

As she hung up she was smiling.

'I thought it felt like a sugar snow, with these warm days and freezing nights. How would you both like to go and help with the sugaring on Uncle Frank's farm?'

Tirza and Simon both jumped up. This was great news. Harriet's sister Helen lived just over the state boundary in New Hampshire. Helping with the maple syrup harvest meant at least three weeks off school, a trip to Uncle Frank's farm and all the fun of sugaring off. It was hard work, of course. Heavy and tiring, and lasting into the night, but their cousins would be there. Some years they weren't needed, if the sap yield was poor. But this year conditions were ideal, and Uncle Frank wanted every pair of hands he could get. He would pay them, too. Not much, but enough to start Tirza thinking about a proper anchor for *Stormy Petrel* instead of the sling-stone she used at present. Simon was pining for a new rifle, a proper one of his own, not a hand-down from his father. They looked at each other joyfully.

'Let's see,' said Harriet. 'It's Thursday today. If you go to school tomorrow and take excusal notes for Miss Bennett... then tomorrow evening, if we do the milking early, we could drive over in the pickup. We'd get there about eleven, say. Your dad and I could stay till Sunday midday. Sam can manage till then. We'll lend a hand at Helen's, then we'll leave the two of you, and come back to fetch you when you're not needed any more.'

She turned to Tirza. 'Do you think Abigail will let you go?'

'Certain sure,' said Tirza confidently. Her grandmother would never, not under any circumstances, have let her off school for three weeks in the ordinary way of things, but Abigail had been a farmer's wife on this very farm for thirty-five years, and she knew that when the land demanded it, everything else had to be abandoned.

On Friday evening they set off, about an hour after dusk, with their supper in a big wicker basket entrusted to Tirza and Simon in the back of the truck. Tobias had rigged up metal hoops over the truck bed and lashed a tarpaulin on to them, making a kind of tent. There was straw on the truck bed for warmth and Harriet had packed them around with blankets. The tented space under the tarpaulin gave an illusion of cosiness, but the air still felt bitterly cold on their faces and hands. Temperatures of ten below freezing had been forecast for the night.

Harriet opened the sliding window in the back of the cab as they bounced down the track towards the farm gate.

'Are you going to be all right? Are you sure now? If you start feeling too cold, just tap on the window and one of you can change places with me for a while.'

'We're fine,' said Tirza.

'When can we eat?' said Simon.

'Not yet awhile. Sakes, son, you just ate a ham sandwich not ten minutes ago.'

The truck turned from the farm track on to the Portland road. They could not see anything from inside their moving tent, but they could tell roughly where they were just from the feel of the road. Tirza buried her hands under the blankets and warmed them between her knees.

'Tirza,' Simon said suddenly out of the dark, 'do you reckon you'll have any babies?'

'Babies? I don't know. I don't know as I want to get married. Why?'

'Wouldn't you be scared?' He cleared his throat. They did not usually discuss anything so personal. 'I was thinking, after Dancer's foal was born... It hurts so much. And all that blood.'

An embarrassed silence lingered in the air. Tirza drew her knees up to her chin and wrapped her arms around them.

'Probably I won't get married, so it won't happen, will it?'

◄◆►

The next morning Tirza woke stiff from the long journey in the truck. Together with Simon she had spent what was left of the night rolled in blankets on the floor of Aunt Helen's shuttered porch along with their cousins Sue and Frank Junior, who had given up their bedrooms to the adult relatives, and Lou, Peggy, Maribell and Sammy, who had arrived the day before with their mother Una and their father Harold, Harriet's brother. Lou was seventeen and near enough grown up. He was going to college in the fall, unless he was drafted. But the rest of them were all close in age. Helping with the sugaring was one of the rare times they had a chance to meet up.

Tirza rolled over, groaning. She and Simon were the only ones left in the tangle of blankets on the floor. The banging of Aunt Helen's gong rang out from the kitchen, and she realised she had already half heard it in her sleep. She rose to her feet stiffly, picked up her bundle of clothes and stepped over Simon to reach the door. Everyone else was up and dressed, so she hurried in the bathroom and reached the kitchen as the others were sitting down in rows at the big kitchen table.

Uncle Frank and two of the farmhands came in the back door, stamping the snow off their boots. It was getting light outside and they had already been into the maple woods, drilling more trees.

'We'd best make a quick breakfast,' said Frank. 'I want to get all the drilling finished today. Tirza, you can follow me and hammer in the spiles in the Windy Top orchard.'

After breakfast Tirza collected a big basket of metal spiles from the sugarhouse and followed her uncle through the snow up the hill to the highest orchard of the farm, halfway up the mountainside. The divisions of the rock maple forest were called orchards, but bore no likeness to a fruit orchard on a regular farm. They were simply sections of trees, separated from each other by boundaries visible only to Frank and his hired men, each containing about two hundred trees. The basket was heavy and Tirza was out of breath by the time they reached Windy Top. Yesterday someone had brought a load of galvanised sap buckets up with the tractor and left them in a heap beside the path.

Frank took a brace and bit out of a holster hitched to his belt and ran his hand over the bark of the first maple, like a doctor feeling a patient. The places where sap holes had been drilled healed over with scar tissue and remained dry for the rest of the tree's life. It would take twenty-five years before the trunk could be drilled even near to an old hole. Frank looked absorbed, running his fingers over a likely spot for a new bore hole. He was the fifth generation to sugar on this land and his knowledge was in his fingertips.

He began to drill, angling the hole slightly upward.

'Remember when you were first here?' he said. 'No more than three or four you'd have been. You were worried the drilling would hurt the tree.'

'Ayuh.'

'I recall saying, No more than cutting your fingernails hurts you. These trees are like members of the family. I wouldn't hurt a one of them any more than I'd hurt you.'

'And you said that trees are faithful to you if you're faithful to them.'

'Well, that's true. My grandfather's grandfather tapped these trees, most on 'em, and we're still eating their syrup today. If the trees were hurt when we tapped them, they'd not give us the sap, now, would they?'

Frank drew the bit gently out of the tree and went round to the other side to find another likely spot. Tirza pushed a spile in as far as it would go, then tapped it home with a wooden mallet. While her uncle drilled the next hole, she walked back to the path, picked up two buckets and shook the snow out of them. She hooked one bucket below the first spile, then inserted a spile into her uncle's second drill-hole.

Neither Tirza nor Frank was given to talking unnecessarily. They worked their way through the trees, exchanging occasional remarks but mostly in silence. The maples were all natural-grown, not planted groves, so the trees grew irregularly. Tirza thought she might have missed one on her own, but Frank moved surely from one to the next as if he had a map in his head.

It took them until dinnertime to drill half the orchard, then they walked back down the mountain towards the farmhouse. Tirza went into the sugarhouse to refill her basket with more spiles while Frank checked on the progress of the syruping. The sugarhouse was a long low shed, with a corrugated tin roof and pine shingles on its walls weathered to the colour of maple cream. Inside was the evaporator – a great ramshackle tin-plate construction made by Frank's father and stretching nearly the length of the sugarhouse. The firebox had to be kept fed with four-foot logs day and night until sugaring was finished. Peggy's face was flushed with the heat as she lugged a rough pine branch across the floor.

Lou was sitting up on the high evaporator chair, his feet on a level with Frank's eyes.

'She's starting to foam maybe too much, Uncle. Want to look?'

Frank climbed up, checked that the temperature gauge was steady on 219 degrees, and peered in at the boiling sap, which had been run down into the evaporator from the holding tank.

'Hmm. Yeah. Tirza? Hop along to the kitchen and ask your Aunt Helen for a piece of fatty salt pork.'

Tirza put down her basket and hopped. If the sap started to form too thick a foam coating on top, evaporation slowed down and the risk of burning increased. She came back with a salted pig's leg and passed it up to her uncle. Then she grabbed the spreaders between the legs of the evaporator chair and climbed up on the other side – it was like a pair of ladders with a chair on top. The smell of the boiling sap, which filled the whole farm, was intense here – sweet yet pungent.

She hung on to Lou's neck and leaned over as Frank dropped the pig's leg gently into the evaporator. Almost at once the scum of foam began to recoil from the fatty meat, shrinking away to the sides and gradually disappearing. Frank looked at his watch.

'Another half-hour, then we'll run her off. You're doing fine, boy. I'll send someone out to relieve you so's you can get some dinner. Peggy, you girls make up the fire once more, then cut along and have yourselves some food.'

'I'll wait till you run off,' said Lou. 'I'd like to watch it.'

'OK. Say, Tirza,' said Frank, climbing down to the floor again, 'come over here. I've got something I want to show you.'

They went over to the end of the sugarhouse where buckets and spiles were piled and rows of earthenware gallon jugs were lined up on a table. From the floor Frank heaved up a section of tree trunk about three feet across and a foot thick and balanced the weight of it on the edge of the table.

'Have a look at this.'

Tirza looked where he was pointing. A segment of tree and bark had been sliced off, and on the pale inner wood there was a discoloured mark like a rough V shape.

'This was an old tree past sapping that we cut down in Windy Top last fall. About where we stopped drilling just now. We were running it through the circular saw for planks when I saw this, so I cut that section out of the trunk to keep.'

'What is it?'

'Well now, sometimes we find spiles accidentally left behind in an old tree, where the tree has healed over them. The modern metal ones play hell with the saw.' He laughed ruefully. 'The older spiles were carved out of white ash and they don't do any harm. But this is older still, and I've only seen one like it once before, about twenty year ago.'

'Is it the mark of a spile?'

'It's an Indian sap hole. They'd cut a deep V and fix their buckets under. Well, I don't suppose it'd be a bucket. Some kind of bark cup, maybe, or a gourd. That mark was made two hundred and fifty, three hundred years ago, by the Abenakis sapping these selfsame trees. We learned how to do it from them. Couldn't really better what the old red men did. Those Abenaki great-grandaddies of yours, they made this.'

Tirza ran her finger along the ancient mark.

'They maybe used baskets for the sap,' she said. 'Girna says their baskets were so fine woven, they would hold water.'

'Just remember, when you're pouring syrup over your pancakes,' said Frank. 'The Indians were living with these trees and caring for them before a white man ever set foot in New England.'

By the next day all the trees were drilled and running, and apart from those working in the sugarhouse everyone was up in the orchards carrying buckets. Tirza was in Three Springs this time, collecting sap near Sue and Frank Junior. They worked their way through the trees from the path to the far end of the orchard where the sugar maples ended at a slide of loose scree as the side of the mountain fell away. Sue was working the trees below Tirza, Frank Junior the ones above, but they moved at about the same pace and could call remarks back and forth to each other. The buckets were not very full this morning, the first day after the trees had been tapped. The two highest orchards, standing in the cold air at the top of the forest, were not yet running as freely as those lower down the mountainside.

Just below them on the path the collection tank had been parked. A big three-hundred-gallon tub on wheels, it had been hauled up here first thing by tractor and would be hauled down again at midday. It was hard work lifting the buckets high enough to tip into the tank.

Waiting for Frank Junior to pour his sap in, Tirza asked, 'Are you going to stay on the farm when you grow up, Frank? Will you carry on sugaring after your dad?'

Frank looked at her as if she was demented.

'Of course. What else would I do? My ancestors have been sugaring on this land since before the War of Independence.'

'So would I, if it was mine,' said Tirza, thinking of the Abenaki scar in the old maple. 'I think it's a great life.'

'It's hard too,' said Frank, watching her pour the clear sap from her buckets. 'Don't never know what the weather will do, and sugaring's all to do with the weather. Get a quick soft spring and the run is over soon as wink. Get a bitter spring and the sap hardly rises, sluggish as a snail. Have a dry summer the year before, the trees don't make many leaves, then sure thing, next spring the sap will be thin. Still and all, I wouldn't want to live anywheres else, be anything else.'

He gestured around at the trees, standing stately up from the snow with the sun slanting through their bare boughs and the sugar sap drip, dripping with a metallic ring into the empty buckets.

'Can't beat it,' Tirza agreed, and went back to carrying.

After dinner she lingered long enough to see the run-off in the sugarhouse before climbing back up to Three Springs. The morning's sap had boiled for about four hours and Uncle Frank reckoned it was now up to eighty-five per cent sugar content. It was strained off through a series of troughs, and the top trough of the evaporator was refilled from the holding tank to start the next cycle. Larry, one of the hired men, was filling gallon jars from a spigot which ran off the bottom trough. He poured a little into a battered tin cup and handed it to Tirza.

'Let that cool, now, or it'll burn the tongue offen you.'

Tirza carried the cup outside and plunged it up to the rim in a bank of snow. Gradually the syrup stopped steaming and when she laid her hand against the side of the cup it was just warm. She stuck her finger into the syrup and licked it off – the first syrup of the season. It tasted sweet, but with a clean, smoky, maple taste that was like nothing else in the world. She sipped a little from the side of the cup and rolled it around on her tongue with her eyes shut. Sweet things usually made her feel sick. But maple syrup was different – like drinking the flavour of the forest. It made you feel your roots running right down into the earth, like the maple trees drawing up the spring water and food from the soil, even though they grew on such hard rocky ground. Behind her eyelids she could see the Abenakis, tasting the first syrup of the season, gift of the gods of the forest, promise of spring, promise of life returning after the bitterness of winter.

<hr>

Tirza and Simon stayed four weeks at the sugaring. Some of the casual labour which used to come and work in a heavy season was not to be had this year – the men had gone to war, or joined the women in armaments factories which were paying good money. So the school-age boys and girls were needed as they had never been needed before.

At last, though, the run was over, the spiles pulled from the last trees, the sticky buckets piled up for the long business of washing up, the last tankful of sap boiled down to syrup.

'Four hundred and thirty-seven gallons,' said Uncle Frank at supper, 'not counting what's set aside for our own use. It's a record year.'

He looked at all of them, family, neighbours and hired hands sitting around the table. Their eyes were red from working through the night and bending over the fire or the evaporator, their hands were stained and their hair and clothes sticky with sap. They were exhausted, but pretty pleased with themselves.

'Sugaring-off party tomorrow,' said Frank.

The night after the party, lying for the last time on the floor of the closed porch, Tirza watched the frosty sky through the opening where Aunt Helen had folded back one of the shutters to let in fresh air. She yawned and the three stars she could see in the patch of sky swam in front of her eyes. She wished sugaring could go on for ever. Because Harriet had brought bad news. Martha and Billy were arriving next week to live at the farm.

Chapter 5

Intermezzo
Scotland: Spring 1980

COLIN TENNANT PROVED to be a dapper man of fifty, with a balding head and a cheerful manner. Tirza reckoned he would meet life's trials head on and bounce back from any adversity. She liked him better than she had anticipated. The gallery was a grand building on George Street, one of the classical, porticoed houses of Edinburgh's New Town, built in the eighteenth century after the draining of the Nor' Loch and the exodus of the upper classes to the more salubrious lands to the north of the mediaeval city. The entire ground floor of the gallery was to be given over to the exhibition of her work and when she saw the grandeur of the surroundings and the eagerness of Colin and his staff to carry out everything according to her wishes, she regretted her earlier churlishness.

The question of whether the arrangement of the exhibition should be chronological or thematic had mostly resolved itself, since the chronological stages of her work fell naturally into themes, as she had moved from one type of assignment to another.

'Did you work as a freelance right from the start?' Colin asked. They were lunching in a tiny Italian restaurant in one of the many streets which form a grid linking George Street and Princes Street.

'Yes.' Tirza wound tagliatelle round her fork and fielded it deftly. She had been taught the trick by an Italian-American sergeant during a spell at base camp just outside Saigon.

'I left high school before I was seventeen, and I'd toyed with the idea of going to college and getting some qualifications, but my father couldn't afford college fees. So I took a vacation job that summer to earn some money. And I thought it would give me time to decide whether I really wanted to spend another four years cooped up studying.'

She put down her fork and gazed past him out of the window, where the Edinburgh traffic ground slowly past.

'I was working as a waitress in a diner in New Jersey and I got to taking pictures of the people who stopped by. Truck drivers, mostly, and some families. Big families, without much money, the kind that stop at diners and fill the kids up with hamburgers and french fries. I'm talking about the days before the giant multinational franchises, you understand.'

She took another mouthful of pasta and washed it down with Frascati.

'I was planning all along to be a photographer, and if I'd gone to college I would have done courses which were relevant. Though in those days you couldn't take the sort of things you can now, like a degree in photographic studies.'

'So did you sell those summer photographs?'

'Sure did. Not to the people I photographed. That was my first idea, but they were mostly just passing through, and too poor anyway to be wasting their money on photographs they didn't need. It was one of the truckers who suggested I should try selling them to a magazine. Of course at that age you think you're going to go straight to the top and sell to *National Geographic*, but competition is fierce, and they wouldn't have looked at anything from a teenage kid. However, he showed me a trucking magazine – it's defunct now – and they paid me my first ever money.'

'For pictures of lorry drivers? Can we have some of those for the exhibition?'

'Sure, no problem. Of course that went to my head. Three photographs earned me more than a whole week of waitressing. I was nearly stupid enough to give up my job on the spot, but luckily I had the sense to stick it out till Labour Day, and it's a good thing I did, because I didn't sell anything else for a couple of months.'

She smiled wryly.

'I'd have had to come begging for my job back, or starved. You see, I hadn't taken into account the fact that the boss gave me my meals and an army cot in the kitchen to sleep on. So even though my wages for a twelve-hour day in dollars and cents could have been carried by a fairly muscular mouse, I had food and shelter. Then at the end of August I sold some of my studies of hot, tired, travelling families to an upmarket arty magazine, and they paid real money. I decided to give up the idea of college. If I could already make money taking photographs, why waste more time?'

Colin topped up her glass and they ordered tiramisu and coffee.

'Did you stay on at the diner?'

'No, my job finished after Labour Day, when the vacation crowds dropped off, so I bought myself a better camera and got a job as a staff photographer on a small-town newspaper in Rhode Island. Lasted two weeks.'

For a while they were busy eating. Then when the waiter had refilled their cups, Tirza sat back against the plush bench, stirring her coffee idly and gazing into space.

'I was useless as a staff photographer. I was bored out of my mind, taking shots of bouncing baby competitions and the retiral of Mr Smith from town hall or Mrs Brown from grade school, complete with gold watch and attendant colleagues. And of course I couldn't stand the discipline – it was worse than being back at school. So I quit. For a while life was pretty hand-to-mouth, but I survived, and got some overseas assignments, and I built up a network of editors who would take my work. Then after the Vietnam war broke out, I persuaded one of them to make me their official war photographer and correspondent. It was a middle-sized town newspaper in middle America. All their staff reporters were middle-aged men with middle-sized families living in comfortable middle-class neighbourhoods. They weren't clamouring to be sent to cover Vietnam. But I had my own reasons for wanting to go, which we will not discuss.'

'Forgive me,' said Colin, running his finger around the lip of his cup, 'but weren't you afraid? Or were you too young to realise what you were letting yourself in for?'

'That's very flattering of you, Colin, but I was in my thirties by then. No, I knew what I was letting myself in for. Or thought I did.'

She swallowed once, briefly, as memory surfaced.

'Now, as for how this applies to the exhibition, I think all the stuff prior to Vietnam can go in one room, and within that we can arrange it by theme. The truck drivers – I went on photographing them. Still do, sometimes. Great faces. The families. Then there's a whole series on Harlem. Later I hiked around for several years and took shots of forgotten places and forgotten people – Cajun country, the Indian reservations, the last throes of the sharecroppers in Louisiana and Georgia. In the mid-fifties I went down to Mexico and then South America. Even got up to Alaska eventually and shot the Inuits and a few crazy prospectors still around hoping for gold. Now there were some faces!'

She pondered briefly.

'Between '59 and '62 I had a couple of trips to the Middle East and spent four months in India.'

Colin was taking notes in a black leather notebook.

'Then Vietnam?' he asked. 'A whole room to itself.'

'Yes. I was there from '63.'

'I'd like to reproduce extracts from some of the pieces you wrote, and mount them amongst the pictures.'

'Fine.'

The waiter reappeared with the coffee pot. Tirza shook her head at him, but Colin nodded.

'Right. Now after Vietnam – Africa?'

'No. I was in Vietnam till '68, then I went on a short assignment to South America for part of '69. After that I was back and forth between Cambodia and Vietnam from '69 to '73. I suppose we ought to display all the Vietnam and Cambodia material in one room, and put the '69 pictures with the earlier South American ones. Then there's the work I did in Africa – central Africa and the Horn. That was '73 and '74.'

She paused, scraping at the dregs of coffee with her spoon.

'I went back to Phnom Penh at the beginning of '75, to cover the final throes of the conflict. That was when a group of us – Western journalists and photographers, and some of the French diplomats – were caught up in the fall of the city to the Khmer

Rouge. We spent a fairly unpleasant time holed up in the French Embassy until we were expelled. They forced us to make an unspeakably nasty journey in open trucks – getting lost in the jungle, alternately broiled and soaked to the skin. These fanatical boys of ten or eleven kept their AK47s pointed at us the whole time. Every time we hit a pot-hole, we expected the guns to go off, but eventually we made it to the border with Thailand.'

She laughed recklessly.

'At least you valued every moment you managed to stay alive. Then I had another spell in South America for the rest of the year, mostly photographing street kids. That whole situation has got worse and worse since I was there. And there are some studies of shanty towns. Interesting to compare with the shanty towns that sprawl out around the cities in Africa. We could almost have a section on shanty towns all over the world, but maybe that would break things up. Forget it. Not a good idea.'

'OK. Then India?'

'And Pakistan and Bangladesh. I'd been working out there a couple of years when I took ill and had to come back.'

'What about the recent Scottish work? Max says you've published hardly any of them.'

Tirza smiled.

'Max is fed up with me. We've recently sold a few to the Sunday travel supplements, but that's all. I'm thinking of putting together a book.'

Colin's head came up like a gun dog fixing on a pheasant.

'Why don't we bring it out to coincide with the exhibition?'

'You're joking. Books take for ever to put together and print.'

'Leave it to me. If you've got the shots, and can provide minimal text – just a caption indicating where they were taken – I can have it ready for the opening. You have to remember this is Edinburgh. There are a lot of small, efficient publishers right here in the city, and several specialise in high-quality glossy art work. They publish catalogues for exhibitions at the Festival, amongst other things, and one or two of them have done work for me before. It won't be a problem.'

———◆◆◆———

After the two days spent with Colin and his staff in Edinburgh, Tirza went back to the island. Grace welcomed her with surprising warmth, weaving affectionately around Tirza's feet while she unpacked, and settling in her lap each evening. Angus Maclean, the postman, had been feeding the cat, but she seemed to have missed Tirza's companionship. During the next week Tirza put together the collection of Scottish photographs with captions for Colin. She had intended to spend longer over the planning of her book, but once she began she found that it came together easily and she enjoyed the sense of urgency which had been missing from her life since she had come to live on the island.

At the end of the week she fixed the outboard on her boat and crossed over to the mainland to send off the parcel, rigid with layers of cardboard and brown paper.

'That will be £2.50,' said Mrs Maclean, 'if you're sure you want to spend all the extra on sending it registered.'

Tirza smiled. 'Oh yes, it's worth it. It's a small price to pay to ensure I don't have to do all that work again.'

Mrs Maclean was clearly longing to know what was in the parcel, but she was too polite to ask. Tirza took pity on her.

'It's just something to do with this exhibition I'm having in Edinburgh.'

'You are having an exhibition in Edinburgh?' Mrs Maclean was impressed. Like the other locals she did not know quite what to make of the American lady who seemed to have no visible means of support.

'An exhibition of photographs, yes. At a gallery in George Street.'

'Fancy!' It was known that Miss Libby took photographs, but Mrs Maclean had not suspected anyone might want to exhibit them. She stored away this information for later dissemination.

Once her parcel was despatched, Tirza found it impossible to work. She was restive by day, despite the recurring bouts of tiredness that still afflicted her, and at night she lay awake turning over in bed, unable to relax her tense limbs. The last of the snow had melted and the microscopic wild flowers that lurked amongst the scrub and heather of her island were beginning to grow, but she could not summon the energy to crawl about photographing them from ground level. The gulls were holding raucous assemblies, fighting for dominance and pairing off, and the curlews which had nested last year at the foot of the rising ground in the centre of the island were back in the same spot.

The days began to lengthen and a little warmth crept hesitantly into the sun. With surprising speed the book proofs arrived and she checked them in a single day. Max telephoned about interviews he was organising.

'Colin is going to book you into a hotel in Edinburgh for two weeks at his expense – starting a week before the opening so you can sort out any final details of the exhibition. I'm setting up the magazine and newspaper interviews for that week. We've got six newspapers – all broadsheets – and three magazines so far. I'm hoping that BBC and ITV news will cover the opening, but you can never count on it, not if some big news story breaks. And I've sorted out one TV interview and two radio interviews for the period around and just after the opening. And *Kaleidoscope* will be covering it.'

'Heavens,' said Tirza, trying to sound impressed but feeling a sinking sensation, 'you have been busy.'

'Well,' said Max, and she could hear a smirk in his voice, 'I am *rather* pleased with myself. Mathilda Goldberg will be doing the TV interview. I think you'll find her quite reasonable. That will be the day after the private view.'

A sudden thought struck Tirza.

'Just a minute, Max. This isn't going to be a *live* interview, is it?'

'Now, don't worry. There will just be a small studio audience, and it will be done in Edinburgh, so you don't have to come down to London. Piece of cake.'

'Max,' said Tirza, 'I could kill you.'

———◆———

After the stress of overseeing the hanging of her photographs in the gallery, the thought of the private view – on the evening before the exhibition opened to the general public – seemed at first almost a relief to Tirza. She had not realised in advance just how disconcerting it would be to see her life's work laid out like this – not only for the judgement of others but as a forced reassessment of what she herself thought she had been doing all those years. Her 'juvenilia', as Colin called them, were hung together in a corner just inside the door of the first room. He saw no reason to make any particular show of them, and she found that by walking swiftly forward whenever she entered the room she could avoid looking at them altogether.

During the week they were mounting and arranging the exhibition she was too much occupied to think very much, but as the first guests filed in from the warm spring streets she suddenly felt nothing but dread. Max had forced her to go shopping for an appropriate outfit with his assistant, Nina, a smart young London woman whose clothes were as slick as her hair and her *maquillage*. She had peered through her huge round glasses at the clothes Tirza was wearing and made small bleating sounds of distress. They had compromised on a trouser suit of pale green linen which felt comfortable, as long as Tirza did not look at herself in a mirror, where a strange creature (new haircut) looked back at her with hostile eyes.

The reception seemed to drag on for hours. Tirza felt the muscles of her face growing tired from maintaining a fixed smile and she heard herself repeating the same banal mutters of thanks for the praise the guests seemed to feel bound to bestow on her. After a while she realised that the hired waiters had been topping up her glass of champagne just too often. The next time one passed with a tray she substituted her glass for one of orange juice and clung to it firmly for the rest of the evening. Gradually she managed to back away from the crowd into a corner of the room displaying her pictures of India and Bangladesh, from where she could see Colin and Max dealing expertly with the guests, without any need for her presence. A door behind her led into the hallway. The ladies' cloakroom was opposite. Tirza retreated thankfully into this sanctuary with her orange juice and a bowl of crisps she found on a table in the hall.

'For heaven's sake,' said Nina in exasperation when she found Tirza there nearly an hour later, 'what are you doing in here? Practically everyone has left. Come on, we're all going off for dinner.'

'I couldn't possibly eat any dinner,' said Tirza. 'My head is splitting. I just want to go to bed.'

'Too much booze on an empty stomach,' said Nina, taking

her firmly by the elbow. 'You'll feel better when you've had something to eat.'

They made their way to Colin's favourite restaurant in Rose Street – Tirza, Max and Nina, Colin and the gallery staff, and a few of the guests who had lingered to the end and then attached themselves to the party. Tirza sat silent in the midst of their excited chatter, nibbling at her trout with almonds. She felt hungry and yet nauseated by the sight of food.

'Now, don't forget your interview tomorrow,' Max was saying. 'Nina will put you into a taxi at ten. Or would you like me to come with you?'

'No, thank you, Max,' said Tirza clearly. 'That will not be necessary. And I think I'll be getting back to my hotel now. I want to get some sleep before making a spectacle of myself tomorrow. Can I pick up a taxi outside here?'

One of the guests stood up as well. Martin... something. 'I'll give you a lift,' he said. 'I've got my car just round the corner. The North British, is it, where you're staying?'

Martin's car was low-slung and sleek and black under the streetlights. Tirza sank down into the seat, which was almost on a level with the pavement. She closed her eyes as Martin started the car and drove off through the empty streets.

It was difficult to climb up out of the car when they reached her hotel, and Martin put a solicitous arm under hers.

'Thank you,' said Tirza, a little brusquely. 'I'm most grateful.'

'The pleasure was entirely mine,' said Martin, suddenly and unexpectedly putting his arms around her.

Tirza went rigid. Sweat began to pour down her back and she arched away from him. Then she raised her hands and pushed him hard in the chest. She was breathing fast in short gasps.

'Hey, no need to get so high and mighty,' he said in tones of offended arrogance.

'Take your hands off me,' said Tirza furiously. She twisted away and ran into the hotel. The man at the reception desk was reading a thriller and looked half asleep. He seemed to notice nothing amiss with her. With a professionally bland smile, he handed her the key to her room, wished her good-night, and turned back to his book.

In her room Tirza threw down her handbag and jacket and

kicked off her shoes. The bathroom held a faint scent of good quality hotel soap, and the virginal white towels were mossy thick. She washed her face and hands over and over until she felt clean. Then she sank into the armchair, wrapping her arms around herself and rocking back and forth on the cold imperial damask. Hating herself.

———◆◆◆———

Tirza had been interviewed on radio, off and on, for years, but she had never before agreed to a television interview. Radio interviews were easy. You were shown to a reception area outside a studio, where the interviewer could be seen like an overblown tropical fish behind the thick glass window, kitted up with headphones and mouthing into a microphone. At an appropriate moment, during a break or a record, you were shown in, sat down and did a voice test on the mike – enumerating solemnly what you had eaten for breakfast. A couple of days ago, going through this charade in the local radio studio, Tirza had intoned, 'Soft-shell crabs, little-neck clams, salted eel bait, two ton of cod.' The interviewer had not batted an eyelid, fiddled with knobs and said, 'Let's try that once more.'

TV was different. She had donned the green suit again and for once had taken the trouble to put on make-up, but as soon as she reached the studio she was whisked away to the make-up room, where they wiped her face clean and started again from the skin up, through several layers. She lost count of how many. Relaxing in the comfortable chair with her head back was deceptive. It almost made her feel she was here to be cosseted, instead of being put on display like a circus animal. They tried to ply her with 'hospitality' – gin and tonic, vodka... It was not yet eleven o'clock in the morning. She shook her head; it was still aching from last night.

She was introduced to Mathilda Goldberg, who seemed pleasant enough, though too absorbed and anxious about the programme to show much personal interest in Tirza. For which she was grateful. Then a woman holding a clipboard and various men with their sleeves rolled up fussed around with the position of the cameras and the arrangement of the seating area. It began to get very hot under the lights. The studio audience was admitted and the woman with the clipboard explained proceedings to them. Then suddenly they were on air.

In an instant Mathilda changed from a harassed presenter to a charming hostess, introducing Tirza and talking about the exhibition. The questions were skilful, drawing out Tirza's reluctant answers, enhancing them. Mathilda smiled easily. Tirza began to relax. She knew that Max had briefed Mathilda not to ask questions about Vietnam, and she did not – or at least not directly. But she skated around the subject, so that Tirza became more and more uneasy.

'Cambodia. I believe you went there in the aftermath of the Vietnam conflict,' said Mathilda, 'yet I notice that many of your pictures show peaceful city streets, rather than the killing fields.'

Tirza felt again the strange atmosphere of Phnom Penh, the sleepy French colonial town, lovely with ironwork balconies and heavy with the scent of blossom. It had reminded her powerfully of the old parts of New Orleans. Mathilda Goldberg must have glanced only casually at the Cambodian pictures. Nina said that she had looked in at the private view for about twenty minutes, during the time Tirza was hiding in the ladies' cloakroom.

Tirza cleared her throat.

'The war in Cambodia was really an extension of the Vietnam war, not its aftermath. The whole of Indo-China was disintegrating. In fact, events during this last year or so are all part of the same pattern. Vietnam's invasion of Cambodia. The Khmer Rouge retreat to the jungle.'

She paused.

'What I was trying to capture, in the pictures of Phnom Penh, was the gradual destruction of what was once one of the most elegant and cultured societies in the world. It was heart-breaking. The Cambodians were a wonderful people – charming, funny, very attractive. Great company.'

Mathilda cocked her head intelligently and expectantly, so Tirza went on.

'In the third photograph in the sequence you'll see a very beautiful young girl coming down the steps of a house with a wide veranda. She's wearing a silk sarong and carrying a paper sunshade. I seem to remember that she was on her way to the Bibliothèque Nationale. She was the daughter of a local doctor.

Much further on in the Cambodian sequence – amongst what you might call the "killing field" photographs – you will see several that look as though they were taken at a demolished factory.'

Tirza stopped. The scene sprang up so clearly before her that she could smell the foul odour of burnt flesh and explosives. The wall of one of the buildings had collapsed behind her just after she had taken the last picture.

'It was, in fact, a fine suburb of the town – after Pol Pot's soldiers had razed much of it to the ground during the final siege. The crowds being herded down the street were the inhabitants of Phnom Penh, driven out of the city to work as slaves in the countryside, where most of them died. In one of the pictures there's a gaunt woman with a terrible scar down her face, dressed in rags. It's the same girl. She had been taken prisoner the previous year. The village where her family had a country house fell to the Khmer Rouge. She was forced at gun-point to become one of their army whores, till she caught syphilis. The scar was a knife slash from an over-enthusiastic client. After that she had no way left to survive but by begging. For me that girl – she was only nineteen in the second photo-graph – says everything that needs to be said about war.'

Mathilda gaped at her. She fumbled for a question, forgetting her carefully prepared script.

'Tell us about how you started as a photographer. How old were you, and what was your first camera?'

It was an innocent enough question, and Tirza should have seen it coming. She felt as though she had been kicked in the stomach. Max knew he was supposed to warn people not to ask questions about her childhood. She cleared her throat.

'My first camera was a Box Brownie. I guess that was most people's first camera in the forties. I was just going on thirteen.'

'Did you buy it yourself?'

'No,' said Tirza with difficulty. 'No. It was given to me. By a British airman who was convalescing near my home after being rescued at sea. He left Maine soon afterwards and I never knew what became of him.'

⎯⎯◈◈◈⎯⎯

By nine o'clock the next morning Tirza was driving north

towards Perth. She had rolled down the windows and opened the roof, and from the spring-warmed Fife countryside an interwoven fabric of scents floated in – newly ploughed earth, young leaves and the distant salt-scent of the sea – filling her with a heady sensation almost like the beginning of joy. She had left the city behind with thankfulness, and with it the tensions of the last week and a half. The same sense of escape lifted her spirits as when she had run down the path from school after it closed for the summer. She had arisen from her tangled bed before seven, showered, thrown her belongings into a suitcase and gone down to breakfast. While eating she had dashed off quick notes to Max and Colin, saying (not altogether truthfully) that she had been called back to the island urgently. Colin might believe her. Max would not, but would be resigned, as always, to what he regarded as her eccentric behaviour. Sometimes she wondered why he continued to act for her. Certainly his commissions had been substantial in the past, though he had not earned much recently. She suspected he felt towards her the same tender but irritated responsibility he would have felt towards a wayward child.

Setting up the exhibition had been a strangely unsettling experience and one she had not as yet come to terms with. During the difficult evening of the private view she had begun to feel that it somehow diminished her work. Classified, listed, displayed, it became too cold, too analytical. It endeavoured to make coherent sense of the incomprehensible, the instinctive and the intuitive after which she had been striving all these years.

Just before she had retreated from view during the party, she had overheard two women discussing a photograph of a girl, aged about ten, whom she had photographed in Calcutta when Tirza herself was already in the first, feverish stages of malaria.

'Isn't she sweet?' one of the women had said.

'Yes, Tirza Libby certainly has a talent for bringing out the charms of the world's down-and-outs, hasn't she? You might almost see a child like that in your own street.'

'Well, not quite!'

And they had laughed.

Tirza had photographed the girl on a day of searing heat as she stood patiently outside the railway station. Like many of the

Chapter 6

Maine: Spring 1942

MARTHA HALSTEAD MADE her way to Maine by train with her five-year-old son Billy. It was a hot and maddening journey. Their departure from Washington was delayed because a troop train was scheduled to leave first, and several politicians were due to come and see it off. The official cars had been held up by a snarl of traffic. Everyone waited. The station, packed fuller than at the start of the school summer vacation, grew airless. Every seat was taken and GIs put their kit-bags down anywhere they could find a piece of wall to lean against, and fell asleep – their mouths hanging open and the sweat patches spreading on their uniforms. Passengers arriving for later trains fell over the sprawling legs, clamoured for Cokes and coffee at the food stalls and used up more of the air.

When a man got up from a seat on a bench to go and complain to one of the station officials, Martha seized the space just ahead of an elderly woman with a stick. She fixed her gaze on the ceiling, ignoring the woman and trying to keep Billy on her lap. He squirmed and protested that he was too *big* to sit on her lap, that he wanted a seat of his *own*, *why* couldn't he have a seat of his own? He glared balefully at the woman sitting next to Martha, who had propped her swollen legs up on her suitcase. To make his point, Billy began to kick Martha's shins with his heels.

At last the politicians arrived, accompanied by newsreel cameras. The train departed to the playing of a dispirited band, and the crowds thinned a little. Martha's train left an hour and a half late, which meant she missed her connection in New York and had to wait another two hours there. Billy demanded more and more Kool-Aid, then wet his pants and was outraged when she changed him in the women's washroom. Martha longed grimly for her maid, Lulu-May. She had handed over the insalubrious parts of Billy's care to Lulu-May when he was three weeks old, and she had *never* had to deal with anything like this before. She had wanted to bring Lulu-May to Maine with her, but her maid had been surprisingly determined not to come.

'I'm sorry, Miz Martha, but my mommy is hankerin' for me to go back home. My sister has gone and got herself in trouble, and the baby's due in three weeks. And there's nine of my brothers and sisters still at home, and the youngest ain't but three. My mommy wants for me to get a day job in Charleston and help her the rest of the time. I'se just goin' home like you is, Miz Martha.'

Offers of better pay and shorter hours could not move her. Now, rolling Billy's sodden clothes up in a ball and stuffing them down in a corner of his suitcase with distaste, Martha reflected that at least she could pass him over to her mother at the end of the journey. Harriet would not mind the dirty jobs associated with a child. Not after some of the things she had to do on the farm. Martha still wasn't sure she was doing the right thing, going back to Maine, but she had felt trapped, living in their latest apartment with Billy. If things didn't work out she would look for somewhere else to wait out the time till Will came back and they could pick up the easy, sociable life they had had to put aside for the war.

She unwrapped a piece of Lux soap from her purse and washed Billy's hands and her own, fastidiously, then dried them on a small towel. Everything felt dirty – the seats in the station, the handles of the faucets, the air itself. After wrapping the soap in greaseproof paper and stowing it with the towel in her purse, she gathered up their luggage and steered Billy out into the waiting room again. It had been Lulu-May's idea to bring the soap and towel. The girl was no fool. But she had behaved like one in giving up her job.

By the time they had waited again in Boston and taken the last train up to Portland, it was dark and Billy had, blessedly, gone to sleep. Martha looked out of the window as the train pulled into Union Station and saw her father standing under a dim dangling bulb. The relief at the thought of handing over responsibility warmed her to him, despite the fact that he had come to meet her in his dungarees and working boots.

'Hi, Dad,' she said, brushing his stubbled cheek briefly with her smooth one. 'We've got three suitcases with us. I sent a trunk on ahead. Did it get here?'

'Ayuh. Yesterday.'

Martha frowned briefly, but held her tongue. She had lived away from Maine dialect long enough to be ashamed of it. Tobias gripped the smallest case under his arm and picked up the others in either hand.

'I've got the pickup out front.'

'Haven't you got a real car yet? Honestly, Dad.'

'No place for a car on a farm, Martha. You know that. Don't have enough gas to run the truck and the tractor as 'tis.'

He did not mention that he had been stuck in Portland for five hours waiting for her, without gasoline to go home and come back. Five wasted hours when he could have been getting on with the spring ploughing and the milking.

Billy was tugging at his mother's skirt and whining.

'I wanna go home, Mom. Can't we go home?'

Martha took him by the hand and began to lead him towards the waiting Ford truck.

'I don't want to go in that truck,' said Billy on a rising shriek. 'I want to go in a car.'

'Come on, now, Billy boy,' said Tobias with an attempt at cheerfulness. 'You can sit with Mom and Grandpa up front. We'll be home in no time. Grandma's got a bite of supper ready and then you can have a sleep in your bed with the striped cover. You remember. Tomorrow you can see the new foals – two baby horses.'

'I hate horses,' said Billy. 'And I hate you.'

◆◆◆

Abigail had decreed that the house on the wharf needed repainting. The snow and winter winds, and the year-round erosion of the salt spray, had taken their toll. The surface of the paint was blistered and fading. In some places whole patches had started to peel away, revealing the silvered clapboards beneath. Nathan wished, silently, that he had never allowed his mother to persuade him to paint it in the first place, when Louisa's health was failing after she gave birth to Tirza. When Abigail was first widowed, she had stayed on at the farm. But when Louisa fell ill she lost no time in moving into Nathan's house on the wharf front, before anyone could suggest that Louisa's own mother, Christina, should come to care for her. One of the first things Abigail had done was to insist that the old grey clapboard house should be smartened up with a coat of white paint and blue frames for the windows and doors.

'It will cheer Louisa up,' she had said firmly, but Louisa had not lived to see the job finished, and Nathan had gone on with the painting mechanically, too numb to give any thought to what he was doing. Several of the houses in Flamboro were painted, but the rest retained the soft dove-grey of the natural wood. Once you painted, however, you had to keep repainting, unless you were prepared to live with years of peeling paint until the wood was restored to its natural state again. Nathan painted about every four years, but for the last year before each repainting the house looked shabby and drove Abigail into bouts of irritation.

The ice was breaking up in the harbour and the fishing season would start soon, so Nathan was devoting every available minute to the decorating. Tirza had helped with the work this time, and proved herself almost as useful as a man. She was slower than he was, but she was gradually mastering the skill of loading her brush fully without it dripping all over her clothes and wasting paint on the ground below. Unlike Abigail, Nathan had no worries about allowing Tirza to climb a ladder. She was more agile – and probably safer – than he was himself.

She had hardly been up to the farm in the last couple of weeks. At first Nathan thought it was because she genuinely enjoyed the house painting, but he had begun to suspect it had something to do with Martha's arrival. He knew the cousins did not get on well and was sorry for it. He didn't find Martha easy himself. Still, it was good to have Tirza's help. He would be able to get off to the fishing at least a week earlier than he could have done without it. This afternoon they were working on the last of the walls, the side of the house furthest from the boat shed, and would be able to start on the blue paint tomorrow.

'That's lookin' mighty fine,' said a voice from below Nathan's feet. Ben Flett was peering up at him from the board sidewalk. Nathan held the brush away from himself and looked down.

'Nearly done.'

'That girl of yours is doin' all right, ain't she?' Ben gestured at Tirza, who was balanced at the top of another ladder at the far end of the wall, slapping the paint on to the barge-board under the eaves.

'Does not bad for a kid,' Nathan agreed. 'You been out yet?'

'Fixin' on startin' tomorrow.' Ben held up a bucket full of a dark grey mass. 'George Towson owed me a bucket o' bait from last fall. Just goin' to bait up my pots now. How long before you'll be ready?'

Nathan groaned. 'Three, four days yet, I reckon. Pesky job, this. I hate it, every time.'

'Why not lay out your pots and then paint between whiles, before you haul? Kill two birds.'

'Not a bad idea. I might just do that.' Nathan shrugged comically. 'If my mother doesn't start creating!'

Ben chuckled, waved to Tirza, and went on down the wharf to where his lobster pots were piled up near his boat. Nathan wedged his elbow against the side of the ladder, pulled a handkerchief out of his pocket with his free hand and wiped the sweat off his forehead and upper lip. At midday there was some heat in the sun now, and the last of the thick plates of ice lingered only in the crannies of the shore which always lay in shadow. The harbour was mostly filled with glass ice, sharp-edged enough to slice into a boat's hull like butter. Following Ben's progress along the harbour front, Nathan could see the sunlight glinting off the broken shell roadway. There was plenty of activity down by the boats. Somebody – probably Eli's grandson Arthur – was stripped to the waist. Arthur had an eye for the girls and he was a good-looking fellow. Muscled like that movie actor who played Tarzan. Paint trickled down between Nathan's fingers and along the back of his hand, and he tilted the brush in irritation. Time he was down there getting his own boat ready.

Tirza climbed down her ladder and shifted it a couple of yards so she could reach a new section of wall. She tilted her head back and looked up at him.

'Why don't you go and bait your traps too, Dad? I can finish this wall by myself. Ben's right – we can do the rest of the painting between runs if I help you on the boat as well as here.'

'School on Monday.'

'We could go out early to lay some of the pots, before school. And I could come home in the lunch recess to help with the painting.'

'Maybe. You're right, though. I could get the baiting done if you'll finish this wall.'

Nathan slapped the last yard or two of paint on his section and climbed down the ladder, a little stiff from perching so long in one position. He went into the shed to clean his brush, then came out and watched Tirza at work back up near the peak of the gable.

'You're a fine help, girl,' he called, then set off with relief down to the wharf.

Unlike her father, Tirza enjoyed the painting. She liked to see the tired-looking house brighten up, and she found the view of Flamboro from the top of the ladder intriguing. She could look down into back yards where people moved about thinking they were unseen; she could peer into the cockpits of the fishing boats in the harbour, and she could see further out to sea than usual. The islands offshore seemed nearer. The half-dozen houses on Crab Island stood out clearly and she could make out the end of a ruined barn on Mustinegus. The headland south of Flamboro hid Libby's Beach and Todd's Neck from her, but she thought that if she could climb up inside the steeple of the church to where the bell hung she might even see that far.

The greatest advantage of helping with the painting was having a valid reason for not going up to the farm. Normally she might have felt guilty about this, because she knew Harriet was grateful for the work she did. But, she reasoned, Martha was the daughter of the house. She could help out, for once. Tirza had ridden her bike over to the farm the day after Martha had arrived, two weeks ago, out of curiosity. Perhaps her cousin might have changed. She would never admit it, but she longed for Martha to like her. Every time Martha came on a visit, she had this brief irrational hope that things might have changed.

Martha was not on the porch when she arrived, nor in the kitchen with her mother, and certainly not anywhere about the farm buildings.

'Where is she, then?' Tirza asked Harriet.

'Who?' said Harriet crisply. 'The cat's aunt?'

'Martha. I thought she came last night. Isn't she up yet?'

'She got up about ten, I guess. She's in the parlour.'

'In the parlour?' Tirza gaped. The parlour was only used at Christmas. Even Martha didn't use the parlour. She usually sat on a rocker on the porch or retreated to her room.

Tirza padded along to the parlour in her socks and peered round the door. Martha was there all right, lounging on the horsehair-padded chaise-longue and painting her nails from a bottle of bright scarlet varnish balanced on a small side table amongst ancient family photographs in shades of sepia and cream. She looked discontented.

'Hi, Martha.'

Martha jumped and cursed as the brush slipped and ran a jagged line over her cuticle. Tirza was not familiar with the word she used.

'What are you doing, creeping up like that? You've made me ruin this nail. I'll have to take it all off and do it again.'

'Sorry,' muttered Tirza, taking a few hesitant steps into the room and bumping into the corner of the parlour organ, which was only played when Abigail visited.

'What do you want?'

'Just came to say hello. Have a good trip?' Tirza asked desperately.

'We had a horrible trip,' Martha enunciated slowly, swabbing the ruined nail with cotton soaked in varnish remover. 'All the trains were late, we were kept waiting for a lot of stupid congressmen in Washington, and everywhere was packed full of GIs with their kit-bags tripping everyone up.'

She peered at the nail to see if it was cleaned to her satisfaction, then picked up her cigarette from an ashtray and inhaled deeply. It was stuck into a long tortoiseshell holder, and she flourished it as she spoke.

'Still as skinny as ever, I see.' She narrowed her eyes.

'Honestly, with that awful haircut, anyone would think you were a boy. When I was your age...' she smiled reminiscently and drew on her cigarette, 'there wasn't any doubt whatsoever.'

Tirza hesitated just inside the door, hurt and baffled. Nothing she did or said would ever appease Martha. Why did she go on trying? She started to sidle backwards out the door. Martha ignored her and began to repaint her nail. Suddenly Tirza was thumped hard in the back, stumbled forward, tripped over a rug and went flying on to her face. Billy ran past her and banged into Martha.

'Hell!' she said, her face furious. 'That's ruined it again. Get off, can't you?'

'I'm bored. What can I do? Can we go to the movies?'

'There aren't any movies here, only in Portland. Get off my foot. Take him outside, will you, Tirza, and find him something to do? I'll never get these finished.'

Tirza led Billy away and handed him over to Harriet in the kitchen. Sam was hitching the team up to the plough in the yard and would not appreciate Billy underfoot, getting into danger. He was a fool around horses.

Tirza left the farm quickly and hadn't been back since.

Now, as she dipped her brush into the paint can, she caught sight of Simon walking down the coastal path toward Flamboro. She waved at him, but he had not seen her, up the ladder. She shouted as he drew level.

'Hey, I'm up here.'

'Oh, hi,' he said, but did not slacken his pace.

'Aren't you stopping?'

'Mom sent me to see Mrs Larrabee. You want to come?'

'Wait a minute. I just need to paint this last few yards.'

'Hurry up.' He perched on one of the trestles that had supported the dories during the winter, while Tirza painted the last strip rapidly, backing down the ladder till she reached the ground. He fiddled impatiently while she cleaned her brush and wiped her hands on a turpentine-soaked cloth, then they set off down Shore Road towards Mrs Larrabee's house. The oyster shells of the road crunched underfoot with their familiar warm-weather sound.

On a curly ironwork bracket projecting from the front of one

of the white-painted houses in Shore Road hung a sign which
declared in flowing letters:

Flamboro Fancy Good & Novelties
Real Maine Crafts

Mrs Larrabee would not be opening her store for a month yet,
but anyone local who wanted to purchase something went
round to the kitchen door. Simon stepped inside and called.

'I'm through in the store, dusting,' shouted Mrs Larrabee.
'Come right on in.'

Tirza and Simon walked through the kitchen and along the
hall to the front of the house, where the parlour had been turned
into a store ten years ago. After her husband had been lost at sea,
Marion Larrabee had extended her interest in collecting knick-
knacks and ornaments into a tidy little business. There were
enough summer visitors with money to spend to keep her busy
during the three months she opened the store each year. She also
hired a display case in the Mansion House, which brought folk
over from Todd's Neck, and her sister in Portland had a shelf of
items for sale in her ladies' dress store. Local people rarely felt
the need of shell-covered boxes or peg-dolls dressed as fishermen, but Mrs Larrabee's stock could be useful for birthdays and
Christmas.

'Come in, come in,' said Mrs Larrabee. She wore a wrap-
around apron covered with large pink roses. With a long-handled
feather duster she was flicking delicately round her stock.

Although Tirza could not see the point of most of Mrs
Larrabee's goods, she found some things fascinating. There was
a wind-up canary in a brass cage which sang almost as well as a
real one. It had stood just inside the window for as long as she
could remember. She always hoped no one would buy it. When
she was small she had been allowed, as a treat, to wind it up, but
she felt she was too old to ask now. There were one or two
paintings on the walls that she had grown fond of over the years,
too. Most of the paintings were crude daubs by 'artists' who
stayed along the coast every year. When they asked Marion
Larrabee to sell their pictures on commission, she never had the
heart to turn them away. These, too, lingered on the walls, but

Tirza no longer noticed them.

Her eyes were always drawn to a pair of real Maine scenes. Without knowing the reason, she could sense that these paintings were of a different order. When she looked at the other pictures, she was conscious only of the texture of paint on canvas. But here the paint seemed to dissolve before the breathing life behind, like mist clearing from a pane of glass. One portrayed two barefoot boys herding the cattle home for milking. The older boy carried a thin switch and the younger one had a pail of blueberries. Both of the boys had a jaunty, devil-may-care attitude she liked. The other painting simply showed an old dory with its powdery white paint flaking off in the sun. Part of a net was draped over the gunwale, and it looked so real you could smell the hot painted wood in the sun and the tarred fishy reek of the net. There were oars and floats piled up on the shingle beside the boat, and the sea beyond was calm and brightly lit. Mrs Larrabee had told her that these two pictures were by a young man who had much admired Winslow Homer, the Maine artist who used to live not far away. The young artist had died before he was thirty. She had decided to keep the paintings for herself but hung them on the wall of the store to encourage people to come in. There was also a small painting of a wild, storm-driven sea. It was only a foot wide, but Tirza felt herself dragged into it as though the whole ocean lay just beyond the frame. She marvelled at it, but it frightened her.

'It was brought in by some people who said they had found it in their attic,' Mrs Larrabee had told her. 'Sold it to me for twenty dollars. Too much, I guess. I've tried to sell it for twenty-five, but no one seems to want it.'

Tirza noticed that several items had been taken out of the glass display case and were laid out on the counter.

'What are you doing with those?' she asked. They were mostly toys: clockwork tin cars and a fire engine, a china-headed doll with a stuffed canvas body and no clothes, a knife with several blades.

Mrs Larrabee pulled a face.

'German things. I'm not holding any more German stock now – I won't have anything to do with the enemy. I thought I would get rid of those. Would either of you like anything?'

'Can I have the knife?' Simon swooped before Tirza could say anything. She hankered after the knife herself.

'Surely. Tirza? Anything you'd like? How about this doll? That isn't rightly stock.'

Mrs Larrabee picked up the doll by the waist and held it aloft between her finger and thumb. It was seven or eight inches high, with the lower arms and legs as well as the head made of china. The moulded hair was glazed black, the eyes blue and the white complexion was faintly tinged with pink on the cheeks. It was a curious old-fashioned thing. Tirza had never seen anything quite like it.

'This used to be a doll of mine. Oh, I had a famous collection! Over fifty dolls in every size and shape you can imagine. My favourites were the French ones with wax heads. Their faces were so soft and lifelike. And they had real hair. I had one that was dressed from top to toe in silk – bonnet, bloomers, petti-coats, dress, coat. Real swansdown on the muff and coat.'

Mrs Larrabee laid the china-headed doll on Tirza's palm.

'Captain Penhaligon brought me this one back, one voyage. She came without clothes and somehow neither my mother nor I ever made any for her. I found her a few years back, wrapped up in tissue paper in my handkerchief drawer as good as new. I thought I'd add her to the stock, but no one has been interested in her. I suppose it's all these dolls made of composition now, isn't it? And dressed to look like Sonja Henie or Shirley Temple. Still, she's an interesting doll with a bit of history, if you'd like to have her, Tirza.'

Tirza mumbled embarrassed thanks and slipped the doll into her pocket. She didn't know what she was going to do with it. She would have preferred the pocket knife.

'My mom sent me to buy some table napkins,' said Simon, shuffling his feet. 'According to Martha only country hicks sit down at table without napkins.' His tone was heavy with sar-casm, and Tirza realised he was furious at being sent on such a fool's errand. Mrs Larrabee pulled open a drawer and began laying out sets of napkins – seersucker, printed cotton and em-broidered linen. Simon looked at them wildly.

'*I* don't know.' He held out two dollar bills. 'That's what Mom gave me. Can I get some with that?'

Mrs Larrabee picked out some cream-coloured napkins printed with strawberries.

'These are a dollar fifty for eight. How about these?'

'Great.'

⋙⋘

In Flett's General Stores, Mary Flett was showing Abigail and Miss Catherine a copy of the Portland paper which had just been delivered.

'It says here that now the ground has thawed, the army is going to be setting up coastal defences along all the beaches. Do you reckon that means around here? Like Libby's Beach?'

'Oh, I don't think so,' said Abigail dismissively. 'We'd have been told.'

Miss Catherine shook her head.

'I don't know what things are coming to. My Clement always used to say the US should keep out of other people's wars. He was too old to serve in the last one, but his younger brother was drafted and served in the trenches. He wasn't ever the same afterwards. Shell-shocked, they called it. Used to have scream-ing nightmares, and sometimes he'd just get the shakes, for no reason at all.'

Suddenly she recollected that Mary's Pete was out there somewhere on a naval ship.

'Of course, we're all in it this time, if they're putting up defences on our beaches. The trenches in the last war – that was some different.'

Charlie came in from the storeroom with a fifty-pound bag of feed on his shoulder and swung it to the ground with a thud.

'Since Pearl Harbor, we don't have a choice,' he said. 'It's our war now and we have to fight it. Don't see how they can guard the whole coastline, though. Three thousand five hundred miles of coast in the State of Maine, what with all our bays and inlets. And two thousand islands. 'Twouldn't be possible.'

'They'll have gun emplacements,' Bert Swanson called through the open door. With the warm weather of the last few days he had moved from the Liars' Bench by the stove and taken up his position in his favourite rocker on the store porch. 'On some of the headlands, that'll be. To shoot at enemy aircraft.'

'German aircraft won't be able to fly as far as here,' Charlie

106

shouted back. 'It's ships they'll be watching out for. Or submarines, more'n likely.'

'Well,' said Abigail decisively, 'they'll do none of it on our property without permission, and that's flat.'

<hr/>

Tobias was walking back up the farm track for his dinner after a tiring morning planting cabbages. He had made a start yesterday, even though it was Sunday, with Simon and Sam helping. The weather was right and he was in a hurry to get ahead. Today Simon was back at school and Sam had been summoned to visit his ailing mother, who had taken a turn for the worse. He had gone by bus to Augusta, and wouldn't be back till nightfall. There was nothing for it but to get on as best he could, though it was really a two-man job.

At the end of the morning he had unhitched Dancer from the seed drill and turned her into the pasture with Lady and the two foals. He walked along the dusty track towards the farmhouse, conscious of the sun on his back marking a real turn in the weather. Outlanders, mocking the weather here, said that Maine had two seasons: winter and July. But Tobias knew every shade and tint of his local climate, which varied even from field to field, and from the fringes of the pine woods to the sandy coastal strip. It felt as though it was going to be a fine summer, but he was reserving judgement a while yet.

Looking up, his attention caught by a sound ahead of him, he was astonished to see a jeep approaching from the direction of the farmhouse, bumping over the ruts of the track. This was private land, and anyone driving down the track must first have come through the gate down on the county road, clearly marked LIBBY FARM ONLY, then driven through the farmyard past the house and come through the second gate on to the track. Tobias quickened his step, a sense of irritation rising in him. He had seen army jeeps careering round the roads in the last few weeks. They were driven by soldiers barely older than Simon, who spat tobacco juice over the side and seemed extremely cocky.

He stopped in the middle of the track, where boggy ground on either side would prevent the jeep from driving round him, and waited. It slowed down and halted circumspectly a few yards away. There were two men in it: the driver, a young sergeant, and a lieutenant, who might have been as much as a year older.

'Excuse me, sir,' said the lieutenant, 'but we have to go on down here.'

'You'll do no such thing without an explanation,' said Tobias hotly. 'This is private property.'

'Oh, uh, are you...' the lieutenant consulted a piece of paper, 'uh, Mr T. Libby?'

'It depends who's asking.'

'The US army, sir. I have a permit to gain access to all coastal paths, and I understand this farm track meets up with the coastal path running north to Flamboro and south to Todd's Neck.'

'I'll see that permit.'

The young lieutenant docilely produced an official-looking document. He had been told to be polite but firm with the local farmers. Tobias scanned the sheets of paper quickly. They seemed to be in order.

'Yes, I'm Tobias Libby, and this is my land you're on.'

The lieutenant jumped down from the jeep; the sergeant gazed into space, masticating gum like a cow chewing the cud.

'We have to carry out a preliminary reconnaissance of the coastal area, sir,' the lieutenant explained, 'to decide on the best placement for guns. Sure, we have plenty of maps, but with coastal erosion and all...'

'No erosion along here,' said Tobias, slightly mollified by the young man's conciliatory tone. 'Your maps are probably pretty correct. But a lot of the ground just up from the beach is marshy. And between the marshes and the beach are the ledges – sharp, shelving rocks. Nowhere flat to give you a base. It's like that all the way from here to Todd's Neck. Inland from the marshy strip it's pine woods, and that's all my property. In the other direction the path goes up along a steep cliff edge, very narrow. The property there belongs to the Tremayne family. I wouldn't say there's anywhere suitable till you get to Todd's Neck in the one direction or Flamboro in the other.'

He considered.

'I suppose there might be a suitable area on either end of Flamboro bay, but it's all built up with wharves and fish houses.

You'd need to talk to the selectmen. My brother is one of them, Nathan Libby. Most of the land on Todd's Neck belongs to the Mansion House Hotel, and I doubt they'd be pleased if you wanted to set up a gun there.'

'Well, maybe we could just take a walk along there and have a looksee?' said the lieutenant. 'If I'm not keeping you?'

Privately, Lieutenant Benson hoped they could get on without the farmer's slow, deliberate musings, but he was prepared to humour him if he had to.

'Just going up to the house for my dinner.' Tobias debated with himself. He wasn't sure how friendly he wanted to be with these soldiers. Anyone else, he wouldn't have hesitated.

'I'll just tell my missus I'll be half an hour. Then why don't you both step in for a bite?'

'Thank you kindly. We'd appreciate that.'

Tobias warned Harriet to expect two extra for dinner, then he climbed into the jeep behind the soldiers and they bumped their way down the farm track until it met the coastal path.

'Has your family lived here for long?' Lieutenant Benson asked as they passed the meadow, where the two foals raced off at the approach of the jeep.

'Round about three hundred years. Some of us have farmed and some have fished, and back when whaling was a profitable business some of us shipped on whalers. So now I'm a farmer and my brother's a lobsterman, but he part owns the farm. Where do you come from yourself?'

'Oh, I'm a city slicker. Born and bred in Baltimore. Just had a little over a year at Johns Hopkins before Pearl Harbor. I enlisted straight after. Hoping to see some action soon, if I get over to Europe.'

Tobias made a snorting noise at the boy's enthusiasm. He hadn't served in the last war, working as he was on his father's farm, but five of his classmates had seen action in Europe and never come back.

'And you?' he asked the sergeant, who rolled his gum into his cheek before answering.

'I'm from Chicago. Never seed anything like this in my life before.' He gestured with one hand at the ocean opening up before them. 'We thought Lake Michigan was big, but, babe, I never pictured anything as big as this.'

He brought the jeep to a halt where the farm track petered out and twisted his head over his shoulder to look at Tobias.

'Don't it give you the creeps living here with all that water and those woods and not a soul in sight? I'd go crazy in a week.'

Tobias looked at him in astonishment. Flamboro was a flourishing little town, there were busy farms all around, and in summer Todd's Neck had visitors strung round the small beach and the golf course like beads on a string.

'I thought the Midwest was full of wide open prairies and nothing to be seen for miles.'

'Wouldn't know. Ain't never been outside Chicago before this. In Chicago you got plenty life, plenty people, always something going on, places to go – get a drink, shoot some pool. Cain't figger out what people here do all day.'

He looked at the finger of pine woods reaching down to the ledges, dark and cool between the trees even now with the sun at its zenith.

'Gives me the creeps,' he said, and shivered.

They got out of the jeep and Tobias led them about halfway along Libby's Beach in the direction of Todd's Neck. The woods drew back from the shore after that single projecting copse, leaving a basin of marshland lying in a long oval between the ledges and the wood shore. It was covered with rough sea grasses, bayberry and wild cranberries. Now, in spring, it still squelched underfoot. By midsummer it would have partly dried out and some areas would remain fairly firm until the fall rains started. The whole mile-long area was threaded through with thin streams running down from the higher ground of the woods. These spread into flat pools and drained off, in places, through old worn cracks in the rocks of the ledges. At the centre, well in from the shore and near the ruins of an old fort, lay a small lake, known as Libby's Pond.

'I see what you mean,' said Lieutenant Benson. 'There's nowhere suitable here. But we'll have to sandbag all the way along.'

'Sandbag?' To Tobias, sandbags were used along the seafront in Flamboro in seasons of dangerous flood tides. He could not see any rationale for them here. Did the army propose to try to keep the sea out of the marsh? It flooded naturally at such times, but you might as well try to bale out the sea as sandbag the marsh.

'Foxholes. We'll dig foxholes all the way along this stretch of beach and reinforce them with sandbags. We won't be manning them all the time, only if there's an invasion alert. Then we can put men into them to pick off any enemy bastards coming ashore.'

Tobias didn't think it would be easy to construct foxholes here, but perhaps the army knew something he didn't.

'And it's like this all the way along to Todd's Neck?'

'That's right. The shore changes there. The neck is really a kind of island joined on to the land by a causeway. It's very rocky and steep, with sheer cliffs dropping into the sea, except for a couple of small beaches. No marsh. You might be able to get the jeep along the coast path, but it would be easier to go round by the county road.'

'Oh, we'll get the jeeps along here all right when we're building the foxholes, but today we'll go by road and talk to the hotel manager. Let's have a look at the path in the other direction, beyond where we left the jeep.'

They retraced their steps past the jeep and began the climb up towards the Tremayne property. The path was so narrow they had to walk in single file. When they reached the top of the headland, Lieutenant Benson looked speculatively at the great empty house.

'Not occupied, you said? We may want to commandeer that.'

Tobias looked alarmed.

'Oh, I don't know. The Tremaynes are a very powerful family. They live in Boston all the time now, but they know politicians...' His voice trailed away.

'Well.'

Lieutenant Benson studied the ground to his right. The strip of land holding the path was not more than two or three feet wide with no protection on the seaward side, where it tumbled away in a vertiginous drop to knife-edged rocks below. The ocean pounded against them, a swirling mass of white and green, and fell back with a sound like a huge animal sucking and slurping at its kill. The inward side of the path was bounded by a low stone wall marking the edge of the Tremayne garden. He could have stepped over it, but on the other side the ground dropped four feet to the lawn. There was nowhere here they could set up a gun without building up a massive level area to support the concrete base, which would involve all kinds of problems. With the solid rock under the path and the drop on the inland side, it would not even be possible to dig foxholes.

They walked further until they could look down at Flamboro encircling its bay below them. The wharves and harbour walls were cluttered with all the working gear of a busy fishing port. To site a gun here would mean knocking down at least one fish house. Lieutenant Benson lifted his eyes and looked across to the far end of the town where the church stood out white against the deep green of another pine wood.

'What about over there, just beyond the church? What's over there?'

'The burying-ground. Then the woods.'

'The burying-ground, eh? There will be flat ground there. And it will be away from the houses. That might be just the place.'

Tobias looked shocked.

'You can't set up a gun in the burying-ground!'

'Why not? It's not going to disturb the inhabitants, is it?'

The sergeant gave a snort of laughter – his first contribution to the conversation since they had left the jeep.

'We could promise not to do any dummy runs during church service, couldn't we, sir? Cain't promise for the real thing.'

They walked back to the jeep in silence. Benson was calculating what difficulties might be involved in gaining access to the burying-ground. If the locals proved too obstinate, he had the power to commandeer it anyway, but he would prefer to avoid that. He asked Tobias the name of the minister.

'Reverend Bridges,' said Tobias, much troubled.

'We'll go over and have a word with the reverend this afternoon,' said Lieutenant Benson, jumping nimbly into the jeep beside the driver. 'After your wife gives us lunch. That'll save us going back to camp, and I take it very kindly.'

Tobias climbed slowly up into the back of the jeep and before he could sit down the driver started manoeuvring it round, cutting up the thin turf and sending a spray of sand flying out from the wheels. Tobias was flung suddenly down into the hard seat, with the breath knocked out of him. As the jeep rattled back up the farm track, the debris flung up from the wheels changed from sand to grey, dusty soil. Tobias wondered how much damage would be done to his track by a fleet of jeeps driving back and forth for the building of foxholes.

They sat down to dinner around the big kitchen table, although Martha had tried to persuade her mother to lay the dining table for the soldiers.

'They'll just have to take us as they find us,' said Harriet, somewhat crossly. Monday was sacrosanct as washing day, and she had been put out when Tobias had delayed dinner half an hour and assumed she could feed two extra men at a moment's notice. With Martha and Billy here she had two additional sets of sheets and towels each week, as well as their clothes. She and Patience had just finished the washing in the big tubs in the wash-house and started on the wringing when Tobias had put his head round the door. She had hoped to have everything up on the washing line by dinnertime, but had been obliged to get out the ham she had boiled for tonight's supper, peel extra potatoes, and open some of her canned green beans. She was just ready when the men appeared.

Martha, glad of any diversion from the boredom of farm life, had laid the table with one of her mother's best tablecloths and the napkins bought by Simon at Mrs Larrabee's. She found a few daffodils in the garden and put these in a vase taken from the china cupboard in the parlour and barely used since her parents' wedding twenty-eight years before.

'Sakes!' said Harriet, pushing her hair back from her hot face and carrying over the big lidded dish of potatoes. 'What are you doing, girl?'

'Just trying to make things look a bit more civilised.'

Before Harriet could retort, Tobias came in, long-faced, with the two soldiers.

Throughout dinner, Martha talked animatedly. Harriet couldn't remember seeing her so lively or so helpful except when she and Will Halstead were courting. After the bad temper and sulks of the last few weeks, she seemed like a different person. Watching Martha prettily drawing out the silent sergeant and talking animatedly to Lieutenant Benson, Harriet felt something like pity for her daughter. She was made for a different life from her parents'. No wonder she was bored and discontented here. She needed young people around her. Young men, Harriet corrected herself. Martha had never enjoyed sharing the limelight with other young women. Her face was flushed with colour and her eyes were bright as she argued playfully with the lieutenant about their favourite Clark Gable movies.

'Say, is there a movie house anywhere round here?' Lieutenant Benson asked. 'Seems like there's nothing to brighten life up.'

'In Portland, yes. Not anywhere nearer. And I can't get into Portland except by bus.' Martha made it sound like the trans-Siberian railway. 'In Washington, of course, we had a car, but it was an air-force car and had to go back when my husband was posted overseas.'

'Gee, that doesn't seem fair on the wives. Maybe you would do me the honour...' he suddenly sounded like something out of a Clark Gable movie himself.

'Yes?'

'Well, we get some extra gas, and I can get the use of a jeep. How's about us going to the movies in Portland one day?' He turned to Harriet. 'I promise to get her safely there and back, ma'am.'

Martha looked put out, but Harriet said gravely, 'Thank you, Lieutenant Benson. I'm sure you will.' The boy must be at least five or six years younger than Martha.

Just then there was a wail from the wash-house, where Billy had been banished to eat his dinner with Patience. He came hurtling through the door, and then stopped, eyeing the strangers dubiously.

'Who're you?' He sounded belligerent.

'Now, Billy,' said Martha sweetly, 'this is Lieutenant Benson and Sergeant Klinsky. Say how-do-you-do.'

Billy climbed on to her lap and glared at the men with his thumb in his mouth.

'My poor little boy,' said Martha sighing and resting her

cheek against the top of his head. 'He doesn't understand this war and he doesn't know what is happening to him.'

Lieutenant Benson had registered the size of Billy with some surprise.

'Why, Mrs Halstead, I couldn't imagine you having such a big boy.'

Martha's jaw hardened a little, but she smiled at him. 'He's big for his age – he's only five. And I was just eighteen when I got married, wasn't I, Mother?'

'Yes, indeed,' said Harriet, rising to clear away the plates and avoiding Tobias's eye. She did not mention that Billy was not born until Martha was nearly twenty-one.

'Now, gentlemen,' she said, 'I hope you can manage some of my dried-apple pie and cream.'

Chapter 7

Maine: Spring 1942

EARLY MORNING WAS the best time of all to be out on Flamboro Bay. Now that the fishing season had started, Tirza was up and dressed by five each morning. Ten minutes later she carried her crab line, baited the night before, down to her dory which she kept moored just below the house, between *Stormy Petrel* and *Louisa Mary*. For bait she used eel, which she prepared herself. Sometimes she caught her own eels, but more often she traded crabs for eels from Eel Joe, an old fisherman who lived south of Todd's Neck.

Eel Joe had been a trawlerman for fifty years, and had retired to live with his married daughter in Portland six years ago. After a couple of months he could not endure it any longer. He found an old lobsterboat wrecked on a waste stretch of shoreline south of Todd's Neck, removed the superstructure and – with the help of his former shipmates – turned it upside down. He cut a window and a door in the stern and fitted up the inside using materials salvaged from the boat's cabin. With an iron stove installed, its chimney poking through a hole cut in the hull, Eel Joe's shack was a snug if somewhat odoriferous home.

To eke out his small pension and to keep himself occupied, Joe trapped eels in a small tidal lake behind his cabin. He also maintained a weir in the cove, where he caught the small herring called brit, which was the lobstermen's favourite bait. During the fishing season he motored around the shore to Flamboro every few days with his baskets full of eels and kegs of brit to sell to the fishermen. Once a week he hitched a lift into Augusta and sold a bushel of fresh eels to an expensive new

French restaurant which cooked and served them with fancy sauces swimming in wine and garlic. Flamboro declared the idea disgusting, but thought Joe had pulled off a smart deal.

Tirza didn't think she could ever face eating eel. Not after her long and messy struggles with that most slippery and energetic of creatures. Joe sold his eels live, so the first job was to kill them, an unpleasant process which Tirza, as a fisherman's daughter, ought to have been able to accomplish unmoved, but disliked intensely. Then the eels had to be chopped up with a small axe into short lengths and packed into big earthenware jars with coarse salt. The smell was a concentration of putrescence, as if the sea had vomited refuse, and the salt ate into her skin like caustic soda.

To bait her crab line, she scooped pieces of eel out of the stinking jar. By now they were covered with a thick, sticky slime under the outer coating of gritty salt. She tied one end of a foot-long piece of string around each segment of eel, then tied the other to the crab line, spacing them a couple of feet apart. Each end of the crab line was weighted with lead, and had a painted wooden float to act as a marker; at intervals, pieces of old cork floats were fastened along its length. Although Tirza had no licence for lobster fishing, nobody needed one for catching crabs, and the fishermen respected her claim to the small inlet below Christina's land where she had been laying her line for the last three years.

Carrying her crab line coiled up in a bushel basket down to her dory in the early morning light, Tirza felt herself more alive than at any other time except when she was sailing *Stormy Petrel*. She had become oddly conscious of her body lately – its spring and strength, and its moments of aching sensitivity, when her skin became as thin and delicate as the wing of a moth. Energy fizzed inside her, making her break out into a run and building up behind her ribs like an overfilled balloon. That spring she felt as though she was buoyed up with some secret expectancy. What she was expecting, she couldn't have said, but she woke each morning thinking, *Yes*, as she looked out eagerly at the new day. At times this sense of something just around the corner of her life tormented her. There seemed to be no reason for it – her days stretched ahead with no new undiscovered country on the horizon.

She lowered her basket into the dory, untied the painter and rowed out into the bay to the sound of the land birds singing the dawn chorus and the sea birds shrieking and swooping over the ocean with all the fresh enthusiasm of early morning. The sun, lying low out to sea, shot through the waves with arrows of light, cool and piercing, flicking up glittering shards of silver against the deep, melded blues and greens where the sea-bed dropped steeply offshore beyond the harbour. Depending on the state of the tide and the direction of the wind, it took her between fifteen minutes and half an hour to row round to her crabbing cove. The land here dropped into the sea from the edge of the woods in a tangle of broken rocks and ledges which provided a favourite place for crabs. Tirza threw the first end of her line overboard near the inner end of the cove, then worked the dory parallel to the shore using one oar like a paddle near the stern and allowing the rest of the line to pay out slowly until she reached the other end. As each piece of bait dropped into the water it left a scummy circle of grey salt mixed with slime which slowly spread and dispersed on the surface.

Close under the lip of the land, where she laid the first end of her line, the sea lapped against a narrow, little-used path skirting the wood-shore. Christina's wood crowded down to the water's edge, and spring tides found their way over the path to lick around the rough trunks of the firs, and rub like a cat up against the smooth silver bark of the birches. Tirza would have known, with her eyes shut, how much of her line she had laid, for as she worked her way along it the scent of the woods gave way to the slithering smell of the rock weed that clung to the out-flung boulders lying off the end of the point. At low tide they just skimmed the surface, their heads breaking through the ringed waves. At high tide they disappeared, hiding treacherously low, so that only the dimple and flow of the water hinted at their presence. In her dory, Tirza was safe enough. The pattern they made, scattered around the point, was as familiar to her as the rooms of her home. But ships had foundered here, making for the shelter of Flamboro harbour.

School had not yet finished for the summer, so she lifted her line just three times during the day: after breakfast, during the dinner recess, and finally in the early evening. This meant that much of her bait was eaten by crabs which dropped off and swam away long before she could net them, but in a good season she managed to catch enough to sell to Charlie Flett for the store and to the Mansion House Hotel, which had been a customer since last year. The family always had all the crabs they wanted to eat, and Tirza handed over a quarter of the money she earned to Abigail.

Crabbing was an honest kind of hunting, Tirza had once said to Christina. The crabs were neither hooked nor scooped up in a trawl net. At any time they could decide to let go of the bait and simply sink to the bottom. It was greed that kept them holding on to the succulent chunks of eel as she lifted the line, and if their greed was stronger than their instinct for escape, then Tirza reckoned she had won in a fair fight.

'Honestly, Girna,' she said, 'and don't tell my dad, I think catching fish on a line or with a net is cheating. The fish has no chance to get away. Well, almost none. I know the undersized ones are thrown back. But I don't think it's a fair fight.'

This did not stop her helping her father, and even laying a trawl line for mackerel herself when they were abundant, as they sometimes were in that mysterious way of fish. But whenever she unhooked a fish she felt vaguely guilty. It was the same with the lobsters. A lobster, once inside a pot, could not escape. But she knew that it was the lobstering that kept food on the table and a roof over their heads, so she said nothing to Nathan about her quixotic notions.

Her crab line laid, that morning in May, Tirza began to row lazily back home. As she drew level with the church and burying-ground, high above her head on the flat promontory adjacent to Christina's wood, she looked up and tried to imagine a big anti-aircraft gun up there. Tobias had come round to see Nathan after the soldiers had visited him, and at first Tirza supposed they were talking about a man sitting up there with a rifle. Tobias explained that this would be a huge gun, a kind of modern cannon, mounted on a swivel base where the gunner could sit and swing the gun from left to right and up or down to fix it on an enemy aircraft or ship.

Nathan had shaken his head at the news.

'I can see why they would want to site a gun up there. There's a natural platform of flat ground and it's raised up enough to allow a good view out to sea. But to put a gun in the burying-ground – that's going to mean trouble.'

'I told him it's town meeting on Friday and we would discuss it then. But I think they'll set it up whether we agree or not.'

—◆◇◆—

After breakfast Tirza went out in *Louisa Mary* to help her father lift, empty and rebait his lobster pots. They could haul about a third of his gang before she had to leave for school. *Louisa Mary* chugged slowly from one of Nathan's lobster floats to the other. He brought the boat softly alongside the float and put the engine into neutral as Tirza leaned over the side, reached below the float with the gaff to catch hold of the rope leading to the pot, and looped it over the winch to haul it aboard. If there was a lobster inside – and often there were none – she would remove it through the hatch in the top, then measure it with the brass rule from the eyes to the beginning of the tail and put it into one of the kegs wedged in the cockpit. There were three kegs: one for Massachusetts lobsters over three and three-eighths inches, one for Maine lobsters over three and one-eighth inches, and one for dumbies which had lost one or both claws. The bait bag then had to be refilled with the stinking bait that tempted the lobsters into the trap, and the whole set – pot, line and buoy – thrown overboard as Nathan engaged the engine again. If Nathan had been on his own – and most lobstermen work on their own – he would have had to leave the wheel each time, deal with the pot and the catch, then return to the wheel, taking about three times as long, so he was glad of her help.

'That's all we'll manage before school,' said Nathan, straightening with a grunt and pressing his hands into the small of his back.

'Don't you have some more, over beyond Mustinegus?'

They were a couple of miles offshore, near the west side of the island.

'Ayuh, but I'd best get you back if you want to lift your crab line before school.'

Nathan put the wheel over and headed back in the direction of the harbour.

'Don't see why you don't get Simon to help you. Pay you

back for all his farm chores you do.'

Tirza laughed.

'Well, I did try. Two years ago, when I first started seriously. But he's useless in a boat. Clumsy as a cow. Dropping the oars overboard. Setting the dory pitching so I thought we'd go over. Lost more crabs than he netted. I gave up on him.'

'He didn't mind?'

'No, sir! He told me, just a couple of months ago – soon as he steps in a boat, all he can think about is drowning. I don't want a Jonah like that aboard.'

Half an hour later, Tirza pulled her dory up to the float at one end of her crab line and shipped her oars. She reached down into the sea and took hold of the line in her left hand. With her right she picked up the crab net. The line had to be raised to the surface with infinite slowness and patience, so the crabs would notice no more movement in the water than the waves. Peering over the side Tirza could see – when the bait was three or four feet below the surface – whether there was a crab clinging to it. If there was, she lifted the line even more slowly and at the crucial moment slid the net below the crab so that when at last it let go of the bait it could be scooped up and into the boat. With all her experience Tirza still lost some crabs in those last vital seconds, and it was this uncertainty which made crab fishing exciting. She also had to be careful to work so that her shadow was not cast over the wrong patch of sea, alerting the smarter crabs.

This morning was a good day. She had landed twenty good-sized crabs and thrown back three small ones. As she rowed back again to Flamboro wharf in time to walk up to school, the crabs crashed about in the bushel basket, rattling their claws and blowing bubbles. Tirza tied up the dory, tipped the crabs into her holding cage which was anchored just below the surface next to the wharf, and grabbed her burlap bag of school books from beside the boat shed. She forgot to wash her hands, and walked unconcernedly along Schoolhouse Lane in an aromatic cloud of eel bait, crab and seaweed.

◆◆◆◆◆

Flamboro annual town meeting was held in the town hall, a modest building about half the size of the school, which stood

121

next to Flett's General Stores. During the rest of the year it was used for meetings of the selectmen, the church wives' group, the Fourth of July party committee, and occasional sociables or barn dances. On Friday morning Mary Flett and her sister-in-law Hilda, wife of Ben, swept and mopped the hall with particular care. Miss Molly arrived as they were finishing, bringing with her a big bunch of tulips from her garden.

'I know they don't last long in water,' she said apologetically as she arranged the tulips in a vase on the table set up at the head of the hall, 'but they'll last today out. We want everything to look as good as possible, don't we?'

Flowers were not usually in evidence at town meeting, although a dollar supper in aid of the church was part of the proceedings. This evening, however, two army officers were coming to explain the plans for the anti-aircraft gun to the townspeople, and Flamboro intended to put on a good show. There had been talk of little else in the town all week, ever since Tobias had brought the news. Opinion was sharply divided between those who thought any army activity in the buryingground was sacrilegious – the very work of the devil – and those who argued, first, that a gun up there was better than one down in the harbour if the enemy started shooting back and, second, that soldiers passing in and out of Flamboro might just bring a bit of trade to the town.

Miss Molly could see arguments on both sides. As a sea captain's daughter, she viewed the threat of German ships as he would have regarded pirates. In an emergency, even the use of the burying-ground might be justifiable. But she did feel uneasy. The thought of careless army boots amongst the quiet mounds and furtive cigarettes stubbed out on gravestones appalled her.

There was a buzz of activity around the town hall all day, as the women carried over their contributions to the dollar supper and stayed to set out dishes and gossip. The annual town meeting marked the first community get-together of the year, and a ripple of cheerfulness ran through the town. The school children were let out a quarter of an hour before time and raced home to finish their chores so they could secure good seats. They had no official part in the proceedings and could not vote, but there was always plenty else going on. Before six o'clock the trawlers began to return, an hour or two earlier than usual for this time of year. Each boat puttered in surrounded by its own cloud of seagulls who screamed and swooped as the fish were gutted and the offal thrown overboard.

Heads turned as the two Libby families entered the hall. Martha had not walked into Flamboro since arriving back at her parents' home, and this was the first time the town had seen her since last summer. She followed Harriet down the central aisle between the rows of folding chairs, her high-heeled sling-backs tapping sharply on the wooden floor amongst all those men's boots and the sensible lace-up shoes of the women. The teenage girls poked each other in the ribs, whispering as they studied her flamboyantly rolled hair and her bright red jacket with its big padded shoulders – pinched in to a narrow waist and flaring in a flounced peplum that emphasised the curve of her hips. Her navy skirt was shorter and tighter than any of them would have dared to wear. Without the slit up the back it would have been hard for her to walk. And the seams of her silk stockings looked as though they had been drawn up the backs of her legs with a ruler and a black pen.

Abigail's mouth was tucked in disapprovingly, but she had no opportunity to vent her feelings about her grand-daughter's appearance. She noticed the appreciative grins of the men in the hall, and raised her chin higher. She would not tolerate being made a laughing-stock, and if Harriet did not put a stop to this flaunting behaviour, she would.

'Good evening, gentlemen.' Nathan greeted the two army officers, who were standing speaking to Ben Flett. 'Nathan Libby.' He held out his hand.

'Captain Brian Tucker,' said the older man, shaking it. 'This is Lieutenant Clive Benson.'

'How d'you do,' said the lieutenant. 'I believe I met your brother the other day – Mr Tobias Libby of Libby's Farm?'

'That right,' said Nathan. 'Now, if you would just like to take these two seats at the side here, while we conduct the election? Two of our selectmen have finished their term of office and we have to elect their replacements. We'll let you have your say before we deal with some minor items of business. Afterwards we have to report on a number of financial matters, and I believe it wouldn't be right for you to sit in on those discussions, but you'd be very welcome to join our dollar supper afterwards.'

Charlie Flett, one of the retiring selectmen, called the meeting to order, and as late arrivals found seats, Christina O'Neill made her way to the front of the hall, where a few solitary chairs were still unoccupied. Despite a warning glance from Abigail, Harriet motioned Christina towards the seat beside her. Harriet always felt obscurely guilty about Christina, as well as embarrassed by her. It was true that she was generally so busy about the farm that she had little opportunity for visiting, but that didn't stop her lingering for a chat with Mary at the store or calling upon the Penhaligon sisters. Yet she had not visited the cabin in the woods once in the last twelve months. Christina looked perfectly respectable today. She had plaited her greying black hair and wound it round her head, and she was wearing shoes, though no stockings. Her skirt had been torn at the hem, but was mended – somewhat clumsily and with a thread which did not altogether match the fabric. Harriet smiled at her hesitantly as she sat down.

Three men were nominated for the two vacant posts. The votes, written on slips of paper and deposited in a tin pail, were counted amidst a soft buzz of conversation and the two winners were announced – Hector Swanson and Walter Pelham. There was a brief, polite round of applause as the two men took their seats. Charlie and Eli, the retiring members, shook them by the hand and joined their families in the main audience.

Nathan invited Captain Tucker to explain to the people of Flamboro the army's plan for coastal defences in the area. No one was unduly disturbed at the thought of the row of foxholes. However, they were not ready to accept a gun in the buryingground so easily.

'We must have at least one gun along this stretch of coast,' said Captain Tucker earnestly. 'It's for your own protection. You don't want Nazis coming ashore from submarines here, do you? Or Nazi planes flying over to bomb your homes? With a gun located up on the high ground beside the church, our gun crews will be able to defend you against either.'

He smiled reassuringly.

'The only other possible site is at the end of one of the

harbour walls. There's two arguments against that. First, being lower down the gunners would have a narrower area of visibility and range of fire. Second, if any fire is returned, the gun position would be just too close to the houses along the harbour front. I do urge you to choose the burying-ground rather than the wharf.'

He sat down, looking patient and attentive. You would almost believe, thought Nathan, that he is really giving us a choice. And, of course, we could argue that the gun could be placed down on Todd's Neck or further north, round in the next bay. But that would be a lot less convenient for them, with no tar road to bring men and ammunition in and out. The argument and the questions went on for some time, but eventually even the dissenters agreed, grumbling, to locating the gun in the burying-ground.

The meeting turned to several smaller matters, then the report on the annual accounts. Restive children were sent to amuse themselves outside until supper was served. The army officers withdrew and some of the women excused themselves to start heating soup and making coffee in the kitchen attached to the hall. Simon and Tirza joined the exodus, having no interest in the discussion of a year's income and expenditure.

'Where's Billy?' Tirza asked Simon as they came out into the mild evening air which smelled of seaweed and tar instead of the hair oil and Woolworth's perfume wafting from the teenagers who had been sitting behind them. Wayne's fifteen-year-old sister Clarice, in the officers' honour, had painted her mouth in a Cupid's bow of Ruby Delight lipstick and dowsed herself in a perfume which smelled to Tirza like sheep-dip mixed with very cheap candy.

'Patience Warren came to baby-sit for the evening. She wanted to come to the dollar supper, but Martha paid her extra.'

'Hey,' said Wayne, who was sitting on a bollard at the water's edge.

'Hey,' said Tirza. They joined him.

'Hope they don't take too long,' said Wayne. 'I'm starvin'. Ma brought meat loaf and some great brownies.'

Tirza stood flicking flat stones and oyster shells across the harbour while the boys discussed food. The tide was up and just on its breathless moment of turn, so the surface was calm in the lee of the harbour wall, but she could not achieve more than three bounces. Growing bored, she perched on another bollard, swinging her legs and watching the hall for any sign that the meeting was finished. She noticed that Martha was standing just at the edge of the light from the door, smoking and talking to Lieutenant Benson and Captain Tucker. Then Miss Bennett came to the door and clanged the school bell.

In the well-mannered but urgent scramble for the head of the supper queue, Tirza managed to find Christina.

'Was it very boring?' she asked. 'All that money stuff?'

'All that money stuff, Tirza, is part of the responsibility of every citizen. If we don't take the trouble to participate in community decisions, we have no right to consider ourselves part of it.'

Tirza thought about this.

'But you live away from the village, in the woods.'

'That doesn't mean I have forgotten my responsibilities. Mind now, move ahead. It's our turn to help ourselves.'

As always, the Flamboro dollar supper was a feast, with all the contributors striving to outdo each other. Captain Tucker and Lieutenant Benson departed at ten, feeling well satisfied with their evening's work. They had persuaded the people of Flamboro into believing the location of the gun was their own choice, they had eaten an excellent meal in return for a nominal contribution to the local church, and they had persuaded the glamorous Martha Halstead to come to the movies with them in Portland on the following Saturday, on a double date.

'Have you got a girl lined up for yourself?' Tucker asked as they climbed out of their jeep just inside the gate of the camp.

Lieutenant Benson, who had been the first to ask Martha out, and thought she was his date, looked surprised. But he supposed the captain could pull rank on him.

'I dunno. I'll need to look around. I guess I'll find somebody.'

The following week the army started work on the foxholes. As Tirza was riding her bike over to the farm on Tuesday after school, she found three jeeps parked where the farm track met the coastal path. She laid her bike down on the rough grass and walked along the ledges above Libby's Beach. At regular intervals, the land had been ripped and torn. In the sandy ground just behind the rocks, holes about six foot square and five foot deep had been dug and then lined with large burlap sacks filled with sand. On the seaward side more bags were heaped up to form a parapet, three bags in height, as additional protection. Tirza peered down into the first one. As she watched, the soil settled, trickling between the sandbags and dusting the floor of the hole.

She walked along in the direction of Todd's Neck and reached the group of soldiers shovelling sand off the beach into sandbags to line the latest hole they had dug. One of the soldiers seemed more slightly built than the others. When he turned and heaved his bag on to the barrier in front of the foxhole, she saw with a shock that it was Simon. He had a cigarette in the corner of his mouth. When he saw her he jumped, choked, and began to cough. He spat out the cigarette and ground it out on the rocks with his heels. Tirza could only stare in astonishment.

'What are you doing?'

'Just lending a hand.'

But he knew that was not what she meant.

'I promised I'd come over and help with the milking today. Have you done your chores?'

He grunted incomprehensibly and began to fill another sandbag.

'Hey there, little lady,' said one of the soldiers, 'you wanna help us too?'

Tirza looked at the havoc they were wreaking on this quiet place, until today untouched and uncultivated by any man's hand, and shook her head. The systematic way they were desecrating the land made her feel physically sick. She turned away and almost ran back to her bicycle.

◆◆◆

It was the last day of school and Miss Bennett had abandoned any hope of serious lessons. She handed out the eighth-grade report cards and then gave them a short lecture on the future. Some of them were going on to high school in Portland in the fall, amongst them Tirza, Simon and Wayne. Most of the girls and many of the boys who lived on the inland farms were leaving school for good. This grieved Julia Bennett, and she had tried when she first came to Flamboro the previous year to persuade their parents that the children would have a better future if they were allowed to continue their schooling. She met a mixture of responses. Some parents were genuinely regretful. They wanted a better life for their children than they had had themselves. But many of them were still hanging on to their farms precariously, after the lean years of the Depression; some who had once owned their own farms were now tenants. Other families regarded all schooling as a waste of time, especially for girls.

'Don't see no need for all this schoolin' myself,' said Mrs Potts, Eileen's mother. 'Once they can read the instructions on a feed sack and know enough arithmetic to figger out how much to charge for eggs, ain't no reason to learn more. It's always bin enough for me. I coulda done with Eileen helpin' round the house these last two years, but her pa said as how we should let her stay to the end of grade school.'

The fishing families seemed less reluctant to allow their children to go on to high school. Julia Bennett could not work out why this should be so, but in the end she put it down to the fact that, although Flamboro was small, it was a town of sorts, with plenty of social activity amongst the citizens. The fishermen listened to the radio for the weather forecasts and they listened to the news. Flett's Stores, too, was a great centre for discussion about the wider world and the progress of the war. While the more remote inland farms, cut off from their neighbours for much of the time, might still be living in the nineteenth century, Flamboro and its fishermen were more in touch with today. Although to Julia Bennett, who had grown up in Philadelphia, Flamboro often seemed old-fashioned to the point of quaintness. She had intended to spend just one year here, until she could find a job teaching somewhere more exciting, but Pete Flett had changed all that. To her surprise she had grown fond of the town and as absorbed by its daily activities and gossip as any of the long-time residents.

'So whatever you decide to do with the rest of your lives,' she wound up her little speech, 'I hope you will retain happy memories of your time at Flamboro School. Those of you who are leaving school, remember that learning goes on for the rest of your lives. You should go on reading books on your own – history, literature, science, there's nothing you can't tackle. And if you decide in a year or two that you would like to go back to school, it's always possible to approach the high school authorities to see if you can attend.'

She glanced round at the smaller group who would be catching the bus to Portland every day from September.

'As for those of you who are continuing with your studies, remember what a privilege it is, and make sure you make the most of the next four wonderful years. By the time you leave high school you'll be almost grown-up, with all the work and worry that entails. Enjoy these years, and use them well. Now, off you go, and have a good summer.'

'Thank you, ma'am! And you, ma'am,' they shouted. Some of them left small gifts on her desk – flowers, half a dozen eggs. Simon brought one of his mother's cakes. Tirza had selected and polished up some large oyster shells to use as pin trays, and had filled each with fudge Miss Catherine had helped her make. Let loose on the bright May morning they went careening out of school half an hour ahead of the younger pupils, drunk on the knowledge that they had put a large span of their childhood behind them.

Simon and Wayne started a mock wrestling match in Schoolhouse Lane. Eileen and Johnny were walking along with their arms blatantly wound round each other. Eileen looked at Tirza patronisingly.

'I really pity you, Tirza Libby,' she said, 'havin' four more years of schoolin' ahead. Sakes, I'm glad I'm done with all that.'

'Well,' said Tirza defiantly, 'at least I'm not so behind at school as you. When I'm the age you are now, I'll already be halfway through high school.'

Eileen was determined to have the last word. She smiled graciously. 'Of course, I was fergettin' you're such a child, Tirza. Only twelve, ain't you? What a baby!' And she sauntered off with Johnny, her nose in the air.

For a minute Tirza was furious, then she laughed. Who cared about Eileen Potts? She slung her bag over her shoulder and went leaping up the hill over the heath and through the blueberry thickets to Christina's wood. The bushes were covered with masses of their waxy bell-shaped creamy flowers. There would be a good blueberry harvest this year. During the last two weeks the heath had burst into spring flower, so that she danced through golden ponds of cinquefoil and woolly gold heather, and skirted the spreading constellations of white stars where wild strawberries could be found later. Fuzzy ladies' tobacco brushed her bare feet and she stopped to pick a bunch of violets, whose purple black reminded her of the dark colour of the deep ocean. Nearby a sprinkling of tiny white blossoms marked out the clumps of gold thread, whose roots Christina said could be used to stop a wound bleeding.

The clearing around Christina's cabin was filled with dappled light and shade where the sun slanted down through the surrounding balsam firs and pines and oaks and reflected upwards from the cove where Tirza laid her crab lines. Christina had a small rectangle of herb garden along one side of her house where she grew lemon balm and sage and borage, southernwood, thyme and marjoram, pennyroyal and thoroughwort, and half a dozen different kinds of mint. She was not much interested in garden flowers, despite her knowledge of their wild relatives, but a few of the old cottage flowers grew by the door: hollyhocks, climbing garlands of morning glory, and the wild eglantine rose, all surging into growth with the warmer weather. The rest of her cultivated ground was taken up with a vegetable plot and the traditional mounds planted in the Indian fashion, each with corn, beans and squash, an ancient tradition in which every crop supported and nourished the other. The early leaves were just poking through the rich, crumbly soil of the mounds and there was new growth on the perennial herbs.

As Tirza came nearer to the cabin she caught a clean sharp scent on the air which pricked in the back of her nose. She put her head inside the open door, where the scent became intense enough to make her eyes water.

'You're making spruce beer!'

'Yes. Come in and you can help me strain it off.'

The mixture, made of the green tops of the black spruce, with spices and treacle, fermented with yeast, needed to be strained into a large bowl. Tirza held the sieve steady while Christina poured, then she held it aloft, shaking out the last drops of the spruce beer. There was a row of pottery flagons on the table beside the bowl. Tirza inserted a funnel into the neck of the first, then Christina ladled the beer in till the flagon was full.

'There are some stoppers over there, on the shelf.'

Tirza brought back a handful of corncob stoppers and sealed the first flagon. The bowl of spruce beer filled five of the flagons, with a cup or two left over.

'Can we try some?'

'It's better when it's had a little time to mature, but I guess we can taste a bit to see if it's all right.'

The spruce beer, sharp and tasting of spice, was pronounced a success as they drank it from two mugs, accompanied by a slab of buttered cornbread. Later, it would become slightly fizzy.

'You're the only person I know who makes spruce beer,' said Tirza, wiping the foam from her upper lip on the back of her hand.

'Doesn't Catherine Penhaligon make it?'

'No. She does make root beer, though.'

'I've always preferred spruce beer. Seems to me it has a cleaner taste.' Christina smiled across the table at her. 'So, is school over for a while?'

'Ayuh. Nearly three months of vacation!'

'Then you'll be off to high school in Portland.'

Tirza pulled a face. 'Don't particularly want to.'

'Nonsense. Make the most of your chances while you can.'

'You sound like Miss Bennett. She was preaching at us today.'

'I expect she talked a lot of sense.'

'Girna,' said Tirza slowly, 'have you seen what they are doing up along Libby's Beach? Those foxholes the soldiers are digging? Seems to me they're wrecking the land. No one's ever touched that land, Indian or settler. Those marshes have always been there, haven't they? And the fishing pools and cranberries?'

'So I've been told. I had a walk along there yesterday evening. I think, in time, the land will heal itself. The soldiers are only using sandbags, remember. They aren't pouring in concrete or lining them with corrugated tin. In years to come, when the war is over and folks have forgotten why they were dug, the burlap of the bags will rot away and the sand will settle. Then the holes will gradually fill up with blown soil and sand. After that the sea grasses and the marshy reeds will grow over them so you'll never see them. Why, by the time you are grown-up, they'll have disappeared.'

She smiled and laid her hand on Tirza's.

'Don't you worry your head about the land. The land knows how to heal herself.' Her smile faded. 'No, it isn't the land I worry about, it's the people.'

'What do you mean?'

'Damage to people isn't so easily healed, and it leaves scars that can mar a life. I think changes are coming which Flamboro will find difficult to manage.' She gazed away from Tirza, out through the open door of the cabin towards the lower end of the clearing and the sea. 'I think people may get hurt, and I don't just mean our young men who have gone away to the war, like Pete.'

She sighed. 'Still, no use grieving for what may never happen.'

───◆───

At six o'clock on a Saturday evening, Harriet tapped hesitantly on Martha's bedroom door. She had left Billy playing in the bath with three celluloid ducks which had once been Simon's and to which he had taken an unexpected fancy. Martha was in her room getting dressed up to go to the movies again with Captain Tucker. For the last two Saturdays she had gone out as part of a group; tonight she had a date with Captain Tucker on his own.

'What is it?' called Martha. She sounded as though she had a mouth full of bobby-pins.

'Can I come in?'

'I guess so. Is Billy in bed?'

Harriet opened the door and stepped in. Martha was seated in front of her dressing-table mirror, building up her hair in a raised pompadour over a roll of net that required a great deal of strategic pinning. She looked irritated at being interrupted.

'Yes?'

Harriet perched on the edge of Martha's bed. When she was sixteen, Martha had insisted on having a lot of frills in her bedroom: the bedspread was frothy dotted white muslin that was a nightmare to iron, the window curtains were made of the same stuff, and so were the curtains of the half-tester and the skirt of the dressing table. There were a lot of little cushions about, several of them heart-shaped. As Martha had married and left home just two years after this decorating phase, the room had never been changed, but Harriet sometimes wondered whether it was quite the style Martha would choose nowadays, with her sophisticated tastes and her smart clothes.

She twisted her hands in her flowered apron and hesitated over how to begin.

'I'm in a hurry, Mother. Was there something you wanted to say?'

It would have to do as an invitation to speak. Harriet plunged in, clumsily.

'It's about this Captain Tucker.'

'Don't you like him?'

'Oh, he seems just fine,' said Harriet hastily. 'A very nice young man. It's just that, well...with Will away, overseas...'

Martha said nothing. She had finished rolling up her front hair and now brushed the long back hair sleekly down over her collar. It still retained that wonderful glinting gold. Harriet could not help but be proud of it.

'I just feel that... that Will might not be very happy, at you going out with another man while he's away.'

Martha applied scarlet lipstick, blotted it, applied a second coat. Then she swung round on the revolving stool and faced her mother. Under the practised make-up she looked out pleadingly.

'Oh, Mother, it's just because he's away that I *have* to go out, don't you understand? I'm so scared. If I sit around here all the time, I start imagining things – the Nazi planes shooting at him, his plane coming down in flames. But when I go out with Brian and the others, I can laugh a little, have a bit of fun, and forget things for a while. Can't you see?' Her bottom lip trembled.

'Oh, honey,' said Harriet, crossing the room and kneeling down beside the stool. 'I'm so sorry.' She put her arms around her daughter. 'I do understand. Only I think you ought to go out in a group, don't you? We don't want people talking.'

'Oh, I don't care about that,' said Martha scornfully, disentangling herself from her mother's embrace and standing up. 'There's nothing going on, I assure you. Brian is just good for a night out in Portland.'

She slipped her feet into her high-heeled shoes, blew her mother a kiss and tapped jauntily downstairs. As Harriet went into the bathroom to lift Billy out of the bath she heard the rhythmical tooting of a jeep horn coming up the farm lane.

Tirza woke suddenly. Something had shocked her out of sleep and she lay for a moment confused, wondering what time it was. Rolling over, she peered at the luminous dial of the alarm clock on her nightstand. It said twelve thirty. Then she realised what sound had woken her: a truck, rattling over the shell-covered rutted Shore Road at the back of the house. It was braking now, stopping nearby. Footsteps pounded along the side of the house and up the steps to the porch. Not running exactly, but hurrying. There was a sharp knock at the door.

She sat up in bed. The boats which fished inshore would not leave for some hours yet; a few that went further afield had left before dark. It couldn't be news of a missing boat. Anyway, the truck had not come along the harbour front. She realised now that she had half heard it in her sleep coming down Schoolhouse Lane, from the direction of the main road. There was a creak of protesting bed springs as her father got up. Tirza heard him push up the window and lean out.

'Who's there? What is it?'

'Nathan?' It was Tobias's voice. 'Can you come down? I'm sorry to wake you like this, but...'

'I'm coming.'

The window slid down again and Nathan went downstairs. Tirza heard the door open and the murmur of voices at the foot of the stairs. She crept to her door and opened it a crack. As she did so, she saw Abigail open the door of her bedroom, which was at the back of the house. Abigail joined her sons in the hallway, then all three of them moved into the kitchen.

Tirza's heart was pounding. Something serious must have happened up at the farm to bring her uncle down to Flamboro in the truck, hours after both households were in bed. With her laced fingers pressed against her chest, she strained her ears to hear what was going on, but it was useless.

Nathan and Abigail both came back upstairs and Tirza could hear drawers opening in Abigail's room, a shoe dropped in

Nathan's. They were back downstairs in minutes and the front door closed behind them. Running across to her open window and leaning out, Tirza was just in time to see all three of them rounding the corner of the house. The truck's engine spluttered, coughed and started, and they were gone.

She sat down on her bed in astonishment. Then she threw off her pyjamas and pulled on her clothes, banging about in her haste. Her bicycle was kept in the boat shed. She did not bother to open the big double doors, but lifted her bicycle up the step into the back hall and wheeled it to the front door. She bumped it down the three steps from the porch to the ground, took a running start and began to pedal along the coastal path.

In all the years she had walked and biked along the path, she had never travelled along it in the middle of the night. Tonight the thick blackness was lit only by a paring of moon and a few pulsing stars between racing clouds, while out at sea an occasional wave turned and foamed under the starlight. Still, she knew the path well and could avoid the larger holes and projecting boulders. When she reached the narrow strip which ran between the Tremayne property and the cliff, she decided she ought to dismount. Walking cautiously, wheeling her bike, she felt suddenly alone. There was no sound but the faint rhythmical ticking from the bicycle wheels and the perpetual crash of the sea, which Tirza never heard, but felt beating in the pulse of her own blood. She glanced across at the Tremayne house and thought how the local children had always called it, jokingly, the Haunted House. It didn't seem quite so much of a joke tonight, with only a thin sliver of moon, half-obscured by clouds, that glinted here and there on the glass of the darkened windows. It was as though someone was moving about those deserted rooms with a flickering candle.

Tirza tightened her grip on the handlebars and concentrated on the path. It would widen out soon, and she would be able to ride again. A sudden movement ahead of her and a rustling in the leatherwood bushes crowded against the stone boundary wall made her jump. Some nocturnal creature, as startled as she was herself, had fled for shelter. Before the path was quite wide enough to be safe, she mounted again and began to pedal hard, down the swoop of ground edging Tobias's bottom field where the rows of young corn whispered, down to the place where a break in the rocks allowed an easy descent to the beach, and then turned to the right on to the main farm track.

The bicycle wheel twisted suddenly, pitching her off on to the stony ground. She struck her chin on something, and she could feel the salty taste of blood where her teeth had cut into her lip. She pulled herself up. The ground here was churned into a tangle of deep ruts where the jeeps had been turning. Usually the ground was bumpy here, but nothing the bike would not have sailed over. Now the path was so broken up she had to wheel it again until she was well past the junction of the two paths. She dabbed her lip on her shirt tail, mounted again, and rode on up the track to the farmyard.

Lights were blazing everywhere in the house. The pickup stood in the middle of the yard, its doors hanging open. The horses and cows were out in the pasture, away from the house, but there were distressed sounds from the chicken shed, like a disturbed hive of bees, and the pig was bumping his shoulder anxiously against the gate of his pen. One of the half-wild farm cats slipped past, eyeing Tirza sideways. It was carrying a rat, which hung limp from its jaws, the long tail trailing in the dust. Tirza shuddered. She could hear voices from the house, and something else.

A terrible thin shrieking noise, like an animal caught in a trap, came from one of the upstairs windows. It went on and on, rising and falling with a strange primitive rhythm. It was interspersed with angry yells, which Tirza recognised as Billy in a furious temper – and perhaps afraid. She couldn't think what could be making that inhuman screaming noise.

As she stood hesitating in the yard, holding her bicycle and wondering whether to go forward to the house or to retreat and make for home, Simon came out of the open back door and sat down on the steps, his head in his hands.

'Simon!' Tirza whispered urgently.

Over the noise he did not hear her.

'Simon!'

He leapt up, peering out from the lighted doorway into the dark yard.

'Tirza? What are you doing here?' He sounded angry, but in

the diffused light from the house his face was tear-stained and blotchy.

'What's going on? What's that noise?'

Simon walked down the steps and across the yard to her. He stared at her wide-eyed in the dark and put his hands over hers on the handlebars.

'Just after Martha got back from her date with Captain Tucker, a telegraph boy came.'

'A telegraph?' Tirza didn't understand at first what he meant. Then her stomach clenched. 'Oh, no. Not Will?'

She saw him nod, silhouetted against the lighted house.

'He's been shot down on a bombing raid over Germany. He's dead.'

They stood in silence, trying to grasp this. Blackness seemed to be seeping towards them from the dark fields and woods. Will Halstead. Dead.

'Martha didn't say anything at first, then she just went berserk, started throwing dishes round the kitchen. Then she ran upstairs and grabbed Billy out of bed and locked him with her in her bedroom. She started screaming like that and she hasn't stopped. Now Billy's yelling – I guess he's terrified. Our dads are trying to get them out.'

Simon raised one hand and ran it over his face. With the other he gripped Tirza's hand tightly.

'I think she's gone crazy.'

Chapter 8

Maine: Spring 1942

Afterwards, PATIENCE WAS to swear her Bible oath that she had not breathed a word to anyone about events at the Libbys' farm that night. Normally she would not have been there on a Saturday. She arrived Monday morning and worked till Friday, sleeping weekday nights on a truckle bed up in one of the attic rooms. Then on Friday evening, with her wages in her pocket, she would walk home to Flamboro. However, since Martha and Billy had arrived at the farm, she had been glad to augment her earnings with baby-sitting whenever the Libby parents could not stay at home to mind Billy. Even on the nights when Patience was sleeping at the farm anyway, Harriet insisted that Martha should pay her for baby-sitting when she was left in charge. So on the Saturday when Martha went out to Portland with Captain Tucker, and Harriet and Tobias had arranged to play bridge with the Fletts, Patience had come back to the farm at six thirty as Harriet was putting Billy to bed. She sat listening to the radio in the farm kitchen until Simon came home and had taken herself off to bed about nine.

At nine thirty, when the Libbys had walked back from Flamboro and let themselves into the house, Patience woke briefly, then fell asleep again. Later, when the screaming began, she was terrified. Uncertain whether to stay where she was or go downstairs, she clutched her pillow to her chest and hid under the quilt. Eventually, after hearing the pickup leave and return, she could no longer endure being alone. Wrapping her house-coat around her, she made her way fearfully down to the landing, where she found Harriet sitting on a chair weeping and

Abigail standing grimly beside her. Wild shrieks were coming from behind Martha's door, mingled with screams of fright from Billy. Through the open landing window she could see Tobias at the top of a ladder, steadied by Nathan at its foot. Tobias seemed to be trying to force Martha's window open.

The eldest of six children and daughter of a trawlerman, Patience was a girl of practical sense when she realised she was confronted with a human crisis and not something out of a nightmare. She went down to the kitchen, stoked the kitchen stove and made a pot of coffee and another of tea. Later the older Libbys drifted in and out of the kitchen and were grateful to her. She saw nothing of Martha, but Harriet carried Billy down to the kitchen wrapped in a blanket. His face was red and puffy with tears and his eyes were wide with shock. Patience made him a mug of hot chocolate and took him on her knee while Harriet collapsed on a chair and cradled a third cup of tea, which she did not drink.

As dawn was lightening the east, Patience heard about the death of Will, falling out of the sky in his burning aeroplane. She cried a little herself, quietly. Will was a decent man. Not handsome, but what her mother called solid. He had always had a kind word for Patience, even when he used to come for his vacations to Todd's Neck as a boy, when she was a little girl with pigtails.

So if it wasn't Patience who let slip the story of that night, who was it? Whatever or whoever, within a couple of days everyone in Flamboro knew that Will Halstead was dead, that his wife Martha was crazy with grief and taking sleeping pills prescribed by the doctor, and that she had reacted to the news by locking herself in her room with her son and threatening to kill them both.

'It's shocking,' said Mary Flett to Miss Catherine as she weighed out flour and raisins. 'He was a fine young man, and he hadn't been over there but two months. There's Harriet's girl a widow at twenty-six and that child fatherless. And if ever a child needed a father's hand, that one does.'

'I feel so sorry for Harriet and Tobias,' said Miss Catherine. 'And two pounds of sugar, please, Mary.' She began to pack her purchases into her basket. 'Will Halstead was a good husband to

Martha, steadying. Now, I don't know... There's many a woman been widowed in this town without losing her mind as well.'

'Women here have always known they might lose their husbands between sunrise and sunrise,' said Mary bluntly. 'You have to accept what the Lord sends. I'm sure Harriet raised Martha as best she could, but that girl always was different, didn't fit in here, and I reckon being away from home so long she's picked up fancy Washington notions.'

Mary was fond of Harriet, and she regarded Martha's hysterical behaviour as some kind of slur on her mother.

'Well,' said Miss Catherine with a sigh, 'no doubt she'll come to terms with it in time. Molly thinks she's been tipped over the edge by guilt – when the telegram arrived, she'd just come back from a night out in Portland with that army captain who was here at town meeting.'

This view gradually took form and hardened as the general opinion in Flamboro. Martha was pitied, but the pity was tempered with reproof. She'd been dating another man when her husband was thousands of miles away, risking his life for his country. Didn't that somehow make her partly responsible for Will's death? And her uncontrolled frenzy on hearing the news, her threat to kill herself and her child – no Flamboro woman had ever behaved with such lack of decency and dignity.

Discussion of Flamboro's first war casualty was interrupted by the arrival of the gun that was to be mounted on the headland beside the burying ground. A number of townsfolk had pictured a machine-gun, like those they had seen in gangster movies, with maybe a stand and a hut for the gunners. They were therefore taken aback when three large army trucks, painted in camouflage patches of khaki, brown and green, drove down Schoolhouse Lane two days after the news of Will's death had reached the town. The trucks turned left at the harbour front and drove up as close to the church as they could, and a party of soldiers piled out of them.

A couple of officers with theodolites directed operations. By the end of the first day, an area had been marked out on the headland, a square hole dug in the topsoil and walled with boards, and concrete poured for the base. The soldiers, who had enlivened things at the Schooner Bar over lunchtime, roared off in the evening, bouncing up the lane round the shoulder of Mount Manenticus to the main Portland road, driving much too fast and killing a racoon which strayed on to the road from the woods round Gooseneck Lake.

Three days later they were back, one group setting up the gun base and mounting the gun, the other group assembling three prefabricated sheds. Simon and Wayne, who hung around the soldiers with the other boys, asking questions, wanted to know what the sheds were for.

'These two smaller ones, for ammunition and gun spares,' said a friendly sergeant. 'The bigger one is for the gunners to use.'

They were allowed to look inside. There were rough bunks, one above the other, against the far wall, a table with a field telephone, and a portable kerosene stove so the men on duty could make themselves coffee. The boys established themselves on the churchyard wall, swinging their legs and watching critically.

'Reckon I could do that,' said Simon, chewing a piece of grass while a couple of soldiers fixed the door of the ammunition shed in place.

'Reckon I could too,' said Wayne. 'Don't look as hard work as fishin', bein' a soldier.'

'I bet I can shoot as well as they can. Been potting rabbits since I was six.' Simon threw away his piece of grass and chose another from the overgrown stems that fringed the edge of the churchyard. 'Though I guess 'tisn't much fun getting shot at in a battle.'

'Nowadays everybody rides in tanks,' said Wayne. 'My uncle over to Kennebunk, Ma's brother, he fought in the last war. He says this one's goin' to be some different. No trenches and all that slaughter. It'll be tanks and aeroplanes and submarines.'

'You wouldn't get me in a submarine.'

'Well...' Wayne reflected, 'I dunno. You can sneak up on the Germans and then let go a torpedo – wham!'

'Ayuh. But what if you get hit, when you're under water?'

Wayne shrugged. 'Drownin' is drownin', in a fishin' boat or a submarine. Don't make no difference.'

Simon did not answer, but he had a sudden picture, sharp and clear, of being trapped beneath the ocean in a holed submarine with the water coming in slowly and no way of escape. He clenched his teeth, and the grass stem snapped, laying a sour-sweet green taste over his tongue.

'Anyways,' said Wayne regretfully, 'I guess the war will be over before we're old enough to enlist.'

'I guess so.'

❖❖❖

Tirza had not joined Simon and the others watching the soldiers installing the gun. She could not understand what they found so interesting about it. The foxholes along Libby's Beach had been bad enough, but it turned out that they were not going to be manned all the time. Once a week a jeep containing two soldiers bounced down the track from the farm to the sea. The soldiers would get out, stretch, have a smoke, and then stroll along the top of the ledges, glancing casually into each foxhole to check that everything was in order. Then they would saunter on. By taking their time, they could make the walk along to Todd's Neck fill the entire morning. Several of the regulars on these patrols soon made friends with the chef at the Mansion House, who would invite them into the hotel kitchen for a bite of lunch.

In the afternoon they would inspect the cove where Eel Joe had his hut, and pass the time of day with him. Their route terminated at the inlet leading into the sea-fed lake where Joe caught his eels. Beyond that the land was too boggy for foxholes and was guarded offshore by rocks like gaping teeth. There was no risk of an enemy craft attempting to land there. The less squeamish of the soldiers would finish the inspection by partaking of a cup of Eel Joe's coffee. There was nothing wrong with the coffee, but the old man, his upturned boat, and his thick white mugs all shared the same potent perfume of dead eel.

As afternoon wore on, the soldiers would usually return along the beach to their jeep and drive back to camp. If, on the other hand, they walked smartly up the coastal path past the Tremayne place, there might be time to go on into Flamboro for a beer before returning. There were some pretty girls to be whistled at, and the townsfolk were inclined to be friendly. All in all, being assigned to inspect the foxholes south of Flamboro was soon regarded as a plum day's job.

Tirza kept out of the way of the soldiers, whether they were inspecting the foxholes or installing the gun or strolling around Flamboro visiting the two bars and peering in the window of Mrs Larrabee's store, looking for gifts for their wives and sweethearts. She resented their presence. Even though they went nowhere near Libby's Beach six days out of every seven, she felt as though they had contaminated it. When she walked that way, she stayed down on the fine silver sand of the beach itself, under the sheltering wall of the ledges, where she could not see the rough ramparts of the sandbags and could pretend to herself that things were the way they used to be.

About halfway along the beach to Todd's Neck the wall of rocks thrust out a wedge suddenly into the sand, before curving back again. Most of the rock along the shore was made up of the sloping layers of granite that form the Maine coastline and lie beneath the soil further inland as well. But here in this one place the rocks were different. Petrified trees which had grown here millions of years ago had left a strange cluster of stumps. Ancient dry land had once spread out where the ocean now rolled. The fishermen hereabouts still thought of the sea-bed in terms of lost hills and valleys, and Christina had told Tirza old Indian tales of the vanished lands under the ocean.

It was at this spot, where she could lay her hand against the petrified side of a tree once surrounded by meadows and valleys, that the sense of time and change became real for Tirza. Once, the thought had simply given her a thrill, as she strove to understand such a gulf of time. Now, though, the ancient trees with their stone roots deep in the shifting sand partly comforted and partly frightened her. They had endured, and they would continue to endure. The coast itself had slipped, heaved and sunk, but only gradually, over aeons of time. But now, it seemed, the war, the army, the strangers coming here, were violently rearranging the face of the land. Tirza felt unsafe.

———◆———

It was about this time that Tirza began to dream.

Usually, her sleep was deep and dark, and she awoke with no memory of the night-time hours. The dreams at first left no more than fragments in her waking mind – a sense of unease, of a conversation interrupted or some task of inexplicable importance left unfinished. Waking, she felt driven to recapture the dream, to complete whatever she had left undone, but sleep would elude her, leaving her tired and peevish.

Later, the dreams became longer, clearer. She was running through blackened streets and the buildings on every side leaned slowly towards her. There were no explosions, no noise, yet she knew that she ran through a bombed city whose walls collapsed lazily, like heavy waves, behind her. As they fell, they threw up spumes of white powder, like wild water out at sea, but she knew she was on land from the heat and the dust-filled air that choked her. She had been charged with some task, and failed. But what it was or where she was going, she could not tell.

It seemed at last that she was dreaming all night. The flight lasted for hours till she woke gasping and exhausted. There were flames now in the city. They reared up behind the buildings, towering into a sky that was silver and black in ragged patches. Her sheets were soaking with sweat in the morning. Her hair plastered flat against her skull.

———◆———

Tirza avoided the farm these days. She had not visited since her bicycle ride in the dark along the coast path, and she had hardly seen the family there. Abigail reported that Martha kept to her room. Harriet and Tobias were busy with the spring seasonal work on the farm, and when Simon came into Flamboro he spent his time with Wayne or hanging around the soldiers, who were now manning the gun permanently, sleeping and keeping watch in shifts.

Nathan was glad of Tirza's help on *Louisa Mary*, and their catches of lobsters were middling good this year. Her own crabbing had fallen off a little after the early days, but it was picking up again. Now that the school vacation had started, the summer people were arriving, and visitors were thronging to the Mansion House as if they had never heard of the war. Tirza planned to lay a second crab line so she would have more crabs to sell to them. Flamboro was accustomed to this annual influx of summer people. Most of them had come for years, and the outbreak of war did not seem to be deterring them. Some stayed in rooms in Flamboro and others rented cottages on the surrounding farms. There were even two small houses in Flamboro itself which belonged to outlanders who spent their summers down Maine every year. One was owned by an elderly couple from Boston who were friends of the Penhaligons, the other belonged to a French family from Quebec.

One bright morning with a promise of real heat later on, Tirza set off in *Stormy Petrel* with two bushels of crabs. She didn't like her fishing gear messing up her catboat, but it was the easiest way to transport the crabs to the Mansion House. As she hoisted the sail the breeze was light, but once she rounded the headland south of Flamboro harbour it freshened and *Stormy Petrel* heeled over. The baskets slid to the lee side and some of the crabs started to scrabble frantically. With her hands full, Tirza had no time to attend to the crabs and as the basket leaned one or two of the bolder ones managed to climb out and skittered about the bottom boards, snapping their claws and blowing bubbles amongst her tackle. Her feet, as usual in warm weather, were bare, so she propped them up on the opposite gunwale and kept one eye on the sail and the shore line and the other on the ranging crabs.

The east-north-east wind carried her past Libby's Beach on one long reach, then she came about and began tacking along the narrow causeway to the island-like promontory of the Neck itself. The Mansion House stood at the very end of Todd's Neck, with its wide wrap-around porch overlooking the ocean. The pier that served the hotel was a little further on, and Tirza headed south again, fetching up against the smart red and white fenders hung alongside the damp barnacled timbers on festoons of rope. The wharf at Flamboro had fenders made of old tyres, but the owners of the Mansion House kept rather higher standards. Tyres or fancy fenders made no difference to Tirza. She took a pride in laying *Stormy Petrel* so gently alongside the piers that she did not even brush them.

She climbed on to the pier and secured the painter to a post with a round turn and a couple of half hitches, then she knelt down and fished around the bottom of the boat for the escaped crabs. She caught three of them and piled them back into one of the bushel baskets. The others could wait till she came back. She lifted the basket out of the boat and, balancing it on her hip, started up the path to the kitchen door of the Mansion House.

'You bring me nice fresh crabs, eh?' said Pierre Lamotte, head chef, standing hands on hips in the centre of his great kitchen and regarding her with his head on one side.

'Great crabs, Monsewer Lamotte,' said Tirza.

Pierre maintained the pretence to the management and guests that he had trained in one of the top restaurants in his native Paris, but late one evening, when Tirza had delivered some of her father's lobsters, he had admitted – after a consoling bottle of Bordeaux – that he had taught himself to cook in his mother's workmen's café in Montreal, a town to which his family had emigrated in the twenties.

'These Philistines,' he said now, shaking a mournful head, 'they do not know a crayfish from a prime lobster. They would not recognise a *filet mignon* if it jumped up and kissed them in the eye, so!' He snapped his fingers in front of her nose.

Tirza wouldn't have recognised a *filet mignon* either, but she certainly understood shellfish. She had a mutually pleasing agreement with Pierre that she would supply as many of her best crabs as possible to the hotel restaurant, and he would pay her only ten per cent less than he would pay the adult fishermen – more than she could sell them for anywhere else. In return she respected his confidences, which were many.

'Is this all you bring me today?'

'I have another basket down in my boat. Some of the crabs escaped. I'll go get the rest of them.'

When she had retrieved the remaining crabs, including one which managed to nip her as she felt for it under the foredeck, Pierre counted out her money from a roll of creased dollar bills and she stowed them in the hip pocket of her shorts. She always delivered the crabs at his quiet period, around ten in the morning, when the breakfasts were cleared, but before the rush for lunches began. The Mansion House had been built to the highest standards of Victorian gourmandising, back in the days when the Todd family still lived here. In addition to the vast central kitchen – where six modern electric stoves now formed an island in the middle with tables and sinks arranged around the walls – there were specialised rooms for every kind of food. Pierre's assistants were busy preparing vegetables in one of these and filleting fish in another, which boasted solid marble slabs and an underground stream to keep it cool. There was a game room and a cheese room, also cooled by the stream, and a whole range of larders. Along the centre of the corridor which ran from the main kitchen between these subsidiary rooms was laid a set of rails, like a miniature railroad track. A heavy wooden trolley, made of solid oak and holding four tiers of shelves, ran on wheels along these rails to serve all parts of the kitchen wing. When Tirza had first been shown the Mansion House's kitchen arrangements she had been astonished, but now she took it for granted.

Having delivered her crabs to the fish room, Tirza sat down with Pierre at one of the scrubbed pine tables in the main kitchen and drank the *citron pressé* he always gave her. There was usually a bowl of leftover dessert from the previous night's dinner as well. Today it was some complicated confection of meringue, hazelnuts and chocolate.

'When will your uncle's strawberries be ready?' Pierre asked, sipping his small cup of black coffee. For a chef besotted with cooking he was remarkably abstemious of both food and drink except when life became particularly trying.

'Not for a few weeks yet. I'll let you know as soon as we start picking.'

Tirza plunged her fork into the hazelnut mixture and sampled it carefully.

'This is great – crunchy and fluffy at the same time.'

'I was *desolé* to hear about your cousin's 'usband, *ma p'tite*.'

Tirza stared down at her plate. She did not know how to respond when people referred to Will's death, but Pierre did not seem to expect anything from her.

'Always it is the young lost in war, and their families left to mourn.' He swirled the coffee in his cup. 'My young brother, 'e went back to France when war was declared. We have 'eard nothing since the Nazis overran the country.'

'Oh, Pierre, I didn't know. You never told me.'

Pierre shrugged, making an odd, despairing gesture with his hands, as though his thoughts slipped away through his fingers.

'Perhaps 'e is safer there than with the Free French in England. Have you 'eard about our new guest?'

Tirza shook her head. The guests at the Mansion House were

of no interest to her, except as consumers of her crabs.

'It is an English pilot. Convalescing.'

'What's he doing here?'

'It is very exciting, very romantic – like a John Buchan novel, yes? This young man, 'e is a fighter pilot, and 'e is in one of these so-called dogfights.'

'Dogfights?'

'*Tiens, p'tite*, do you take no interest in the war? This is when the planes on both sides fight one-to-one in the sky, like old-fashioned warriors. Only sometimes it is not so sporting. Three German planes attacked this pilot's Spitfire, and 'is plane caught fire. 'E managed to land the plane on the water and get out, with 'is rubber raft. Me, I don't see 'ow you can land a plane on water. It seems impossible – you might as well say you can walk on water. But this is what they say 'e did.'

'But why is he here?'

'The plane crashes a long way off the west coast of Cornwall. That is the bottom left corner of England, *tu comprends*? Doubtless you are also ignorant of *la géographie*. Then 'e drifts in 'is raft for a week, and is discovered by one of the convoys carrying supplies from America. The convoy, it was on the return journey west, so the ship's doctor, 'e mends this pilot as best 'e can and they bring 'im with them. They cannot turn back for one man.'

'Was he hurt?'

''E breaks both legs when the plane 'its the sea, and there is much tearing of flesh and muscles. Also, 'e suffers from exposure. They keep 'im in 'ospital for some weeks in New York, then someone suggests the Mansion 'ouse for 'is convalescence.'

'I guess he can't go back to England till he's well.'

'No. 'E still cannot walk properly. In the meantime 'e stays with us, and for once I have a guest 'oo understands good food.'

'Well, I hope he likes my crabs.' Tirza was losing interest in the English pilot. 'What time is it? I have to go help my dad.'

'*Mon Dieu!* It is nearly eleven! Away with you.'

'See you tomorrow.' Tirza picked up her two empty baskets and ran down the path back to the pier.

⋘⋙

It was time to paint the inside of the cow barn. Tobias had

already painted the outside in the same dull rusty crimson as every other barn in the State of Maine. Hector Swanson had just had his barn painted in the same red by the company which made Beech-Nut Chewing Tobacco.

'It's a prime deal, Mr Libby,' Hector had assured Tobias. 'They come back and paint your barn every year for free.'

'Not for free,' Tobias grumbled. 'They cover one whole side with advertising. On my barn that'd be the side facing the road. The same side as everyone coming up the farm track sees when they come to the house. I don't want anything to do with it. I don't even hold with chewing tobacco. Dirty habit.'

'It's the way things are going. Farmers have to be commercial these days. Those who can't move with the times aren't going to survive. Look at all those ruined places up on Mount Manenticus. Nothing left up there but cellar holes now.'

'That was the Depression. And folks trying to farm land that wasn't ever meant for farming. That's timber land.'

'True enough. But if you can cut down on costs, it increases your profit margin, or else it frees the cash for other improvements. Like my new milking machine.'

Tobias snorted. Conversations with Hector always ended up with his new milking machine these days. Hector Swanson was the first farmer in the county to install an all-electric milk operation, and he was as pleased as a dog with two tails.

'I don't know about that,' said Tobias. 'Don't think I'll be going over to the electric. It costs extra diesel to run the Kohler system to produce the extra electricity. Milking the cows yourself doesn't cost anything.'

'It costs your time – or Sam's or Mrs Libby's.'

'Got to pay Sam his wages anyhow. And Harriet and me might as well do the milking by hand as stand around waiting for a machine to do it. Besides...'

He gave Hector an ironic look.

'Read in my farming magazine the other day about a farmer in Kansas. He gets his cows all hooked up to one of those machines and starts it running. There's a storm coming on, but he doesn't think anything to it. Then lightning strikes his generator and all his cows are electrocuted along the wires. Act of God, that's what it was. Whole thing's against nature.'

Tobias was glad he did not have a load of machinery to move now he was going to whitewash the inside of the cow barn. It needed to be done fast, between morning and evening milking, for the minimum disruption. Yesterday Simon had forked the remaining hay down from the hayloft into the hayrack and Sam had hauled it round the back of the barn out of the way. Then the two of them had swept the place clean after evening milking. Harriet, looking round after they were done, had clicked her tongue but said nothing. She tied a bunch of damp rags to the end of a long pole and went round the barn again, sweeping down the spiders' webs and the dust that lurked around the rafters and the window frames. Tirza and Nathan were coming to help with the whitewashing, so with all of them working it should be possible to finish in the one day.

As she had promised, Tirza arrived on her bike soon after five, just as it was getting light.

'Dad's coming along behind,' she said. 'Shall I help with the milking?'

Soon after Nathan arrived, the cows were driven out into the pasture and they were ready to start.

'I can give you a hand too, Tobias,' said Harriet.

'Don't you worry. You've got plenty of chores. And you never did like ladders.'

'Well, that's true. Dinner will be ready at noon.' Harriet smiled at Tirza. 'We haven't seen you for a long time. We can have a good visit over dinner.'

Tirza shuffled her feet. She had been avoiding the farm, avoiding Martha, but she was aware she had not been helping Harriet as much as she usually did.

'I'll come for strawberry picking. And if you need help when you're canning...'

'You don't need to come just to work,' said Harriet kindly. 'I appreciate your company.' She touched Tirza's arm as she headed back to the house.

'Now,' said Tobias. 'We have to paint the milk room last, after the milk is collected.'

Tirza peered round the doorway. The milk had stopped dripping through the strainers into the last two milk cans. Tobias removed the strainers, put the lids on the big cans and hitched them to the hoist. Then he hoisted them up and lowered them to stand in the huge clay trough with the others. The blocks of ice floating in the water chinked against the sides of the cans. Later, when the milk was cool, the truck from Portland would collect most of the cans, except those kept for family use and Harriet's cheese making.

Tobias poured whitewash into old sauerkraut cans, on to which Simon had fixed wire handles, and handed out brushes.

'Simon and Tirza can get started on the tie-up. Sam, you get up into the hayloft and do as much as you can reach from there. Nathan and I will start at the other end of the barn with the ladders and work along the ceiling till we meet up with you.'

Soon there was no sound except the wet slap of their brushes against the plaster and the beams of the old barn. Tirza loved whitewashing. Last year's coat was stained and greyish. Her wide brush laid a dazzling layer of white over the top. It went on so easily you could work fast, and within an hour the tie-up had already begun to look brighter and bigger. What a sense of power! An action so simple, and the building grew larger, billowing outwards like a balloon inflating, the roof taking flight above their heads and soaring upwards.

'Snowball will probably be so startled this evening, when she sees this, that she won't give any milk!' said Tirza.

'Don't suppose cows notice things like that,' said Simon.

Tirza looked at him in astonishment. 'Of course they do. That's why Snowball is some difficult. She's a noticing cow. Smarter than the rest.'

Simon laughed. 'Are you a cow psychologist now?'

She shrugged. 'Just common sense. You watch her, that's all.'

By noon they were more than halfway finished, so after their dinner of cod, boiled new potatoes and young cabbages thinned out from the field, they sat out on the porch for a time while Tobias and Nathan drank a cup of coffee and Harriet and Patience shared a pot of tea. Martha had not appeared for dinner, but Tirza had noticed Patience going upstairs with a tray. Billy, who had been watched closely by Patience all morning to keep him out of mischief amongst the whitewash, ran around the flower beds below the porch with his arms stretched out, making aeroplane noises.

The ground sloped away from the house on this side, down to the orchard which lay on the near side of the farm track, with the strawberry field on the far side of it. In winter you could just make out the county road beyond, but now it was hidden by the trees, which were covered with blossom. As the breeze stirred them, the first petals drifted down, sprinkling the orchard grass and the backs of the half-dozen geese who lived there.

Whitewashing time and apple blossom – it was almost summer, thought Tirza, shutting her eyes against the sun and leaning back on her hands. The old silvered boards of the porch were warm under her palms, and her legs dangled over the edge. Far away she could hear the sound of a big aeroplane.

'Time we were getting back to work,' said Nathan, but no one rushed to move. The sun and the sense of the morning's achievement made them lazy.

'There's an aeroplane coming this way,' said Simon.

'I read something in the paper,' said Tobias. 'They're starting regular patrols up and down the coast, looking out for enemy planes and ships.'

'I guess they've got more chance of seeing them than a couple of GIs up on the church headland with a gun,' said Nathan.

The plane came nearer. It was flying up from the south. A big plane, four engines. Tirza and Simon jumped up and shaded their eyes, searching for a sight of it. They had hardly ever seen a four-engine plane.

'There it is!' cried Simon, pointing. Then Tirza saw it too. They were squinting into the sun, and even the grown-ups were looking too. Billy had climbed up on to the porch.

'Where, where? Show me!' He tugged at the hem of Tirza's shorts. She lifted him up and pointed.

The roar grew louder. The plane was going to fly right overhead. Suddenly the screen door from the living room flew open and hit the wall. Martha stumbled through, almost falling. Her hair was awry and she wore no make-up. She looked strange, wild-eyed.

She ran forward and seized Billy from Tirza, swinging him in the air and clutching him to her so that he gave a startled explosion of breath, too surprised to say anything. She stared frantically around and up at the plane, which they could all see now. Then with a terrible cry she threw one arm over her head, crooked at an awkward angle, and ran back into the house. Harriet started to her feet and ran after her. The others were slower, but in a scramble that was almost comic in its haste they followed behind.

They found Harriet in the kitchen. Martha was under the table, hunched over Billy who was yelling with indignation. She was shaking. Outside, the sound of the patrol plane died away to the north.

⬥

'I reckon it was the plane,' said Nathan to Tobias after they had resumed the whitewashing. The milk had been collected. The family milk cans were standing temporarily outside in the horse trough with a block of ice, and they were working in the milk room. Tirza, painting the door frame of the tie-up next door, could hear them talking quietly together.

'I guess so.'

'Stands to reason. Will dying like that, his plane crashing. She's thinking every plane is like to crash.'

'I guess she isn't thinking at all. She's so scared she just wants to grab Billy and hide.'

'Ayuh.'

They fell silent.

It was the first time Tirza had seen Martha since Will's death and she had been, for a moment, very frightened. Then she had felt angry, though she could not have said why. Once the sound of the plane died away, Martha crawled out from under the kitchen table and released Billy, who ran to Patience. Martha looked dazed, her eyes vacant, like someone who has just woken up. Harriet had made her drink a cup of scalding sweet tea, and after a while Martha had acted quite normal. No one made any reference to her strange behaviour. For the first time in her life, Tirza was sorry for Billy, and she even felt some pity for Martha too, though it was mixed with irritation. Her father and uncle might be right about the reason for Martha's behaviour, but it was stupid. Why should the aeroplane, which was flying along quite steadily, suddenly fall out of the sky? And if it did, why should it fall on Libby's Farm? And a kitchen table wouldn't be much protection. Tirza was scornful.

153

They finished the whitewashing with a couple of hours to spare before evening milking. The stalls in the tie-up were dry enough by then to use, and with care the milk room too. The whole cow barn looked twice the size, with the low-lying evening sun lighting it up and the clean smell of the whitewash filling the air.

Tirza and Nathan stayed to supper and then walked slowly back to Flamboro, Tirza wheeling her bicycle. They had lost a day's fishing, but families need to help each other out at busy times. With Nathan still part-owner of the family farm, they would both lend a hand with haymaking and harvest.

'Dad?' said Tirza. 'Do you reckon Martha is... well... kind of crazy, since Will got killed?'

Nathan sighed.

'She's not really crazy, child. Just crazy with grief. She'll get over it, some day. But we have to be patient meantime. That hiding with Billy under the table – that was just a kind of instinct, like a cat hiding her kittens or a ruffled grouse fluttering around, trying to draw you away from its nest. It's nothing to do with reason.'

'You reckon she'll get better, then?'

'I reckon so. Ayuh.'

<hr>

The herring had come. In one of their mysterious and unpredictable migrations, they were swarming about ten miles out to sea off Flamboro, where they were spotted late one evening. The fishermen needed to move fast, for the fish would disappear as suddenly as they had come – north, perhaps, to the Grand Banks or south towards Rhode Island and Cape Cod.

Mostly, these days, Nathan confined himself to lobster fishing. As a young man he had worked as a trawlerman, first as crew on a boat belonging to another fisherman – George Pelham, the father of Walter. His own father was still alive then and the farm was not large enough to provide a living for two grown sons, once the elder one married. Like many younger sons in the family before him, Nathan had chosen the sea and left Tobias to work the farm. He was a single man then, with no dependants to be left abandoned if he should be lost overboard.

His father had died when Nathan was courting Louisa

O'Neill and the two brothers inherited the farm jointly. Tobias suggested they should sell off a parcel of land halfway across the county which had come into the family with some nineteenth-century marriage. The fields were too far away to use for anything but hay. It was impossible to keep taking horses and machinery over there for other crops. Even for hay it was not worth the time involved. With his half of the money from the sale of the land Nathan was able to pay most of the cost of the *Louisa Mary*, the rest to be paid off to the bank over five years. Together with their lawyer, the brothers devised a fair scheme of dividing any profits from the farm, the majority going to Tobias.

For a year after buying the *Louisa Mary*, Nathan went out inshore fishing with the rest of the trawler fleet from Flamboro, but the boat was not large enough to go further afield. When he married, he applied for his lobster licence. He had known too many trawlermen's widows left to struggle on their own, though in the rough Maine seas a lobsterman's life was hardly safer. The lobsters provided an adequate living most years, augmented by some fishing. In the lean lobster years he fished more often. Tirza's birth and Louisa's death persuaded him that this pattern of work had been the right choice. Some of the men who ran greater risks netted far greater catches and could afford bigger boats. Walter Pelham, who had taken over George's old boat on which Nathan had once crewed, had bought himself a fancy new boat out of Kennebunkport two years ago. Most of the lobsterboats were under thirty feet, the trawlers a little longer, but Walter's *Reliant* was forty-three feet at the waterline. By rights it needed at least three men to handle her and her gear – skipper and two sternmen – but whenever Walter could keep Wayne away from school he dispensed with one of his crew and used Wayne instead. His irregular education had held Wayne back to the same class at school as Simon and Tirza. He was already fourteen and big for his age, but he had not grown into his full strength yet.

When word went round that the herring had been spotted, Nathan decided that he would go after them with the other fishermen. *Louisa Mary*'s net was not very large, but it was as much as he could handle with Tirza's assistance. If the run was as good as reported, it would be worth missing a day or two at the pots in exchange for a sizeable herring catch.

The evening was grey and overcast when they loaded the fish kegs into the *Louisa Mary*. Tirza paused in rolling them down to Nathan, squinting at the sky and sniffing.

'Rain before morning, I reckon. And an easterly.'

'Ayuh. It'll be good for the fishing.'

Bright sun would give away the position of the boat to the fish and could send them darting away like a vast grey underwater cloud before the net could even be laid out. And every fisherman in the southern half of Maine, where the coast faced due east towards the ocean, feared a strong westerly wind, an offshore rote, which could sweep you helplessly out to sea. But it was the north-easterlies that were the worst of all, bringing the severe storms down from Canada and the Arctic.

The weather turned out as they expected. At three thirty the next morning as they climbed aboard the *Louisa Mary*, a fine drizzle was falling from a starless sky. It was not yet dawn and there were lights on in some of the sheds along the wharf, where other fishermen were collecting gear. Tirza stored the basket of food and two thermoses – one of hot coffee and one of cold milk – in the cramped wheelhouse and came out again on deck. She bundled her yellow oilskins into a locker on the port side and turned up the collar of her windcheater. It was not wet enough yet for oilskins, which were heavy and awkward to wear, but the fine cold rain made the day feel like fall after the long stretch of late spring sunshine.

Wayne hailed her from his father's *Reliant*, which was moored alongside.

'Goin' to be a swell day's fishin', my dad says. Shame you ain't got more capacity on that little boat o' yourn!'

Tirza stuck out her tongue at him. This had been a running joke ever since Walter had bought *Reliant*.

'Oh, we're just taking a day off real work,' she said. 'Thought we'd have us a lazy day pulling in fish with a net like you folks, 'stead of our usual high class work.'

'Give over, the both of you,' said Walter. 'Cast off forrard, boy.'

Once *Reliant* was under way, Nathan started the *Louisa Mary*'s diesel engine and they puttered slowly out of the harbour between the winking red lights on the two walls that embraced it like arms. Despite the heavy sky there was only a low swell running before the light onshore breeze. Nathan opened up the throttle and the *Louisa Mary* surged sweetly forward. *Reliant*, bigger and faster, was already disappearing into the darkness ahead, but the *Louisa Mary* was a sturdy little boat, what Nathan called a 'true' boat. This was partly due to the way she sat in the water, and partly to the way she handled, but above all it came from the way she seemed at home in large seas or small, so that those who went to sea in her always felt safe.

Nathan hummed quietly to himself as they headed out to the bearing where the herring had been sighted last night. He would never whistle on a boat, but without thinking he always began this soft contented humming when he had the wheel between his hands and the boat fairly under way. Tirza smiled to herself and poured them each a mug of the heavily sweetened coffee and stirred milk into it.

The grey sky was beginning to lighten ahead of them with the rising sun as they neared the fishing ground and chose a position clear of the other boats. As Nathan throttled back Tirza pulled out her oilskins and struggled into them. The rain was falling more heavily now. The oilskins would protect her from it and, more crucially, from the wet and muck of lowering and raising the net and handling the fish. She had never possessed oilskins of her own. These were an old cut-down set of Nathan's which Abigail had adapted for her. Although they had been shortened to the right length, Abigail had made no attempt to narrow them. The broad back which had fitted Nathan comfortably stood out around Tirza like a yellow tent. They were too stiff to mould themselves to her narrower shoulders and back, and sometimes when she turned she revolved inside them, leaving the oilskins facing east when she was facing north. She looked forward to the day when she would stop growing and could have a set of her own in the right size.

They laid the net out astern and Nathan began to trawl slowly while Tirza kept a look-out for any dangers to the net, unforeseen snags or wreckage. The sea was so murky today there was little chance of spotting anything in time. Below her in the choppy waters she could see the turn and flash of the herring, and if she laid her hand on the ropes holding the head of the net, they thrummed with more than the movement of the boat and the waves.

A hundred yards further out to sea, a wave more solid than the rest rolled over, and a great curved body, gleaming blue-silver like pewter, showed against the deep blue-grey of the ocean.

'Look, Dad!' she cried. 'A whale! First one I've seen this year.'

As they watched, the whale humped into sight, then breached, sending a fountain of spray into the air where it caught a chancy beam of light and glittered briefly. With a slap of his tail and a final heave of his great back, the whale was gone. Nothing was left but a drift of strong fishy breath floating past in the wind. The sight of a whale always filled Tirza with passion. Leviathan, emperor of the seven seas, near enough almost to touch, breathing the air she breathed, anointed with the same ocean spray, then sounding, diving, booming his complex songs down the long channels of the deep.

When Nathan judged they had run long enough, he nodded, cut the throttle, and Tirza engaged the winch that would lift the net inboard. Nathan came astern to help her and as the net swung in over the deck a low shaft of sunlight broke through the cloud and lit up the liquid silver of the herrings, wriggling and flapping in a great mass which bulged the net outwards. Tirza released the foot of the net and the fish showered down around them, leaving them more than calf-deep in the glittering, sea-smelling haul. Nathan laid out the net again as Tirza began to sort and gut. Young fish went overboard, downwind to stop them falling back into the net again. The remaining fish were judged by eye according to size. Out of an empty sky the gulls were suddenly upon them, shrieking and fighting over the guts as Tirza flipped them overboard. Fish scales were everywhere – in her hair, down her neck, flecking her forearms below the rolled-up oilskin sleeves, even clinging to her eyelashes. Nathan joined her until the job was half done, then he went back to the wheel-house and eased the *Louisa Mary* forward again for the next drag, while Tirza finished gutting the fish and tossing them into the kegs.

At around twelve o'clock, Tirza brought out their thick sand-wiches and a piece of custard pie and an apple each. They sat on the lockers, facing each other across the fish kegs.

'This last load will do us, I think,' said Nathan. 'Might even get back in time to haul the pots tonight.' He bit into his apple, then paused, staring over his shoulder.

'Hey, there, look at that! Seems like Walter's caught more'n he bargained for!'

Tirza twisted round and looked where he pointed. The fish-ing had brought them quite close to the *Reliant*. Walter, Wayne and Eli, the other crewman, seemed to be struggling unusually hard to raise their net. Then Walter hung out over the stern while Eli held on to him by the legs. He seemed to be hitting something with the metal-tipped gaff.

'What's he doing?' Tirza asked.

Nathan laughed. 'He's caught himself a dogfish. A good old Maine shark. Oh, Lordee! It's torn some great hole in his net trying to get at the herring. Oh, by dear, I shouldn't laugh. That net's worth a load of money. Poor Walter, that's his fishing done for today.'

They watched the torn net, spilling its fish, being hauled in. Walter looked across the waves at them and made a comic despairing gesture, shrugging his shoulders. Nathan got up, brushing crumbs from his mouth and went to start the engine again, but as he did so a great booming crash rolled through the air, like muffled thunder, and the whole ocean trembled. The *Louisa Mary* bucked like a frightened horse, and Tirza stumbled and fell against the stern, bruising her knees. She saw Walter and the others looking wildly around, and boats further away from them tossing unnaturally on the sea. Half a mile beyond them a grey naval vessel was slipping northwards, almost invisible against the sea. Behind it, a cauliflower mound of white water exploded upwards.

Tirza clutched at the gunwale to steady herself.

'What was that?'

It was terrifying, this noise which seemed to be thrown up by the sea itself.

Nathan, after that first startled moment, collected himself. He left the engine and came back to her. Without a word he began to winch in the net, though it would be barely a quarter full.

'What was it?' Tirza could hear a note of panic in her voice.

'Depth charges,' said Nathan shortly. He released the pathetic catch on to the deck and began gutting.

'Saw something in the newspaper. The navy is starting to drop depth charges as they patrol the coast. To hit the German submarines, if any try to sneak in to the shore. But of course it isn't only submarines that get hit.'

He smiled grimly and wiped his knife on the seat of his pants.

'I guess that's the end of our prime herring run.'

Chapter 9

Intermezzo
Scotland: Summer 1980

THE EXHIBITION OF Tirza's photographs at the gallery in Edinburgh proved such a success that it was extended by a fortnight. Then a gallery owner from Boston, visiting London and reading a review in the arts section of one of the Sunday newspapers, contacted Colin Tennant to arrange a loan of the entire exhibition to her own gallery for two months during the autumn. Max telephoned Tirza with the news.

'And Colin has had to order a reprint of your Scottish book. I eat humble pie. Your stags and heathery crags have gone down a treat with the punters.'

Tirza snorted.

'Jessica has forwarded another batch of fan mail to you today,' he said. 'And I've had some commission enquiries. I'll ring you again when I have more details.'

'OK.'

'Oh, and this woman from Boston, Pam O'Rourke, she wants to know whether you would be willing to fly over and open the American exhibition? Same sort of thing as you did in Edinburgh, but I've warned her that you aren't too keen on television interviews.'

'Max, I'm not sure...'

'No need to decide yet. Think about it. It's a long time since you were in the States, isn't it?'

'Yes,' she said shortly. 'A long time. I've no wish to go back.'

'Think about it.'

<><><>

Two days later the pile of letters forwarded by Max's secretary was brought over from the mainland by Angus Maclean. He had shed his jacket and rolled up his sleeves in the warm June sunlight and came cheerfully up from Tirza's small pier talking as he came.

'Well, it's a braw morning, is it not? The weather forecast says we will be having this fine weather for a week or more. It is the high pressure — stationary, they said, over the west coast of Scotland.'

Tirza smiled up at him. She was seated on a large boulder beside her front door, drinking coffee and eating toast spread with the local honey which was liberally laced with whisky. The cat was spread out in a patch of sun on the thin turf at her feet. When she had first bought the island, Tirza had thought she would remove this boulder, which occupied a prominent position just to the side of her front door. She had discovered fresh marks of a crowbar around its base where someone else had tried before her, probably her German predecessor or his workmen. She soon discovered why they had abandoned the task. The boulder appeared to be welded to the bedrock of the island itself. Having decided she would have to live with it, she discovered that it made an excellent seat for viewing the bay and the ocean beyond. She wondered how many generations of owners, over how many centuries, had sat where she now sat, watching this view which had remained unchanged for millennia, yet which changed with every racing cloud and turn of the running tide.

'Yes,' she said to Angus, 'I heard the forecast at six. But the sun is over-bright for the fishermen.'

Angus passed her the packet of letters and regarded her quizzically.

'You are knowing about the fish, then.'

'My father was a fisherman.'

When Angus was gone and she had finished her breakfast, she skimmed quickly through the letters, most of which she could answer with a standard reply she had evolved since the exhibition had prompted this flurry of correspondence. One letter, however, brought her up sharp.

Dear Miss Libby,

I am taking the liberty of writing to you after first seeing your interview with Mathilda Goldberg on television and subsequently visiting the amazing retrospective exhibition of your photographs in Edinburgh. For many years I have admired your work, without realising who the photographer was. To see so much, of such quality, gathered together in one place was truly rewarding.

It is, however, about a different matter that I am writing to you now. In your television interview you mentioned something from your past which caught my attention. Later, certain pictures in the exhibition confirmed my apparently wild conjecture.

It is, I know, a great deal to ask, but I wonder whether I might pay you a brief visit? I believe there may be a connection between our families, but I would prefer to speak to you about it face to face. It all happened a long time ago, and I may be mistaken, but if I am right I think you might wish to hear what I have to say.

Please forgive me if this sounds extremely lugubrious and mysterious. It isn't meant to. If you are not willing for me to visit your home, perhaps you could suggest a place where we might meet?

Yours sincerely,
Alexander Wrycroft

Tirza read the letter three times. Alexander Wrycroft did not sound as though he was some crazy eccentric, but he was extraordinarily evasive. 'A connection between our families.' What could he possibly mean? 'You might wish to hear what I have to say.' It could be some kind of threat. She had never known anyone called Wrycroft, and her family certainly had no connection with...she peered at the address... something Gaelic and totally unpronounceable in the Highlands. Not very far away from Caillard, as the golden eagle might fly it, over the tops of the mountains. But a long way by car, detouring around the deep sea lochs which cut into this coast like the fingers of two hands plunged into a lump of dough.

That evening, Tirza sat down conscientiously to reply to the letters she had received in the morning's post. All but the one from Mr Wrycroft could be answered swiftly. She folded them, inserted them into envelopes, addressed and stamped them. They made a good, satisfying pile on the corner of the table. She read Wrycroft's letter again, momentarily wondering whether there might be some link with her great-grandfather, Bruce Macpherson, who had emigrated from the Highlands a century and a half before. But she had made no reference in the television interview to this thread in her ancestry. Dismissing the idea, she pulled the pad toward her, picked up her pen, and wrote:

Dear Mr Wrycroft,
  Thank you for your interesting letter. I am so glad you enjoyed the exhibition. I am afraid you must be mistaken about a connection between our families, recent or in the past. I have never known anyone of the name of Wrycroft. Regrettably, it will not be possible to arrange a meeting.
  Yours truly,
  T. Libby

In the morning, Tirza gave all the letters to Angus and forgot about them. She had embarked on a new project – photographing buildings of the west coast – and was away from home a good deal. The deserted cottages along the shore and tucked away into corners of the glens fascinated her. Most of their thick stone walls were still standing to their full height, though many had been abandoned long ago during the Highland Clearances. The roofs, which had been covered with turf or thatched with straw or reeds, had perished long since.

It was difficult to distinguish these long-deserted cottages from those which had been given up as recently as the thirties, although occasionally she was lucky enough to find something lying around which revealed the date of the last occupancy. Sometimes she discovered, amongst the nettles, a battered saucepan in the favourite cream enamel trimmed with green which every housewife had owned in the thirties and forties. Once she found a stained and faded calendar folded open at November 1923. But a well grown Scots pine standing in the front room – the but – was evidence of a longer abandonment.

Hunting down these lost homes, which revealed a much richer, busier life in this now solitary land, reminded her again that some of her own ancestors had been driven from these very hills. Part of her fondness for her island was its isolation from any connection with her past, and the thought of her own deep blood binding her to this place was disturbing. She tried to push it from her mind.

She was not photographing just the empty cottages. There were several of the ancient Z-plan fortified tower houses nearby, and also a few of the grand mock-mediaeval castles in which the rich had played at baronial life during Victorian summers. Small towns and villages had their plain, rather dour buildings, occasionally breaking out into the absent-minded ornamentation of crow-stepped gables. The local villages lacked the charm of villages she had seen in England, which were coherent in shape, clustered round a central green and with big, spreading trees to set off the architecture and provide shelter from sun and rain. The Scottish villages seemed to have grown up heedlessly, their houses deliberately ignoring each other or any sense of cohesion. Sometimes they were simply strung along a road, with an ugly corrugated shed somewhere in the middle to serve as a petrol station. Sometimes the village stood at a cross-roads, but this provided no centre, no significance to the houses, which simply stood there, as if not sure why they had been built in the first place but anxious to be off as soon as possible. The small towns, however, were often arranged around a surprisingly wide main street, with a mercat cross and an ancient building which she discovered was called a tollbooth, where town affairs were decided. They hinted of a community life now lost.

Tirza found these places a little depressing – the villages ungainly and the towns declined – but in her growing collection of architectural studies they made an intriguing contrast to the clusters of empty cottages which were often located in places of great natural beauty. Her own small fishing village, Caillard – given structure and cohesion by the curve of the shore and the double arms of the harbour – was transformed into something almost pretty by comparison.

A couple of weeks later she returned from one of her trips spent photographing suitable subjects for her new collection. She had passed five busy days climbing through waist-high bracken and stumbling over the ridges of old plough-land hidden under the rough scrub and grass now cropped by sheep. She was covered with bites from midges, which had begun their annual plague of the west coast, and as she parked her car in the space she used in the car park behind the Prince Returning, she decided to treat herself to a drink and a bar supper before crossing to the island.

The usual crowd was occupying the bar when she pushed her way through the door. Fishermen, shopkeepers, one or two crofters – some with their wives or girlfriends, some without. Tirza hitched a stool up to the bar with her foot and sat down. Donnie McIver, landlord and barman, came over, polishing a glass.

'And what can I get you, Tirza?' The McIvers were the only village people who would address her by her first name. She had, after all, lived here a mere two years.

'Half a pint of your best bitter, Donnie. No, make that a pint. I've a thirst like a navvy, and I need something to deaden the pain of the local insect life.'

Donnie drew her a pint and set it down on a mat proclaiming the virtues of some bottled beer no one ever bought.

'That'll set you up. Never mind the wee midges. You'll no' feel them at all when you've lived here ten years.'

'Mingies, we used to call them, where I grew up. And, Lord, the horse-flies! They used to come in with a particular tide and stay for two weeks, then they disappeared again. The bites would come up in a red lump the width of your thumbnail and nearly as high too. Most painful bites I've ever had, even including the creepy-crawlies the Far East could throw at you.'

She took a deep swallow of her beer.

'Ah, that would be what we call the clegs,' said Donnie. 'Vicious things.'

'I've met the local breed. Ours were worse. What's on the menu tonight?'

Donnie angled the slate towards her, reflecting that in all the time he had known Tirza Libby, she had never before made a reference to where she had grown up. Since the fuss of the Edinburgh exhibition the village had found out more about her by reading the newspapers than it had ever learned from her directly.

'The scampi isn't much good,' he said. 'It's something Moira bought in from the sales rep and we won't be getting it again.'

'Honestly, Donnie, with all the shellfish out there in the bay, I don't know why you don't catch your own! Bought in from the rep! Well, what do you recommend, then?'

'The chicken casserole is no' bad. Local chickens from Munro's flock, and Moira wasna mean with the wine and herbs. I had it for my own tea. It was just fine.'

'OK, I'll have the chicken casserole, then, with French fries. And some of Moira's trifle afterwards. I deserve it, I've had a tiring few days.'

Donnie leaned through the hatch behind the bar and called, 'One chicken and chips for Tirza, Moira. One trifle to follow.'

He was occupied for a time with his other customers, but returned to chat with Tirza as she ate her meal. The sink was at this end of the bar and he washed up as he talked.

'There's word going round that they are going to make up the road to the north of the village,' he commented.

'But it doesn't lead anywhere.'

'Some people are saying that the laird has sold land along there for holiday cottages.'

'Oh, no!' Tirza looked dismayed. 'Sorry. I suppose it will help your custom, but I'd hate to see the village spoiled.'

Donnie dried the glasses slowly and hooked them into the rack above his head. 'We canna fight progress, but I dinna want the place spoiled any more than you do. It's likely just a rumour.'

Tirza glanced round the room. A man had come in while she was eating, a stranger. He was sitting in a low chair in a shadowed corner near the empty fireplace, apparently watching a darts match, but she was sure he had been looking at her before she turned round. She swung her stool back to the bar.

'Who's that man over by the fireplace?' She did not have to explain who she meant. Visitors were rare here.

'He's come for the salmon fishing. Staying with us. A week's fishing licence, he's bought.'

'Donnie, take a look. Is he watching me?'

Donnie let his eyes roam vaguely round the room, then looked at her.

'Aye, he might be.'

'Creepy.'

'Not at all,' he said gallantly, whipping away her plate and replacing it with a heaped bowl of trifle. 'Why shouldna a man admire a fine-looking woman?'

'Shut up, you daft bugger,' said Tirza, unaccountably blushing as she dug her spoon into the trifle.

<hr />

Tirza forgot the stranger when she took the boat over to the island and greeted Grace, who seemed particularly pleased to see her. The cat even followed her into the bedroom and curled up on the foot of the bed for the night.

'I am honoured,' said Tirza, rubbing behind Grace's ears before switching out her bedside lamp. 'Clearly I should go away more often.'

She recalled the stranger when she returned to the village to shop the next morning. There was an unfamiliar Range Rover parked behind the inn next to her own car when she went to collect a bag she had left there the night before. The Range Rover was fairly new and well cared for, except where heavy mud had encrusted the underside of the wheel-arches. A working vehicle, but one whose owner did not neglect it. The owner himself was nowhere to be seen while she walked about the village buying milk and groceries, and a sheet of stamps from the post office, but soon after she had perched on a bar stool he came in behind her and sat down in the same chair by the fireplace.

'Morning, pet,' said Moira, wiping down the counter in front of her. Moira came from a long way south of here, somewhere in the north of England, Tirza guessed, and her cheerful terms of endearment sounded strange in this reserved community.

'What can I get you?'

'I'll have your salmon salad, please, Moira.'

'We're very honoured,' said Moira, bringing a salad across from the back counter and passing Tirza cutlery wrapped in a green paper napkin. 'Supper last night and lunch today. Last of the big spenders, are you?'

Tirza grinned at her as she forked up the fresh-caught salmon, covered with a light, mustardy mayonnaise.

'Just lazy. And your cooking is so good. It exercises my brain to open a can of baked beans.'

Moira laughed.

'Well, we all have our different talents. Those photographs of yours... well! I saw that feature in the Sunday supplement. I can hardly credit that you're living here, quiet as anything, after you've been in Vietnam and Brazil and India and all those places.'

'Maybe that's why I like it here. We can't spend all of our lives living on the edge of danger. Besides, I was younger then.'

'Get along with you! Those pictures of India were only taken a couple of years ago.'

'Yes, I know. But I've been quite ill since then, and that makes you feel your age.'

'Well, love, I don't suppose it's my place to say it, but I said to Donnie just the other day, I said, Our climate must suit Tirza Libby. She's looking ten years younger than she did when she first stayed here. Remember how I told you about the island that evening? I never thought you'd go and *buy* it! You never can tell where an idle word will lead, can you?'

'No, indeed,' Tirza agreed. 'You never can.'

—◦◦◦◦—

After lunch she went for a walk north along the seafront to the point where the tarmac road dwindled away into a dusty track which led on round the coast to a scattered group of crofts. These had been saved from near desolation by a few determined men and women who had brought the land back into heart. Like most Highland crofts they were dotted about the hillside apparently at random, each surrounded by its small acreage. Some were farmed for self-sufficiency with little in the way of cash crops except a few eggs and chickens. These tended to be occupied by couples where either the husband or the wife had a paid job. In one the husband was the local telephone repair-man and the wife the crofter. In another the husband farmed while the wife worked as a freelance copy-editor.

Three or four of the crofts were fully economic farms. They grew basic food for the family, but more effort went into some specialist cash crop. The Maclarens had a herd of pedigree Nubian goats. Their milk and ice-cream went every other day by refrigerated lorry to Inverness, and once a fortnight Celia Maclaren loaded up her small dented van with cheeses and drove them down to a delicatessen in Glasgow. Another crofter was experimenting with angora rabbits; his wife spun and dyed the yarn, shipping it off to an expensive wool shop in Oxford. On a third croft, almost all the cultivable land was laid out to commercial herbs. The herbs seemed to like the rather poor soil of the hillside.

The crofts occupied a shallow slope which rose gradually to a shoulder of grassy hillside. Beyond this first height the ground seemed to gather together and then heaved itself upwards into the towering summits which formed the western edge of the Highlands. Below the crofts a smooth slope fell away to the sea. Tirza sat down on a patch of warm grass here and looked out over the bay where her island lay like pointed hat with a wide flat brim. Beyond it the ocean stretched to the horizon, interrupted by a long arm of one of the outer isles.

This was where Donnie said holiday cottages might be built. Tirza could see the commercial potential and the temptations it offered. She had never met the local laird, but he was well spoken of. Surely he would not be so unfeeling as to sacrifice all this for money?

'Excuse me.'

A voice almost at her side made her jump. The man had approached soundlessly over the mossy turf, the wind carrying away any noise made by his supple, worn boots on the grass.

'I'm sorry, I've startled you.'

'No, no. Not at all.'

Tirza shaded her eyes with her hand and looked up at him. Dazzled with the reflections of the summer sun on the waves, she saw him first through a mist of jumping lights. He towered above her against the pale blue sky, but she could see now that he was smiling.

'Do you mind if I join you?'

Tirza made a gesture towards the grass.

'Help yourself. It's beautiful here, isn't it?'

For a fleeting moment she wondered whether he was some sort of surveyor, sent to spy out the land for development, incognito. It was the unknown fisherman from the hotel, the owner of the Range Rover with the dried red clay stuck to the wheel-arches. Someone used to driving over rough country, and country with a different soil from here.

He lowered himself to the ground, carefully, as though his back hurt him. When he came down from his height to the level of her eyes, his face – hidden previously in the dark corner of the inn – came into focus. Something about it hit her in the stomach with a sharp physical reflex.

He clasped his hands around his knees and stared out over the bay.

'It's a beautiful island, Miss Libby. I can see why you don't want anyone to trouble you here. But I think we need to talk.'

Tirza stiffened.

'Did you write to me? Is your name Alexander Wrycroft?'

He nodded, and held out his hand politely. Automatically, she shook it.

'I'm sorry,' he said. 'You must find my intrusion very distasteful. But I think, in the end, you will want to hear what I have to say.'

'How did you find me?'

'It wasn't difficult. Although there was no address on your letter, the postmark was perfectly clear. As you know, I don't live so very far away. I farm about twenty miles from Inverness.'

That seemed credible. The car, the boots, the tweed jacket – worn and patched with leather at the elbows, but originally of excellent quality. He was about her own age, tall and sturdy but not heavily built, with an air of tranquillity about him that was reassuring. Tirza realised suddenly that she would like to photograph him, but that face...

'I think it is somewhat inconsiderate,' she replied, 'not to say impertinent, after my letter to you.'

'Forgive me.' He laid his hand on her arm. 'Just listen for a moment.'

Then, in spite of what he said, he was silent for minutes, looking out at the ocean.

'On the television, when you were being interviewed by that woman, you suddenly lost your composure. She asked you about your first camera. A perfectly innocent question, I would have thought. But you were completely disconcerted. Then you said that it was a Box Brownie, given to you by a British airman.'

Tirza twisted her fingers in the turf, pulling up a handful of tiny wildflowers, no more than an inch high.

'Yes.'

'That roused my interest. That, and your name. I'm ashamed to say I hadn't heard your name before, though when I saw your pictures, of course I recognised them. Not much of a reader of the newspapers, I'm afraid. Apart from the farming prices.'

He paused again.

'Anyway, when I could manage to take the time from the spring ploughing, I went down to Edinburgh to see your exhibition.' The steady, disciplined tone of his voice suddenly changed and he beamed at her, that oddly familiar smile, so that she felt sick. 'Wonderful! I've never seen anything like it. Some day, I'd like to talk it all through with you.'

His voice became sombre again.

'I went round everything twice. I suppose I must have spent about three hours in there and I came out almost light-headed with fatigue and hunger. But it was only on my way out that I noticed the little group of photographs half-hidden by the open door in the first room. They're labelled "Juvenilia". Do you know the ones I mean?'

Tirza nodded dumbly, not looking at him.

'When I saw those, I knew my instincts had been right. There he was, large as life. One of the photographs was very clear. He was standing in a sailing boat, with one arm round the mast. I couldn't quite read the name of the boat. There was some sort of tackle hanging over it.'

Tirza's mouth tasted of salt.

'*Stormy Petrel*,' she said.

Chapter 10

Maine: Summer 1942

IN JUNE THERE came a period of hot, lazy days and quiet nights. Work at the fishing and on the farms did not stop, but the long hours of daylight, the sun and the sense of summer stretching ahead slowed the pace. Life moved to a different rhythm. Tobias was haying now, taking his time over it and fitting it around the other chores, like hoeing the vegetable fields and checking on the heifers. This year's calves had now been moved to a pasture on the far side of the county road and needed salt taken over regularly in the hot weather.

Most sunny days there was haying to be done. As well as the main farm, which lay mostly between the county road and the sea, the Libbys owned a sizeable portion of land on the other side of the road, adjacent to Swansons' farm. Scattered here and there around Flamboro there were other parcels of land, some of which had been put down to crops when old Mr Libby had been in charge. When his sons were well grown and he also employed two hired men, it had been possible to tend this land. Now the only practical crop for much of it was hay. Even in a wet summer, Tobias could harvest enough for all his winter needs. In a good year he had spare to sell on.

On the long sun-laden days he and Sam, sometimes with Simon helping, would cut the hay in the morning. They left it lying while the midday heat warmed it and other chores were tended to. Then in the afternoon they would turn it. After a further couple of days, turning and drying, they would rake and then load it on to the horse-drawn hayrack and bring it back to the farm.

During haymaking Tirza had started going up to the farm most days at dinnertime and helping in the afternoon. Tobias used the tractor to tow the mowing machine, then saved fuel during the rest of the haying by using one of the horses hitched to the hay turner and hay rake. He would not allow Tirza to handle the tractor, though Simon now drove it for simple jobs. On level fields Tobias let Simon mow while he and Sam followed behind scything the field edges by hand. Despite her best efforts, Tirza was not yet tall enough to handle one of the big scythes, though she could use a small sickle as well as Simon.

In the afternoons, without the novelty of driving the tractor, Simon lost interest and slipped away to Flamboro. He had made friends with several of the regular crews manning the gun up by the burying-ground – they gave him chewing gum and Hershey bars and taught him to chain-smoke Camels. One of them, a young fellow not much older than he, also introduced him to the trick of chewing a strong peppermint afterwards to hide the smell of tobacco on his breath from his family.

Tirza, walking or cycling along the coastal path to help on the farm in the afternoons, often met Simon going the other way. They rarely stopped to talk, but she had learned that Martha was getting better, had been into Portland with her mother to buy shoes and was now coming out to sit on the porch instead of hiding in her room. But still, whenever one of the patrol planes came over, she lost all self-control. She would grab Billy if he was anywhere near and dive for cover – under tables, into the cellar, once – at Flett's Stores – behind the counter amongst the sacks of feed and flour.

From overhearing talk in the village, Tirza knew that Martha's behaviour had provoked comment. Sympathy for her was increasingly tinged with condemnation. The story of Martha emerging from behind Flett's counter, with grass seed in her hair and best white flour smudging the front of her red cotton dress, had gained some additional colour in the retelling. Tirza knew, because she had been in the store when it had happened.

She was sitting cross-legged on the floor, leaning against the pot-bellied stove – unlit during the summer months – reading a *Dick Tracy* comic borrowed from Johnny Flett and sucking an acid ball. Martha, Harriet and Billy came in to deliver the eggs and buy some dry goods, and right in the middle of the transaction had come the now familiar sound of a four-engine plane flying overhead. Martha had given that shriek — not so loud now, but still disconcerting — and dragged a furiously struggling Billy behind the counter. Mary, startled and jostled as they passed, had dropped one of the eggs she was counting. It spread across the counter and began to drip over the edge in a long slimy trail. Watching over the top of her comic, Tirza bit her lip, caught between shame and laughter. When Martha emerged after the sound of the plane died away she looked a sight, but she was not — as later versions suggested — covered with the entire ingredients for a cake.

'Put her in the oven and bake her right there!' Walter Pelham was heard to crow to some of his cronies sitting outside the Schooner Bar in the long summer evening.

———◆———

One day on her way to the farm, Tirza noticed a faint trail leading through the ragged uncut grass at the edge of the Tremaynes' neglected garden, just where it ran up to the stone wall marking the start of the Libby farm. She could not be sure what animal had made it, but — seeing Simon approach — she walked past without investigating further. Whatever it was, Simon would probably shoot it, and she wanted to have a look for herself first.

When she reached the farmyard, Harriet was just blowing the long note on the dinner horn which had been used by the Libby family for four generations to summon the men in from the fields for their meals. Tirza joined the family for crab cakes, pickles and fresh bread. Harriet's home-baked bread scented the kitchen, and when you broke open a roll, hot from the oven, the yeasty steam filled your nostrils. Abigail said she was getting too old to bake bread, so at home Tirza and Nathan had to eat white pulpy store-bought loaves, which chewed in the mouth like a wash-cloth — fluffy and soft against the tongue at first, then collapsing to a sour-tasting pap.

'Saw Simon going into Flamboro,' said Tirza, with her mouth full of the warm, grainy brown bread which had the finest taste on earth. 'Doesn't he want his dinner?'

'He took some sandwiches,' said Harriet. 'He and Wayne are up to something again.'

Tobias grunted.

'I could use his help this afternoon.'

'I'm here to help,' said Tirza. 'Can I drive the rake again?'

'Ayuh. I'll turn in behind with the bull rake. Sam's needed to hoe the turnips. That rain last week and all this sun, that's bringing up a pesky lot of weeds in the field past the cow pasture.'

Tirza smiled to herself. Anybody but a Maine farmer would be glad of the fine summer weather, with rain only at night for the last three weeks. But if a farmer can't complain about the weather, he can't feel that he is confronting the real challenge of his life.

'Is it the field over to Carey's Corner today?' she asked.

'That's it. If you're done eating, let's get over there. We cut four days ago and we've turned three times, so it's ready for raking. And with this heat it'll be dry enough to pitch and load.'

While Tobias hitched Dancer up, Tirza fetched the bull rake – five feet wide and toothed with wooden prongs as thick as her uncle's thumb. She wedged this on top of the framework of the big hay rake, so it would not fall off as they drove along the road, then climbed up by means of the long horizontal bar to which the sharp, curved metal prongs were attached. These were raised now, and there was just enough room to squeeze in front of them, behind her uncle's back where he sat on the seat. She braced her legs apart, gripping the metal bar with her bare toes, and wrapped her arms around his solid waist. Her nose was pressed against the back of his plaid cotton shirt, which smelled of Swan soap and hay and sweat.

'OK?' he asked.

'OK.'

At the field beyond Swansons' Tobias halted Dancer inside the gate, aligning the rake to run parallel with the stone wall edging the longer side, then climbed down and Tirza took his place. The metal seat, curved like a saddle, was warm. He lifted down the bull rake.

'Get going when you're ready.'

Tirza picked up the reins in her left hand. With the right she reached behind her for the lever handle which worked the prongs of the rake, and lowered them. They hit the dry stubble with a faint twang like a distant banjo. Setting Dancer in line with the first swathe of cut hay, she chirruped her forward. The rake caught on the laid hay, jerked slightly, then began to move forward as the horse plodded along the field.

Driving down the long edge of the field, Tirza felt a sudden wave of happiness sweep over her. The springy bouncing of the rake underneath her, the music of a song sparrow from a sumac growing over the stone wall, the screech of the rake as she raised it to drop a perfect load, and then lowered it again – all these things filled her with contentment.

Through the quiet sunny afternoon Tirza drove the rake up and down the field in parallel lines while Tobias worked behind her, drawing the hay into mounds for pitching on. When half the field was finished, he called across to her to give Dancer a rest at the end of the row. Climbing down stiffly from the hard metal seat, she picked up the bucket which had held their food. She trudged off to fill the bucket for Dancer from the creek at the far end of the field, setting her bare feet carefully between the rows of sharp stubble. On the bank of the creek she lay down on her stomach and splashed water over her head and neck to cool down. Her arms were as brown as varnished wood and spangled all over with glinting fragments of chaff. She plunged them up to the armpits in the cool water.

Back at the other end of the field she set down the bucket for Dancer, who sucked up the water gratefully.

'Hey, hey!' said Tirza, 'Not too fast! You'll blow up like a balloon.'

She lifted the bucket away from Dancer and held it behind her back. The horse looked at her reproachfully, her head hanging and water dripping from her muzzle. After she judged the water had settled in the horse's stomach, Tirza put the bucket down again, and squatted in the shade of the stone wall. Tobias was lying flat on his back with his handkerchief spread over his face.

'Muffins in the waxed paper and lemonade in the bottle,' he said in a muffled voice. 'And an apple. You can have a fifteen-minute snooze if you want.'

But Tirza was not sleepy. She ate her muffins and watched a

lizard basking on a flat stone just a foot away from her. It was about four inches long and the colour of a burning coal. She had seen green lizards before and brown ones, but never an orange one like this. Ordinary lizards blended in with their surroundings, but this fellow stood out like a bright light against the brown of the soil and the grey of the stones lying heaped round the edge of the field. The lizard was as motionless as a statue and when it blinked – the lower lid rising up and meeting the upper lid across its eye – Tirza was startled. She reached cautiously for the bottle of lemonade, trying not to frighten it, but suddenly it was gone. One flash of orange in the uncut hay close against the wall, then it disappeared.

When Tobias had rested enough, they began on the second half of the field. His shirt was patched dark with sweat, but – although the top of Tirza's head felt like a skillet when she touched it with the flat of her hand – there was a very slight breeze up high on the hay rake that made the sun bearable.

'Hay's fine and dry,' said Tobias when they had finished raking the whole field. 'I think we'll get it in straight away. I'll go back for the hayrack. You want to come?'

'Ayuh,' said Tirza, gathering up the paper and bottle and stuffing them in the empty bucket. 'Can I drive?'

'OK. Lucky we don't have many summer people along this road.'

Tirza swung up into the seat again and Tobias perched behind her, holding on by the back of the seat. She drove out through the gate and turned left. A few yards along the county road they were overtaken by a jeep full of soldiers which roared past and cut in close under Dancer's nose. The driver tooted his horn cheerfully and the soldiers shouted a greeting. Dancer, usually calm and reliable, shied towards the sandy ditch at the side of the road and the whole rake lurched sideways. Tirza struggled with the reins, calling out soothingly to the horse and holding her steady. One wheel of the rake dragged along the sandy edge of the ditch, but she managed to turn Dancer back on to the road and ease her down to a walk again.

'Good girl,' said Tobias. He had restrained himself from taking the reins out of her hands. 'Forget what I said about the summer people. None of them are as crazy as these GIs.'

An hour later, when they arrived back at the hay field with the hayrack hitched up to Dancer, it was Tirza's turn to do the heavier work. The hayrack was a wide-bodied cart, extended upwards on all sides by posts that leaned outwards like a sagging, gap-toothed fence, so the top was several feet wider and longer than the bed of the cart. Tirza pitched the hay from the mounded stacks up over the rim of the hayrack while Tobias packed and stowed. She could pitch quite well now – plunging her fork into the mound, lifting it with a twist and then giving it the heave that sent the hay flying off the tines. Tobias fielded and placed each forkful exactly where he wanted it, treading it down and packing it so that the whole mass held together, even though it projected far over the sides. They proceeded along the field together, man and girl and horse. Dancer did not need to be driven. She stopped automatically at each pile of hay until Tobias called to her to get up again.

It took them three trips to carry all the hay back to the farm and unload it. By the time they drove the last load home the breeze was almost chilly against their sweat-drenched bodies. Tirza sprawled on her back high on top of the hay as the rack swayed below her like a ship at sea. She ached in every muscle and sharp bits of chaff had worked their way inside her shirt and shorts, but the soft mountain of hay held her surrounded by its scent of captured summer sun. She could look straight up into the pale, washed-out sky and see the moon rising, shimmering and swimming like a pail of milk, while the sun was still in the sky.

⋘⋙

Next morning, after lifting her lines and delivering her crabs to Pierre at the Mansion House, Tirza walked along to the Tremayne place to investigate the animal track she had noticed the day before. It was difficult to find again and she realised that the light must have been falling at just the right angle to reveal it on the previous day. The track led from the dry stony ground of the cliff path over a fallen patch of the Tremaynes' wall and then, clearer in the juicy growth of weeds and unkempt grass, down to the boundary of the Libby farm. Here the stone wall was in good repair, and the track stopped directly in front of it. Some sort of animal which could jump or scramble over it, then.

Tirza found footholds in the rough stones and hauled herself up. Peering over she could see the track begin again on the other side.

There was a small thicket of silver birch here, on this far side of Tobias's cornfield. It had never been cleared for ploughing because the ground was rough and broken, caving away into miniature ravines between the trees and stubbed with large boulders. Tirza let herself down gently, a couple of yards away from the animal track so that her bare feet would not leave a scent and drive the creature away. The ground was slightly damp under the trees – it had rained a little last night and here the ground stayed moist longer, shaded by the branches.

She crouched down with her chin almost in the weeds and looked along the level of the ground. Christina had taught her long ago to read animal tracks. They were faint and blurred, but Tirza thought they were the footprints of a fox. She crept forward, still half crouched, and saw a hole leading into the bank of one of the ravines. Her nose confirmed what she had suspected. Foxes. She was glad she hadn't betrayed them to Simon. They would be dead by now. But she reckoned there was no need to kill the creatures. This far away from the farm buildings they were not an immediate danger to Harriet's chickens. Much easier for them to steal young birds from the gulls' nests along the edge of the cliff and the rabbits which had taken over much of the Tremayne garden.

Tirza settled herself on her stomach. From here she could watch for the foxes and by lifting her head she could see across the field to where the farm track came down to the head of the beach. There had been no sign of a jeep today, so the soldiers would not be around, inspecting the sandbags and creating a disturbance. Her patience was rewarded almost at once. A big fox, probably the dog fox, appeared at the mouth of the hole and looked warily around. Tirza had been careful to approach downwind, and he did not seem to see or scent her. After spying out the land he trotted off along his track towards the Tremayne place as confidently as a dog in its own garden.

Nothing happened for a long time. In the quiet and warmth under the trees, with no sound but the boom of the breakers below the cliff, Tirza nearly fell asleep. Her eyelids were drooping when she caught sight of movement just inside the hole. One by one, five young fox cubs tumbled out into the ravine, followed by their mother. The powerful fox smell was strong now. The mother fox pinned down one cub with her paw and began to wash it, nibbling and pulling at burrs and ticks in its fur. The cub struggled to get away, then flattened itself resignedly on the ground. The other four cubs scavenged about, nipping at insects and jumping out at each other from behind fallen branches. The vixen released the first cub and started to wash another while two of the cubs chased each other around her brush and over her back.

Tirza was so absorbed in watching them that she did not notice the figures over on the farm track until they were almost at the beach. Then her eye was caught by the flash of sunlight on a white shirt. The man she recognised as the captain who had been dating Martha when the news had come about Will's death. She had seen him in Flamboro since – most recently on Saturday night when the soldiers started an impromptu dance with girls from the village. They had installed a wind-up Victrola and a pile of records just inside the door of the Schooner Bar, and danced in the street where there was more room. She had seen the captain jiving with Wayne's sister Clarice, while the Victrola played 'Don't Sit Under the Apple Tree with Anyone Else But Me'.

Walking along hand-in-hand with the captain now was Martha, and Tirza drew in her breath sharply when she saw what her cousin was wearing. When she arrived from Washington, Martha had brought with her a flesh pink two-piece bathing suit. Tirza remembered the first time Martha had worn it to sunbathe on the farm lawn, one of the earliest warm days of spring, back before the telegram came. Harriet had turned pale.

'That thing isn't decent,' she said, shocked. 'You look as though you haven't any clothes on. You practically don't have any clothes on. What will the men think of you?'

'What *will* the men think of me, Mother?' Martha said. She smiled sleekly to herself and ran her hands down her sides.

'They'll think you aren't a decent woman,' said Tobias, backing Harriet up.

Martha tossed her head and laughed scornfully.

'Oh, I don't suppose anyone is going to see me.'

Now here was Martha walking down to the beach, holding the captain's hand and wearing that thing which looked like underwear. She had sandals on her feet and a loose robe thrown round her shoulders, but the wind lifted it and blew it back so that even from where she lay inside the thicket Tirza could see the thin stuff of the bathing suit clinging to Martha's breasts and the high, small round of her stomach. Bare skin showed between the bottom of the bra-shaped halter and the top of the pants, which dipped a little over her stomach. As Harriet had said, the colour of the fabric made it look as though she was stark naked.

Tirza felt a hot flush of shame swamp her, so that her skin burned. The couple disappeared over the ledges on their way to the beach. Suddenly the dog fox appeared again, loping back along his track to the den. He was carrying a dead crow in his mouth. Its head dangled back from his jaws, and one wing swept the dust.

Simon had left the farm early that morning. He was bored with haymaking. At first he had enjoyed driving the tractor, towing the mowing machine through the standing hay and watching it fall to the sharp blades, swish, swish, swish, in a fast rhythm the old horses could never have achieved. He liked the smell of the engine too, and he had discovered that he was quicker than his father to spot the source of the problem when the tractor gave trouble.

After a while, though, the monotony of going up and down the field began to drive him crazy. And sitting with Sam and his father when they took a break from scything the edges of the field, listening to their slow, careful talk, started his arms and legs fidgeting as if he had no control over them. He didn't want to have a break from driving the tractor. He wanted to continue until the job was finished. Why were they always so slow?

He couldn't stay in the house. He always seemed to be in the way of Harriet and Patience's chores. And now that Martha had emerged from her room and sat about in a rocking chair on the porch, she embarrassed him. He could not forget the night the telegram had arrived, or the occasions since, when she had run shrieking from the sound of a plane flying overhead. He tried to keep away from her. Then Billy, who never seemed to be able to play by himself like other children – except when he sneaked off to forbidden places like the pond or the lime pit – would come and plague Simon. He would walk into Simon's room without knocking, or grab his comic book so roughly out of his hand that it tore. The farm, which had once fitted round him like a comfortable old suit of clothes, now chafed and irritated him.

He had done his early chores this morning, feeding and watering the chicks and cleaning the tie-up after his father and Sam had finished the milking. But after breakfast, when he should have been going down to the haying with them, he had sneaked away and come to Flamboro. Now he was lying on his back on the stubby turf of the headland beside the concrete base of the anti-aircraft gun, smoking a Camel. Here he felt relaxed and peaceful, though he found it difficult to smoke in this position. The smoke kept going accidentally up the back of his nose, making him choke, but he had seen the soldiers smoke in this casual, sophisticated way, and he was determined to master it.

The crew had shared their lunch with him, heated up on the kerosene stove. Jim called it 'shit on a shingle'. Creamed chipped beef on toast. He and Danny were sitting on the gun base with their legs dangling and boasting about the girls they had knocked up. Simon wasn't quite sure what this meant, but he wasn't going to show his ignorance by asking. He had a pretty good idea anyway. His attention was caught by something Danny said.

'Trouble is, ain't nowhere private you can take a broad round here. Back home, we had an empty house on our block ever'body used.'

Simon rolled over, coughed on the cigarette smoke and sat up. 'I know an empty house you could use.'

The two young soldiers gaped at him, as if one of the gravestones had spoken.

'The Tremayne place,' said Simon, eager to show he could be useful.

'That old spooky place, along the cliff towards the beach?' asked Jim.

'Yeah. It's been empty for years. The doors are all locked up, but I can show you how to get in.'

They exchanged glances.

'No fooling?' Danny asked cautiously.

'Cross my heart,' said Simon so earnestly that they grinned, and he felt foolish. 'No one goes there. The kids round here all think it's haunted, so they keep away. And the manager gave up looking after it years ago.'

'What about the owners?'

'Oh, they moved away to Boston around when I was born.'

'OK, kid,' said Jim tolerantly. 'When we go off duty you can show us this place of yours. If you're sure no one else knows how to get in.'

'Only my cousin, and she never goes there.'

<hr/>

When Tirza was coming away from the Mansion House later that week, she cut through the garden as she carried her empty baskets back to *Stormy Petrel*. Now that the summer weather was here, most of the guests had gone down to the beach by mid-morning. Some stayed on Todd's Neck, prepared to put up with the narrow cramped beach to save walking any distance. Others – usually the families with children – hung themselves around with picnic baskets and bags and towels and hiked off to Libby's Beach, whose mile-long stretch of wide silver sand tempted them away from the hotel.

Tirza was not supposed to go into the formal garden, but it was a shortcut back to the pier and she rarely saw anyone there in summer except a few old ladies nodding over their books, or a couple of old men playing chequers on one of the curly cast-iron tables. So she was surprised when she rounded the tall hedge enclosing the rose garden and collided with a youngish man. Her baskets hit something hard and the man staggered. A long thin object went flying. Tirza saw it was a crutch and stooped to pick it up. He took it from her, balancing awkwardly with the other one under his armpit.

'Sorry,' she said.

'Thank you,' he said simultaneously, and they both laughed.

'I didn't see you.' She swung her baskets up on to her hip again. 'I'm not really supposed to come this way.'

He sniffed, as though she carried some aroma with her.

'You must be the kid who brings the crabs for the chef.'

'Ayuh.'

'What did you say?'

He stared at her, half smiling. She felt a blush rising up her neck.

'Nothing. Yes.'

'That wasn't what you said.'

'I said, "Ayuh."' She glowered at him. 'Haven't you ever heard that before?'

'Well, no, I haven't. Ayuh.' He tested the word on his tongue. 'It's a Maine word? Meaning "yes"?'

'Yesss,' said Tirza, hissing it out affectedly.

'Where I come from, people say "Aye". Bit the same, isn't it?'

'I thought you were foreign. You talk funny,' said Tirza challengingly.

'Mmm.'

She turned away and headed towards the small side gate of the garden, which opened on to the path to the pier. He eased himself awkwardly round on his crutches and began to limp along beside her. Tirza found herself pulling ahead of him and felt impelled to slow down. She held the wicket gate open while he swung himself through.

'Much obliged.'

They started along the path. It was covered with some kind of fancy gravel which clogged his crutches and slowed him even further.

'What's your name?' he asked, rather breathless.

'Tirza,' she said shortly.

'That's a funny kind of a name.'

'It is not. It's a good Bible name.'

'Well, is it, now? Can't say I've ever come across it.'

They had reached the pier. Tirza stepped on to it, and leaned over to put the baskets in the bottom of *Stormy Petrel*. She untied the painter from the post.

'What's *your* name, then?' she asked, balanced with one bare foot on the pier, the other foot holding the boat steady by the gunwale.

'My name's Sandy.'

'Sandy? *Sandy?*' She laughed. 'That's not a name, that's a beach.'

He grinned at her.

'It's a name where I come from. Short for Alexander.'

'Well,' Tirza conceded.

He watched her hoist the sail and ease *Stormy Petrel* out into the ocean. He raised his hand to her once, and she raised hers in return. As she was about to round the end of Todd's Neck she glanced back. He was still standing there on the end of the pier, balanced on his crutches.

<hr>

Once a year, the Shakers paid a visit to the Mansion House. Their community lay inland, some miles away, and they started before dawn with their old-fashioned horse-drawn buggies and carts, reaching the hotel about midday on a Monday in late June. They stayed until midday on Saturday, packing up and driving back in time for the Sunday services at their community.

During the time they stayed on the coast, they camped in their wagons, rolling themselves up in their blankets and sleeping cheerfully on the hard boards. They cooked over open fires and sat down sedately to eat on the grass with the same solemn prayers as they spoke in their bare scrubbed refectories. Tobias Libby always gave them permission to park their vehicles and graze their horses on a small meadow at the far end of the Libby land, nearest to Todd's Neck. It was separated from the main farm by the marshy ground and pine woods which lay behind the beach; farm machinery could only reach it by driving along the county road to the Todd's Neck turn. The meadow was the only piece of open ground on either side of this by-road until you reached the narrow isthmus of the Neck itself.

Harriet always said the Shakers were good folks, for all their queer ways, and she would send them round milk and eggs every day, and sometimes some fresh baked loaves or a joint of bacon. Ever since Tirza could remember, they had been coming. This summer she wondered briefly whether the war would stop them, but no, Tobias had received the usual formal letter requesting permission to use his field again. It meant moving the bull, but that was the only inconvenience. Sam walked up one morning along the ledges to fetch old Duncan back to the farm, leading him by a rope through his nose-ring. In the midsummer heat the bull was placid and followed Sam at an easy amble along the coastal path until he saw the first of the foxholes. Then he dug in his feet, lowered his head and snorted.

'Come on, you silly critter,' said Sam. ''Tain't nothin' but a few holes in the ground.'

But Duncan, who had known this path all his life, was not to be persuaded so easily. He balked and side-stepped, waltzing around the edges of the foxholes all the way back to the farm track, till Sam was red-faced and worn out. His flushed colour was not due just to the struggle. There were soldiers on the beach, enjoying time off sunbathing and paddling about in the edge of the heavy surf. Afraid at first of the great Holstein, they had started up a volley of jeers and catcalls when they saw the hard time Sam was having. During the trudge up the farm track from the sea Sam rehearsed in his mind all the sarcastic things he would have said if he had thought of them in time. Behind the barn there was a small area of grass where the bull was sometimes kept, enclosed by an electric fence. Sam shut Duncan in with relief, checked that he had salt in the lick and water in the trough, and put his head round the kitchen door.

'That's the bull back, Mrs Libby.'

'You've been a time, Sam.'

'Ayuh. Fool beast was scared of them foxholes. Sooner these soldiers clear outta here the better, I say.'

'Well,' said Harriet, who agreed with him for reasons of her own, 'I guess we'll just have to endure it until the war is over.'

The next day the Shakers arrived and, as in every previous year since they had been old enough to walk that far on their own, Tirza and Simon carried a couple of large chip baskets of food along to the field where the wagons and buggies were now parked in a wide circle.

It was the first time they had done anything together for weeks, and Tirza felt unexpectedly shy of him. Simon, however, swung along quite cheerfully. The visit of the Shakers, though repeated every year, was enough out of the ordinary to bring a little liveliness into life. They did not talk much. Out at sea the naval patrol boats were doing a depth charge run, and they could sense the explosions through the soles of their bare feet on the sandy soil as much as from the sound, which hit the eardrums like a wave of heavy pressure. On the horizon they could count the dim outlines of six naval vessels. Further out part of the superstructure of another just showed above the curve of the ocean as it disappeared over the horizon. Slightly nearer than the naval ships a cluster of inshore fishing boats out of Flamboro was trawling dispiritedly.

'Dad's mostly given up trawling,' said Tirza, watching the boats as she walked.

'Why's that?'

'It's these depth charges. Ruins the fishing. Kills some fish. Scares the rest away. The catch is down to about one-third of what it ought to be.'

'That's bad.'

'Ayuh. At least Dad has a lobster licence. I don't know what the others will do, who don't have one.'

They walked on and a patrol plane droned overhead, flying along the line of the path they were following. It passed them and faded into the distance. They both thought, but did not speak, the same thing.

The Shakers were glad to see them. They shook them both formally by the hand and invited them to sit down while the baskets were unpacked.

'We are most grateful to your mother, young man,' said Brother Ethro, who appeared to be some kind of leader, though it wasn't clear whether the Shakers believed in such a thing. 'Won't you join us? We are just going to have a little of Sister Dorcas and Sister Hannah's cakes after our long journey. We'd surely be glad to have you share with us.'

They accepted, feeling it would be discourteous to refuse, but Simon fidgeted through the preliminary prayers and Tirza's mind wandered. The cakes, though, were delicious. Afterwards, they helped erect the stalls in the hotel ballroom. These consisted of no more than boards laid on trestles, but over each was spread a blue-and-white checked blanket, topped with a fine starched embroidered cloth. The Shakers believed in a stark simplicity of life, but that did not seem to blunt their skill in producing beautiful things.

On these stalls, arranged around the edges of the room, they laid out the crafts they had brought to sell, to help support the community. There was the elegant Shaker furniture: candle tables and rocking chairs, a baby's cradle, stools and small chests. There were woven goods, worked over the winter, both thick woollen blankets and fine table-linens. There were all kinds of practical items: sturdy Shaker brooms and brushes, garden and farming tools, and pieces of harness. Simon picked among these, looking for unusual items but failing to find any. Most of the Shaker tools were old stalwarts that had proved their worth over generations, but sometimes they came up with a new invention, for they were practical people and believed that the invention and design of a useful new tool was as good a way of worshipping God and giving thanks for His created Earth as spending the same number of hours in prayer. 'Hands to work and hearts to God' – that was their motto.

Tirza liked the small fancy items best, especially the boxes which were made by wrapping thin wood round an oval form and pinning the overlapping tongues of wood in place with slim brass rivets. The wood was beech, hand cut as fine as cardboard, so the boxes were light to hold, but springy and resilient. Mostly they were left the natural colour of the wood, but some were painted in clear strong colours: oxblood red, the green of spruce trees in midsummer, or a rich deep blue the colour of Gooseneck Lake on a fine day. One set of five, piled one on top of the other in diminishing sizes, had been painted with scenes of houses and barns and orchard trees.

'Them's where we live,' said a girl about Tirza's age, who had been setting up the stock on this stall with her, but had not yet spoken.

'In your community?'

The girl nodded.

'I haven't seen you here before,' said Tirza, 'though I've seen the Shakers every year.'

'My daddy just brung us to the Shakers last fall. That's Ma over there.' The girl nodded towards a thin, tired-looking woman spreading a cloth on the next stall. As she nodded, her over-large poke bonnet slipped off, exposing wispy brown hair. She pulled it back on again.

'He said as how it was gettin' beyond him to feed the twelve of us any more, with Ma expectin' again. So we druv up in our buggy all the way from West Virginny. My daddy said as how the Shakers would give us a home and feed us an' all. Then two days after we was there, he took off again. We ain't seed him since.'

'That's too bad,' said Tirza sympathetically. 'What did your mother do?'

'Oh, I reckin she didn't take it too bad. She was purdy thankful. I guess she finds it kind of peaceful with the Shakers. When he was in licker, my daddy sure did beat up on us. Ma says as how she's had enough of men to last a lifetime.'

Tirza was puzzled. 'But there are men Shakers too.'

'We live separate an' sleep separate, an' Ma reckins that fine by her.'

'Will you stay a Shaker always, then?'

'Oh, yezum. I don't want no eleven babies!' The girl laughed merrily. 'Here, I got to go help Ma. Be seeing y'all.'

━━◈━━

The next day when Tirza delivered the crabs, she found the man called Sandy waiting by *Stormy Petrel* when she returned to the pier, the long way round this time, avoiding the formal garden.

'Good morning,' he said.

'Morning.'

She climbed down into the boat and began to cast off. He put out one crutch and held the gunwale against the fenders.

'I don't suppose you'd consider taking a passenger?'

She stared up at him in astonishment.

'What do you mean?'

'Give me a lift round to Flamboro? I'm bored out of my mind toddling around the garden here with all the aged pensioners. I can't climb on the rocks and my crutches sink into the beach. I thought if you would give me a lift to the village it would be a change of scene.'

'How would you get back?'

'Taxi?'

'There's no taxis in Flamboro!' She laughed at the absurdity of the idea.

'Well, the hotel would probably send a car for me.'

She looked doubtful.

'There's gas rationing now, you know.'

His shoulders drooped.

'Yes, you're right. Stupid idea. Forget it.'

Suddenly Tirza felt sorry for him. She thought how bored she would be, stuck here on crutches, with nothing to do and the fine summer going on all around.

'Come on,' she said. 'I'll take you for a sail and then I'll bring you back.'

'Really? But aren't you very busy with your crabs and everything?'

'Doesn't take every minute of my day.'

She threw a hitch round the post again and climbed on to the pier. It required some manoeuvring to lower Sandy into the boat, but with Tirza putting her shoulder under his armpit and half lifting him, they managed it at last. She stowed his crutches forrard, partly under the deck, and told him to sit amidships.

'Have you ever sailed before?'

'A little, in a friend's boat, but only on a loch, not on the open ocean.'

'On a what?' Tirza was busy hoisting the sail and easing *Stormy Petrel* away from the pier.

'Loch. A kind of lake.'

'Well, this is no lake. Keep your head down below the boom.'

Once they were fully under way, Tirza sat on the windward side deck, with her toes curled round the gunwale on the lee side for support and with the tiller under her arm.

'You're him, aren't you?' she said. 'That English airman Pierre told me about. They picked you out of the sea after your plane went down.'

'That's it. But...' he pulled a comic face. 'A *British* airman, if you don't mind.'

'Why, what's the difference?'

'I'm Scottish. Which means I'm British, but not English.'

'Oh.' Tirza wasn't interested. 'Head down.'

She brought the boat about and began to head out to sea.

'I tell you what. There's an island about a couple of miles offshore. Mustinegus Island. Would you like me to take you out there? It's uninhabited now, though there used to be two or three farms there.'

'Sounds fine to me.'

He felt in the pockets of his loose cotton jacket.

'It's a good thing I was hopeful about you agreeing to take me aboard. I persuaded the chef to make up a packet of sandwiches and some fruit.' He took them out and laid them on the bottom boards of the boat. 'And I got a couple of bottles of beer from the bar. Or maybe you aren't old enough to drink beer yet.'

Tirza looked at him, startled.

'No.' She shook her head at him. 'I don't drink beer.'

'Oh, well. Sorry. I suppose I should have brought a Coke.'

As she headed on a long tack which would take them almost to the island, Tirza pondered this briefly. What kind of girl did he think she was, to be offering her beer? She was glad none of her family had heard him or they might not be too pleased that she was taking him out to Mustinegus Island all by herself. But she soon dismissed it from her mind, concentrating on her sailing.

The boat was awkward to handle with a man's weight fixed amidships. Tirza was anxious that *Stormy Petrel* shouldn't seem sluggish but would show off what a fine boat she was to this slightly odd but attractive stranger. Luckily the breeze was brisk enough that the boat soon picked up speed, but not so strong that she would have to ask Sandy to shift about as they sailed. It occurred to her a little late that a partially crippled passenger might be dangerous in the wrong weather conditions. The direction of the wind, though, favoured them, and the heat of the sun, blazing down from a cloudless sky and dancing off the waves, was modified by its cool breath coming from further out at sea.

After ten minutes Sandy took off his jacket and folded it up.

'It's good to get away from the hotel for a bit. They're very kind to me, but it's dull there on my own, and immobile. One minute I'm sitting around an airfield in the south of England waiting to be scrambled to fight the Jerries. The next I'm doing an impersonation of Long John Silver three thousand miles away in a stately New England hotel amongst the geriatrics.'

Tirza thought he exaggerated a lot, and didn't understand everything he said, but she only commented, '*Treasure Island*. That's a great book.'

'You've read it?' He looked pleased and rather surprised.

'Sure. Robert Louis Stevenson. I've read his *Kidnapped* too.

And *Travels with a Donkey*. But not *Dr Jekyll and Mr Hyde*.'

'Well, now.' He looked at her appraisingly, as if he had noticed her for the first time. 'And what books do you like best?'

She regarded him a little scornfully. 'Depends on how I'm feeling. I like different things for different moods. Or different weathers. Or different seasons. Miss Bennett – she's our class teacher – she had us write a theme this year on "My Favourite Book". Plain silly I thought. So I wrote about why I feel like certain things at certain times.'

'Sounds very interesting.'

'Oh, it was interesting, all right! She gave me a D grade. Said I hadn't answered the question.' She grinned at him suddenly. 'I didn't care. I liked writing it.'

'I'd enjoy reading it.'

'Well.' She was suddenly shy and became busy coiling away loose ends of rope.

'So tell me some of the things you enjoy reading,' he said. 'Never mind about ranking them in order.'

'Sometimes I just want to read poetry. It's so spare and clean. Like a boat with good lines, you know? I've been reading a lot of Robert Frost lately – he's a New England poet. But I like the old poets too. Chaucer is great. I like getting my tongue round the old words, and he tells good stories. And I like Shelley's "Ozymandias". It makes you think. All these kings and presidents and such, with their puffed-up words, conceited as a turkey-cock. What do they amount to in the end? In the end, nature will take over everything. Only here in Maine it will be the forest, not the desert.'

'What about Shakespeare? Don't you like him?'

'Oh, I don't count him just in with the others. He's some different. I've read all his plays now. Maybe one day I'll get to see one.'

'You've never been to one?'

'In Flamboro?' She laughed.

'Portland, then.'

'Maybe I'll go some day, I don't know. My dad and my grandmother wouldn't be interested. My other grandmother might be, I suppose, but she's never suggested it.'

Sandy opened his mouth to ask about these relatives, but just then she had to bring the boat about on to a new tack which would fetch them in to a small cove on the island. By the time the boat was quiet again, heeling over as the wind grew fresher, he had moved to something else.

'Do you read any other novelists, apart from Stevenson?'

'Of course. I like those nineteenth-century English ones.'

'British.'

'Oh, shucks!' She laughed. 'You know, Dickens and the Brontës. I didn't like Jane Austen at first, but I read *Northanger Abbey* this spring, and it was really funny.'

'What about the Americans?'

'Mark Twain is great, but I thought *Moby Dick* was awful slow. I never finished it. And there's that novelist F. Scott Fitzgerald, have you read him? *Tender Is the Night*?'

Sandy, his eyes dancing, agreed that he had.

'I just read it, though I didn't understand everything,' she confessed. 'I'm used to people thinking I'm crazy because I read so much,' she continued, misunderstanding his expression, 'but I read *fast*. I don't spend so much time on it, except in bed at night. And, besides...'

'What?'

She was embarrassed. 'Well, when you're reading, you can go anywhere, can't you, away inside your head? You can be anyone.'

She looked at him, suddenly making some kind of mute appeal for recognition, for kinship. He smiled back fondly.

'That's exactly right. That's just how I feel myself. But what an unusual fellow you are, for a crab-fisher laddie.'

Tirza half rose, staring at him.

'What did you say?'

'I said...' He saw the blood rising from her neck and flooding her face, and the curve of her cheek as she turned away from him. 'My God, you're a girl!'

Tirza ran the boat ashore on the beach and jumped into water up to her thighs. In silence she hauled *Stormy Petrel* further up and tied the painter around a tree. Sandy, stranded in the bottom of the boat with the sail flapping above him and the boom jerking back and forth, could do nothing but wait. Tirza waded out to the boat again and lowered the sail. As she reached out her arm to gather in the folds of cloth he could see, which he should have noticed before, that her shirt clung to the small curves of budding breasts. He felt foolish and humiliated, sitting there, and did not know how to make it up to her.

Grimly Tirza helped him over the edge of the boat and through the shallows. She took his jacket and the food from him as she handed him his crutches, and led him to the edge of the shingle beach where short grass grew between bayberry bushes. Here he collapsed on a projecting boulder and caught her by the wrist. He pulled her down beside him and she came down awkwardly on her knees.

'Tirza, I'm so sorry. It was stupid of me. I can't think... Your name, I don't know why, I thought it was a boy's name. Like Ezra. And your hair is so short.' He ran his hand over the dark stubble her father trimmed for her every Saturday night. She jerked her head away and tried to stand up, but he kept a firm grip on her wrist with the other hand.

'I know I'm skinny,' she said bitterly. 'You don't have to explain.'

Sandy's eye gleamed briefly, but she did not see it.

'You'll grow.' He laughed softly. 'Of course I should have realised. No boy of your age would have been so kind. Or have read so shrewdly. How old are you, anyway?'

'Twelve. Going on thirteen in the fall,' she said gruffly.

'That's a wonderful age and an awful age. Neither one thing nor t'other. Neither child nor adult. I remember it vividly. And, oh Lord! I offered you a beer! What would your mother say?'

'I don't have a mother, but my grandmother would go crazy.' She gave a small muffled laugh.

He slid his hand down from her wrist and took her hand in his.

'Am I forgiven?' He lifted the hand, brown and weathered but – now that he looked at it – definitely a girl's hand. He kissed the palm lightly.

She turned and looked at him suddenly, her lips slightly parted, her eyes astonished.

'Yes,' she said faintly. 'Of course you're forgiven.'

'Good.' He laid her hand tenderly on the top of the boulder and patted it, then struggled to his feet. 'Let's make a fresh start. Tell me about this island.'

Chapter 11

Maine: Summer 1942

THE COVE WHERE they landed was on the north-west corner of Mustinegus. The island, a rough oval in shape running north-south, resembled a meat platter, raised on the east side and tilting down on the west. This tilting of the land meant that most of the island turned its back on the Atlantic gales, cradling the warm old farm lands to the west and south. The eastern side was still clothed with ancient woods of spruce and fir, with a few deciduous trees scattered amongst them, oak and hickory, rock maple and sumac. These woods ended abruptly at the top of the steep cliffs which dropped a hundred feet or more into roaring Atlantic breakers. Over millions of years the sea had worn hollows and caves in the eastern cliffs which echoed and redoubled the fury of the waves, so that the whole island was alive with the sound. To Sandy it felt like standing in the centre of some primaeval orchestra where both players and instruments were the forces of nature.

Tirza led him along the faint traces of a path to the edge of the forest, above the cliff.

'Be careful!' she said, raising her voice over the sound of the waves. 'It's a long way down.'

Steadying himself with a hand on a huge rock maple whose roots twined out of the side of the cliff and back again, seeking anchorage and nourishment, Sandy peered over into the boiling icy cauldron at the foot of the cliff. He thought he had no fear of heights, but a feeling of vertigo swept over him immediately. Flying itself had never worried him, though he had a healthy fear of the German fighter planes. But the sheer raw power of that pounding ocean, every hour of every day for ever... the thought of it numbed him. He eased himself back from the cliff and gripped his crutches with hands that were trembling.

Tirza turned away from the woods and made her way back to the path.

'This leads to the first of the farms. Most of the berry bushes are along here.'

A hundred yards further on, she pointed to a great thicket of low, sprawling bushes which spread their fresh growth across a level stretch of ground and lapped around the feet of the surrounding trees like water.

'Blueberries. Some of the best in these parts. Hardly anyone ever comes to pick them now, though I sailed over last year and picked for one day.'

Sandy leaned over as far as the crutches would allow and lifted a branch.

'There doesn't seem to be much here.'

'These little green berries, see? They'll fatten up more yet, and turn dark blue when they're ready.'

'When?'

'Oh, a couple of months yet. It looks like a good year. I might come out again.'

'Are there any other sorts of berries?'

'There aren't any cranberries worth picking. They need boggy ground. We have them on our marsh up behind Libby's Beach.'

'That's your land, is it?'

'My uncle and my dad own the farm. My uncle Tobias farms it and my dad is a lobsterman.'

'So that's how you come to be a crab-fisher.'

Tirza shrugged.

'You don't need a licence for crab-fishing. I earned the money to buy *Stormy Petrel* that way.'

'It must be hard work.'

'I don't mind hard work.'

They walked on towards the ruined farm and Tirza pointed out cloudberries and wild raspberries.

'It's the blueberries that are the best, though.' She stopped beside the fallen remains of a stone wall. 'This was one of the farms.'

It was a forlorn place, with the wooden barn collapsed and the roof of the house sliding off. Weeds grew thickly where the cows had once been brought in for milking. A faded green shutter, hanging on by one hinge, swung to and fro with a plaintive sound.

'When did people last live on the island?' Sandy asked.

'I think the other two farms were abandoned about twelve-fifteen years ago. People settled here when the colonists first came to New England, and they stayed right on till then. My grandmother said that when the Depression came, two of the families decided to quit and move to the mainland. The soil is good here, but it was tough having to go back and forth by boat to the mainland with the produce.'

'And this farm here?'

'They were cousins of the Swansons, who own a farm near us. It was the hurricane of '38 that drove them out. I don't know if you heard about it, but it did an awful lot of damage. I can remember it. I guess I was about eight or nine. Boats picked up and thrown miles inland. Pieces of straw driven into hardwood trees like nails. This family managed to get off the island with their cows and waited out the storm with the Swansons. It was a crazy storm. In some places one part of a forest was blown down flat but all around the other trees weren't touched. Or one house would be smashed into matchsticks and the ones on either side were fine. After the storm the family came back, thinking the forest would have taken the brunt of the storm and the farm would be safe. They found there wasn't a tree down in the woods, but most of the roof was off the farmhouse and the barn was just as ruined as you see it now. And all the sheep were gone. Not a tuft of wool to be found. Nobody knows if they were swept away or if they were so scared they ran into the sea. So the family gave up the farm and moved away.'

'That's a sad story.'

Tirza looked at him straight. 'It's a hard country to live in. Folks who come here in the summer only see that it's beautiful. They don't understand that it's a dangerous country too.'

They poked around the farm for a while, then went down to a grassy space just above the low tumbled rocks of the west shore facing the mainland. Sitting here they ate the sandwiches Pierre had provided and Tirza bit into an apple while Sandy drank his beer.

'Before the settlers arrived,' said Tirza, 'the Abenaki used to come here in the summers.'

'Who?'

'The local Indian nation. They spent their winters inland, hunting otter and beavers. At the beginning of spring they came back to their summer settlements on the coast to plant crops and catch fish. They would come out here in their birch-bark canoes to catch seabirds and collect their eggs. And hunt seals – the seals still bask on those rocks along the cove where we landed.'

'How do you know the Indians came here?'

'My grandmother told me.'

'The one who wouldn't have approved of the beer?'

'Oh, no. That's my dad's mother – my Libby grandmother. She's lived with my dad and me since my mother died. I meant my other grandmother, Christina O'Neill. She studied law at Vassar and married the schoolteacher, and now she lives in a cabin in the woods on the far side of Flamboro. One of the Abenaki summer villages used to be in her forest, near where her house is now.'

'She sounds an interesting person.'

'She's half Abenaki,' said Tirza, a little defiantly.

'Is she, indeed? So you're... a quarter Indian? No, an eighth?'

'Ayuh.'

'And it was an old tradition that they used to come out here to the island?'

'Oh, it's more than a tradition. I've found arrowheads and fish-hooks here. And part of a broken cookpot once, too.'

Sandy became excited.

'Any chance we might find more? Where did you find them?'

'Just a piece from where you're sitting. Under that thicket of birch, where the ground is soft. You see that mound? There's an Indian shell heap under there.'

Sandy limped over to where she pointed, and began stirring up the soil with the end of his crutch. There was nothing to be seen but dead leaves and broken shells and an earthworm heaving itself hastily out of the way. Tirza watched him tolerantly for a while, then she knelt down at his feet and began patting the ground with her palms and digging gently with a piece of stick. After a few minutes, she picked something out of the ground, squinted at it, blew off the worst of the dirt, then carried it down to a rock jutting out over the water.

'Have you found something?' Sandy was incredulous.

She did not answer, but lay on her stomach, rinsing the object in the sea. Then she rolled over and held it up to him, a glinting silver-grey object, its wet faceted sides catching and reflecting the sun.

'It's an arrowhead. Well, I'm damned! Just like that! How did you do it?' He cradled the arrowhead in his palm, tilting it to catch the light. It was perfect, an exquisite gem not more than an inch long.

'I just seem to have a feel for it,' said Tirza, getting up and brushing the bits of dead leaf off her shorts. 'That would be used for shooting birds – ducks and such. That's why it's so small.'

'It's beautiful. What workmanship! Think of making that with nothing but stone tools.'

'Doesn't make any difference. A well-made stone tool is just as good as any metal tool you care to name. Girna has an Abenaki knife made of obsidian. Don't find it round here. Obsidian was traded hundreds of miles, it was so precious. She thinks it's a surgeon's knife. It cuts so fine, it makes a steel knife seem like a blunt saw. What matters in making a tool is the skill of the maker's hands and the strength of his spirit. That is what the Indian nations believe.'

'Yes,' he said, looking at her thoughtfully. 'Yes, I'm sure you're right.' He held the arrowhead out to her delicately between finger and thumb.

'Oh no. I want you to keep it. To remember the island.'

'I shall treasure it,' he said. He wrapped it in his handkerchief and placed it carefully in the pocket of his shirt.

◆◆◆

On the last morning of the Shakers' visit, Tirza wandered around the stalls looking at the remaining goods on sale. Quite a few pieces of furniture had been sold, including the cradle and most of the chairs. The hotel guests and other summer people had bought practically all the embroidered tablecloths and oval boxes. It was on Saturday that most of the local people came, too busy during the week to spare the time. Farmers' wives were fingering the fine woollen blankets, checked or striped in green and blue. Some of their husbands were there too, looking at the tools. She saw Walter Pelham counting out the money for a new spade.

Abigail had sent Tirza to buy a broom. The Shakers were famous for the quality of their brooms, and Abigail bought hers nowhere else. Tirza had been given strict instructions as to width of head and length of handle, but she didn't find brooms very enthralling. Instead she lingered by the small wooden goods: flatware trays, darning mushrooms, rolling pins, babies' rattles, and the thin oval boxes. No one had bought the set of five boxes painted with country scenes. For the first time she noticed that the tapering pile had to be arranged the right way round, because the scene was carried on from one box to the next. Someone had disturbed the pile. Carefully she turned two of the boxes round so that they matched up with the other three.

'Hi there.' It was the girl from West Virginia.

'Hi.'

Even after nearly a week of living rough in a wagon, the girl looked immaculately clean and tidy in her floor-length mauve dress with its white collar and long white apron. Only her poke bonnet was wayward. Tirza was suddenly conscious of her work-grimed hands and less than clean shorts. She put her hands behind her back.

'Have you had a good week here?'

'Great. Kinda like a vacation, y'know? Not so many chores here as in the community. Y'all sure are lucky to live here all the time.'

'I guess so.'

'I just wish...' The girl looked yearningly out of the window at the ocean.

'What?'

'Why, I just wish I could go swimmin'. Ain't never seed the ocean before. I'd like to feel the sea water on my skin. But Brother Enoch says it ain't seemly.'

'It's pretty cold,' said Tirza by way of comfort.

'I wouldn't care. Used to swim nakid in the crick at home.

Jumpin' Jehozaphat but that was cold!'

The girl suddenly seemed to hear herself and clapped her hands over her mouth. Her eyes rolled around, checking to see if she had been overheard. She mumbled something and ran off. Tirza touched the pile of boxes with her fingertip and sighed. Then she turned away to look for Abigail's broom.

'Hello there.'

Sandy hopped across the slippery ballroom floor cautiously. He was getting more proficient, but the rubber tips of the crutches squeaked and slithered on the polished wood.

'Are you interested in the boxes? I noticed them myself.'

'I like the farm scenes,' said Tirza. 'It looks like my uncle Tobias's farm. And these boxes are so light, you wouldn't believe.'

She picked up the smallest one and handed it to him. He balanced himself carefully and took it from her.

'Amazing. I wonder how they make them.'

'I guess they steam the wood before they bend it. Like boat building. You can do most anything with wood when it's steamed.'

She placed the box carefully back on the top of the pile, aligning the painting.

'So long. I've got to buy a broom for my grandmother.'

'The Indian grandmother, or the teetotal grandmother?'

Tirza laughed.

'Not my Indian grandmother.'

She walked back along the beach, because she was stopping off at the farm to help with the start of the strawberry picking. When she reached the farm, Harriet, Tobias, Sam and Simon were all in the strawberry field which lay just inside the farm gate, next to the county road. Tirza left the broom on the porch and collected a basket from the grain shed.

'There aren't many ready yet, are there?' she said to Harriet as she squatted down in the adjacent row.

'No, but it's going to be a good crop later. Just see how many more are coming.'

Strawberry picking, Tirza had found, was almost the only thing that became more difficult as you grew older. She could still remember herself as a small child when she had first helped with the picking. She must have been about five. It had been easy then to squat down and pick straight into the basket – her eyes on a level, it seemed, with the plants themselves. She couldn't really have been that low down, but she knew she had never felt tired at the strawberry picking in those days, only baking hot in the sun and ready for a drink whenever one was offered.

Nowadays she just could not find a comfortable position. It was even worse than last year – she must have grown some since then. Her clothes always seemed to be too short in the wrists and the leg, and every winter when she tried to force her feet back into her boots it caused Abigail much irritable comment on the subject of expensive shoe leather.

The extra inches she had gained hindered her whichever way she turned. First she hunkered down with her knees up by her ears, but after a time a sharp pain started up in her thighs. Then she tried kneeling, but the ground was full of tiny stones which cut into her knees. She sat sideways in the space between the rows with her legs stretched out in front of her and twisted round to pick, but that started up a pain in her back. She saw that the others were shifting their positions as often as she did, all except Sam. Despite his lanky length and his angular elbows and knees, Sam was able to fold himself up into a compact bundle like a grasshopper sitting in the sun, and he worked his way along his row faster than any of them.

Tirza paused for a moment and popped a particularly succulent strawberry into her mouth. She closed her eyes and chewed slowly, rolling the flavour around on her tongue. Strawberries always tasted best out here, freshly picked with the heat of the sun still on them. She leaned back on her hands and felt the soil as warm as a blanket between her fingers. She could hear a cricket chirping somewhere over near the orchard and Tobias humming softly under his breath the way her dad hummed at the lobster fishing. A herring gull wheeled and shrieked overhead, then veered off towards the ocean. With her eyes closed, she could hear the boom of the sea and in the opposite direction over on Swansons' farm a half-grown lamb calling to its mother. For a moment she felt inexplicably happy. Then she opened her eyes, turned round to crouch over the plants and began picking again.

They stopped work at noon. The first flush of ripe berries had been picked and the plants could be left another few days before they would need to be picked again. They carried their baskets up to the kitchen, where Harriet would sort out boxes of the finest berries to sell to Flett's Stores and the Portland buyer. The rest would be canned or made into jam, though everyone was worrying about sugar since rationing had started at the beginning of May.

'I wrote down a low-sugar jam recipe off the radio,' said Harriet, shaking her head, 'but I don't know. Would the jam keep? I reckon it would go mouldy without enough sugar.'

'Grandma says she's going to do all her fruit canning without sugar this year,' Tirza volunteered. 'So she can use the sugar ration for jam.'

'Ayuh, I was thinking on that. And that reminds me.' Harriet tipped a couple of pounds of the best strawberries into a small basket. 'Take these home with you, Tirza. Abigail will be glad of them for dessert tonight.'

'Come with me to the milk room,' said Tobias, 'and I'll give you a can of cream to go with them.'

Tirza started off on her homeward journey loaded down with the strawberries, the cream, the broom and a bag of chocolate brownies Harriet handed her at the last moment. She was thankful she had not ridden her bicycle that morning. As she passed the Tremayne house, she had a feeling that something looked different about it, but it was only as she started down the steep part of the path into Flamboro, carefully balancing the can of cream, that she looked back and realised what it was. One of the shades at an upstairs window had been raised.

<hr />

On Sunday morning, Tirza was surprised to see Sandy in church. He sat in a pew across the aisle from the Libby family, and gave her a smile as she came in. Afterwards, as the congregation lingered in the pleasant sun outside, discussing plans for the annual Fourth of July party, he came over to her. He was managing with one crutch now, and was holding a brown paper package by its string in his other hand.

Tirza introduced him, first to her father and grandmother, then to the family from the farm, who were all present except

Martha, who had not been near the church since Will's death.

Tobias shook Sandy's hand with a look of curiosity in his eye. The story of the injured British pilot was common currency in Flamboro, but he had not been seen in the town before. Tirza felt a certain possessiveness towards him.

'This is Sandy, Uncle Tobias. He spent a week at sea in a rubber dinghy before he was rescued.'

She knew they were all longing to hear the story first hand, but their old-fashioned New England politeness prevented their asking outright. She had not liked to question him about it herself.

'You're staying at the Mansion House, are you, Mr... er...?' said Abigail. Tirza knew him simply as Sandy and had not thought to find out his last name.

'Fraser. But, please, call me Sandy.'

When he smiled, his whole face lit up, and his eyes crinkled at the corners. Tirza noticed that now he was getting a tan, the smile lines at the corners of his eyes were etched faintly in paler skin against the brown. She wondered how old he was. Much younger than her father and uncle, that was clear. Perhaps about the same age as Pete Flett, who was twenty-three. Though those crinkles might mean he was older. She focused on what was being said. Her grandmother was inviting Sandy to join them for Sunday dinner, and he was accepting.

'I'll just need to tell them that I won't be going back in the hotel car,' he said. 'Perhaps Tirza could give me a lift in *Stormy Petrel* afterwards.'

She saw their heads swivel round as they stared at her. She had not mentioned before that she had met Sandy, or that she had taken him sailing with her.

'No need for that,' said Tobias. 'We came in the pickup today because I had a load to bring into town from the farm. We can take you back with us. 'Tisn't much further along the road to Todd's Neck.'

'I wouldn't want to use up your petrol ration. How about it, Tirza?'

'Oh, I'd be glad to take you.'

What was *petrol*? she wondered.

Sandy went to speak to the hotel driver and Tirza waited

behind to show him the way while the rest of the family walked along the harbour front to Nathan's house. Today was one of the regular Sunday visits by the farm family, and Tirza dreaded that it would be very dull for Sandy.

'There,' he said. 'That's taken care of. Now, before we catch them up, I have something for you.' He led her to a pile of lobster crates on the wharf side and sat down to ease his legs. She perched beside him.

'Here.' He handed her the parcel he had been carrying all this time. 'Something in exchange for the arrowhead, though not as special, I'm afraid.'

Tirza took the parcel silently. She did not know what to say. Nobody gave her presents, just like that. Only for birthdays and Christmas, and then they were usually practical things. She untied the string carefully, wound it round her hand and put it into the pocket of the skirt Abigail obliged her to wear to church. She folded back the brown paper and found the largest of the Shaker boxes with painted scenes.

'Oh, Sandy, it's wonderful.' She turned it in her hands. It was even better than she remembered.

'Open it.'

Inside was the next smallest box. Inside that, the next one. And so on until she reached the smallest one.

'Open that one too.'

Inside the last box was a snapshot of Sandy, dashing in uniform and standing beside a small aeroplane. On the back he had written: 'To Tirza with affection from Sandy, because she has a forgiving nature.'

'Something for you to remember me by, when I'm gone,' he said.

Tirza cradled her lapful of boxes and kept her eyes down, unable to look at him.

'They're wonderful, but I don't think my grandmother would let me accept them.'

'Does she have to know?'

Did she? Tirza felt her chest churning with some feeling she had never experienced before. Why should Abigail have to know? She wanted the boxes and she wanted the photograph, and above all she wanted to go on being friends with Sandy. If she rejected his gift, he might be upset or angry. She lifted her head and her eyes met his. Her cheeks were burning, but she held up her chin defiantly.

'No. I don't suppose she has to know. It's nothing to do with her.'

Reverently she fitted the boxes one inside the other and wrapped the paper loosely round them again.

'I'll put them in the locker on *Stormy Petrel* for now,' she said. 'And I'll take them inside later.' She tucked the photograph into the pocket of her blouse, where it gave her a queer feeling, as though it was burning through to her.

Sunday dinner was transformed with Sandy sitting down at the family table. He kept them all laughing with his outrageous stories of RAF leave in London, and treated Abigail with such deference that she soon relaxed and laughed along with the rest of them. Simon, emboldened, asked about the Spitfire's crash into the sea. Sandy gave them a highly coloured version enlivened with comic details, but underneath it all Tirza realised how near he had been to death. She wondered suddenly whether the cheerful way he told the story was shaped by the terror of the real experience. Sometimes she would whistle a defiant tune when she was most afraid. She watched him, wondering. She had never felt this close to a grown-up before. His accident, his dependency on her when they had sailed in *Stormy Petrel*, all made him seem vulnerable, as though he wasn't much older than she was herself.

Sailing back to Todd's Neck that afternoon, they were both quiet. Sandy lay back in the bow of the boat with his eyes shut. He looked drawn and tired, and Tirza nursed the boat along as gently as she could. When she came about for the final run in to the pier, however, the waves slapped once broadside on and threw up a fine spray which landed on his face. His eyes fluttered open, looking dazed and disorientated, and she realised that he had been fast asleep. He smiled apologetically.

'Tried to do a bit too much today. Sorry to be such a boring companion.'

'That's OK. Are you feeling all right?'

'My right leg is hurting a wee bit. I'll lie down when I get back.'

She gave him her shoulder to lean on, from the pier to the door of the hotel. His feet dragged and she felt a tug of pity and concern. On the threshold he squeezed her shoulders.

'You're a dear girl. A real chum.' Then he disappeared into the draped and polished interior of the Mansion House.

◆◆◆

The Boston ladies had decided to invite some of the soldiers to tea. 'Our visiting heroes', Miss Molly called them. Miss Catherine was not quite so sure about this description, but agreed that a few select young men might be entertained. It would give Susanna something to look forward to. Simon and Wayne were consulted, as they had made the acquaintance of most of the gun crews. Tirza suggested Captain Tucker, and asked if she could bring Sandy.

'He's a visiting hero, too,' she pointed out. 'He's visiting from even further away and he's certainly a hero. He's shot down eight German fighters.'

'Of course you must invite him,' said Miss Molly. 'Now do you think it will be acceptable if we invite them to tea? I am not sure what young men expect these days. I am afraid that we really do not go in for these cocktails they all drink.'

Tirza, Simon and Wayne assured her that a tea party would be very welcome.

'They say as how the food on base is pretty borin', Miss Molly,' said Wayne. 'There's plenty of it, but Jim says he sure does miss his ma's home cookin'.'

'Make one of your lemon cakes, Miss Catherine,' said Tirza. 'Oh, and could you make blueberry muffins? Sandy says he's never eaten muffins. And he'd never heard of putting blue-berries in cakes. He says blaeberries grow in Scotland, and bil-berries in England, but I don't know if they're the same thing. He says they're so small nobody bothers to pick them.'

'Well, they can't be a patch on our Maine blueberries, then,' said Miss Catherine complacently. 'Than which there is *nothing* better. I have a few Mason jars left from last year's canning. I'll certainly make some blueberry muffins. And some chocolate drop muffins as well.'

'Flett's is clear out of chocolate drops,' said Simon. 'It's the war.'

Miss Susanna, sitting in her chair and finishing off the last of her oak tree rug, tapped the side of her nose with her finger.

'Kitty has a secret store of chocolate drops.'

Miss Molly clicked her tongue disapprovingly and muttered something about hoarding.

'Molly Penhaligon!' said Miss Catherine indignantly. 'It is not hoarding. I just saw all these big bags of chocolate drops for cooking when I was down in Boston last month, and I thought I'd stock up the larder. You're fond of chocolate drop muffins yourself.'

Simon was scratching his head, wondering how to make a delicate suggestion. He knew the soldiers would prefer beer, but did not like to suggest it.

'Er, I'm not sure how many of them drink tea...' he began.

'Don't worry,' said Miss Catherine briskly. 'We shall provide coffee as well.' She looked at him shrewdly. 'We shall not be providing strong drink. It will do them no harm to drink coffee.'

Miss Susanna gave Tirza the ghost of a wink.

'The new rug is great,' said Tirza, stroking the soft, tight loops. 'What are you going to make next?'

'Ah, I have an idea for that. But there is a problem. I can't seem to get hold of any burlap.'

'It's the war,' said Miss Catherine. 'All the burlap is going for war use – kit-bags and such. Sandbags.'

Tirza paused in polishing the best Penhaligon silver, brought out for the party. Sandbags? But she didn't say anything.

◆◆◆

Six soldiers were invited to tea, four o'clock sharp at the Boston ladies' house. Jim and Danny from the gun crews, Captain Tucker and the lugubrious Sergeant Klinsky, and Tommy and Irvine who did the regular inspection run along the foxholes. It was to be a democratic party, a mixture of GIs and officers. Simon, Wayne and Tirza were to be there to pass the food and help out, and Tirza was to bring Sandy round in *Stormy Petrel* and manoeuvre him up the steep path. He had now abandoned the crutch and could manage with two sticks, but was still suffering from a good deal of pain in his damaged legs. The broken bones and raw wounds had more or less healed, he explained to Tirza, but the torn nerves and muscles were taking longer to recover.

'You ought to get my grandmother to look at them,' she said.

'Your beer grandmother?' he asked innocently.

'No, of course not, you dope! Girna. Christina O'Neill.'

'Ah.' He cocked his head curiously on one side. 'Is she some sort of native healer, then?'

'She knows a lot about plants and things,' said Tirza shortly, wishing she had not mentioned it. 'Please yourself.'

'Don't be cross.' He took her by the wrist. It was so slender, despite the work she did, a man's work, that his finger and thumb encircled it.

Tirza felt a shock run through her. It happened whenever he touched her, and left her legs shaking. She tried to pull her arm away, but he held on.

'We'll go and visit your grandmother after this tea party, shall we? I would like to meet her very much, whether or not she can help the pain.' His voice was sober, without a hint of its earlier teasing note.

Often, she felt awkward and unsure how to take him. Sometimes he said the opposite of what he meant – but he wasn't lying exactly. She had read about British irony, but had no experience – here in plain-talking, uncomplicated Flamboro – in recognising it. It made her feel uncomfortable. At other times, when he was straightforward and serious, the things he said echoed her own thoughts so exactly that she wanted to touch his hand and say, 'Yes. That's just how I feel.' But natural shyness and reserve held her back, and also this strange spark that jumped between them, as if she had touched the electric fence round the bull's pasture.

The soldiers arrived promptly for tea, their hair slicked down with brilliantine and their fingernails scrubbed. For most of them, the army was their first experience of being away from home. In their off-duty hours they had drifted into wildness, away from the restraints of curtain-twitching neighbours. Drink was cheap and it wasn't difficult to find girls who were naive but willing. However, they were on their best behaviour now, sitting stiff and nervous on the edge of the brocaded chairs in the Penhaligon drawing room (opened up for the occasion) and balancing cups of coffee on their knees. Captain Tucker, a little older and more experienced than the others, seemed more at ease.

Tirza and Sandy came in after the others. There were beads of sweat standing out on his upper lip by the time they had made the climb up the sloping garden and the long flight of front steps, but he smiled and shook hands all round as if he felt no pain at all. Watching him, Tirza could see that his manners and his *way* of speaking were different from the other men. It wasn't simply his English accent. (*Scottish*, she corrected herself.) It was the way he spoke to people. Friendly without being too pushy. That was the nearest she could come to it, though she knew that did not begin to describe it. Formal, but relaxed. It baffled her, as she kept a proprietorial eye on him. She wished she could learn to speak to strangers like that.

The talk, at first, was inevitably about the war. There was a rumour that a submarine had been detected by the naval patrols about ten miles off the coast and hit by depth charges. Patches of oil had appeared on the surface, but no one knew for certain whether any serious damage had been done.

'Nothin' ever comes within sight of our gun,' said Danny longingly. 'Wouldn't I just like to have a shot at them Krauts myself!'

Sandy was questioned about the RAF. He had been in the Battle of Britain and described it vividly, yet it somehow seemed unreal to Tirza, like a radio play. She couldn't connect this man, sitting and enjoying Miss Catherine's blueberry muffins dripping with Harriet's home-churned butter, with life and death duels over the skies of England. Captain Tucker wanted to know about the crash. Sandy gave an even livelier account than he had done at the Libbys' table, till they were all laughing at his attempts to catch fish, using one of his socks. Tirza didn't believe a word of it, but she laughed as much as any of them.

'Now, I have something I want you all to do for me,' said Miss Susanna. 'I'm planning my new rug, and I thought I'd do something different this time. A patchwork affair, like the old wedding quilts when all the bride's friends each worked a section.'

'How do you mean?' asked Simon. 'I can't hook rugs.'

'You could soon learn. But no, I was thinking more about the designing. I've drawn up a grid for the pattern, and divided it into ten rectangles, for the ten of you here today. So it can be a kind of memorial of this one day in June 1942. I want you each to draw something – a picture, or your initials in a pattern, or anything you like. Then I'll convert it into a plan for the rug when I can get some burlap. I'll want you each to hook one little bit, later, just to show you've had a hand in making it.'

Danny and Irvine looked as though they had been clubbed and Tommy gazed into space with bemused eyes. But Jim looked interested.

'I'll have a go,' said Sandy. 'I can't draw, but I'll have a bash at sketching my old kite – my Spitfire.'

'I hear those are great little planes,' said Sergeant Klinsky, as though he hoped to change the direction the conversation was taking.

'I suppose I can try,' said Captain Tucker slowly. 'I've got a fist like a leg of pork.'

Simon, Wayne and Tirza exchanged glances.

'You'll be OK, Wayne,' said Tirza. 'At least you can draw.'

They went through into the dining room, where a sheet of brown paper, cut to the size of the finished rug, was laid out on Captain Penhaligon's vast mahogany table and weighed down with a book at each corner. It had been ruled out with a faint grid of lines to represent the weave of the burlap, and divided into five rows of two rectangles, with a border around each.

'I'll work a rope pattern in the borders, I think, to link the pictures together,' said Miss Susanna, who was leaning on Miss Molly's arm.

Sandy took the thick pencil she offered him and sketched a single-engine plane, filling one of the frames. He added the RAF emblem of circles on the wings and put a few wiggly clouds behind it.

'How's that?'

'Just what I want. Now sign it with your initials.'

He wrote a flourishing 'A.F.' in the corner and passed the pencil to Wayne. Encouraged, Wayne stuck his tongue out between his teeth and produced a workmanlike drawing of a trawler. He signed it too, and gave a sigh of relief.

'That's excellent, Wayne,' said Miss Molly. 'I didn't know you were an artist.'

Wayne turned red and shuffled his feet.

One by one they filled in their frames. Tirza did her best to draw *Stormy Petrel*. Sergeant Klinsky, unexpectedly, drew a vase of flowers, which leaned a little to one side, but Miss Susanna said, 'Good. Let's not have transport in all of them.'

Danny attempted to draw the gun, but it might have been a stick of celery; Jim carefully outlined an American flag.

'About the only thing I kin do,' he muttered to Danny.

Captain Tucker pondered a good deal, then he produced quite a passable likeness of Flamboro church, although the weathervane was almost as high as the spire. Tommy, over six feet tall, with muscles like a wrestler and tattoos on the backs of his hands, drew the rear view of a rabbit. He reddened as he leaned back and looked at it.

'Teacher taught me how to do that in kindergarten,' he mumbled. 'Don't reckin I've drawn nothin' since.'

That left Irvine and Simon to complete the last row. Irvine sucked the pencil, then began to draw a series of arcs. 'A rainbow,' he explained. 'I calculate that'll let you use plenty of colours. And I guess we're all looking for the pot of gold when peace comes after this durn war.' He handed the pencil on to Simon.

Simon writhed with embarrassment.

'I *can't*, Miss Susanna,' he said. 'I can't even draw a straight line in math. Using a ruler.'

'No need to worry if your lines aren't straight. Hooking along the weave of the fabric will make them come straight.'

'I don't know what to do.'

'Oh, go on,' said Wayne. 'Do *something*.'

'You could draw the farm,' said Tirza, oddly insistent, as if this was important. 'The cow barn.'

'Aw, Tirza, it's a peculiar shape. All those angles the roof makes.'

'Here,' said Miss Susanna, 'I'll help you get started. If we draw the front, where the big double doors are...' She took his hand and guided it. 'Now, just run some lines back from that to make the side.'

Awkwardly, he did as he was told. It was no work of art, but it was unmistakably a cow barn. Encouraged, he drew a tree with a stick-like trunk, a lollipop top and little circles all over it.

'An apple tree,' he said triumphantly, throwing the pencil down.

Tirza opened her mouth to say that the orchard trees were a long way from the cow barn, then she shut it again.

'Initials,' said Miss Susanna.

After their artistic efforts, the soldiers began to relax. Yes, they could just manage another piece of cake and some more coffee, and when Miss Catherine brought in a strawberry shortcake smothered in cream, the Boston ladies' first party for the visiting heroes came to a satisfying climax.

After they left the Penhaligons' house, Tirza and Sandy went round to Schoolhouse Lane and started up the rough ground towards Christina's wood. Sandy seemed rested after sitting and was only limping a little.

'Are those blueberries?' said Sandy, pointing to a cluster of growth below them, where the ground was green and boggy.

'No, those are cranberries. Haven't you ever seen cranberries?'

'I don't think they grow in Britain.'

'Those are OK, but we have much better ones in our marsh. They're not ready yet. These are blueberries, just ahead of us.'

'Right, I see. They're like the ones on the island.'

He stood still, breathing heavily. 'Is it far to Mrs O'Neill's house?'

'Not far. But here, you better lean on me.'

When they reached the cabin there was a thin wisp of smoke rising from the chimney, but Christina was sitting outside in the clearing above the cliff shelling peas. Tirza introduced Sandy, and Christina set aside the bowl of peas before she took his hand. She looked keenly into his eyes.

'So you are the young man from Scotland. My father came from the Highlands. I see you are in pain. Won't you come inside?'

She led Sandy into the cabin, still holding him by the hand, and made him sit on the edge of the long cedar linen chest which she kept covered with a rug to make a seat. While Tirza wandered around picking up books and examining the latest pressed wildflowers, Christine took him through the details of his injuries and the treatment he had received.

'Well.' She tossed her greying braids over her shoulders. 'I'm going to have to look at both those legs. Get your pants off.'

Sandy looked startled, and glanced at Tirza. Christina laughed.

'Tirza has spent half her life on the farm; bare legs won't worry her. But if you're over-modest, go into my bedroom. There's a towel there you can wrap around yourself.'

Sandy did as he was told, and came limping back, clutching a towel around his hips.

'Lie down there,' Christina commanded, 'and stretch out your legs.'

Tirza, stealing a glance sideways, was shocked by the terrible red gashes across Sandy's legs, puckered as if gathering threads had been run through them at irregular intervals and drawn tight. The new skin, fragile as petals, was shiny.

'It was the torn metal that did this, I suppose,' said Christina.

Sandy nodded, looking awkward and uncomfortable lying there. 'And the impact broke bones in several places, though the last X-ray showed them healing all right.'

Christina knelt down on the floor beside him. She closed her eyes and ran her hands over his legs from thigh to calf, probing the muscles and bending each knee. Then she cupped each heel in the palm of her hand in turn and rotated the ankle. Sandy winced occasionally, especially when she massaged the muscles at the back of his calves.

With a click of her tongue, she got up and took down some bundles of dried leaves which were hanging from pegs in the rafters.

'Put the kettle on, will you, Tirza? And pick me some fresh sage from the garden.'

When boiling water was poured on to a selection of leaves Christina had pounded in an earthenware bowl, an aromatic steam filled the cabin. Sandy breathed it in deeply. Even the smell made him feel better. He was not sure what he was expecting – rattle dances, mumbo-jumbo? This dignified, middle-aged woman was not at all what he had pictured. Her only eccentricities seemed to be a habit of going barefoot, like Tirza, and her decision to live alone in the woods. He lay back, less tense now than when he was waiting to see what she was going to do. Much of the cabin was lined with bookshelves, he noticed. It was clear where Tirza had caught the habit of reading.

'Now,' said Christina. 'This has cooled a little, but we must lay it on as hot as you can bear, just so long as we don't scald you.'

She began to coat his legs with the pulpy mass, which felt unbearably hot at first, but soon imparted no more than a comforting, deep-penetrating heat. Over the poultice she laid moss, and then took a length of surgical bandage from Tirza and wound it round everything to keep it in place. Sandy started to wonder how he was going to make his way back to the hotel wearing nothing but his shirt and underpants, a towel and two huge, white-bandaged legs.

As if she had read his thoughts, Christina fixed him with a humorous eye.

'Don't worry. It would be better if you kept these on all night, but I'll take them off when they're cold, and give you some salve to rub in when you go to bed tonight. You can stay long enough to eat supper with us, can't you?'

'Yes,' said Sandy, sinking back and enjoying the warmth and softness of the dressings. 'That's very kind of you.'

Christina pinned the end of the last bandage in place and wiped her hands on a towel. She looked down at the young, strained face.

'Put a blanket over him, child,' she said to Tirza. 'I hope he'll sleep for a while. Then come outside and help me finish those peas.'

Tirza fetched a blanket from Christina's bedroom. Sandy's trousers and socks were lying neatly folded on the bed. The blanket was one of the old Indian ones, frayed at the corners but rich with patterns which held meanings hidden from her. Sandy was breathing deeply, his dark lashes lying still on his cheeks. Tirza felt an unexpected rush of tenderness as she tucked the blanket carefully over him. People looked younger when they were asleep. He might have been no older than Simon. Then she went outside to help Christina.

By the time supper was ready and the smell of grilled herring and corn stirabout filled the cabin, Sandy began to wake up. Tirza came over with a cushion in her hand and smiled at him.

'Now you're just to sit up carefully.' She wedged the cushion at the end of the chest where it met the wall, and helped him into a sitting position so he could lean against it.

'Why, Mrs O'Neill,' he said, 'I believe I'm feeling better already.'

Tirza passed him a tray of food and he started to eat hungrily.

'Please call me Christina.' She had wound her braids at the nape of her neck and looked more formal now. 'I hope it will give you some relief and start the healing process. Your muscles were very tense and knotted. And there are torn ligaments that will take some time to heal. I'm afraid you'll be limping for a good few weeks yet. I think you should come back in a couple of days. Come in the morning, so we can leave the poultices on for longer.'

'I always wondered whether there was something in this herbal medicine.'

'Oh, yes,' she said dryly. 'Herbs have wonderful therapeutic powers that most people have forgotten in this modern age of chemical medicines. Did you know that the properties of aspirin were known to the Indians? They derived it from the bark of the silver birch. I wish I knew more about the uses of herbs and other plants. Pennyroyal, bergamot, thoroughwort – they all have excellent properties. Arnica. Camomile. But I'm ignorant about so many of them. Southernwood I know only for its lemon scent, which lasts for months, folded amongst linen. And of course it was given as a pledge of love.'

She grinned. 'Whether for its permanence or for its astringency, I'm not sure. My mother taught me what little I know, but I'm afraid that, like so many youngsters, I was rather scornful of my parents' skills and heedless of what they could teach me. I thought my future lay elsewhere.'

'Tirza tells me you studied law at Vassar.'

'I did. That was enough to show me that I'd been following a naive daydream. I thought I would be able to fight for the cause of justice and protect the innocent. But when I came to realise I might just as often be called upon to defend the wicked, and exercise persuasive arguments on their behalf, I lost the taste for it. By the time I came back here, both my parents were dead, so I had sacrificed a great deal for a misguided ambition.'

After their meal, Christina removed the poultices from one leg and Tirza from the other. Tirza noticed that the skin was a better colour. The newly healed scars were no longer so red and angry looking, and the flesh seemed firmer and more healthy. She laid her palm against Sandy's thigh, where the worst of the scars cut a jagged line down to his knee. The skin felt pleasantly warm now.

'Does it feel better?' she asked.

'Much better.' He grinned at Christina. 'You may not be a tribal medicine man, but you seem to have healed me.'

Tirza was afraid her grandmother might be offended, but she only laughed.

'Go and put your clothes on, you young rascal, and Tirza can take you home.'

Chapter 12

Maine: Summer 1942

THE MORNING BEFORE Independence Day, Tirza got up as usual at five o'clock, dressed, and let herself quietly out of the house on the wharf side. However, she did not go as usual to pick up her bucket of baited crab line and row her dory round to the cove below Christina's forest. Instead she climbed the path over the promontory south of Flamboro and took the cliff path alongside the Tremayne place towards Libby's Beach. Had anyone observed her, they might have noticed a certain furtiveness about the way she glanced over her shoulder at the sleeping town before she disappeared from sight behind the clump of birches at the point where the path levelled out and followed the narrow strip of rock between the Tremaynes' land and the precipitous cliffs.

No one, however, was watching. Danny and Jim, who were coming to the end of the most wearisome watch at the gun platform, from 10 p.m. to 6 a.m., had a desultory eye on the sea, but the lack of activity offshore had robbed their spells of duty of any interest and they spent their time in somnolent inactivity. There had been light enough for them to scan the ocean through their binoculars for about an hour now, though looking east into a sun rising through sea mist dazzled their eyes and confused their perceptions. What seemed to be likely black shapes on the horizon reproduced themselves on the front of Flett's Stores below them on Shore Road, or danced elusively from the schoolhouse roof to the sloping garden of the Penhaligon house, betraying themselves as negative spectres of the sun imprinted on their eyeballs.

They yawned and stretched and cursed the length of the watch, and sipped at their scummy tin mugs of cold coffee and lit another cigarette from the burning stub of its predecessor, and swore that they had the most God-forsaken duty of the whole God-damned war.

The spots on the horizon which were not a trick of the sun were the now-familiar outlines of the offshore fishing fleet, heading home, but Tirza was long gone before the fishermen were near enough to shore to notice her making her way purposefully towards the foxholes, which drew a dotted line marking the division between the granite ledges of the beach on the one side and the lush grasses, scattered with brackish pools and interspersed with wild cranberries, which formed the marsh on the other.

Nor did any of the lobstermen see her. They were swimming up from sleep, but slowly. On long, easy summer days they could take their time, stretching out the working day with the sun. They yawned and turned over, or groped with bony feet for carpet slippers and wandered down to the smell of bacon and eggs frying.

No one observed her from the Penhaligon house. The three sisters slept more lightly now in old age, but each preserved the fiction of sleeping in order to spare the concern of the others. Miss Susanna kept a thermos of tea in her room, which she measured out sparingly during the night whenever the pain woke her. Miss Catherine, who slept better than the others during the dark winters, found herself restive on light summer mornings, and would creep down to the kitchen before six to start coffee percolating, where she would be joined half an hour later by Miss Molly, who kept up the pretence by feigning surprise at finding Kitty there, at being there herself, at the clock for telling what must surely be the wrong time.

In the Mansion House Hotel, guests and staff were still sleeping, and no one took a quick glance at the morning from any of the few side windows which overlooked the length of the beach stretching away from the base of Todd's Neck, so Tirza was unseen also from here. In his room facing east toward the ocean, perched above the steep cliff which ended in a tumble of ragged rocks, Sandy had spent an undisturbed night for the first time since his crash. Whatever Christina had put into her poultice and the cream he had applied later, it had eased the pain enough to allow him to sleep.

Even Pierre, in the best of the staff bedrooms, would not wake for another hour. The Mansion House began serving breakfast at the civilised hour of eight o'clock. Unlike the fishermen's houses in Flamboro and the farms inland, the hotel was silent, with no stirring, no early risers.

Tirza could not be seen from the Libbys' farm, because once she reached the junction of the coastal path with the farm track, she turned away from the fields and followed the sandy path to the beach. It zigzagged down between banks of sweet briar which scrambled over the projecting rocks and were warmed by the early sun to a fine heady perfume. The smooth silver sand of Libby's Beach was fringed with a scalloped edging of translucent clam shells and the mysterious whorls from the interiors of broken snail shells, and in the low early light Tirza could see bubbles breaking up through the wet strip left by the receding tide. Below the revealing bubbles lived short-necks and blue clams in such profusion that she could have dug them up from the sand with her toes.

No one saw Tirza, which was as well, because she was about to do something she would never have done for herself. She was about to commit theft.

She had made her choice of foxhole. Not at the beginning of the line, and not at the end, because, she reasoned, these were the ones Irvine and Tommy and the others were likely to pay most attention to. Halfway along the line they would be sauntering, lighting a cigarette, busy talking. She had seen them often enough. And there was one particular foxhole... She found it again with satisfaction, climbing up the sharp ledges of granite with the skill of practice. If you placed your foot unwarily, the knife-edged layers of rock could cut into a bare foot like butter. But if you climbed crabwise, placing each foot on familiar small niches and plateaux in the rocks, your flesh met only the ancient flat surfaces of the layers.

The foxhole she had selected had been sited carelessly, too close to the boggy ground, and the marsh was already sucking it away from underneath. Below her feet as she perched on the edge of the hole looking down she could see the sandbagged sides bowing inwards, starting to collapse. On the seaward side the raised parapet was sagging to the left and sliding almost imperceptibly into the hole. She examined the top layer of sandbags. Several were poorly woven, with ugly irregular threads distorting the fabric. Another was marked by a large black stain the shape of Texas. Two more seemed suitable.

With some difficulty, she heaved one of the big sacks over to examine the underneath. There was a small snagged patch. It might be possible to mend it. Sand trickled from the bag over her toes and was lost in the bottom of the foxhole. The tops of the bags were not secured. She had thought they might be sewn or tied in some way, and had made sure her knife was in the pocket of her shorts before she set off, but the tops of the bags were simply twisted and tucked under, the whole structure kept in place by one sandbag leaning on another. What appeared to be solid was nothing but shifting, unreliable sand, momentarily held in place by a fragile casing of loose burlap, but ready to collapse and slither away at a touch. For the blink of an eye, Tirza was seized with the joyful notion of setting the whole deceptive mile-long rampart sliding into oblivion, like a child's sandcastle overtaken by the tide. Then she saw that, pleasing though this might be, it would destroy – in the very moment of triumph – the effectiveness of her plan, which was to steal and remain unnoticed.

She turned over the second good sandbag. The burlap was even, unmarked, unsnagged. Perfect. She heaved the bag away from the foxhole to the top of the ledges and aimed the open end at the beach, then she hitched up the bottom so that the sand cascaded down. It stood out, a different colour, darker than the fine dry sand abutting on the base of the ledges. Probably the sand from the bag was damp, holding the rain from two nights ago at its centre. The remaining bags on the parapet she dragged around a little to disguise the fact that one had been removed, but the whole structure was so precarious she was afraid of pulling it all down. No one, she was sure, would notice the gap. She picked up the empty sandbag and jumped down on to the beach. A few well-aimed kicks dispersed the darker sand till it was barely visible, and the rising sun would soon dry it out.

Tirza held up the empty bag and scrutinised it. If it was opened out flat, it looked plenty large enough for Miss Susanna's rug. She gave it another shake, to get rid of the last of the sand, then folded it up and tucked it under her arm. Time she was turning back and getting out her crab line if she was to catch anything in time for her mid-morning delivery to the hotel.

◆◇◆

Tobias had been elected once again to head the committee organising the Independence Day party, and he was determined that, war or no war, everyone was going to have a day to remember. Even in his boyhood at the turn of the century the people of Flamboro and the surrounding farms had gathered on Libby's Beach for the celebrations, so by long custom the Libby family were, in a manner of speaking, the hosts for the event. The essential elements had hardly changed in the last forty years: races and games on the sands for the youngsters during the day, a big campfire lit ceremonially at noon and kept going till after dark, a clam-bake and hot dog roast, and after sunset fireworks let off from a roped area of the beach by a responsible group of men. The big rockets, aimed out over the sea, brought everything to a spectacular close about ten o'clock.

There had been trouble this year about the campfire. It might be a breach of the new wartime regulations to have a fire burning at night which could serve as a beacon for enemy ships. Tobias had been obliged to visit the army base and plead the case for the Independence Day campfire.

'Seems to me,' he had said bluntly, confronting a dubious-looking officer, 'that we're in this war to defend the whole notion of what we're celebrating on the Fourth – freedom of the individual, freedom from tyranny. If Hitler can stop us celebrating Independence Day on a beach in Maine, just by being there, over in Europe, almost looks like he's got us licked already.'

He had been referred to another officer, and then to a third, bringing out the same argument each time, standing squarely before them, a solid, determined man in overalls and blunt, heavy work boots, until eventually they realised they would never get rid of him until they gave in. It was a victory of a kind.

The second problem was obtaining fireworks. He had scoured local suppliers – who told him there was a war on – and had driven to Portland and Augusta and Rockland and Kennebunk, gathering fireworks one by one until he had enough to make a good show. The more difficult the quest, the more grimly determined Tobias became to make this the greatest Fourth of July celebration Flamboro had ever seen.

All the planning and arguing and searching occupied his mind, helping to crowd out the black depression which had been settling there. When the news had first come that Will had been shot down, Tobias – unreasonably, he now saw – had clung on to the belief that it was all a mistake, that Will was just missing in action. He had always believed he was as ready as the next fellow to confront trouble and deal with it. But somehow the scrap of telegraph paper arriving that night had seemed unreal to him. He had been totally unable to connect it with any sense of Will as a person, a tall, thin young man, balding early, grave and kind, who had always seemed older than his years.

When Martha became hysterical that night, his main reaction had been one of annoyance. The stoical women of his family had never behaved in such a way. He already disapproved of her dating the army officers. An innate fatalism now began to whisper to him that if Martha had lost her husband, she had brought it on herself. As the weeks went by and it was borne in on him that Will really had been killed, he found his emotions dulled and numb. He even began to look upon Martha's witless flight at the first sound of a passing plane as some maddening but unavoidable natural phenomenon.

Lately, he had become aware of other things. Harriet was looking tired. Tobias would have been the first to admit that while he noticed every detail of change on his land or in his stock, he was inclined to take his wife for granted. Thinking back over the last months, he remembered her, bright-eyed and rosy in the frosty air up at Gooseneck Lake on the day of the skating party. And laughing, licking sticky fingers at the sugaring-off party over to Frank's place. Since then, fine lines had appeared on her face, and her eyes looked dull. Even he had noticed that she moved more slowly, as though her body hurt her, though she continued to do much of the milking, tended the chickens and helped in the fields when needed, as well as looking after the big farmhouse with only Patience Warren's help. Billy and Martha had made a lot more work for her, he knew. More cooking, more washing, more cleaning. Now she was well into the summer canning. No wonder she was tired. He was tired himself.

And there was Simon. The boy had always been reliable in the past, doing his chores without too much chasing, working on the farm during the busy seasons unquestioningly. Now he was forever disappearing, leaving his chores half done, avoiding the haymaking and the hoeing of the turnip and cabbage fields. Yesterday he had even complained about taking salt to the young heifers in the field over by Swansons, a job he had always loved since he was a small boy. Tirza was putting in more work on the farm this summer than Simon.

Tobias had never thought much about Simon's friendship with Tirza. The cousins had grown up like brother and sister, and he knew Abigail considered this had turned Tirza into a tomboy. Tobias wasn't so sure. He reckoned that would have happened anyway. It was in Tirza's nature. He'd never before considered what influence Tirza might have on Simon. Now the boy had no time for Tirza and was constantly hanging out around the soldiers. It made Tobias uneasy. Not that he had anything against the GIs. They were just young men a long way from home, but some of them were kind of rough, and he suspected they were filling Simon's head with wrong notions. And he had caught a scent off the boy. Tobias had a highly developed sense of smell. It was one of the first warnings he had when one of the animals was falling sick. He could pick up a difference in the scent of the beast. It was the same with his son. He knew that the boy was smoking and drinking beer, however much he tried to disguise it with those peppermints. He hadn't wanted to worry Harriet with the knowledge, but it was one more burden he was carrying around.

※

A few days before the Fourth, Tobias had been in Flett's, explaining to Charlie how much still needed to be done.

'Spent so much time wrastling with the army and chasing all over the state looking for fireworks, I've done nothing yet about the campfire,' he said, half in complaint, half in apology.

'Maybe I can help,' said Julia Bennett, who was at the next counter with Mary, examining a sprigged cotton for a blouse. Her eyes were bright. A letter had come that morning from Pete – his ship was safely in port for repairs, and she had just mailed off a reply from the post office end of the store.

'A lot of the schoolchildren are at loose ends this summer,' she said. 'When they aren't working with the fish or on the farms, they don't have much to do. Now the bus service has been cut back because of gas rationing, they can't get to Portland for the movies, and there doesn't seem to be much in Flamboro for them.'

She smiled at Tobias.

'I can round up any number of them to collect wood for the campfire. Where do you usually get it, and where do you want the fire built?'

'The kids can show you where we build the fire,' said Tobias. 'Same place as always. There's a kind of semicircle of rocks that makes a natural windbreak. We pick up all the driftwood we can find, and bring fallen branches from the woods beyond Flamboro. You need to ask Christina O'Neill's permission first. The wood belongs to her. And you can borrow my logging scoot.'

Charlie offered to take charge of the clam-bake. Everybody would be out with buckets, shovels, clam rakes and forks on the Fourth, digging clams till they had enough. But someone was needed to set up the bake itself, make sure it was built so it wouldn't fall over, provide the tarpaulin, and collect enough seaweed to pack in layers with the clams to keep the steam in and add flavour.

————◆◆◆————

Tobias still had a million things to do, and went down to the beach straight after milking on the morning of Independence Day to check on the campfire. To his surprise he found Charlie there before him, already digging out a pit for the clam-bake about ten yards further along the beach. Together they inspected the construction of the campfire.

'Not bad,' Tobias conceded. 'Reckon that'll burn up all right.'

'She's no fool, that girl,' said Charlie. 'She got the kids to pile the extra fuel round behind the rocks away from the sparks. Should be plenty to keep it going long enough.'

They poked at the carefully built wigwam of logs which reached above their heads. It stood firm. Most of it was fallen wood from Christina's forest, hauled all the way to the beach by Julia Bennett's team. Here and there the darker clumps of fir and pine were interspersed with the bleached-bone colour of drift-wood. One piece rose from the apex of the pile like an out-stretched arm, its polished contours rippling under the sunlight like the muscles of an athlete. Near the base of the pile Tobias could make out some pieces of broken fish box, gone overboard from a trawler, and a huge shattered timber, nine or ten inches square in section and nearly eight feet long, which had once formed part of a sizeable ship.

'Ayuh.' He was satisfied. 'It'll do. I calculate your Pete's done all right for himself with that schoolteacher of his.'

Charlie grunted. He found he was uncharacteristically super-stitious these days. He did not want to talk about the future for fear of ill-wishing it. He turned back to his pit.

'We'll line this with stones now, shall we? Then there'll be less to do later. Give me a hand to fetch them over from the pile by the ledges. That's where we left them last year.'

—◦◦◦—

'So what goes on at this Independence Day party, Monsieur Lamotte?' asked Sandy. He was breakfasting alone on the veranda of the Mansion House before the rest of the guests stirred. Pierre had personally brought the grilled trout to the table and stayed to gossip. He shrugged.

'They run about on the sand and throw rusty 'orseshoes at a post, then they eat overcooked clams and watch a few fireworks. Nothing of any interest to you, Monsieur.'

'You sound very sour about it. Aren't you in favour? It's a bit like Bastille Day, isn't it? They celebrate throwing us out of America and you celebrate throwing your kings out of France. You must share some common feeling.'

Pierre shrugged again.

'Me, I see no point in ruining the digestion with shellfish which could be transformed with proper care and a good sauce. It gives me pain to see the waste.'

'But I heard some of the Flamboro ladies provide other edibles as well.'

Pierre tucked in the corners of his mouth sardonically.

'*Eh, bien.* Edible they may be, for those with taste-buds like the flannel of a lumberjack's shirt.'

Sandy laughed. 'Come now, you're surely not jealous? And I believe you even have the day off, with most of the guests going to the beach party. Isn't Matthew going to cope in the kitchen on his own?'

'It will do 'im good to take responsibility for once. It is part of 'is training.'

'So what are you going to do on your day off? Do you have a little lady friend in Flamboro or Portland?'

Pierre looked offended.

'My fiancée is in Montreal, Monsieur. I do not betray 'er.'

'Well, come with me to the beach party, then, and we'll sample the clams together. In fact, you could even show your generosity by contributing to the feast. I'm sure the hotel management would approve. An act of good will towards the locals. One of your famous desserts...?'

Pierre shook his head, laughing ruefully.

'You are outrageous, Monsieur. I 'ave told you the clams are dreadful, sandy and overcooked. And the *potage* of the local women – old-fashioned peasant stuff.'

'You'll come, then.'

'*Tiens*, it will be for amusement only.'

<hr>

Miss Molly opened the back door to let Sir Percy out into the garden for his morning stroll. He was an exceptionally large black cat with a white shirt front and a good opinion of himself. In the first dewy morning he enjoyed a quiet saunter down the steps, a peaceful investigation of the boundaries of his domain and, if the sun was right, a short nap on the roof of the lumber shed. This morning, aware of an atmosphere of more activity than normal in the kitchen, he took his time stepping over the threshold, so that Miss Molly was obliged to stand waiting, holding the screen door against its spring hinge to stop it snapping shut on his tail. When he reckoned he had made his point, he stepped forward. It was unwise to try her patience too far, or she would scoop him up in an undignified position and deposit him on the grass.

As he lowered his gaze to the second step, a great brown fuzzy thing caught his eye, and he recoiled, making a faint 'eek' noise. Then, recovering himself, he jumped down and sat disdainfully on it.

'Heavens, Percy, what have we here?' asked Miss Molly, easing his portly backside over on to the step and pulling the object from beneath him. She shook it out and fine dry sand cascaded over him, some of it getting in his eyes. Outraged, Sir Percy shook his head and shot off the steps to take refuge under an azalea.

'Look at this, Kitty.'

Miss Molly held up her find. Miss Catherine looked round from spooning coffee into the percolator.

'What is it?'

'A rather sandy burlap sack. Neatly folded and left on our back step. Bearing a stamp saying *US Government Property*.'

Miss Catherine put down her spoon and fingered the sack.

'The sand will soon wash out, and with the seams unpicked...'

'Just what I was thinking. Susanna can hook her patchwork rug after all.'

Miss Catherine began to make toast.

'It will probably be her last one.' Her voice shook, but she went on laying the breakfast for the two of them, and a tray for their sister.

'I know.' Miss Molly caught hold of her hand and pressed it lightly. 'She knows that too. Someone very kind has made it possible for her.'

'Take it and show her,' Miss Catherine urged. 'She was feeling very down last night.'

'I will.' Miss Molly laughed suddenly. 'Sand and all.'

As the sound of her feet went sturdily upstairs, Miss Catherine felt the sand left on her hand by her sister. She rolled the grains between her fingers, looking out of the window.

'I wonder who,' she said to herself.

◆◆◆

By ten o'clock Tirza had lifted her crab lines, delivered early to the hotel and sailed back to Flamboro without staying to talk to

229

Pierre. There was too much of interest going on in Flamboro today. She joined Wayne, Simon, and Wayne's older sister Clarice on the back steps of the Pelhams' house. Mrs Pelham passed them out a plate of cookies and a jug of grape Kool-Aid. The cookies, part of a batch she was baking for the party, had charred along one side, so she told them they could have the better bits to eat. She had no intention of producing damaged goods in front of the other women at the picnic. Tirza picked the burnt edges off her cookie and threw them to the gulls which stood in a line along the fence. They swooped, screaming and jostling as though she had thrown them a bucket of herring. Maybe they were being sarcastic. She took a drink of her Kool-Aid. Mrs Pelham never mixed it up properly, so that gritty lumps remained undissolved which you had to squash against the roof of your mouth where they released intense bursts of flavour.

Simon and Wayne were arguing about which of them would win the 200-yard race in the afternoon.

'Bet you a dollar I win,' said Wayne.

'It's a deal,' said Simon. 'I can beat you easy, any day.'

'Boys!' said Clarice contemptuously to Tirza. 'Whadda you bet somebody else wins. Morton Harris is as fast as either of them. Wastin' their money.'

'Hmph,' said Tirza. She wasn't much interested.

'So why aren't you chasin' after that English flyer today?' said Clarice. Her voice was acid. 'I declare, you make an exhibition of yourself, Tirza Libby.'

Tirza turned round slowly. She could feel heat rising in her face as if a fire had been lit under her chin.

'What did you say?'

'You heard me. All the girls in town have bin talkin' about it. I'd be ashamed,' said Clarice virtuously, as if she did not spend every Friday and Saturday night jiving at the Schooner Bar.

Tirza said nothing, but she put her glass of Kool-Aid down on the step and began to bite on her thumbnail.

'He's much too old for you,' Clarice said loftily. 'He's thirty if he's a day. He must be *mortified* at the way you carry on.'

Simon had overheard her, for he turned around and stared, then he laughed.

'Don't be a dope, Clarice. Tirza just took him sailing a couple of times, and they went to see Christina O'Neill. You only have one thing on your mind.'

'Sakes, Simon, I don't know what you mean.'

Clarice, Wayne and Simon all exchanged a knowing look, then fixed their gaze pityingly on Tirza. Abruptly she got up and walked away, sticking her hands in the back pockets of her shorts and whistling one of her father's aimless airs. She felt clumsy and humiliated, half understanding what they were talking about, but pushing it away from her mind.

⋖⋗

'It will do just fine,' said Miss Susanna. She had unpicked the side and bottom seams of the sandbag and Miss Catherine had washed it. They laid it out in the sun on the grass to dry, where it steamed gently. 'There's even enough spare to turn the edges under. It was Tirza, of course.'

'Do you think so?' Miss Molly said.

'Oh, yes.'

'You're probably right. The combination of audacity and kindness suggests our Tirza.'

'It should be dry enough by mid-morning for me to mark out the pattern before we leave for the party.'

'Susanna! You're never planning on going.'

'Of course I am. I've not missed an Independence Day party in my life, and I'm not fixing on doing so now. That nice Captain Tucker is going to collect all three of us in his jeep at eleven and drive us round through Libby's Farm and down to the ledges. I won't need to walk but a few hundred yards.'

'I don't know...' said Miss Molly.

'Of course she should go,' Miss Catherine said. 'We don't get that many chances to have fun at our age. We'll take three of the folding garden chairs and we'll do just fine.'

⋖⋗

Martha had decided she would, after all, go to the party. She kept changing her mind until the very morning. She had not been out in company since Will's death, but she had visited the beach several times with Captain Tucker in his off-duty hours, and she knew she looked good in her new two-piece swimsuit. Lately she had begun to crave attention and admiration again.

Otherwise, she would have to stay in the empty farmhouse while her family and Patience, and even Sam, spent the day eating and playing games and watching fireworks. The thought of being cooped up alone in the house while all the township was enjoying itself was too much for her. Grudgingly, as if she was doing them a favour, she told her parents she would come – for a little while, anyhow.

She chose her outfit with care. Underneath, she would wear her swimsuit, for sunbathing. It wasn't likely she would swim. She had agreed to go in once or twice with Captain Tucker, but the sea was freezing and today it would be full of kids screaming and fooling around. Over her swimsuit she put on an outfit of shorts and a little square top made of pink seersucker and trimmed with white. The shorts were *very* short and showed off her long legs, and the gap between the shorts and the brief top revealed glimpses of her bronzed midriff as she moved. She brushed her long blonde hair till it gleamed, and then pinned the top hair over the net supports which raised it in two large rolls above her forehead. Carefully she scrutinised herself in the mirror. Last night she had painted her finger and toenails in a shocking pink which made them stand out when she ran her hands down the paler pink seersucker, smoothing it over her hips. She slipped her feet into sandals and put on a pair of sunglasses.

Though the kind of entertainment planned was not what she would have chosen for herself, Martha found she was looking forward to the day. Things seemed less black now. It was fun to have some freedom as if she was a girl again, to go out when she liked and not always be looking over her shoulder at what the other officers' wives might be thinking. Maine and her parents' home was boring beyond belief, but (something she kept to herself) life in married housing had begun to pall months ago, and she probably would have come up this summer anyway, just to get away from it. Will had been very kind, of course, but he was dull. For so many years her ambitions had all been focused on a huge white wedding. She had never really given a thought to what would come after. Within weeks of her honeymoon she had felt the first itch of discontent. Will was too bland, too admiring. She wanted a bit of excitement in her life. A bit of danger, even. When she had started going out with Will, it had seemed thrilling – his rich family, his big house in Boston, his long vacations at the Mansion House where he had invited her to meals involving more knives and forks than she had ever seen in her life before. But after her marriage all of that had become dreary, till her life felt just like a flat page from a magazine – apparently full of glossy life but as thin as paper.

When these thoughts skittered unbidden through her head, she would shiver suddenly, as if she had seen an omen of ill luck.

If only she could shake off the fears that came upon her, she would be all right, she would be fine. Sometimes in the night she would wake up sweating and shaking from a dream whose details fled at once, leaving nothing but a deep sense of menace. Worse was the sound of low-flying aeroplanes which patrolled the coast by day. In her saner moments, she knew she must look a fool, but blind terror seized her as soon as the thrumming of the engines filled her ears, blocking out everything else, even thought. It was like the nightmares suddenly made real, and she knew she must hide or go crazy.

<hr>

Harriet, packing up her baked goods with Patience in the kitchen, and fending off Billy, who had his fingers into everything, was feeling better than she had for weeks. It seemed like a good sign, Martha agreeing to go to the Independence Day celebrations, almost like old times, when she had been one of the shrieking children running races and toasting hot dogs over the campfire. Though there was still a shadow of unease at the back of her mind. To Harriet there was something unseemly about Martha going off to the beach with Captain Tucker. Oh, she had noticed it, all right! Martha might think she could fool her mother, but Harriet had known her too long, known that particular look of calculated innocence that meant Martha was up to something. Still and all, she was thankful they were past the stage of Martha locking herself away in her room. Will's death she tried not to think about.

Tobias was looking better, too, she thought. For a time after that awful night he had gone quiet, but the busy summer season on the farm kept him occupied in the fields, so that he had few moments for brooding. By the time he came in after evening milking and they had eaten their supper, there was only time to listen to the latest news broadcast before bed. The war news was universally grim, but at least it took their minds partly from their personal worries and made them feel a kind of companionship with the families of all the other boys.

She tried to pretend to herself, whenever she could, that nothing had happened. That Will was simply away somewhere. And sometimes, to her discomfort, she found herself forgetting about Will, no longer able to see his face properly in her memory. It was as though Martha and Billy had been living at the farm always, and Will was no more than an easily forgotten ripple in the course of their lives. She was horrified by her own callousness.

'How do I look?' said Martha. She stepped into the kitchen and twirled around, her flared shorts spinning out and showing her long brown legs. She looked cheerful and normal, like the teenage girl she had once been, enchanting all the young fishermen and farmers in the area.

'Fine!' Harriet said, too heartily.

'Can I have a cookie?' said Billy, pulling at Harriet's skirt and looking discontented. He was no longer as pasty-faced as he had been, but he had not lost the whining note to his voice.

'Once we're on our way,' said Harriet, brisk now. 'Grandpa and Simon have already gone down to the beach to see to all the arrangements, so we need you to help us carry the food. We'll have a cookie when we get to the top end of the turnip field.'

Billy looked slightly mollified. Most of the time he was in the way on the farm. Too young to join Simon and his friends and bored with hanging around the women in the house, he was constantly complaining, 'What can I *do*?'

The women and Billy set out with the baskets and buckets of food, leaving Sam to finish his chores and join them later. As they turned on to the track to the beach, Hector Swanson came up the drive with his wife and young baby, taking the shortcut through Libby's farm.

'Fine weather's holdin', Mrs Libby,' said Harold cheerfully, 'though they do say there's a storm coming up. Tail end of one of the hurricanes down Florida way.'

'Eh, well,' said Harriet. 'Long as the hurricanes themselves stay away. I'll not forget '38 in a hurry.'

Halfway along the track, at the top of the turnip field, Harriet handed round oatmeal cookies to encourage Billy, and they met Simon coming back towards the house.

'I'm getting a couple more shovels to dig for clams,' he said through a mouthful. 'And our old clam rake. Ben's broken the handle of his, and some of the soldiers are there too, wanting to help.'

At the junction with the coast path four jeeps were parked on the torn and rutted ground, and when they climbed down between the briar roses they could see groups busy digging for clams, gathering seaweed for the clam-bake and laying out food on cloths in the shelter of the petrified trees.

'What are those people doing on the rocks?' said Martha. 'Isn't that the Cannucks with the summer house in Flamboro?'

'Sakes,' said Harriet, setting down her burdens and pressing her hands against the small of her back, 'I do believe they're collecting snails. Mary says those Frenchies *eat* them, common slimy snails off the rocks. I couldn't fancy it myself.'

'Morning,' said Nathan, coming past with a bucket of clams to rinse in the sea. His bare feet, projecting from his rolled-up trousers, were white beside Martha's suntan. 'They *are* collecting snails. I'm surprised the Cannucks want to come to the Independence Day party, but it seems they don't hold it against us.'

'They don't expect us to eat the snails too, do they?'

'Shouldn't think so. They're building another small campfire over there, to boil the snails, and they've been gathering wild garlic to eat with them.'

'Ugh!' said Patience and Martha together, and grinned at each other, for once almost friendly. Then Martha dropped her bucket of cakes and pies and strolled off to join Captain Tucker and his friends. Patience knelt on the sand and began to unpack the food on to the rugs laid out by Mary Flett and Josie Pelham.

'Where's Tirza?' Harriet said.

'Gone to fetch that British airman from the Mansion House,' Nathan said. 'She's bringing him round to the beach in *Stormy Petrel*, so he doesn't have to climb over the rocks from Todd's Neck.'

'You don't think...' said Harriet.

'What?'

'That maybe she's spending too much time with him? He's a very good-looking young man. I thought she might be...'

Nathan laughed. 'Our Tirza? She's a good little fisherman and a hard worker. She isn't like these silly girls who are always running after the fellows. No, she's just made a kind of pet of him. Like a favourite dog.'

'Hmm.'

More people were arriving from Flamboro now, and Harriet abandoned the subject.

<hr />

'The Fourth of July,' said Tirza sternly, 'celebrates our independence from England. When we broke away and became a nation.' Her voice was emphatic. 'If you are coming, you'd better remember that.'

They had rounded the end of Todd's Neck and were heading in towards the beach. It was swarming with people. The whole population of Flamboro had turned out, and the farming families from miles around. A line of visitors from the Mansion House was snaking down the tumbled rocks at the southern end of the beach, and as they watched another group of soldiers arrived, their voices loud enough to be heard even over the crash of the waves.

'Oh, I will,' Sandy assured her. 'I have to tell you, there are people in Scotland who'd like to regain their independence from England.'

'What do you mean?'

'We used to be an independent sovereign nation, with our own king and our own parliament.'

'I didn't know that.'

'So I won't be offended or tactless.'

'OK. Now stay put while I pull her up on the beach, then I'll give you a hand.'

'I can manage now. Just let me get my legs over the side at my own speed.'

<hr />

It must have been about noon, with the tide just beginning to run out and the first of the hot dogs, speared on straightened coat hangers, sizzling over the campfire, when Ben Flett said,

'What's that ship gettin' up to?'

Only a few people nearby heard him. The younger children were running races, shrieking along the wet sand like a crowd of demented gulls. One or two heads turned to look where he pointed. Nathan frowned and shaded his eyes with his hand.

'It's a US navy ship. Is it one of those landing craft? It's got that squared-off bow.'

Walter screwed up his eyes and looked.

'Reckin it's comin' in. They won't be tryin' to land here, surely?'

The men watched in silence as the ship headed on a course directly towards them.

'I don't know what their draught is,' said Nathan, 'but that's some old shallow just off there...'

As he spoke, they all saw the shudder which ran through the ship.

Ben jumped to his feet.

'She's touched.'

'Damn fools,' Walter said.

In the next few minutes the rest of the townsfolk on the beach became aware of what was happening offshore. The landing craft seemed to free herself for a moment, then grounded again, well out from the beach where a sand bar reached a long way into the ocean. The sand lay silted over one of the ancient mountain ridges which formed part of the underwater land-scape. A little to the south or north, the naval ship would have been able to come in much closer without touching. Soldiers could be seen standing around uncertainly on deck, some of them peering apprehensively at the long drop down into the sea. Even while everyone watched, the waves curling on to the shore were receding. There was a strong ebb tide running, and the drop here was more than twenty feet.

The observers on shore saw the bow of the boat – a flat door like the back of a removal truck – drop down into the water, raising a splash as high as the deck. It led down from the ship like a ramp, its lower end hidden below the sea. Down this the soldiers made their way, some swaggering, some hesitantly, into the waist-high surf. Holding their rifles above their heads they waded ashore.

'Wonder what they're thinkin' to do now,' Eli said.

The soldiers milled about, their drab uniforms swirling into the holiday clothes of the party-goers like brown sugar stirred into some exotic drink. Within minutes they had been absorbed into the crowd. It was perhaps between twenty minutes and half an hour since the landing craft had first shivered against the sand bar, and already she was standing awkwardly out of the sea, listing a little to port as the tide sucked away from her sides.

'Well,' Nathan said.

'She'll be stuck there best part of twelve hours now,' said Ben.

'Ayuh. Somebody's going to be in mighty trouble.'

The officers of the ship were keeping out of sight on the bridge, but the soldiers were laughing and piling their rifles up on the ledges out of the sand, happy to make the most of the unplanned vacation.

'Hey,' a dapper young GI said to Ben, 'is this a Fourth of July party?'

'Sure is. Won't you join us?'

'You bet. What's that steaming heap of seaweed and tarpaulin?'

'Clam-bake. If you and your buddies are hungry, we'd better get you digging for more clams.'

'Sure. Lead on.'

It was not long before a second clam-bake was constructed and the pungent odour of hot clams and seaweed drifted along the beach. The soldiers stripped to the waist and ran races against the men of Flamboro. Then someone brought a rope and lined up a tug of war. By the time everyone was eating clams and bowls of Miss Catherine's home-made Boston baked beans, it would have been difficult to separate townsfolk and summer people from soldiers. The French Canadians found some of the GIs willing to try their boiled snails. They sat in a circle round the iron pot with bent pins to excavate the snails from their shells and a dish of melted butter and garlic to dip them in. Even Mrs Larrabee, who had spent a year in Quebec as a young woman, tried the snails and declared them tasty, but no one else from Flamboro was prepared to risk it.

After dinner, which stretched on till four o'clock, most people sat around too full for energetic activity. Some of the younger children fell asleep on rugs in the shade of clumps of rock, and Miss Susanna, stretched out on a deck chair under a big golf umbrella, put back her head and closed her eyes. A few of the men had set up a game of horseshoes, and the only sounds on the beach were the soft murmur of voices and the metallic ring of the horseshoes striking each other or the goal post.

Tirza lay flat on her back with her legs in the sun and her head in the shade of the petrified trees. She had eaten so much her stomach felt stretched, and she had decided to keep very still until the overeaten feeling went away. She opened one eye to look at the horseshoe players and saw Simon throwing, his shape bordered by multicoloured lines that shimmered and danced around him, making him look as insubstantial as the rainbow on a waterfall. She closed her eyes again. Near her feet, Sandy was sitting with his sticks on the sand beside him and his arms around his drawn-up knees. He was talking to Pierre and one of the soldiers so quietly that she could only catch an occasional word, but she heard 'Hitler' and 'Churchill'. War talk. The rest of her family were off to the left, at the end of the beach nearer the farm, but Tirza was staying near *Stormy Petrel*, to keep an eye on her.

With the heat and the food, she felt herself drifting off, but somewhere, as she went slipping under the edge of sleep as if she was swimming under water, she felt a throbbing. It seemed to come up to her from the hot sand under her calves and the cool sand under her head. The slight breeze fanned a wisp of her hair across her face. Since Sandy had mistaken her for a boy, she had refused to allow her father to cut it. Now she simply chopped ragged bangs for herself at the front. The back had grown down into a rough pageboy shape. The sand was filtering into her hair and it seemed – in her half sleep – that the individual grains of sand were dancing against her skull with the vibration which came with the throbbing sound. Slowly she sat up, shaking the sand out of her hair with her eyes still shut. When she opened them the scene on the beach swam into focus: people lying strewn about, almost like the pictures of London in the Blitz which she had seen in the newspapers.

She shook her head again. The noise grew louder. It was one of the patrol planes coming low up the coast from the south.

Tirza looked around, wondering where Martha was. She saw Sandy and the soldier tilt their heads back, and the soldier pointed as the heavy, four-engine plane pounded into sight from the direction of Eel Joe's cove.

Suddenly there was a piercing scream from the other end of the beach, and the figure of a woman came racing towards them. Martha looked as though she was naked, but Tirza realised she was wearing the flesh-coloured swimsuit again. Her long blonde hair was loose and streaming down her back, but she ran clumsily, her arms and legs ugly and uncoordinated. Halfway along she stooped and grabbed Billy, who had been building a sandcastle with one of the children from the Mansion House. He had been well-behaved all day, but now he gave a shriek of pure rage as Martha's careless feet ploughed into the castle, scattering the painstakingly constructed ramparts. She whirled around, a confused look on her face, then scrambled up over the ledges and flung herself into a foxhole. As the plane came level with Libby's Beach, Tirza could just see the top of her cousin's head where she crouched behind the sandbags. Filled with shame she turned away and stared blindly out at the stranded ship.

'Who on earth was that?' she heard Sandy ask.

'Me, I 'ave no idea,' said Pierre. 'Some crazy woman?'

'Crazy or not, she's a stunner. I wouldn't mind an introduction.'

'Monsieur Sandy, take my advice. All women mean trouble. Crazy women the most trouble.'

Sandy laughed and punched the chef on the arm.

'I don't believe you're a misogynist.'

'I 'ave my fiancée in Montreal who is a sensible woman with a good *dot*. When I 'ave saved enough for my own restaurant, we will marry. Other women, I leave alone.'

◆◆◆

Out to sea, the afternoon light began to pearl over, thickening along the horizon and then filling up the eastern sky like a milky liquid in a glass bowl. There was a fog building out there, some miles out to sea, while over the land the westering sun went down pink and gold in a clear sky. On the face of the fog wall rainbows shimmered, sheets of brilliant colour a mile high, stained-glass windows in the sky. As the air grew cooler, mosquitoes began to filter out gradually from the marshy ground behind the shore line, and the sound of hands slapping on bare arms and thighs accompanied the replenishing of the huge campfire and the setting up of the fireworks.

People became more energetic as the evening stole in. Charlie produced a big iron cauldron and hauled a holding trap of lobsters out of a rock pool where he had kept it all day, while along at the south end of the beach someone had set up a Victrola and soldiers were dancing with girls from Flamboro, joined by some of the summer people. After the lobsters had been boiled over the campfire, they were handed out along the beach, and groups of people gathered round bowls of melted butter, cracking open the shells and dipping the meat into the butter.

When at last Tobias judged that it was dark enough, he gathered his team inside the rope barrier which had been rigged around the fireworks area. With a long taper, Walter lit the first row of rockets, which shot up to explode in constellations of red and gold. They fanned outwards and wavered in the night sky like giant feathered clusters of dandelion seeds, then fell hissing into the sea. The crowd greeted them with an involuntary 'Aah'.

Wayne and Simon, wriggling under the rope, began setting off Chinese crackers they had bought themselves. The unexpected bangs, going off at a distance from Tobias and his helpers, made several people jump, and a child began to cry. Then another wave of light sprang up – magic fountains arranged in a square, which spurted sparks in gold and amber, silver and red, one colour after another, like demented volcanoes. Tobias was getting into his stride now.

Tirza felt her elbow taken from behind in the dark. She knew from the lingering scent of his aftershave that it was Sandy.

'Are you wanting me to sail you home?' she asked, without turning round. Another flight of rockets soared into the sky and hung there, a Milky Way, a solar system, a universe of hopeful stars.

'No, no, I'm doing fine.' He stepped up beside her, leaning on his sticks. 'Spectacular, isn't it? Wonderful show. No, I was wondering if you could tell me who that girl was? That beautiful blonde who leapt into the foxhole when the plane went over.'

Tirza, inexplicably, felt her mouth go dry.

'Why do you want to know?' she said evasively.

'Just wondered.'

She considered. Sooner or later someone would tell him. It was useless trying to avoid it.

'That's my cousin, Martha Halstead.'

'Halstead?'

'Halstead is her married name. She's Simon's sister.'

'So she's married? I saw she picked up a little boy.'

'That's her son, Billy. He's five. You met him at our house.'

Tirza fought with her conscience and lost.

'Her husband was killed a couple of months ago, flying with the air force on a bombing mission over Germany.'

'Poor blighter.' Sandy seemed to consider for a minute. 'Why did she do that? Hide in the foxhole?'

'She's been kind of crazy ever since,' said Tirza clearly. 'Whenever a plane comes over, that's what she does. Hides. Crazy.'

'Not surprising. The Blitz has affected some people like that, too. Would you introduce me to her?'

'Why?'

'Oh, well... Wife of a fellow airman.' His voice sounded false to Tirza. 'You know.'

Tirza sighed. 'Oh, come on then.'

She began to walk quickly up the beach at a pace she hoped he could not match, but hopping and stumbling he almost managed to keep up with her. They came upon Martha sitting on a rug with Harriet and Billy. She had put on her short pink seersucker top as the air had grown cooler, but not her shorts, so that her long legs seemed to emerge straight from the frilled hem of the top.

'This is Martha,' Tirza said ungraciously. 'Martha, this is Sandy.' She turned her back on them, and watched the fireworks.

Martha did not get up, but stretched out her soft hand, tipped with its immaculate nail varnish.

'Hello there,' she said in that husky voice she adopted when speaking to men, which made Tirza feel sick to her stomach. 'I've heard all about you. Where have you been hiding all this time?'

Tirza heard her shift her position and pat the rug.

'Why don't you sit down here and watch the fireworks with us?'

Sandy, awkwardly because of his sticks, lowered himself to the ground.

'Tirza darling,' Martha said, 'could you move out of the way? You're blocking our view.'

Chapter 13

Maine: Summer 1942

TIRZA HAD LIFTED her crab line and delivered one bushel basket, not entirely filled, to Pierre. Her catch had been falling off lately. Perhaps the depth charges offshore had started to affect the coastal marine life too. The lobstermen were complaining of poor catches, while the fishermen who normally trawled inshore were being forced to lay their nets further and further out to sea. Apart from Walter Pelham's *Reliant* their boats were not designed to work so far offshore, and a layer of anxiety lay over the town like a thin summer fog. There seemed to be little choice for the men. The inshore fishing was wiped out. Some days dead fish could be seen floating on the surface just off the harbour. Other times a flotilla of corpses came in on the tide and fetched up in rock pools and sheltered coves. The gulls were benefiting, growing fat on the easy pickings.

It was the morning after the Independence Day party and the beach was deserted as she coasted past on a long reach back to Flamboro. Part of the baseball diamond was still scored into the sand above high-water mark, and the charred remains of the great campfire filled the breeze with their pungent savour. A lone Lucky Strike packet washed sluggishly at the edge of the waves, catching the alert yellow-eyed attention of a herring gull.

<><><>

In the days following the party, a sense of anticlimax settled over Flamboro and anxiety deepened. The war news continued to be grim. The party seemed now like a last defiant fling in the face of tragedy. One spark of cheerfulness remained alight, however. Pete Flett had been given a few days' shore leave while his ship was repaired in the naval dockyard at Bath, and he arrived home in the middle of the night, having hitched a lift from Portland station on one of the fish trucks which collected the early morning catch. His ship had been grazed, was all, he declared, by a German torpedo, but some plates were buckled and she had been leaking as they limped back home, escorting the empty cargo ships which had delivered food and war supplies to a beleaguered Britain.

Two more families with sons away in the navy took some comfort from Pete's breezy way of talking about convoy duty, though Nathan shook his head and smiled doubtfully when Tirza told him about it.

'Well,' he said, 'Pete doesn't want his mother worrying. But I reckon there's a lot more to it than he's letting on. The convoys go up near Greenland and Iceland. It hardly gets dark at this time of year, so they're sitting ducks for the U-boats. When the winter comes, there'll be more than the Germans to contend with. There'll be Arctic storms, November at the latest. Same as the old whalers had to endure.'

Pete was contemptuous about the landing craft which had grounded on the sandbank off Libby's Beach.

'Some tomfool wartime captain,' he said. 'Can't read his charts. That bar has been there long as anyone can remember. It's marked on all the charts. How long were they stuck there?'

'Till the middle of the night,' said Wayne.

They were sitting with Pete on the porch of Flett's General Stores and Post Office, though Julia looked as though she wished the others would go away.

'After the fireworks the soldiers stayed dancin' and smoochin' with the girls,' Wayne said. 'Clarice,' he added scornfully, 'reckined it was great. My sister is so *stupid*. Anything in a uniform.'

'Well,' said Julia, holding tightly on to Pete's hand, 'a uniform is very handsome. It's just a shame that a war has to go along with it.'

She and Pete looked at each other in what Simon called a moony way, then Pete said, 'Clear off, kids. We've got things to talk about.'

Tirza wandered off on her own. She thought she would visit a patch of blueberry bushes which grew on the edge of the

Tremayne property near the foxes' den. For some reason these blueberries always ripened earlier than other bushes, and she was planning to take a pailful to the Boston ladies. Miss Susanna had retired to her bed after the Fourth of July, though Miss Molly had said yesterday that she would be sitting downstairs today and she wanted Tirza to come round and hook part of her section of the patchwork rug.

As she climbed the cliff path she became aware of a powerful smell, like rotting fish but worse, much worse. The ordinary clean sea-smell of fresh-caught fish had been part of Tirza's world all her life, and so had the rotten filthy smell of the bait shed. Also, since the depth charges had started killing off the fish, everyone had become familiar with the sight and smell of the clumps of dead fish washed ashore at certain spots around the coast – the cove below Christina's wood, the curve of Libby's Beach where it met the natural causeway of rock leading to Todd's Neck, and round in Eel Joe's bay. These were the places where the sea gave things up, where for centuries people had gathered driftwood or searched for the men lost at sea.

But this smell was different. It seeped into her nostrils like smoke as she climbed the steep part of the path to the top of the cliff. Then as she topped the rise it hit her, a wall of stench so solid you would have sworn you could reach out and touch it. She clapped her hand over her nose and mouth. Ahead of her the bare path led over the thin grass of the cliff edge. On the right a song sparrow was perched on the stone wall, singing as though all was well. In every direction, there was nothing out of the ordinary to be seen.

It could come, then, only from below the cliff, where the ocean flung itself on jagged rocks, inch by inch over the years undercutting the cliff. Tirza put down her blueberry pail, lay on her stomach and wriggled cautiously over the tufts of spare grass until she could put her head over the edge of the cliff. Down below, something seemed at first to have changed the lie of the land. Instead of the usual ragged jaws of broken rocks, all she could see was a great smooth mound of grey boulder lying where the sea broke against the foot of the cliff. A giant of a boulder perhaps fifty feet long. As the waves broke over it and sucked back again, the boulder – as large as some of the smaller islands out in the bay – lolled sideways, then washed back. The sun ran glimmering over its slippery side, turning it almost silver in places. Then it rolled once more, and Tirza realised that it was not a boulder mysteriously misplaced, but a whale. A dead whale.

She could see one of its eyes now, staring dull and blind at the sky. Its tail lay flaccid amongst the vicious rocks. Whales sometimes became stranded, she knew that. But they were apt to beach themselves where the shore sloped gradually and the tide rose and fell many feet, trapping them unexpectedly in shallow water. She had never heard of one coming ashore like this at the foot of a cliff amongst broken rocks. Surely the creature's subtle senses would have warned it off a high shore?

There was no sign of injury, but it was undoubtedly dead. Suddenly she remembered the depth charges. Had the whale been killed by them? Bombed from above as it swam innocently in its native ocean? Or killed by the pressure from the explosion which could rattle windows even on shore? Or had it simply been stunned, so that it swam in confusion, deaf and blind, until it foundered on these terrible rocks? A powerful wave of grief and anger rose up in her.

She crawled backwards away from the vertiginous cliff and stood up. Uncertainly, she looked around. She supposed she would have to tell someone, not that there was much anyone could do. No one could reach the whale where it lay, either from the top of the cliff or from the sea, which was studded here with treacherous underwater reefs. For some reason, perhaps simply because it was the nearest house, she looked over towards the Tremayne place. That shade was still raised. Could Simon have been back there, since their visit all those months ago? As she watched, she thought she saw a movement inside the window, a pale gleam like bare flesh against the glass. Then it was gone. She shook her head. Probably just the reflection of a cloud, but maybe Simon was there. She set off at a trot, jumping the stone wall and crossing the parched knee-high grass of the ruined lawn.

When she reached the cellar door, she saw that it had been wrenched right away from its frame and lay on the gravel path, leaving the dark hole of the cellar fully exposed. She couldn't think why Simon would have done that, but it did look as though he might be inside. She made her way through the cellar full of flowerpots to the wine cellar and the coal store. There were bottles lying on the floor with their necks broken off, and a dense smell which rushed from her lungs straight to her brain, weirdly dizzying. Flies crawled about in sticky dark patches of liquid on the concrete. At the top of the cellar steps the door stood ajar. The abandoned kitchen looked the same, but when Tirza came out into the main hall of the house, she sensed something in the air that made her pause. There was a feeling in the house as though there were people here, more than just Simon. And a smell too. Not just the closed-up, abandoned smell the house had had before, but other smells – cigarettes, and dimestore perfume, and an acrid musky smell.

'Simon,' she called out uncertainly. Then louder, 'Simon? Are you there?'

There came a rush of sounds, rustling and smothered voices and a small crash as if someone had dropped a shoe.

'Simon!'

She started up the stairs. As she rounded the bend in the staircase at the half-landing, she came face to face with two people. One was a girl from Flamboro, some friend of Clarice's. Her hair was all over her face and she was buttoning up her blouse. The other was a soldier she had never seen before. He was carrying his uniform thrown over his shoulder and wearing nothing but a pair of khaki underpants. He reached out and grabbed her, pulling her against him so she could smell him, and it seemed to her that he smelled even worse than the whale. That, at least, had been a smell from the sea. The man smelled of the cheap hair oil that slicked down his black hair, and of old ashtrays, stale sweat and that same foul musky odour. The hair on his chest was thickly matted and scurfy.

'Hello there, darlin',' he said, taking a handful of her hair in one hand and pushing his face up against hers. 'You come for some too, have you?'

Then he thrust his other hand between her legs, groping and probing with his fingers. Instinctively she doubled up. She twisted away, yelling something, she didn't know what, then she kicked him with her heel on his bare shin, ducked under his arm and ran. Stumbling, half falling down the wide staircase. Behind her she heard them both laughing.

———◈———

It was a symptom of the times, Harriet thought, that she should be sitting in church in her Sunday clothes at eleven o'clock on a weekday morning watching her best friend's son getting married. With barely twenty-four hours' notice, Pete and Julia had informed their families and friends that they had decided to have the wedding at once, while Pete was home, since they didn't know when he would next have any leave. Julia's parents had arrived overnight on a train from Philadelphia. Mr Bennett was white-haired and distinguished looking. Her mother, small and plump, seemed the kind of woman who under normal circumstances would have joyfully organised a full-blown wedding with half a dozen bridesmaids and two hundred guests. Instead, she looked hollow-eyed and grey with fatigue after the journey.

Julia, wearing her mother's wedding dress – hastily taken in that very morning to fit her – was too lively and too bright of eye. Pete was square-jawed and sombre. Mary told Harriet that he had been against the wedding at first.

'He said he didn't want to leave her a widow. But Julia said she would rather be married to him for two days than not at all, so they agreed it in the end. It's terrible they have to think like that, and all these young girls, widowed... Oh, Harriet, I'm so sorry!' Her hand flew to her mouth.

'It's all right, Mary,' Harriet said. 'Martha and Will had eight years together. They were luckier than some.'

Sitting here now, watching Pete slip the ring on Julia's finger, Harriet wondered what her daughter was thinking. Martha had taken a seat in the pew in front of her parents, next to that British airman Tirza had been so taken up with. Since Martha and he had wandered off down the darkened beach on the night of the Independence Day party, Harriet had seen them together twice. Captain Tucker hadn't been around. Sandy – that was the airman's name. He was sitting with his arm across the pew, curved behind Martha's shoulders, almost an embrace – a disgraceful way to behave in church. Harriet caught back a sigh that rose involuntarily to her lips.

All of the Libby family had come to Pete's wedding, except Tirza, who had run home yesterday morning, Abigail said, complaining of pains in her stomach. She had taken to her bed and been there ever since, refusing all food and only drinking a little water.

'Well,' Harriet said delicately, 'she's going on thirteen, she's about the right age...' She wasn't sure how much Abigail had informed Tirza about the facts of a woman's life.

'No,' said Abigail briskly, 'I don't think it's that. Indigestion, I expect.'

It wasn't like Tirza, though. Harriet could not remember her ever being ill, except for a bout of measles. Tirza and Simon had both caught it during their first month at school. On her way to the wedding, Harriet had looked in on Tirza, who lay curled up in a ball, with her face to the wall.

'I'm OK, I'll be OK,' she said snappily. 'Have you seen the whale?'

'You saw it, then? Was that what upset you?'

'No!' Tirza shouted. 'I told you, I'm sick to my stomach.'

'There've been crowds going to see the whale. Everybody from round about, and summer people from as far away as Camden.'

'That's disgusting.'

'Well, you don't often see a whale up that close,' said Harriet mildly. 'It's just harmless curiosity.'

'I hope they all fall over the cliff,' said Tirza angrily. 'Why can't they leave it alone? Why can't people just leave people alone?'

She buried her face in her pillow then, and Harriet thought she might be crying, so after a minute she withdrew tactfully.

Something was definitely wrong with her, and Harriet didn't think it was stomach ache. Tirza had always been such a straight-forward girl, even-tempered and poised, grown-up for her years. Yet she still had a kind of childlike innocence that made her vulnerable. This time Harriet was unable to suppress her sigh before it escaped and Tobias looked at her in surprise, with his eyebrows raised interrogatively. She shook her head and picked up her hymn-book.

The Fletts and the Bennetts had organised a hasty wedding

party in the back yard of the store, but the young couple left very soon for a few hours of honeymoon, which they were spending no further away than the Mansion House. As a wedding present the four parents were paying for them to have two nights of privacy there.

'After the war, there will be time to be thinking about dishes and sheets and all those matters,' Mary said to Harriet, wiping her eyes as Pete and Julia drove away in Charlie's battered old Dodge.

'Where is Julia going to live?'

'We wanted her to come to us, but she is staying on in her rooms at Marion Larrabee's. I suppose she likes her independence.'

'Will she go on teaching school?'

'Oh, yes.'

'Different from when we were girls, isn't it?'

'No harm for a girl to have a job of her own, as long as she gives it up when the babies start coming.'

———◈———

After three days Pierre came to Flamboro to scold Tirza for failing to deliver her crabs. The Mansion House, he pointed out, had come to depend on her and she was jeopardising his reputation as the finest seafood chef on the Maine coast. She looked at him wanly and said she supposed she could manage to deliver the next day. She was sitting in the parlour, a room she hated, with a blanket wrapped around her. Despite the July heat outside, she was cold.

'Bien. I rely on you.' Pierre searched his mind for some gossip to cheer her up. 'Our friend Sandy, 'e 'as made a conquest.'

Tirza lifted expressionless eyes to his face.

'The beautiful woman on the beach – I did not know that this is your cousin, p'tite. Twice they 'ave dinner in the 'otel, and they go for moonlight walks along the cliff. Très romantique.'

Tirza stirred inside her blanket.

'So what?' she said rudely.

Pierre peered at her shrewdly.

'Come – the nose, it is not out of joint? You are 'is friend. This is just a little romantic adventure. It shows 'e is nearly well again. But then we will all 'ave to say au revoir to 'im. You know this very well, *ma p'tite.*'

Tirza set her jaw. 'I'll see you tomorrow with the crabs.'

———◈———

Tirza could not escape Sandy's new infatuation with Martha. When she encountered him in the garden of the hotel the following morning, he seemed not to have noticed that she had been missing for several days. He took her by the arm and told her how lucky she was to have such a beautiful girl for a cousin. He began to enumerate all the aspects of Martha's beauty, but Tirza shut her ears. She had heard all this before. Instead she hurried towards the pier, dangling the bushel baskets from her hands so that they banged painfully against her ankles. Sandy limped determinedly beside her.

'Unfortunately, I'm still a little limited in getting about. And now Martha has said she doesn't want me to keep ringing her at home, says her parents have been making disapproving noises. But I know you are on our side, Tirza. So would you take her this letter?'

He held out one of the stiff, cream-coloured hotel envelopes. It was bulky with the letter inside. Tirza shifted the baskets to *Stormy Petrel* and took it reluctantly, not looking at him.

'That's a grand girl! And you won't delay, will you? If you stop off at the far end of the beach on your way home, you could just nip up to the farm and slip it to her privately, couldn't you?'

Tirza climbed wordlessly down into the boat and cast off. She pushed the letter into the pocket of her shorts and laid out her oars.

'Why are you rowing instead of sailing?'

'No wind,' she said shortly. 'Haven't you noticed?'

It always astonished her the way he went around deaf and blind to the weather she could read like a child's primer.

'Oh. Well, it'll be easy to stop off, won't it?'

'Just add more to a long journey,' she said, manoeuvring the boat away from the pier and bending to her oars. She wasn't going to let him see her face.

When she reached the farm Martha was lying back in a rocking chair on the porch in a blue sun-dress with a scoop neck. She had her eyes closed but she was humming some dance tune softly to herself. Tirza dropped the letter on her lap without a word and Martha's eyes flew open. They were exactly the colour of her dress and Tirza had to admit, silently, that she was as pretty as any film star. Martha looked at the writing on the letter and gave a complacent little smile.

'So, you're the mailman, are you?'

She didn't thank Tirza, but she pushed a jug of iced tea towards her on the metal porch table. Tirza was hot and thirsty from all the rowing, but there was no spare glass on the table, so she picked up the jug, tilted her head back and poured the tea into her open mouth.

'For heaven's sake, Tirza,' Martha cried, as some of the tea splashed down on to her forearm, 'what do you think you're doing?'

Tirza set down the jug and wiped her mouth with the back of her hand.

'Will there be a reply?' she asked coolly.

'Oh, well, if you can wait.'

'No. I can't.'

Tirza turned on her heel, jumped off the porch steps and stumped away down the farm track again, her bare feet raising spurts of grey dust in the heavy air. She rubbed her hand over her face again. It was just sweat getting in her eyes.

She decided to retrieve the blueberry pail she had abandoned near the Tremayne place and take a couple of quarts to Miss Catherine for an early batch of blueberry muffins. Someone had kicked the pail aside under a scrubby bayberry bush. There was an interlaced web of footprints in the dust of the clifftop path where people had come to view the dead whale. Empty cigarette packs lay beside a box which had held Kodak film. A sickening smell of decay engulfed the whole place. Tirza climbed over the wall and found the blueberry bushes at the top edge of the gully where the foxes had their den. Today any scent from the den was overwhelmed by the odour of the dead whale. There was a good crop of fat blueberries, though, and Tirza crouched down, picking at a steady pace. Grimly, she pushed away the thought of the house behind her.

By the time she slid *Stormy Petrel* off the beach, there was a line of cloud building on the horizon and enough wind had picked up to allow her to sail slowly back the rest of the way to Flamboro. She made a wide berth round the headland to avoid the reefs. From out at sea, nothing could be seen of the whale, but even here the scent of rotten sea creature hung in the air.

The Boston ladies were delighted to see her, though she felt as though she carried the smell of the whale on her hands and in her hair. Miss Catherine swooped on the blueberries and carried them off to the kitchen. Miss Molly led her out to the wisteria-covered arbour in the garden where Miss Susanna was sitting propped up by pillows, but looking very spry, surrounded with her orderly piles of fabric strips. She had the new rug laid over her knees and was hooking part of Simon's red barn.

'Just the person I wanted to see,' said Miss Susanna. 'Everyone else who drew part of the pattern has hooked a bit on the rug. You're the only one left. Come and do part of *Stormy Petrel*.'

'Sorry,' Tirza mumbled. 'I should have been to see you sooner.'

Miss Susanna smiled as she selected some white fabric strips for the boat hull and a light tan for the sail.

'Don't you worry. I know perfectly well where the burlap backing came from, and I'm very grateful.'

'Well,' said Tirza. She laughed suddenly. 'If those soldiers leave good burlap lying around on the beach, what can they expect?'

'After all,' said Miss Susanna, 'it's Libby's Beach. Who has better right to the salvage than a Libby?' Her laugh rang out as she handed the hook to Tirza. 'Best not make a habit of it, though. They might notice if the whole line of foxholes disappeared.'

'I promise. Though most of the bags aren't good enough to use.' She struggled with the hook. 'I don't know how to do this right.'

'Here, let me show you. You need to hold the strip quite taut with your left hand while you hook with your right.'

It turned out to be easier than Tirza expected. By the time the other two sisters came out with plates of blueberry muffins and a jug of iced tea with mint floating in it, she had hooked the whole of the boat hull, the sail, and a fragment of blue sky. The blue was part of an old pair of her own dungarees.

Miss Susanna laid the rug aside and gave it a little pat.

'I'm glad I had this idea for the rug. When it's finished it will be like a piece of this summer, captured for ever on canvas. When you are grown up, Tirza, you'll be able to look at it and remember all that has happened this year. Such a strange year. So many changes.'

Tirza said nothing.

'Have you noticed?' asked Miss Molly. 'She's added the whale, here in the bottom border.'

'Except I've drawn him alive and spouting. That's how we want to remember him, isn't it?'

'Yes,' Tirza said. 'I think he was killed by the depth charges. I hate them. They're ruining the fishing. And I don't like the soldiers everywhere, spoiling everything. I wish they'd all go away.'

Miss Susanna sighed.

'In wartime life is bound to change. But when peace comes, I'm sure everything will be all right again.'

Tirza shook her head dumbly.

—◆◆◆—

Martha must have found some way of replying to Sandy's letter. Perhaps she just posted it. But whenever Sandy could waylay Tirza near the hotel, he asked her to take more letters for him. She changed her times of delivering the crabs to Pierre in order to avoid him, or landed on the north side of Todd's Neck near the beach instead of sailing around the headland to the pier. This meant hauling the heavy baskets of crabs up over the broken rocks and then along a path through the woods. It left her hot, breathless and cross. One day Sandy came upon her by chance in the woods where she had put down her basket to suck a finger which a particularly vicious crab had nipped.

She was inwardly cursing all crabs and their aggressive habits as she looked over the headland cliff. A scum of dead fish was bobbing about below, covering the water between the rocks. More damage from the depth charges. When the tide went out most of them would be trapped to rot in the sun. The ledges here were angled up at their seaward end and sloped towards the land, so that pools were left when the tide went out. The cliff was almost as high as the one where the whale had washed ashore, although the path was wider and not so treacherous underfoot.

'Hello,' said Sandy. 'You're a stranger.'

She jumped, taken by surprise. The soft pine needles scattered on the floor of the wood had made his approach silent. She did not answer, but continued to suck her bruised finger and gaze out to sea.

'What's so fascinating out there?'

He shifted both sticks to one hand and put the other arm around her shoulders, not for support, but companionably. If he felt her stiffen, he gave no sign.

'Scenting the weather,' she said gruffly. 'Reckon there's a storm coming up.'

'How can you tell?'

'Just a feeling in the air. Heavy. And an oily look out to sea, on the horizon. And she's smurring up to the south-east. But not too soon. *Short warning, soon past; long foretelling, long last.*'

'You haven't taken me sailing for ages.'

'Thought you weren't interested any more.'

'Of course I am. And I bought a camera when I went to Portland the other day. Just a Box Brownie, and a few rolls of film, but I've been taking pictures – the whale, you know, and some of Flamboro. People too. The lobstermen at work, and Pierre in his kitchen, and your cousin Martha.'

He said it carelessly, but Tirza noticed a change in his voice. She stooped to pick up her basket, so she could pull away from his arm.

'Don't know why you bother.' She swung the basket up and started along the path towards the hotel. He fell into step beside her.

'Something to remember you all by. I can't stay here for ever. You know that.'

Tirza said nothing, but there was a twisting deep in her stomach, and she shivered.

'I want to take a picture of you and *Stormy Petrel*,' he said. 'Will you let me do that?'

'Suppose so.'

'And what about going sailing again? Weren't you going out to Mustinegus Island to pick blueberries some time soon?'

'Ayuh, I was fixing on going tomorrow. But I reckon you've got better things to do.'

'Tomorrow?' He smiled. 'Tomorrow would be fine. When?'

'I'll bring the crabs round first. Meet me on the pier at eight.'

'Eight! Do we have to leave so early?'

'Eight's not early. And it gets some hot picking blueberries by midday.'

'All right, you're the captain.' He gave her a mock salute. 'I'll get Pierre to give us a picnic – and no beer, I promise.'

For the rest of the day, Tirza felt more cheerful than she had done since Independence Day, though she kept a sharp eye on the horizon where the line between sky and sea still had that slick oily look she distrusted. In the evening she cycled over to the farm to borrow some extra blueberry pails.

'Just thought that there's likely to be a good crop,' she said to Harriet, 'going by what I saw a few weeks back. I'll bring you some too.'

'Much obliged,' said Harriet. 'I'm having a day off myself tomorrow. Martha and I are taking the pickup to Portland. There's a summer sale on at Porteus, Mitchell and Braun. I'm looking for bedlinen and Martha wants clothes for herself and Billy. That child has really grown some this summer.'

They both looked across the yard at Billy, who was carrying feed to the hens.

'I guess he's getting used to the farm,' Tirza said.

'Settling in, settling in. He's going to spend the day with Joey tomorrow.'

Tirza strung some of the blueberry pails on her handlebars and tied the rest to the carrier over her back wheel. All the way back to Flamboro she thought she sounded like Walter's old pickup which was falling apart because he'd spent every penny on *Reliant* and had to keep his truck together – as Nathan said – with string and chewing gum.

◄◆►

The next morning Tirza handed over the day's crabs to Pierre at seven thirty and was back on the pier by twenty to eight. If Sandy didn't come on time, she would not wait for him, she told herself. But a couple of minutes later he arrived with his new camera hanging in a case from a cord round his neck and a satchel full of food on his shoulder. He passed these down to her, followed by his sticks, then eased himself in a sitting position out to the edge of the pier with his legs dangling above the cockpit of *Stormy Petrel*.

'Don't help me,' he said. 'I can do it if I don't try to rush things.'

He leaned forward and grabbed the mast with one hand, then lowered himself carefully into the boat while Tirza leaned outward to balance his weight. He collapsed awkwardly into the bottom of the boat laughing.

'Did it! Not very elegantly, I admit. Still, I'll soon be fit and fighting again.'

Tirza stowed his sticks under the side deck and put the camera and lunch in the watertight locker under the foredeck. After she had hoisted the sail and set a course out to sea, she perched on the windward coaming and looked at him.

'Do you mean that? Are you really going to be fit to leave soon?'

'Well, it's a manner of speaking. The doctor reckons just a few weeks now. Much as I'd like to stay, there's a war on and every pilot is needed. I'm older than most of the boys who are flying, you know. Eighteen, nineteen, they are. I've more experience. And it's good for morale, too, when the youngsters can see that a few of us do manage to survive to my advanced years.'

'How old are you, then?' Tirza asked. She knew it was rude to ask a person's age, but he almost seemed to be inviting her.

'Thirty-two. Ancient.' He glanced casually towards the approaching loom of the island. 'How old is your cousin?'

'Simon? Thirteen and three-quarters.'

'No, I meant... Martha?'

'Oh. Martha will be... twenty-seven next birthday.'

'Twenty-seven. And you'll be thirteen soon, didn't you say?'

'In a few weeks. My birthday is the first of October.'

'First of October.' He smiled. 'Is it, indeed? I might just be here still. And when is Simon's birthday?'

'Eighteenth of December. He always complains it's too near Christmas.'

'So it is. And Martha's birthday?'

'Oh, that was back in February. Tenth of February.' Tirza couldn't see the point of all this. The Libby family did not make much fuss of birthdays. But she asked politely, 'And when's your birthday?'

He grinned again. 'First of October. Same day as you. Now there's a coincidence.'

Tirza put the helm over and brought *Stormy Petrel* fluttering into the wind with just enough way on to ground her softly on the beach. She felt obscurely flattered that she shared a birthday with Sandy.

'So that's when you'll be thirty-three.'

She jumped into the shallow water and began hauling the boat further on to the beach.

'No. I should have said I'm almost thirty-two. That's the age I'll be then.'

He swung his legs over the side in a businesslike way.

'Now, let's see which of us can pick the most blueberries.'

At the top of the rise above the ruined farmhouse, the blueberry bushes stretched away in all directions. As they approached the thicket, a cloud of curlews which had been feeding there rose like a summer blizzard in flashes of silver against the sun. The bushes they revealed were so thickly studded with fruit that the island seemed to be covered with expanses of blue water, dotted here and there with woods. Tirza gave a grunt of satisfaction. She plucked a berry off the nearest bush and examined it. It was the size of a small cherry, with a dusky blue bloom to the skin like some exotic butterfly. Tirza tasted the berry, rolling it over in her mouth.

'Ayuh. Just right. Ripe enough, but not gone too far.'

Sandy picked one to taste.

'These must be related to our blaeberries,' he said, 'but they never tasted like this. Look at the size of them!'

They crouched down and began to pick. There was never any question who would pick most. Tirza had first gone blueberrying at the age of two, and she knew instinctively just how to cup the berries and how much pressure to apply so that they came away sweetly from the branch without disintegrating. Sandy's fingers were soon purple and spattered with small seeds, while Tirza's hands moved rhythmically over the bushes.

The rich winey smell of the blueberries rose around them as they pushed further and further into the thicket. It mingled with the astringent scent of the pines, sun-warmed overhead, and the strong smell of the deep ocean coming in with the onshore wind. For a long time they were silent, except for the rustling of the bushes and the plop of the berries into the pails. Then Sandy straightened his back and groaned a little, and Tirza straightened to keep him company.

'Don't strain your legs, now.'

'No, just a bit cramped.'

He shaded his eyes and peered out through the trunks of the trees at the sea.

'The waves seem big today. Yet there isn't all that much wind.'

'That's what we call an old sea. Means there's been a big storm somewhere. The ocean is stirred up right from the bottom and it goes on rolling for a while. Like a bucket when you start it swaying. The water keeps slopping back and forth.'

'I see. I remember stirring up the bath water when I was a lad and then getting in a panic when I couldn't stop it splashing over the edge. I knew I'd be in trouble.'

'This is the hurricane season,' said Tirza. 'It's probably the leftover edge of one that's blown out south'ards.'

'You don't often get them here, do you?'

'Sometimes. They start down in the Caribbean and usually they've worn themselves out before they reach Maine, but we can get the edge of one, or sometimes a real bad one like four years ago.'

She bent and began picking again. The hot still air, the rich scent of pine and blueberries, and the buzzing of bees in the carpet of wildflowers about their feet gave the island a strange, isolated air, like some dream landscape. After a time, the flock of curlews overcame their fear and settled at the far end of the blueberry thicket, feeding up for their long migration south. Gulls, too, made sudden squawking forays, waddling boldly amongst the bushes nearer to hand and eyeing them with their bright cold gaze.

Suddenly Tirza stilled. She put out a cautious hand and caught Sandy by the wrist. He looked at her enquiringly and she jerked her head slightly to the left. Trotting out of the pine woods above the eastern cliff came a big dog fox. He looked in their direction but seemed unperturbed. The bushes swayed as he waded into them and began to tug the berries off the branches. Sandy chuckled softly. For a moment the fox paused with a cluster of berries hanging from his jaw. Then he resumed his meal, quite unafraid. Half an hour at least passed while they continued to pick – man, fox and girl – then the fox lifted his head as though he heard something they did not, and trotted off into the trees again.

Sandy let his breath out in a gust as though he had been holding it.

'Extraordinary! How did a fox manage to come out to the island?'

'Oh, there's a whole tribe of foxes. And rabbits too. I reckon their ancestors came over when there used to be regular boats carrying goods and crops. Probably stowed on board. Plenty for them to eat, and nobody to trouble them. I guess he's so tame because he isn't used to folks chasing after him.'

'Let's have our lunch,' Sandy said. 'I'm famished.'

They sat down in the smaller cove by the site of the old Indian settlement to eat the picnic Pierre had packed for them. Then Sandy took a photograph of the cove with the ruined farmhouse in the background, and several of Tirza sitting on the Indian shell heap and standing on the rocks at the water's edge.

After lunch they finished filling the blueberry pails and Tirza showed Sandy round the rest of the island. She could see that he was walking much more easily now, and that meant only one thing: he would be leaving, as he said, before long. She didn't want to look ahead to that, or to the thought of days empty of any hope of being with him.

At the southernmost tip of the island, beyond the tumbled walls of the third deserted farmhouse, there was a small boggy patch with cranberries growing in it.

'Shall we pick these?' Sandy asked.

'They won't be ready yet. Anyway, the ones on our marsh are much better. Even those I showed you near the schoolhouse.'

Sandy picked one of the hard shiny berries and held it up between his finger and thumb.

'It looks like a bead.'

'When I was little, I used to make myself necklaces out of them. They're some hard.'

Sandy put the berry into his mouth and bit on it.

'Ugh! That's disgusting!'

'Told you they weren't ready.' Tirza laughed at his expression. 'You can't eat them raw anyway. Bitter as sorrow, they are.'

They walked back across the island, following the remains of the disused farm track and pointing out to each other the paths made by other creatures – the fox, probably, and the rabbits, whose holes could be seen in the sandy banks.

'Porcupine too, most likely,' said Tirza, 'though I've only ever seen one over here. Could be the Indians brought them over. Then they'd be easy to catch, for eating and for their quills.'

'Have you ever eaten porcupine?'

'Never have, though the Indians did. And they used the quills for decoration on boxes and head-dresses, and ceremonial clothes.'

By the blueberry thicket they collected the filled pails, which Tirza had covered with flat stones in case the fox or the gulls came nosing around. When they reached *Stormy Petrel*, Sandy said he must have a photograph of Tirza sailing her, so she had to push off and sail parallel to the shore until he was satisfied with his picture. When she came back to pick him up, she eyed the camera longingly.

'Can I try it? Haven't ever used a camera.'

'Of course you can. What do you want to photograph?'

Tirza considered, standing on the beach with the painter in her hand.

'You go and stand in *Stormy Petrel* and I'll take the two of you together.'

'OK.'

He showed her how to aim the camera by looking into the viewfinder, where the world swam grey and soft-edged, like a scene under water. Then he pointed out the button to press and climbed into the boat, propping his sticks against the gunwale.

'How do you want me? Like this?'

He flung an arm around *Stormy Petrel*'s mast like an embrace, laughing. Before Tirza could think whether she had aimed the camera right, she clicked the shutter.

'Oh, I hope I didn't spoil it!'

'Of course you didn't. Tell you what. Let's sail back to Flamboro instead of the hotel, and you can take some more pictures there.'

They made a rapid journey back to the mainland, before the rising wind. Tirza was quite relieved to make fast to the wharf and after she had passed the pails up to Sandy she stared out to sea again. There was an ominous greenish-grey light along the horizon.

For a while they pottered around Flamboro, Sandy explaining about focus and shutter openings on complicated cameras.

'You know as much as I do now. Luckily a Box Brownie is about the easiest camera to use, and you don't need to worry about all that. Why don't you take a picture of those lobster pots?'

'A photograph of lobster pots!' She was astonished.

'They're very decorative, with their bowed tops and those netting funnels at the ends – what do you call them?'

'Heads.'

'And the carved floats all in different colours. Do the colours mean something?'

'Each lobsterman has his own design. So when they're laid at sea, nobody can mistake which is which. Then there's no excuse for poaching.'

'I see. Well, it's a pity the colours won't show up. You *can* get colour film, but it's fearfully expensive. Only for professionals. Go on, take the lobster pots.'

When she looked at the wharf-side heap of pots through the viewfinder, she suddenly saw what he meant. The arrangement seemed to separate itself from the daily toil of her father and the other men and become an intriguing pattern in its own right. She would like to talk to Girna about this. Her grandmother had often tried to interest her in drawing wild flowers and animals, but Tirza didn't have the talent or the patience.

Afterwards Tirza persuaded Charlie Flett to pose on the porch of the store, though he was much embarrassed.

'I don't know what Mary would say,' he complained. 'Getting my picture took in my work clothes. I've just been moving barrels out of the storeroom.'

'You're just fine,' said Tirza, who was gaining confidence. 'Sandy is letting me take some pictures of Flamboro the way it is every day. Nothing fancy.'

At last they had finished the third film and Sandy said he must be getting back to the hotel. Tirza realised with a start that it was time she did the evening lift of her crab line, and she cast an anxious eye out to sea again, wondering how long it would take her to sail to Todd's Neck and back, and then attend to the crabs. The wind had shifted several points to a south-westerly, and was strengthening all the time. The lobstermen were in harbour already, hurrying back before they could be caught by an offshore rote. Most of the trawlers were coming in over the harbour bar in a cluster now, with one or two tagging along behind, still a mile or two out.

For the first time Sandy seemed to notice the weather.

'I don't think you should try to sail me back,' he said. 'Look, there's the Portland bus about to leave. I'll take that up to the county road and then hitch a lift as far as I can towards Todd's Neck.'

'But your legs...'

'Much better. The doctor says exercise is good for me now. Don't worry, I'll take it slowly. I don't want to think of you out at sea in this.'

Tirza nodded. She was secretly relieved.

'It's been a wonderful day,' he said, touching her lightly on her bare arm. 'Thank you.'

'Your camera,' she said, shying away from him and lifting the strap of the big case over her head.

'Right. I'll put a fresh film in, and we'll take some more another day, shall we?'

———◈———

Tirza had never under-run her line so quickly. She lost at least four good crabs and a couple of throw-backs through hurrying too much. They didn't seem to be biting very well anyway, and she only had six crabs in her basket when she wound the line down and rowed the dory back to the wharf. She checked that both *Stormy Petrel* and the dories were securely moored fore and aft, then deposited the crabs in the holding trap and left her line beside her jars of bait in the bait shed. She went to pick up some of the full berry pails from where she has left them near the *Louisa Mary*.

'It's looking some bad out there,' she said to Ben Flett, who was tidying away the gear on his boat and roping down everything in sight.

'Ayuh. Best take your sails and loose gear indoors tonight,' he said.

'Is everyone in?'

'Everyone except *Reliant*. Walter has been takin' her further out than the rest of us, since the fishin' has been poorly. Reckon he went out past Matinicus last night. Ain't seen him since.'

It took Tirza four more trips to carry all the blueberries, the sail, rudder, oars and centreboard up to the house. Then Nathan helped her unstep the mast and rope the tarpaulin cover down over the cockpit of *Stormy Petrel*. Between them they carried the mast up to the boat shed.

'It may not amount to anything,' said Nathan as they came into the kitchen, 'but better safe than sorry.'

'There's a weather warning on the radio,' Abigail said. 'They say the hurricane running up the coast is beginning to die out, but they're forecasting severe gales at least. Maybe even the last of the hurricane.'

Nathan shook his head.

'I don't like to think of Walter out there with only Eli and Wayne to crew. Walter's a pretty man with a boat, but Eli is past seventy and Wayne's nothing but a boy.'

◆

Darkness fell early. Tirza did not see the clouds finally come up. Instead the whole sky closed over suddenly, as if something had been clamped down on top of it, cutting out the evening sun. Abigail switched on the kitchen light while they ate their supper, like the middle of winter. Looking out of her bedroom later, Tirza could see fragments of leaves and twigs whirling in the band of light cast by her window. Instead of blowing steadily in one direction they spun in tiny circles, no more than six inches across, so that the air seemed to seethe like boiling water.

Under the harbour lights she could see clumps of men gathering, the light reflecting from their sou'westers and oilskins. *Reliant* was four hours overdue.

It was unbearable to stay inside with this sense of approaching calamity. She knew Abigail would forbid her to go out of doors, so she crept downstairs quietly in her bare feet and slid past the kitchen where her grandmother was dozing over the newspaper. Her cut-down oilskins hung on a hook inside the boat shed door. She put them on and let herself out into the night.

The men and boys were gathered on the wharf, the women stood in separate groups nearer the seafront houses. Nathan and Ben and a few others had stepped down on to the lobster car, as if the few yards this brought them nearer to the sea somehow made them feel better. Now she was outside, Tirza caught the full force of the wind and had to clamp her sou'wester down on her head with both hands to stop it blowing away. She caught sight of Simon on the fringe of the crowd and struggled over to him. He grabbed her by the elbow as a gust threw her sideways, almost off the wharf.

'Watch out! You'll do no good ending up in the harbour.'

'What's happening?'

'Your dad and Ben were talking about going out to look for them, but it would be suicide. Latest news is, the last of the hurricane is headed right this way.'

Tirza was silent. There was nothing to be said. Either *Reliant* had foundered already, and Walter, Wayne and Eli were lost, or she was out there trying to battle her way in. It seemed unlikely. If she had still been afloat, she would surely have made harbour by now, even with the offshore rote. She couldn't have been fishing a whole four hours further out to sea than the rest of the fleet.

The church clock struck eleven. The force of the wind was increasing and the group of watching women persuaded Josie Pelham to wait inside Flett's Stores. She went stoically, her hands twisted in her apron but her face set in dignified lines of resignation. Clarice, trailing behind, was puffy-eyed as if she had been crying, but she walked now with her face averted and she shook off Jim from the gun crew who tried to stop her with his hand.

Tirza wondered whether the gun crew had left their post. And there were other soldiers in the crowd too, more than could be on duty tonight. The news of the missing boat had somehow reached them and they had gathered here with the other watchers. Nathan and Ben climbed the ladder from the lobster car up the side of the spindle-legged wharf, which rose high above the level of the water. The tide was at full ebb, and the reefs offshore would be at their most dangerous.

'Eli's bin fishin' sixty-five years,' Ben volunteered, 'since he were ten. Barrin' six years when he shipped on a whaler back in the nineties.'

There was a sudden violent surge in the wind, followed by a curious sound, like a great zipper being torn open. A cloud passed through the harbour lights like a flock of birds, and Tirza saw that a patch of shingles had been ripped off the bait shed roof. They were slicing through the air as deadly as knives. Instinctively, the Flamboro people ducked, but the soldiers were not so quick, nor was Reverend Bridges, who had joined the crowd. The minister was an inland man and he looked merely astonished when a shingle flying at ninety or a hundred miles an hour struck him on the head. He collapsed at Charlie Flett's feet. At the same moment one of the soldiers who had instinctively raised his hands to protect his face gave a shriek. Blood was pouring down his arm where a shingle had sliced across his wrist.

The injuries gave them something to do. The soldier was helped into Flett's Stores and two of the men carried the minister in and laid him on the Liars' Bench. He was bleeding where the shingle had cut his temple. All the watchers from the foreshore crowded in behind. There was not much anyone could do, but there was a sense of doing something, just by being there. Mary Flett, who had been a nurse before her marriage, cleaned and dressed the wounds while Charlie lit the pot-bellied stove. It might be August, but the hurricane had sucked cold air into its vortex, and everyone found they were shivering.

The church clock struck one. Mary had ushered Josie Pelham and the other women into the Fletts' apartment above the store and she brought down jugs of coffee and plates of hot biscuits to the men. The minister was sitting up now, pale and a little confused, while the soldier, it seemed, couldn't stop talking.

'Durndest thing I ever saw,' he said. 'Like a knife-throwin' act at one of them there Wild West shows. Hurtlin' through the air.' He seemed to fancy the word, tasting it on the tongue. *'Hurtlin'* through the air. Nearly sliced my hand right off.'

'Jest be thankful it didn't cut your head right off, Chuck,' said one of the other soldiers dryly. 'Elsen you would of had to stop talking.'

Everybody laughed, with a nervous, anxious sound.

The church clock struck two. Gradually people began to drift away. Nathan, who seemed to notice Tirza for the first time, hitched her up from the floor by her elbows.

'Your grandmother is going to tan the backside off the both of us,' he said. 'Come on. There's nothing we can do till first light.'

'Doesn't seem worth going to bed now,' Tirza mumbled. 'It almost is first light.'

They stumbled back together along the seafront. The lamps along the harbour looked sickly now that the sky was no longer so black dark. The wind was abating and a few stars flickered briefly between the torn shreds of the clouds. Out at sea beyond the islands there was a thread of paler sky along the horizon, where mountainous waves heaved and collided.

'Can I come with you when you go out in the morning?' Tirza asked as they hung up their oilskins on the boat shed door.

'Hunting drowned men is no job for a girl,' said Nathan bluntly.

She raised her chin defiantly. 'I can be just as brave as any man. Wayne is my friend. And my eyes are sharper than yours.'

Nathan sighed and passed his hand wearily over his face.

'Oh, child, I don't know. I fear to think, sometimes, what your mother would have made of the way I've raised you. I don't feel I've done right by you, treating you no better than a boy.'

Tirza put her arms awkwardly round his solid, barrel-shaped body and laid her cheek against the rough wool of his working sweater which smelled of lobsters and tar. He had never had time yesterday evening to change out of his hauling clothes.

'You've raised me just fine, Dad. Maybe I'm not pretty and

elegant like Martha, but I like things the way they are.'

He tousled her hair roughly. Then held up a strand of it between his fingers.

'Hey, now. Look at this! It's getting so long, we'll soon be able to knit bait bags out of it. Come on, time you were in bed.'

—◇◇◇—

Sandy had caught the bus from Flamboro up to the Portland road and walked about a quarter of a mile when he was lucky enough to pick up a lift from an elderly couple driving back to the Mansion House. He settled with relief into the back seat of their Cadillac, thankful that American cars had so much more room than British ones. He rested his sticks against the edge of the seat and stretched out his legs. In his eagerness to be his normal, active self again, he had overdone things today. All the stooping over the blueberry bushes had strained the muscles up the backs of his calves and thighs, and he had aggravated matters by the walk on the uneven sandy edge of the road.

'There's a hurricane warning, have you heard?' said Mrs van der Welden.

'No, I hadn't. A real full-blown hurricane?'

'No, no,' said her husband. 'Only out at sea, and it's dying away. Nothing to worry about.'

Sandy sat back and looked out of the window as they turned on to the Todd's Neck road past the far end of Libby's wood. Tirza had told him, just before he got on the bus, that one of the fishing boats was late in to harbour.

He forgot about it when he reached the hotel and found a letter from Martha awaiting him. He had left before the mail had been delivered that morning and to his surprise he had not thought about her all day. Now, however, he carried the letter up to his room and tore it open. A wave of heat ran through him as he smelled her scent rising from the paper. She had spent today shopping with her mother and he thought she might have stayed away on purpose to provoke him. It was the first time since they had met that they had not spent at least part of the day together.

To their mutual frustration, they had not found anywhere they could meet in privacy. Neither of them had a car. Sandy still had difficulty moving about. And anywhere they could reach was so public. Martha had a suggestion.

> *My family owns a piece of land on Todd's Neck, just above the path leading down to Libby's Beach. My grandfather was going to build a big house there to rent out to summer people back in the 1890s, when Todd's Neck became so fashionable, but all he ever finished was a summer cottage. It hasn't been let for a couple of years. I can get the key. I don't know why I didn't think of it before. I'll meet you there about eleven o'clock – you can't miss it. The last building before the big rocks.*

Because he was so tired, Sandy went to bed early, but was woken in the middle of the night by the sound of his open window banging about in its frame. He limped across the room and looked out over the ocean. Far out to sea there was nothing but blackness. Usually there was enough moonlight and starlight to cast a sheen over the sea. Tonight only the nearer reaches caught a few scraps of reflected light from the hotel, and they showed a white mass seething like a badly poured pint of beer. He recalled what Tirza had said about an 'old' sea. Clearly new forces had stirred the ocean up again. He felt sorry for any poor fellows who might still be abroad on it. He closed and latched the window, and went back to bed.

Harriet was lying awake in the old brass four-poster bed at the farmhouse. Tobias had dropped off to sleep at last. Simon had telephoned them from Flett's Stores during the evening to say that he was going to wait in Flamboro for news of Wayne and his father, and after they had come to bed both Harriet and Tobias had pretended to be asleep, each for the other's sake. Tobias was now breathing heavily, interrupted by small, gasping snores, so Harriet could stop pretending.

The hurricane four years ago had been a terrifying experience. Flamboro and its boats had got off fairly lightly, but further along the shore large lobsterboats had been picked up and thrown five miles inland. And at the farm the roof had been torn off the chicken shed and most of her hens killed. Growing up under the shore of the great woods of north-west Maine, Harriet hated the sound of a high wind. Her uncle had been crippled by a tree falling in such a wind and her own father had just escaped with his life from another tree fall which knocked him unconscious for three days. For most of the night she lay awake, thinking of the *Reliant*, and fell asleep near dawn to dreams haunted by mountains of grey water rising and curling over her head.

Chapter 14

Maine: Summer 1942

*L*OUISA *MARY* AND the rest of Flamboro's fleet were out beyond the islands by the time the sun dragged itself clear of the horizon ahead of them. There was a sullen choppy sea running and the wind kept veering as though the air had been left in a state of confusion by the passing of the hurricane. The sky was sullen too, so that even when the sun came up its light was veiled by a thickness in the air that might have been cloud or fog or even the fine debris scattered through the high air by the storm.

Tirza sat hunched on the foredeck in her oilskins, staring out over a sea steep enough to hide the whole of the *Reliant* in the trough of a wave. Nathan stood on the engine housing to peer over the wheelhouse, steering with his feet. They had already salvaged one piece of wreckage – some broken fishing gear – but it was impossible to tell whether it belonged to *Reliant*. The fleet of small boats had started the search in some sort of order, but by now they were scattered across several miles of sea, those with more powerful engines surging ahead. Whenever one of the fishermen caught sight of something on the surface of the waves he changed course to investigate, so gradually the boats had become separated.

About a hundred yards away Tirza thought she could make out a patch on the water that was a darker grey than the rest of the sea. As the next wave heaved it up she could see that there was something, wide and flat, floating out there. She shouted above the noise of the engine and pointed. Nathan put the wheel over and headed *Louisa Mary* where she indicated.

As they approached, Tirza realised that the wreckage could not be anything to do with *Reliant*. It was an inflatable rubber raft, with ropes festooned around the sides, of the kind used by the navy. It might, however, come from some other victim of the storm.

'It's a life-raft,' she shouted over her shoulder as Nathan throttled back. 'From a naval ship, I guess.'

'Too small.' He had spotted it now, bringing *Louisa Mary* round in a curve to approach it from leeward. 'Could be from a plane, though.'

Cautiously he nosed the boat nearer, afraid of puncturing the fragile craft. Then he cut the engine when *Louisa Mary* had just enough way on to bring her alongside.

'There's a man inside.' Tirza's voice was hoarse. 'He's in uniform. I think he's dead.'

Nathan reached out with his gaff and pulled the life-raft over by means of one of the rope loops. His face was grave as he studied the man.

'Ayuh, he's dead all right.'

The face was blackened and bloated, the tongue protruding between the teeth and the eyes staring. The young man had contrived a partial shelter for himself out of a parachute, and a few pitiful possessions lay around him – an empty metal box which had contained emergency rations, some photographs and a flying helmet. He had taken off his boots and his bare feet looked surprisingly pale and tender. If she kept her eyes from his face, Tirza might have imagined that he was sleeping, for he lay curled on his side like a young child.

'I don't recognise the uniform,' she said shakily. Nathan was hanging over the gunwale making a towline fast to the bow of the life-raft. With the man so obviously dead, it wasn't worth the risk of trying to lift him aboard so far from land in a heavy sea.

'It's German,' he said shortly. 'He's a German airman.'

Tirza felt a jolt in her stomach like an electric shock. She had been feeling pity for the man, but he was the enemy.

'Do you think he crashed in the hurricane?'

'No. He's been longer dead than that. Died of starvation and thirst and exposure. No knowing how long he's been in that raft or how far he's drifted. Might have been tossed around for weeks.'

Tirza felt suddenly sick, and bowed her head on her drawn-up knees. Nathan gripped her shoulder briefly, then pushed the raft away with the gaff so that it swung slowly round to the stern of *Louisa Mary*. He started the engine and laid a course back towards Flamboro at half speed. The raft jerked, bobbed, then came obediently round behind the lobsterboat.

'Aren't we supposed to be searching for Wayne and the others?' asked Tirza dispiritedly, keeping her eyes averted from their macabre tow.

'We have to take this back first. We'll come out again after.'

———◈———

Late in the afternoon two boats from Casco Bay which had joined in the search found *Reliant* stranded on her beam ends on a shoal off Mount Desert Island. It was not clear whether the accident had occurred here, or whether she had been blown on to the shoal by the hurricane subsequently. There was no sign of her crew. Two life jackets were still in a locker inside her cabin. None of the fishermen or lobstermen wore life jackets while they worked – they were too much of an impediment. But most boats carried one for each man, and while running home before a storm a cautious man would don one. There was no way of telling whether the crew of *Reliant* had been taken unawares, with no time to put on their life jackets. Perhaps Walter had told Wayne to put one on when the weather blew up, but he and Eli had not bothered.

When Josie Pelham heard of the single missing life jacket, her face lit up for a moment, before freezing over again. Even in summer it was doubtful anyone could have survived twenty-four hours in the ocean in a life jacket. Before nightfall word came that the Casco boats had managed to tow *Reliant* off the reef. She was not badly holed. They had pumped her out and were towing her back to Flamboro. There was an unspoken thought in the air – the value of the boat would make some financial provision for the widow and her daughter.

A subdued air hung over Flamboro in the days that followed. The people of the town were accustomed to death at sea, but that made it no easier to bear when it struck. The circle of women closed protectively round Josie and Clarice, and the young soldiers who called with gifts of chocolate and nylons were politely but firmly turned away. Doggedly, the men of the town showed their concern in the work of repairing *Reliant* and finding a buyer. Negotiating the best possible price gave them the satisfaction of doing something practical for Josie.

The military authorities took away the body of the German airman and all his gear, but before they came Tirza and Nathan dried out his personal belongings in the kitchen. There was a packet of letters and a diary written in German, the ink smudged with water and the pages sticking together. The photographs had fared better. They showed what must be the man's family. A middle-aged couple with two grown-up children – the boy might, in better times, have been the airman. A young woman with blonde braids wound round her head and a baby in her arms. The woman was smiling but the baby eyed the camera with deep seriousness.

Tirza, amid conflicting feelings of rage and pity, found the photographs a painful reminder that the young man was not so different from Sandy or Will. She wanted to think of him as a monster, daring to come here, despoiling the coast of Maine, bringing bombs and death, but she kept coming back to those photographs, which filled her with a strange sense of shame.

The officer in charge of the detail which removed the body questioned both Tirza and Nathan closely. Nathan gave him as near as possible a chart location for the spot where the life-raft had been found, and Tirza described what she had seen, but there was not much they could add to the mute testimony of the man himself. He wore an identity tag which they had not touched. They both felt relief when the military ambulance drove away.

———◈———

A week after the hurricane, when hope had been abandoned of finding any of the crew of *Reliant*, Reverend Bridges announced that Josie had asked for a memorial service to be celebrated in the church – the local custom when a drowning at sea meant a normal funeral could not be held. The following morning, however, Eel Joe's outboard motor was heard puttering into the harbour. On board his boat, lying between the fixed boxes in which Joe stored his eels, was the body of Wayne Pelham, still wearing his life jacket.

Joe had found Wayne in one of the places where bodies and objects washed overboard were known sometimes to come ashore – the angular dent in the shoreline, not large enough to be called a cove, where the rocks at the base of Todd's Neck met Libby's Beach. The body had fetched up there and lodged amongst the sharp rocks, hidden from most directions. Joe had found it when he landed there to fish for porgies with a hand line and in scrambling over the rocks to a convenient ledge caught sight of a corner of the bright yellow life jacket. There was no knowing how long Wayne's body had been trapped there.

That night, Tirza awoke still tangled in a dark net of dreams. She lay staring upwards, to where the rough beams would be, floating above her in the moonless air. The old dream of the burning city lurked in fragments in the corners of her mind, but something else had followed, something that had left her cold and clammy, although the air of her room as her breathing steadied was mild.

Faces had drifted up towards her from the sea-bed, drawn up as she winched a lobster pot aboard *Louisa Mary*. Or was it one face? Already scarred by scavenging sea creatures, it seemed at one moment to be the face of the German airman, at the next, Wayne's face, laughing and jeering at her.

'Goin' to be a swell day's fishin', my dad says. Shame you ain't got more capacity on that little boat o' yourn!'

'But a shark's torn your net,' she said. 'It's the end of the herring run.'

———◆———

When the shadows were drawing in the next afternoon, Tirza stumbled into the clearing around Christina's cabin. Her grandmother was sitting in her old wicker chair with a book in her hands, but she was not reading. Tirza knelt down on the ground beside her, hunching up, huddled against the coarse russet cloth of her skirt. Christina put her book down on the rocky ground and laid her hand gently on the downturned dark head.

'We have to learn to accept it, my darling. The only thing we can be sure of in our lives is our death at the end of it.'

Tirza's shoulders jerked rebelliously.

'He was only fourteen, Girna. Why did he have to drown? Why poor Wayne? What had he done?' She drew a long breath, and her head trembled under Christina's touch. 'I'm sorry about his dad too – of course I am – and Eli, but they were grown-up. They'd had plenty of time. Grandma says...' She gulped. 'She says it's God's chosen who die young. It's a *blessing*, she says, to be spared growing up. I *hate* her! I *hate* her God! It's all lies. Isn't it, Girna?'

She raised a tear-stained face pleadingly.

Christina twined a lock of the soft, unkempt hair around her finger and looked down at her.

'It was the Indian belief that when a person dies, it is the same as when a flower dies or a tree dies. We all take sustenance from the earth, we all return to it. And by the earth they meant the whole of the created universe, of course. Man has a spirit, but so has every deer or eagle or whale or oak or clump of wild cloud-berries. When the material body dies, the spirit wanders but is free to return again in the same or another form, and pass through the cycle of life again. They had a saying: "Next time it will be better."'

'But what about *now*?' Tirza cried. 'It's *now* I want to know about.'

Christina shook her head. 'I don't know. We have to accept and keep on living, however much we rage against what happens to us in life, Tirza. Remember that all life is a circle, with the flowering tree of the soul at its centre and its four quarters which sustain that tree: the south with its soft warmth, the west with its nourishing rain and the east that brings peace and light. But there is the north, too. The north sends the great winds that train us to be strong and courageous. All life is made up of these elements. Without them it is incomplete. A broken pattern. Try to hold a little of Wayne in your memory. That way, he goes on living as long as you do.'

———◆———

The following day, the funeral for Wayne and the memorial service for Walter and Eli was held in the white clapboard church on the headland overlooking Flamboro harbour. The women had brought armfuls of flowers from their tiny gardens, tended with such care and difficulty on the poor sandy soil of the town. Mostly, they were the old cottage flowers – hollyhocks and delphiniums, portulacas, black-eyed susans and lupins. The children had gathered wild flowers from the field edges up behind the town, and Miss Molly had recklessly cut large bunches from the old-fashioned scented rose bushes brought back from England fifty years ago by Captain Penhaligon. Everyone was there, even Miss Susanna, driven the few yards to the church gate and half carried into the church by Nathan and Charlie. Her skin was so pale that it looked transparent, but although her eyes were more deeply sunken even than a few weeks ago, they were as bright and alert as ever.

'I believed I should be the next to require the minister's services,' Miss Susanna murmured to Harriet. 'I thought my heart would break when I heard about young Wayne and the others. After a lifetime of knowing the sea's implacable hunger, I still find myself crying out against it.'

Christina was sitting on Miss Susanna's other side. She took her hand.

Tirza, in the pew behind, could hear their soft voices. She looked up at the plain white ceiling of the church and the windows of clear glass against which the flowers arranged on the sills laid patterns of colour – branches thick with lilac blossom looped and fretted with vines of the wild white morning glory, and stiff furred sheaves of hollyhock, whose flowers looked fragile against the parent stems. Outside the window to her right a late golden robin was singing. The melody rippled and bubbled like a spring of fresh water, as if nothing was wrong, as if this summer – as if the life of the village – could go on unchanged. She wondered if Wayne's spirit was around here somewhere, watching what was happening, or whether he had already chosen another body, as a fox, maybe, or a herring gull. Something independent and fierce and quarrelsome.

The murmuring stopped as the minister walked up the aisle, and the service began. The members of the congregation lifted their voices in a hymn that held a particular significance for the people of Flamboro, for whom the rocky land and rocky ocean were the foundations of life itself.

> 'Rock of Ages, cleft for me.
> Let me hide myself in Thee.
> Unknown waves before me roll,
> Hiding rock and treach'rous shoal.'

Later, Nathan stepped forward to read from the Psalms in memory of his friends and the young boy now lying in the plain pine casket in front of them all.

> 'If I take the wings of the morning and dwell in the uttermost parts of the sea; even there shall Thy hand lead me, and Thy right hand shall hold me.'

Chapter 15

Intermezzo
Fall 1980

Boston
September 1, 1980

Dear Ms Libby

I enjoyed our meeting last month at Max Prescott's office in London. It was great to hear from him that you've agreed to come over for the opening of the exhibition on September 14. I've booked you a hotel suite here in Boston for the first five days, September 11 to 15. After that, we'll talk about what you'd like to do. I hope maybe you'll visit with me and my family at our country place in Vermont. We would just love to have you do that.

I've lined up seven interviews with national newspapers and magazines, and have another three possibles. There will be four radio slots, and I've been lucky enough to get you on the Gary Gemmings Show. Max has told me you don't care for live TV interviews, but don't worry! The Gary Gemmings Show is pre-recorded, and if anything goes wrong, they just do it over.

The radio interviews will be done in studios right here in town, and most of the journalists have agreed to meet with you at your hotel. Two of them, however, want to get some shots of you in the gallery, so for those interviews I thought we'd use my office here. I hope these arrangements suit you, but if not just let me know and we'll change anything you want.

My assistant has booked your flights from Edinburgh to London and London to Boston, and your tickets will be waiting to be collected at Edinburgh airport. (See enclosed sheet with details.) She got you an open-ended return ticket, since we weren't sure what your plans might be after you finish here. I'll meet you with a car at the airport and drive you to your hotel. I look forward so much to seeing you on September 11.

Yours truly,
Pam O'Rourke

Ballinuig,
Inverness-shire
5 September

Dear Tirza,

Yes, I do think that you're right to go to Boston. I'm sure it won't be the ordeal you say that you envisage in your panic-stricken moments. What are a few wealthy Bostonian matrons compared with the Vietcong or the cut-throat drug dealers of Colombia, that you should give them even a passing thought? Go and be polite for a few hours, say your piece nicely for the journalists, and then enjoy yourself! I wish I were coming with you. From all that I've heard, New England is beautiful in the autumn. Will the leaves have started changing colour by the time you're there? Once you've finished all your official duties, it will be almost October, so I'll be picturing you amongst flaming scarlets and oranges, photographing white clapboard churches. Or would that be too obviously beautiful for you? Anyway, you're bound to find something of interest, to contrast with our bleak Highland scenery.

We're well into the harvest here. I've been sitting on a combine from 5 a.m. till 10 p.m., and I'm now writing this with one hand and forking up scrambled eggs with the other, which was all I could be bothered to cook. My backside is so tender I've put a cushion on top of the kitchen chair. It makes me ache all over to think of farmers a generation ago, who had to sit on those bare metal seats, exposed to everything that the wind and weather could throw at them. I dare say we're getting very soft nowadays.

Douglas is arriving tomorrow, at the end of his year's VSO at the orphanage in Pakistan. He'll give me a hand with the harvest until he starts university in a month's time. Alison has been a great help over her summer holiday, but of course when the schools started a fortnight ago she had to go back to work. I hope it won't be too long before you meet them. They're not bad kids. When they were smaller, I used to wonder whether losing their mother so young would leave a permanent scar, but they seem OK. It helped having my mother with us till she settled in Edinburgh with her sister three years ago.

I've looked through the dusty old boxes in the attic, as I promised, but found nothing relating to Maine. All I have is the large manila envelope I told you about before. I looked through the contents again, especially the photographs. There is that one of you in *Stormy Petrel*. I don't want to part with it, but I'll have a copy made and give it to you when we meet.

Thank you for agreeing to have dinner with me in Edinburgh before you set off for the States. I'm looking forward to it more than I can say.

Take care of yourself.

Yours aye,

Alex

Boston

15 September, 1980

Dear Max,

Well, the launch went off successfully, I think. I promise I did you credit. I confronted all those faces and did not retreat to the Ladies, though I felt like it a few times! I suppose I'm accustomed now to the more restrained British way of doing things. Over here I have felt once or twice that I was being devoured. Truly, I can't understand people's attitude. It's the photographs that are important, not me. They're here to look at them. Instead, people seem to want to *touch* me all the time. Disconcerting, and enough to drive me back to Scotland, if Pam weren't so kind and excited about it all.

Tell Colin that the American edition of the book is selling well – they've already had to order a reprint. I've been approached by one of the big publishers over here to do a large-format book based on my work over the years. I've referred him to you, so you should be hearing from him soon. Also, a local Boston firm has a proposal for a calendar – alternate views of New England and Scotland. I'll need to think about this. I don't yet have any work on New England. He's also got your address.

In a couple of days I'm going with Pam to her family home in Vermont. She's been very insistent, and it will be good to get away from the crowds and the city. They go there as often as possible, and want to fit in a quick visit before their children start back at their private schools in Boston. I plan to take some pictures of the countryside and the farming community, then I may rent a car and drive around a bit when the O'Rourkes come back to Boston. I'll let you know when I'm more certain of my plans.

See you before too long.

Love,

Tirza

Portland
September 16, 1980

Dear Miss Libby

I hope you will forgive my writing to you like this on behalf of one of my clients. The exhibition of your work (of which, may I say, I have long been an admirer) and your own visit to this country having been reported extensively in the newspapers, my client has asked me, as his legal representative, to contact you. Indeed, for the last year he has been anxious to reach you, but it has proved somewhat difficult to trace your whereabouts.

It appears from the interviews I have read that you plan to stay in New England for a few weeks after the opening of the exhibition. I wonder whether I could prevail upon you to pay a visit to our office in Portland, so that we might discuss certain matters which will be more appropriately dealt with in person? Alternatively, I could call on you in Boston, but if Maine is on your itinerary, it might be more satisfactory to be able to view all the relevant documents here in the office.

Perhaps you would be good enough to call me, or to inform me where I may contact you, so that we can arrange a meeting.

I remain yours very truly,

Gabriel C. Foss, Jr.

Dear Alex,

We've been here five days now. You would love it. The woods have all the colours you were expecting and I had forgotten. Strange, isn't it, the tricks memory plays? Some things I remember so clearly. Others I have forgotten, till something jogs the brain, like an electric shock, and then – click! – the memory is there again. That's how it has been with the sight of the woods in full autumn splendour.

A couple of odd things have happened since I called you from Boston. First, a letter from a Portland lawyer was forwarded to me here from the gallery. It's very portentous and breathes heavily of 'matters to discuss' and a client who is anxious to trace me. He wants me to meet him in Portland or Boston, but divulges nothing. Can't imagine what he is talking about. I haven't made up my mind whether or not I'll agree to a meeting. I don't really want to waste time going back to Boston before I catch my flight home from the airport, but I certainly hadn't planned on going to Maine. I know you say I should go back, but I'm not sure I agree.

The other curiosity is this. Pam and I drove into the nearest town yesterday for groceries and afterwards while she went to the bank I pottered around a second-hand book store, where I found a big glossy book published about five years ago, called *Todd's Neck: Victorian Summer High Life*. Talk about coincidence! I bought it, of course, and though I haven't had time to read it yet, I've been dipping in. It is based on a collection of 1880s and 1890s photographs which came to light about ten years ago, taken by a New York high society photographer who used to summer at the Mansion House on Todd's Neck soon after it was turned into a hotel. The text details the way Maine became the fashionable summer place for the rich from New York and Boston.

I wasn't so interested in that as in the early pages describing the area before it became popular. Apparently the Libby family owned far more land than I realised. From the seventeenth century our land reached from Flamboro down about five miles south of Todd's Neck. The Todds owned most of the Neck itself, but when they overreached themselves in the mid-nineteenth century, one Elias Libby bought a large part of the land from them, except for the area around the Mansion House. I think he must have been my great-(great?)-grandfather. Then about twenty years later the family had to sell land themselves, including most of Todd's Neck and the area south of it.

Now remember what I said just now about memory? I have a very faint recollection of some family property beyond Todd's Neck being spoken of, but I paid it no mind (as we used to say) at the time.

The book also reproduced an 1890 map showing Todd's Neck and Flamboro, with the householders' names printed next to their houses. All the familiar names leapt out at me – Libby, Flett, Penhaligon, Larrabee, Tremayne, Pelham, Swanson. I can't tell you how peculiar it made me feel. There is this map, nearly a century old, and there are the same houses, with the same names next to them. The Libbys at Libby's Farm would be my grandparents. (Or maybe my great-grandparents?) I never knew my grandfather, but my grandmother Abigail lived with us when I was a child. Flett's General Stores and Post Office is shown. Capt. Penhaligon was the old sea captain I told you about, and his three daughters were already grown young women when that map was made. It is really unsettling – like stepping back into history and coming face to face, not exactly with yourself, but with your own shadow.

I never wanted to go back. Ever. But perhaps enough years have passed now. Perhaps I can face it. Perhaps I should face it. The lawyer's letter, and that map – they seem to be prodding me. I think if I don't go, I'll regret it. Be ashamed of myself, even. All these years I've tried to turn my back on what happened there, and by doing that I've frozen part of myself. Perhaps we aren't truly adult until we can face our childhood honestly and without fear.

Anyway, I'll let you know what I decide. I wish you *were* here.

Tirza

Dear Max

I promised to keep you informed of my movements.

I've rented a car, as planned, and will be taking more photographs as I tour around. First, though, I've decided to drive to Maine. Some lawyer in Portland wants to see me, though he won't divulge why. I plan to take my time driving over there, and I've booked in at the Mansion House Hotel, Todd's Neck, Flamboro, for a couple of nights. Not sure how long I'll stay, but I don't expect to be there more than a week. I'll call you from there to let you know my next moves.

Pam O'Rourke has been really kind. Her husband took the children back to Boston in time for school, but we stayed on a few days here, just lazing around and gossiping. I feel thoroughly rested. She's a live wire when she's occupied with gallery business, but when she switches off she has a wonderful capacity for relaxing. She puts it all down to having studied meditation and using aromatherapy! I don't know about that, but this visit to Vermont with her has done me a lot of good.

When are you going off to Tuscany?

Love,

Tirza

Chapter 16

Maine: Fall 1942

THE SUMMER WEATHER never truly returned after the hurricane. There were hot days again, but these spells did not last for long. The wind would get up, or the banks of fog come rolling down from the Bay of Fundy, bringing an underlying chill to the air. Tobias was working every hour of clear weather to bring in the harvest. Tirza's days were full, between the fishing and the harvest, and two weeks or more went by desolately without her meeting Sandy. Harriet and Abigail spent long hours in their kitchens, crimson-faced over their stoves, canning and making jams and pickles. Even Simon was working hard at the harvest, cutting and boxing cabbages and driving the reaping machine.

During the harvest, Tirza saw more of Simon than she had since spring had brought the soldiers to Flamboro. One day they were working side by side in the cabbage field, crumpling sheets of newspaper to make individual nests for the best ones and packing them into heavy cardboard cartons for shipment to a wholesaler in New Jersey. Simon was whistling 'Chattanooga Choo Choo' softly as he worked. He looked cheerful, and not as though he was counting the minutes until he could escape from the farm, the way he had earlier in the year.

'Have you changed your mind?' Tirza said, not sure how much he would confide in her any more. 'About taking over the farm after your dad retires?'

Simon sat back on his heels and looked at her with narrowed eyes. He was passing a big cabbage from one hand to the other, as if he was hefting a basketball.

'You haven't been blabbing to anyone, have you?'

'Of course not.' She was offended. 'I only wondered.'

Simon looked over his shoulder. Sam and Tobias were working along parallel rows, but they were some yards ahead of Tirza and Simon.

'I've been talking to some of the guys.' He had lowered his voice. 'The enlisted men, like Captain Tucker, are some different from the men just drafted into the army because of the war. If you enlist in the regular army, they teach you a specialised skill. Like gunnery, see, or signals. And you can get promotion to officer. If you graduate from high school first, you've got a chance to enlist straight away as an officer, if you pass the exams and all. And there's other possibilities...'

A few days ago, Simon had met the British airman in Flamboro, getting out of the hotel car.

'Good morning,' said Sandy, stopping at the foot of the steps up to Flett's Stores.

'Morning,' said Simon, side-stepping on his way up to the headland to see the gun crew.

'Like a Coke?'

Simon stopped. He was hot from the walk, and Mary Flett always kept a few bottles of Coke in the ice-box.

'Great!'

They sat side by side on the edge of the porch with their legs dangling, all the rocking chairs already being occupied by the porch regulars. Simon gulped thankfully from the thick glass bottle, then pressed it against his hot temples. Sandy was talking about Martha, but Simon let it wash over him; he'd heard it all before.

'So I suppose you'll be taking over the farm eventually,' said Sandy. 'Do you plan to go to college first? Like Hector Swanson?'

Simon looked at him in surprise. He had never given a thought to college. Suddenly he was blurting out his longing to be free of the drudgery and emotional blackmail of the farm, his plans to join the army, the idea of enlisting after high school.

'Have you thought about West Point?'

'West Point?'

'That's what it's called, isn't it? Like our Sandhurst? Sort of university for army officers. If you're serious about joining the army, better go about the thing properly.'

'But... I don't know... Wouldn't it cost a lot of money?' Simon was momentarily dazzled, then downcast.

'I've no idea. I expect there are scholarships. Why don't you ask Captain Tucker? If he doesn't know himself, he'll know where you can find out.'

In the days that followed, Simon had thought of little else. He hadn't managed to speak to Captain Tucker yet, but he kept whispering to himself, *West Point*. That would show Dad. And Martha. And Flamboro. He'd prove he could really amount to something, not stay a dirt farmer all his life.

'Maybe I might even get to West Point.' It burst out of him now half defiantly.

Simon looked more animated than Tirza had seen him for a long time. One thing stood out clearly. He planned to finish high school first. She let out a sigh of relief.

Simon misunderstood.

'You don't need to started sighing, Tirza,' he said irritably. 'I'll join the army if I want, and I'll go all round the world. Get to be a general, maybe!' He laughed.

'No, no, I wasn't complaining or anything,' she protested. 'Only I'm glad you're coming to high school in the fall.'

'Oh, sure,' he said airily. 'Sergeant Klinsky says only a fool would try to work his way up in the army, like him. He's still only a sergeant and maybe won't get any higher. He says, graduate from high school, with some math and physics and stuff, and you're halfway to being an officer.'

He packed the cabbage into the box, and picked up his knife to cut another.

'Anyway, if I eventually decide to retire from the army when I'm forty or something, I could still take over the farm. Dad could run it with hired help till then.'

They continued to work their way along the rows of cabbages, crawling forward on their knees. Tobias wanted a third of the field cut and packed by the time the buyer's truck came at five thirty. Just now they were kneeling near one of the stone piles. Every year men, women and children of the Libby family had picked the stones from the fields and laid them in long piles by the field edges like ancient burial mounds. When a family picked stones, the size each child could lift was decided at the start by the father, who handed out a measuring stick cut to length. That way every member of the family contributed, each according to physical capacity. The largest stones had gone to the building of the stone walls, many of them almost as old as the family's tenure of this land. But even so the stone piles were fifteen or eighteen feet long, eight feet wide, and almost as tall as a man.

You would think all the loose stones in the soil would have been picked up by now, but every winter's frost threw up more to be gathered each spring, and at harvest time, if there had been a long dry spell, the dusty earth crumbled away from the insidious stones, which always moved upwards as if they were living creatures. So when you were on your knees in the dry earth the hard edges of granite pieces pressed into your flesh. You could always stand, of course, and bend double, but that was certain sure to give you a crick back. Tirza often thought there should be some easier way to harvest the vegetable crops, but she had never been able to figure out how.

The weather was a good deal cooler now, with a high white veil drawn over the sky, but down here pressed against the sun-warmed earth and labouring hard she had to keep wiping the sweat out of her eyes. Her hands grew slippery on the handle of the sharp knife she was using to cut the cabbage stalks, and she wiped her palms on the seat of her shorts every few minutes. She would have preferred to be out with Nathan in the lobsterboat, but he had said he could manage the hauling fine on his own, when Tobias came yesterday asking for her help.

'Want to pick crab apples this evening?' Simon asked suddenly. He had lifted the full carton to carry to the edge of the field.

'OK.'

Tirza was pleased. She had been wondering whether he would want to go picking with her this year. The crab apple trees grew on the Tremayne estate. The first time she and Simon – daring each other on – had climbed into the orchard they could not have been more than five and six. They ate the apples that year, despite their sour flavour – that was all part of the adventure. The severe stomach aches they suffered as a result did not put them off going back the following year. By then they knew that crab apples had to be cooked and made into jellies and preserves, so they filled a bucket and brought them home to Harriet with pride.

'Sakes!' she said. 'Where did you find these?'

When they told her, she shook her head.

'Seems to me that's stealing.'

Sam, surprisingly, had come to their defence.

'Them apples just go to waste every year,' he said. 'Fall to the ground and rot away. Feed nothin' but the yellow jackets and such. Tremaynes ain't gonna use them. Don't seem like stealin' to me.'

When Tobias came in, he agreed.

'I hate to see good food thrown away. Tell you what, Harriet. Make them into jelly, and if the Tremaynes turn up, you can hand it over to them, and they'll be grateful.'

Since that time, six years ago now, Tirza and Simon had gathered crab apples every year for Harriet's jelly. They sometimes helped with the chopping too, because at this time of year Harriet could barely keep pace with all her work. And Tirza never quite lost her sense of wonder at the glow of the finished jelly.

After a quick supper in the farm kitchen, they set off. As well as the root cellar under the house, over the horse barn next to Sam's bedroom there was a loft where apples and pumpkins and onions and other keeping fruits and vegetables were stored for the winter. They climbed the ladder to collect four bushel baskets for the crab apples.

This evening the loft was full of a hazy light like dark honey. Motes of dust from the hay stored below swam in the beams which fell slantwise through the window and the cracks where the old boards of the walls had shrunk away from each other over the years. A shaft glittered on Simon's fair hair. The scent of harvest never left this place. Mostly compounded of apples and onions, it carried harmonies of pumpkins, turnips and rutabagas. Potatoes, too, Tirza had noticed, had their own woody, earthy smell. This year's harvest was beginning to fill the slatted shelves, but it would be some weeks yet till the apples from the orchard and the main-crop potatoes would be gathered, and the pumpkins were still fattening. Sam had already braided together a dozen ropes of onions and hung them from old, squared-off, handmade nails that were hammered into the roof beams. More would follow when he had time in the evenings to make them, sitting in the rocker on the porch which he always occupied. Tirza loved to watch the way his bony fingers worked the leaves of the onions together. Although she was able enough when it came to mending nets, she had never managed to plait onions successfully. They always fell apart as soon as she held up the rope to show it off.

Simon ducked underneath the onions and unhooked two bushel baskets from the wall and passed them over to her. Then he lifted down two more for himself and they climbed back down the ladder to the barn. The farm track was already partly in shadow from the pine woods as they headed down to the shore, and mingies were dancing maddeningly around their faces. They slapped and swatted at them, and Tirza kept huffing air out through her mouth in the hope that they would stay away from her face. She led the way into the Tremayne estate by crossing the cabbage field and climbing over the stone wall. It was fairly high here, but she didn't want to go right round by the coast path. Simon might spot the foxes' den. Anyway, the orchards were opposite here, some way in from the shore.

'We never remember the plums,' said Simon, as he said every year. 'The wasps and the birds will have eaten them all by now.'

'Ayuh. Last year we said we'd remind each other.'

'There's been too much going on this year. Maybe next year.'

Although the evening shadows were long, there was plenty of light to see what they were doing, and they moved apart, each selecting a promising looking tree. Tirza managed to fill one of her baskets with the apples she could reach from the ground, but to fill the second one, she climbed up into the lower branches and balanced the basket in a convenient crook where she could pick into it. The half-filled basket was not too heavy to lift down from the first tree, but by the time it was full she knew she would need help.

'Simon!' she called. She could not see him in the dim light. He was probably up in the branches of another tree. She shinnied down and looked around. He had put his two full baskets next to her first one, but wasn't anywhere to be seen.

'Simon?'

'I'm here.'

He came sauntering over from the direction of the house and helped her lift the basket down from above their heads.

'Where did you go?'

'Thought I saw a light in the house. But it was probably just a reflection of the setting sun.'

Tirza remembered broken wine bottles and the half-naked soldier with the girl from the village, and shivered. Suddenly she wanted to be away from here. She didn't want Simon to know that the lovely old house had been so defiled. Between them they carried a basket to the stone wall and passed it over, then went back for the others. After they had climbed over into the cabbage field, Simon peered out towards the darkening sea.

'You'd better get home. Looks like a fog getting up. Don't want Grandma starting a ruckus. I can carry one basket up to the house and get Dad and Sam to help me bring back the other three.'

'OK.' She hesitated. 'It was great to pick the apples with you again,' she said awkwardly.

'Aw, sure.' He looked embarrassed and heaved up one of the baskets. 'Be seeing you.'

Without a backward glance he set off up the farm track. Tirza watched him go. Against the setting sun he looked as insubstantial as if he had been cut out of cardboard. The edges of him were blurred as she squinted into the red-orange light. She wondered whether you could take a photograph of that. Sandy had said you shouldn't point the camera into the sun because it would spoil the photograph, but it seemed to her that you might want to do just that. It was peculiar the way Simon, whose hand, bumping against hers as they manoeuvred the basket out of the tree, had felt so solid and muscular, could be turned by a trick of the light into something as wispy as a shadow. Probably you could paint that, but she wanted to photograph it.

◆◆◆◆

The evening fog seemed to have been just a trick of the weather, because the next few days were hot and bright, almost like July again, although it was nearly Labour Day. Nathan told Tirza to spend her time helping up at the farm. She wasn't catching many crabs now, and the guests at the Mansion House were drifting away. Privately, Nathan thought it would be a good idea for her to be kept busy with Tobias and Harriet, and to see something of Simon. She shouldn't spend so much time fishing with him on the *Louisa Mary*. She was growing up and needed to mix more with other people.

Anyway, when she started at high school in Portland she wouldn't be able to come out hauling with him. She would have to leave on the early bus in the morning and wouldn't return to Flamboro until after he was back in harbour, so he'd better get used to doing without her help right now. He'd managed well enough on his own when she was a baby. It saved him time and physical effort when she helped, of course, but he had to admit that what he liked best about having her on board was the companionship.

If you had told him when he was a young man that he would ever relish the presence of a daughter on his lobsterboat, he'd have laughed aloud. But she was good company. Talking enough for good conversation's sake, but never too much. Oh, she had never been a chatterer. But since the loss of *Reliant*, he had been worrying about taking her out with him at all. It wasn't right to take youngsters to sea and risk their lives. Though folk had been doing it since Flamboro was founded. Boys, at least. Mind, according to Christina the original inhabitants, the Abenaki, had thought nothing of women fishing. They went out on equal terms with the men. Perhaps that was what made Tirza so good in a boat. Perhaps she had inherited her sea craft from her Indian ancestors.

He grinned to himself. That was some crazy notion!

The day before Labour Day Nathan went out as usual to haul his gang of traps. It was hot and sultry, with a dense breathless feel in the air as if the whole world was suffocating – interrupted by sudden gusts of cold air. They had all been discussing it on the wharf side as they collected their bait and readied their boats.

Ben was of the opinion that a thunderstorm was brewing.

'My missus woke with one of her almighty headaches this morning, and that's a sure sign of thunder. Swears by it, she does.'

Arthur shook his head.

'Don't feel like thunder to me. More like one of them settled calms that used to maroon the old windjammers out at sea. I don't see no problem.' He took off his shirt and wiped his forehead with it. After his grandfather Eli had been lost with *Reliant*, he had stopped lazing around so much. He was saving his money for a boat of his own, to help out his whole family. Meantime, he was still crewing for Ben. Since the naval patrols had disturbed the fish, they had to work longer hours for poor catches, but there didn't seem much else any of them could do.

Nathan suspected that it might be a heavy sea fog building up way offshore. Summer was ending, and the season was upon them when areas of hot air and cold air collided, stirring up fog. As he motored out of the harbour, he spotted wisps of steam rising from the surface of the waves. He nodded in confirmation of his own thoughts. That meant the sea, still holding the heat of the last few days, was warmer than the air seeping in from Canada, even though there was barely wind to stir the listless leaves on the trees in Flamboro. Fog was more than likely, he reckoned, before the day was much older. He opened the throttle a little wider, heading for twenty or so pots he had laid out over towards Mustinegus Island.

The first of his floats came in sight – spindle-shaped and painted yellow and red. That British fellow, Sandy, had asked him how he ever managed to locate his two hundred pots. 'In all that waste of water,' he had called it.

Nathan thought about it as he put the engine into neutral and went forward to hook the pot out of the water. The sea wasn't a wasteland to him, for one thing. Out here he could have described all the underwater geography that lay round about. In his mind's eye it was as clear as Mount Manenticus, which he could see rising up on land, with Flamboro just a splash of white like seagull droppings at its foot and Gooseneck Lake over beyond the southern hogsback. These hills and valleys under water, sudden crags and deep rifts where a lobster pot might be lost – he could almost see them. The water lay like a tricky gauze over the top of them, but he had been learning their shapes and patterns since he had first come out in a boat with a lobsterman uncle when he was six or seven.

That was how the knowledge was passed on, he'd explained to Sandy. Oh sure, there were charts, but they only served as reminders. Every man fishing these waters carried his own map of the sea-bed inside his own head.

The lobster pot was empty. He pitched it overboard and headed for the next one. Trouble was, in fog or storm, you could lose your bearings, those unconscious sightings you took from coastline features and from the bell and whistle buoys marking the dangerous reefs. On an ordinary dark night it wasn't so bad. There were harbour lights and lighthouses, and the clusters of windows from the houses in the ports. They all helped you to fix yourself on that mental map. And as for finding your lobster pots – well, you just remembered where you had laid them in relation to that map. Nathan couldn't see the difficulty, any more than he could comprehend how some people had no sense of direction. Mary Flett was like that. Give her a lift somewhere, and she'd be saying, 'Take a left here, Nathan,' and you'd say, 'But, Mary, they live *east* of here, not *west*.' She'd look at you blankly, as if you were talking a foreign language. Which maybe you were.

The next three pots were empty too. And the bait was shredded and disintegrating, so he refilled the bait bags. Then he had a run of good luck. Five legal lobsters, one small one he threw back and one shedder. He held this last one up and examined it in disgust. After a lobster had shed its shell, it started growing fast, before the new shell hardened around it. And during this stage its flesh filled up with water like a sponge. No Maine fisherman would eat a shedder. They tasted like soggy pink felt. There were lobstermen and canners who would pass off a shedder as an edible lobster, but Nathan wasn't one of them. This would be a fine fellow, too, once his shell firmed up. Nathan dropped him over the side with a sigh. Maybe if the lobster stayed in this area where Nathan had a fair number of pots, he'd wander into one again when he would be worth eating.

He put the engine in gear and headed north-east of the island. He had a group of twenty-five pots on an underwater ledge here where the fishing was good. The first one held two females with clusters of eggs under their tails. *Two.* Oh well, one day the eggs would be the catch of the future. He lowered them carefully into the water and watched them scuttling downwards into the murk. It was looking darker down there than it had just a few minutes ago.

Nathan straightened and sniffed the air. There was a damp smell different from the sea smell. It left a slight smoky after-taste on the back of your tongue. The horizon was blurred, as if someone had smudged a finger over half-dry paint. He weighed up the likelihood that the fog would come in rapidly. He was less than halfway through hauling his gang.

Under no circumstances was Nathan a rash man, but he needed all the lobsters he could catch at the moment. Abigail said Tirza must have several sets of new clothes to wear to high school in Portland. She had already dragged her off to buy a winter coat, and he had been taken aback when he saw the bill. Harriet had offered Abigail the pick of Martha's castoffs. There were some sweaters that Abigail judged suitable, but everything else, it appeared, was too 'flashy'. Tirza had looked embarrassed and uncomfortable when she tried Martha's clothes on. Nathan had experienced an odd sensation watching her parade, reluctantly, in one outfit after another. At first the clothes seemed incongruous. He was used to seeing her in grubby shorts or dungarees patched at the knee, or in his old cut-down oilskins. In Martha's clothes she looked, not just older, but alien. More feminine. Mysterious somehow. He was as uncomfortable about it all as she was. In the end he had agreed with his mother about the sweaters, and promised to find enough money to cover a couple of plaid skirts, some saddle Oxfords, and what Abigail called smalls – underwear, socks and handkerchiefs.

It seemed that as soon as he had agreed to this expenditure, the lobsters had taken to hiding away. He glanced at the horizon again. It looked no worse than it had done a few minutes ago. He would carry on, he decided, and finish hauling, but keep a reef watch. If things got worse, he would leave the cluster of thirty pots over to the north-west, in the direction of Casco Bay.

He had lifted four more pots and found three good lobsters when he noticed that the colours of the float on the fourth pot dimmed before his eyes as he dropped it back over the side. He looked up sharply. The horizon had crept up on him. It was no more than a mile away. And Mustinegus to the south had disappeared altogether. He swore under his breath and put the engine in gear. The glass of the compass was misted over with condensation. He rarely used a compass, but he wiped it now with the heel of his hand, then swung *Louisa Mary* round and headed back for Flamboro. The fog came stealing along on his heels.

At first he thought he might be able to outrun it, but the fog, like a great soft animal, rolled over his shoulders, over the cramped wheelhouse, over the bows. Everything ahead was blotted out and he was alone in a grey circle of dank air. He could not even see the bow of the boat. He slowed down. No point in rushing now, and more risk of collision. Most of the time Flamboro boats managed to avoid going to sea in a fog, but every fisherman kept a small foghorn stored in the stern locker. Steering with one hand, Nathan groped under the dragnet and spare gear in the locker until he felt the hard brass edge of the horn. He set it on the bottom boards by his foot and worked it at intervals with his left hand while he steered with his right.

He tried to remember where he had last seen the other boats. Ben had been further out than he was, but had turned back earlier. Probably he was ahead of *Louisa Mary* by now. The Towson brothers both laid their traps not far offshore. There were fewer lobsters there, what with the coming and going of the boats in the harbour, but the Towsons were young still – eighteen and twenty – and neither of them could afford a boat big enough to work further out. He numbered over the other lobsterboats in his mind. He was pretty sure no one was still further out than he was, which meant they would reach the harbour before the fog was too bad. But it also meant more risk of running into one of them. He sounded the foghorn again and strained his ears for any answering boom, but all he could hear was the regular noise of the buoys, shifting and distorted.

The fog had a curious effect on sounds. It seemed to muffle your ears as if they were wrapped up in a thick scarf. You strained to hear through its cloying thickness just as you strained to see through it. And yet some noises came louder and closer than they would on a clear day. The desolate groaning of a whistle buoy could sound near enough to fill you with panic while it was still a safe distance away, and voices sometimes echoed off the walls of fog and rebounded, so they seemed to come first from one direction and then from another. It was Nathan's belief that it was these tricks that fog played with sound, more than the inability to see, which caused accidents. They confused the mind, and a fisherman who would bring his boat safely back to harbour on a pitch black night by the sound of the breakers alone could, in a fog, become as helpless as the most cack-handed novice.

These heavy fogs, rolling in from Newfoundland and Greenland, had a solidity that was almost tangible. Nathan glanced over his shoulder again. Beyond *Louisa Mary's* stern a shape hovered. Darker than the encompassing fog, it reared up and leaned over the small lobsterboat – fifty or sixty feet high. Somewhere in the distance off to starboard, a gull gave a single shriek. A stab of lonely terror smote Nathan like a physical blow, and he crouched over the wheel, shielding his eyes from that monstrous presence in the fog. Then the grey swirling mass around him shifted and backed, and he was alone again in a uniform greyness.

It was a cold fog, coming down from the north-east. Dank and cold where it clung to his skin. Yet he was sweating inside his oilskins and thigh boots. He could feel the sweat gathering on his shoulders and ribcage and trickling down his back to settle in a soaking mass at his waistband.

Ahead and on his port bow – he thought – came the bleat of another lobsterboat's foghorn. Nathan held his breath. He must be near the harbour entrance now. The narrow channel between the two outflung arms of the harbour walls, and the reefs just below the surface on which they were constructed, allowed little room for two boats to manoeuvre during fog. He switched off his engine and allowed the boat to drift slowly under her own momentum.

'Hey there! Ben, is it? Or George? It's Nathan here, bringing in *Louisa Mary*.'

'Ahoy, Nathan!' Ben's voice came out of the fog ahead of him. Thirty yards? Forty yards away?

'Are you over the bar?'

'Ayuh. Just going to tie up to the lobster car. I'll keep sounding my horn and you can follow me in.'

The engine coughed with the damp as Nathan started it again, but then it steadied, and he forged ahead slowly until Ben's boat and the long flat bulk of the lobster car took shape out of the greyness. He brought *Louisa Mary* alongside, just aft of Ben, and threw a couple of turns around one of the upright posts. Dimly through the fog he could see the silhouette of a slim young woman balancing on the pitching deck of the lobster car. Then he realised it was Tirza, with her arms wrapped around her. He climbed out on to the slippery slats and found his legs were shaking.

'Oh Dad,' said Tirza, clutching hold of him. 'I thought you'd done it this time.'

'Nothing to fret about. Easy as pie,' Nathan said.

◆◆◆

Labour Day dawned with a clear blue sky and a sparkle on the ocean that looked like midsummer. It was intolerable to think of school starting tomorrow. Tirza sprang out of bed half an hour earlier than usual, wanting to cram as much into the day as possible. She pulled on a pair of blue cotton shorts and an old shirt of Nathan's. Abigail had cut off the tails and Tirza wore it with the sleeves rolled up, but it still billowed around her like a spinnaker sail in a light breeze. The looseness of it, and the cool air wafting inside it, always gave her a sense of freedom. She laid her crab line and rowed back to breakfast. Nathan was already seated in front of a plate of pancakes and bacon, and Abigail brought the coffee pot to the table as Tirza dried her hands carelessly on the seat of her shorts.

'So how are you going to spend your last day of freedom?' Nathan asked.

'After I've delivered to the Mansion House I'm meeting Simon at Libby's Marsh. He's bringing the cranberry rakes.'

'You don't have to spend the last day of the vacation working.'

'Oh, raking cranberries isn't working. I like going to the marsh. There's always something to see there. The geese will be flocking on the lake, and maybe we'll go over and look at the fort.'

'Why,' Nathan said, 'is there anything left of that still? Seems it was already pretty tumbled down when I was a boy.'

'Sure. It's not too bad. Last year Simon and me cleared all the creepers and weeds off it. Took three days, but it looked great afterwards.'

'Simon and I,' said Abigail automatically.

'Simon and I.' Tirza shook cornflakes into her bowl and poured milk over them, splashing some on the cloth.

'I've always thought,' said Abigail, 'that somebody ought to look at that fort. One of these professors from a museum. I know when I was a girl there was an article in the newspaper about it. Seems it was built in 1690.'

Tirza paused with her spoon halfway to her mouth. She hadn't realised it was that old. The fort stood on Libby property, so probably Libbys had built it when they first held the land, to defend themselves from the Indians. Or maybe from the French. She never could remember the dates of the French wars in these parts. Abigail, of course, had been a Libby herself before her marriage, second cousin to her husband. Born and brought up on the Libby farm the other side of Swansons', near the end of the Todd's Neck road.

Tirza started to eat again.

'I bet Sandy would be interested in it. He's always claiming America is so *new*. I reckon 1690 isn't new.'

'Don't you go hanging round that young man, now, Tirza Libby,' said her grandmother. 'You don't want him thinking you're forward.'

'I don't hang around him!' Tirza was furious. 'I haven't seen him for weeks. How can that be hanging around?'

'Don't shout.'

'Dad?' she appealed to him. 'Dad, I don't hang round him, do I?'

Nathan looked uncomfortable.

'Of course not.'

'If anyone hangs around him,' said Tirza bitterly, 'it's Martha.'

Nathan and Abigail exchanged a glance.

◆◇◆◇◆

At eleven o'clock Tirza met Simon near the foxholes. She had left *Stormy Petrel* pulled up on the beach with her new anchor firmly stamped into a patch of sandy soil just behind the ledges. The tide was coming in so she wasn't planning to run any risks.

Simon was carrying two cranberry rakes and a basket. Tirza had brought one of Abigail's baskets. Although Abigail said she could no longer be bothered with crab-apple jelly, she liked to put up cranberries and cranberry jelly ready for Thanksgiving and Christmas.

Together they picked their way past the foxholes into the edge of the marsh. After the long spell of almost unbroken dry weather, the smaller pools had shrunk to mere patches of darker green amongst the bog grasses. But even now there were treacherous places in the marsh, the pits of quicksand and mud which could engulf a stranger unfamiliar with the tricky paths. Old tradition held that these bog holes were bottomless, but Miss Bennett had told them in school that scientific surveys had established that the 'bottomless' pits in the Maine coastal marshes were never more than sixteen feet deep. Tirza, sitting in the schoolroom and studying the ceiling, had reckoned that sixteen feet was about as high at the ridge-pole of the school roof. If you fell into one of the bog holes, it would not make a lot of difference if it was bottomless or just as high as the rooftop.

The best cranberries grew in irregular thickets around Libby's Pond which lay almost in the centre of the marsh. It was about a quarter of a mile long and pinched in the middle like a Victorian lady wearing a tight corset. Several islands of tufted reeds were scattered along its length, which provided nesting places for marsh birds and ducks during the summer. As they neared the lake, a cloud of red-legged geese rose with a beating of wings and swung overhead. Tirza and Simon flopped down on their stomachs amongst the cranberries at the end of the lake and waited. After a few minutes the geese circled around and came in to land again, throwing up a fine spray as they hit the water. They would feed here for a while, then head south again, for the Chesapeake, perhaps, or even further to the Gulf of Mexico.

'It makes me tired just to think about it,' said Tirza.

'What?'

'Flying all that distance. And how do they *know*? Know where to go, I mean.'

'They fly in formation, following a leader.'

'But how did they work it out in the first place?'

'I don't know,' said Simon. 'Maybe trillions of years ago they only came a little way north of their winter homes. Aha, says one bird, I do believe there's better feeding a ways north of here. Let's just buzz over where there'll be plenty of food for the kids when they hatch out. He's lazy, see. Then when it starts getting cold in the fall, his wife says, I declare, honey, it was a lot warmer where we used to live. I think we should move back south for the cold weather. Come on kids, just follow your dad and we'll be back at a nice snug place for winter.'

Tirza gave a snort of laughter. 'Then the next year, their neighbours want to come too, and the young ones are breeding...'

'And every year they try going a little further...'

'Well, I guess it could have happened like that. Here, pass me a rake. We'd better get picking.'

Down beside the lake, bending over the cranberries, it felt almost tropical. The heat built up in this hollow part of the land, sheltered on three sides by dense pine woods. Even though it was open on the east to the sea, it lay several feet below the level of the ledges along the top of the beach. It was this cup-like formation and the abundance of small streams which created the marsh and also trapped the sun's warmth – even on days like this which felt autumnal on the cliffs and harbour fronts exposed to the east wind.

The cranberries were thick this year. The bright red oval berries, hard as dried beans, popped off their stems and hit the wooden sides of the cranberry rake with a sharp ping, like beads dropped on a plate. Tirza enjoyed harvest time, apart from the back ache, and felt the rhythm of the year like the turning wheel of her life. But gathering the planted crops never had for her the same satisfaction as the harvesting of the wild fruits. There was a kind of thrill to it, as if you had outsmarted the coming winter. And the idea of abundant food, just growing here as it must have done for thousands of years, was oddly comforting. There were blackberries still to be gathered this year, and rose hips. Both Harriet and Christina made winter cordials from the hips. And there were a few hickory trees in Christina's wood. Tirza would need to gather the nuts soon, or the squirrels would have them all. Not that she begrudged the squirrels their share. It always seemed pretty cunning the way squirrels stored up their winter food, just like people.

It was past midday by the time they had filled their baskets and Simon said he had to get back to the farm. He pulled a piece of string out of his pocket and tied the two rakes together by their handles for easier carrying.

'See you tomorrow on the bus to Portland,' he said as he started home along the beach.

'Ayuh,' Tirza said. She felt a sudden sinking in her stomach. The thought of going to high school was not pleasant. New school, new teachers, new classmates. And the long journey by bus twice a day instead of the short walk along the seafront. It was going to change her life considerably.

She walked over to where *Stormy Petrel*'s anchor rope stretched out from the ledges over the water. The tide had risen now and she was afloat in three or four feet of water. Tirza began to pull on the rope to bring her in to shore. As she did so, she saw a figure approaching along the beach from the direction of Libby's Farm. At first she thought it was Simon coming back again, then she realised that it was Sandy.

'Hello,' he called, waving. 'I've been looking for you.'

Tirza stood with her feet in the water, steadying *Stormy Petrel* with one hand.

'Looking for me where?'

'I thought you might be at your uncle's farm. Then I met Simon and he said you had been picking cranberries along here.' He peered into the basket of berries balanced on a flat rock. 'Amazing. I do believe you would know how to live off the land if you had to, Tirza.'

'Not quite,' she said, but she was pleased.

'I have something for you. Got it in Portland yesterday. Do you have time to come up to the hotel?'

'I guess so.'

She lifted the basket of berries into the boat and settled it firmly on the bottom boards. Then she played out the anchor rope again so that *Stormy Petrel* rode offshore. They walked together to the path over the rocks on Todd's Neck. Sandy was using only one stick now, and Tirza noticed that he no longer seemed to be limping.

When they reached the hotel, Sandy collected his key from the desk.

'It's upstairs in my room,' he said, leading the way to the wide curved staircase, whose carpet was so thick that walking was like wading through wet sand. The staircase had fantastically ornamented spindles and balustrades, and in alcoves along the wall stood blue-and-white Chinese jars four feet tall. Tirza had never been in this part of the hotel before, and she stared about her with interest, but she was conscious that the severe-looking woman behind the desk had turned her mouth down in disapproval when she saw Tirza's bare, sand-encrusted feet and the tufts from the marsh grasses clinging to her clothes.

'Here we are,' said Sandy, throwing open a heavy mahogany door and leading the way into the room. Tirza gaped. It reminded her of the bedrooms in the Tremayne house, except that here everything was fresh and clean. The bed was a huge four-poster – you needed a step to climb up into it. It was covered by a hand-made patchwork quilt, so fine she wondered whether it might be one of Miss Molly's. There were festoons of wispy drapes caught back with cords round each of the posts, and a carved oak coffer at the foot of the bed. Two armchairs worked in needlepoint stood either side of the big window. In the corner was an old-fashioned roll-top desk, polished till it glowed, and on each side of the bed a night stand piled high with books. A big wardrobe of the kind Miss Catherine called an 'armoire' completed the furnishings, but there was also a door, half ajar.

'What's through there?' she asked.

'My bathroom.'

'Your own bathroom? Just for you? Can I look?'

'Of course.'

She pushed the door open and stepped inside. Unlike the bedroom, the bathroom was furnished in the most modern style, like a Hollywood movie, with everything in marble. The huge mirrors on the wall showed a skinny girl with unkempt hair, tattered clothes, and a large scab on one knee. Tirza backed away hastily and went to look out of the bedroom window. The view was not very different from the view out of her own room, without the wharf down below. Mustinegus, however, looked a different shape seen from this angle.

'Now,' said Sandy. 'I know you're starting high school tomorrow, so to celebrate the occasion I've got you a present. Shut your eyes and hold out your hands.'

Feeling foolish, Tirza did so. She felt him put a hard, heavy object in her hands.

'Can I look now?'

'Yes.'

It was a camera. The twin of Sandy's own, it seemed. She was astonished.

'Oh, Sandy.' She lifted it lovingly out of its case, where she could see three or four boxes of film. 'Oh, it's wonderful! But it isn't my birthday or anything. I don't know what my dad will say.'

He might say she couldn't accept it.

'You must just tell him it's my way of saying thank you for all the times you helped me when I was ill.'

She laid it carefully down on the bed and flung her arms around him.

'It's the most marvellous present I've ever had. I'll never forget you, Sandy.'

He put his arms around her and pressed her close to him. She could smell the clean, male scent of him, and the spice of his aftershave, and the blood rushed roaring into her ears.

Chapter 17

Maine: Fall 1942

LEAVING FLAMBORO, STARTING high school, felt strange the next day. It was one of those warm fall days that seem like summer, so Tirza was hot and constrained in her school clothes, a pleated plaid skirt, scratchy with newness, a white blouse and a high-necked navy sweater that had once been Martha's. Although the sweater was clean and aired, it carried with it a lingering shadow of Martha's musky perfume which made it seem foreign to Tirza. It stood separate from her like the shell of a dead snail in which a hermit crab has taken up residence, unlike her own worn and faded summer clothes which lay softly against her skin like another layer of herself. Her feet were now encased in knee-high white socks and heavy regulation black and white saddle-Oxfords. After months of barefoot freedom, her toes were agonisingly cramped, and she was conscious of the bulk of the shoes with every step. It felt as though she had to swing each leg like a fisherman swinging a weighted lead line.

The previous evening, Nathan had presented her with a new leather bag for her books.

'Thought this might be useful,' he said gruffly.

The leather glowed where he had secretly buffed and polished it. Tirza, knowing just how many lobsters it must have cost and remembering the terrible day of the fog, blinked back tears and hugged him. She clutched it now on her knees. There was little inside it: a pencil case, ruler and geometry instruments. Her lunch, wrapped in waxed paper and packed in a tin box. The school would provide stationery and books. Despite her reluctance, part of her was curious about the books.

She found a seat near the back of the bus to Portland. No one came to sit beside her. Simon was up front with two other boys, three of them crowded together on a seat intended for two and kidding around in that silly way boys have when they are showing off because they are nervous. The older high school students scrambled aboard the bus at the last minute with studied nonchalance.

Miss Bennett arrived to wish them luck. Of course, she was really Mrs Pete Flett now, but to her former pupils she was still Miss Bennett. She climbed up the steep steps into the bus with some difficulty, because she was already dressed for her own first day of school in a smart new suit with a big jacket and a pencil-slim skirt. Her skirt climbed above her knees as she came up the steps and one of the boys gave a wolf whistle. She blushed slightly and tugged her skirt down, but she did not scold as she would have done just a few months ago. It was this, more than anything else, that made Tirza realise she really was starting a new school.

'I wanted to wish you all the best of luck,' said Miss Bennett. 'And to tell you that I'll be thinking of you this morning.'

'Thank you, Miss Bennett,' they chorused.

'And make sure you are a credit to Flamboro School.'

'Yes, ma'am.'

'And come and tell me all about it when you get back this afternoon.'

'Yes, ma'am.'

She climbed down and the bus driver started the engine. It was an ancient bus which rattled violently when the engine was running. The body panels seemed to be banging against the chassis so hard they would fall off. Miss Bennett gave them a final wave and the bus swung left up Schoolhouse Lane towards the Portland road.

It was a confusing day. Tirza spent most of it in a panic that she would lose her way in the big building with its network of corridors and surging crowds of older students. It was hard to go from being in the senior class of their small village school to being the youngest person in the entire high school. She had grown some during the summer, but she was conscious all day of looking like a grade school child who had wandered into this collection of adults by mistake. She saw very little of Simon. Where they had optional subjects, he had chosen sciences, Tirza had chosen Spanish, French and history. Even with the compulsory classes, like English, she found that she had been placed in a higher academic section than he had. The only class they had in common was civics, where the students seemed to be allocated alphabetically.

It was confusing, too, the way they had to keep packing up their books and papers and moving on to a different teacher, instead of settling into one room for the day. When it was time to board the afternoon bus back to Flamboro, Tirza was exhausted. She caught sight of herself in the plate-glass window of a store next to the bus stop. Her hair was a mess, her blouse was hanging out between her sweater and her skirt, and her face looked pasty white with two dark-ringed eyes peering out of it. She knew she could not really be that white, not with her summer tan, but the image startled her nevertheless. The boys arrived in a rush at the same time as the bus, and pushed in front of Tirza to get on first. This time she sat closer to them, just two seats behind. She did not want to look as though she was hanging around them, but it seemed more reassuring, somehow, to hear their familiar voices. The bus wandered around the dusty back roads in a long zigzag route back to Flamboro, and Tirza spent the time looking through her new books. She ran a caressing hand over their sleek cloth covers, and sniffed the slippery paper which smelled of ink and newness. She had never possessed so many unknown books at once before. The Spanish book had a long introduction which she began to read, all about the history of Spain and the Conquistadors invading Central and South America, and the differences between the Spanish spoken in Spain and Spanish spoken on this side of the Atlantic. Tirza became absorbed in it and read all the way home. It occurred to her as she climbed down the steps that she could probably do a lot of her homework on the bus, to give herself more free time in the evenings.

◄◆►

She had no chance to try out her new camera until the weekend. There had been quite a debate about it at home, while

Tirza held her breath, waiting to find out whether she would be allowed to keep it. In the end, however, Nathan had overruled Abigail's stern objections, yielding to the silent, pleading looks Tirza was giving him. The camera fitted inside one pocket of its carrying case, and there was another one for spare films and other items. Sandy had packed in four films, a small book on photography and copies of the photographs she had taken with his camera.

She studied these critically. They weren't too bad. She had moved the camera on one of them, and a couple were out of focus, but mostly she had managed to capture what she thought she had seen in the viewfinder. The picture of Sandy in *Stormy Petrel* and the one showing the heap of lobster pots were pretty good. On Friday evening she read the photography book in bed until she fell asleep over it. To be honest, it made everything sound more complicated than it had when she was taking pictures with Sandy.

All Saturday, except when she was wanted for her chores, she spent hunting round Flamboro for likely subjects to photograph. She was parsimonious with her film, though, after pricing those for sale in Flett's Stores. And she would need to save up money for getting the films developed. That would have to be done in Portland. It would be difficult, because there was only just time to get from the bus to school in the morning and from school to the bus at night. At lunchtime they were supposed to stay on the school premises, except for the Seniors. Maybe she could make friends with one of the girls who lived in Portland, and persuade her to take the films to be developed.

In the afternoon she took the camera to show Christina.

'That's a very fine gift,' she said. 'If you have the eye for it, the camera can be used as skilfully as a painter uses a brush. What can you see to photograph here?'

They were sitting outside Christina's cabin near the well. She was shucking corn and paused with the cob cradled between her hands in the lap of her apron.

'Well.' Tirza considered. 'There are some clumps of flowers at the foot of that maple. And I could photograph your cabin. And I'd like to take one of you like that, with the corn.'

Christina laughed.

'All right.'

Unlike Abigail, she did not insist on going inside to change her dress and tidy her hair.

'Now, what else?' she said, when Tirza had finished.

'The woods, maybe. Only that's difficult, because you can't really show the whole woods. Unless you sailed out to sea and photographed them from there. Then they'd probably look too small and far away. I don't know how you could do it. Same as the ocean. How can you photograph that? See, this one I tried to take on Sandy's camera – it just looks like nothing, a sort of grey plate. That bump there is Mustinegus, but you can't get any idea of the sizes or the distance.'

Christina studied the photograph.

'I suppose it is a little like drawing and painting. We used to be told to look not just at the objects we were trying to draw, but at the spaces between them.'

She stood up, brushing the corn silk off her skirt and putting the cob down on her stool.

'Now, look at the ocean between this group of trees below us. The maple is quite close, so the leaves would come out large on your photograph. Behind are those two spruces and the clumps of balsam firs, and right at the edge of the cliff there's that hickory, further away still. I think they would give you the depth you need, so your picture has some distance in it. And if you concentrate on the spaces between the trees – the shapes of those spaces – they're filled up with the ocean.'

'I see,' Tirza said, looking into the viewfinder. 'The pieces of ocean make a pattern between the trees, and the trees frame the ocean.' She clicked the shutter. 'I wonder how it will turn out.'

'You must show me when you have it developed. I've never owned a camera, but I'm sure a lot of the principles of art must apply to photography.'

Tirza thought about that when she was trying to read the photography book in bed again that night. It explained focal length in boring detail, but Tirza thought that her grandmother's ideas made much more sense. If you could think of a photograph as a painting, with depth, and light and shade, and balance, then it ought to work out right.

On Sunday, after church and dinner, she slipped out again

with her camera. There had been only the three of them for lunch today, so the washing up did not take long, and she was out of the house by two o'clock. She decided to walk along the coast path and take some pictures of the Tremayne house and the foxes' den (the foxes too, if she was lucky), then see if there was anything of interest along Libby's Beach.

At the Tremayne place she climbed over the stone wall and walked across the neglected garden till she was close enough to fill the viewfinder with the house. She understood by now that if she had taken her photograph from the edge of the garden the house would look like a small box on the horizon. Back in the gully, near the den, she crouched behind the bushes for half an hour until she was rewarded by one of the growing fox cubs coming out to sun himself. At the click of the camera he turned and stared intently in her direction and she quickly took another picture before he retreated into the hole.

Feeling pleased with herself, she wandered along the beach, but it was difficult to see what she could photograph here. The tide was halfway in, there were no fishing boats out because it was Sunday, and no one else was on the beach this late in the year. Then she remembered a spur of rock, the Spouter, which jutted out from the path leading up to the Mansion House from this side of Todd's Neck. It was near to the old Libby property, where Harriet had sometimes taken them for picnics when they were small, and she had been fascinated by the way the breakers shot vertically into the air through cracks in the Spouter, with a great spume of foam. She put the camera back into its case, which she wore round her neck, and began to scramble up the rocks.

The path to the hotel followed the cliff edge here for a short way, then veered across the headland and went south while a narrow, little-used side path led to the Libby summer cottage. As Tirza turned on to this – nothing more than a pale strip in the tough sea-grasses along the top of the cliff – she remembered that it was just below here that Wayne's body had been found washed inshore. She looked down over the edge at the sharp spikes of rock. Due to some effect of geology, the ledges of granite, which lay nearly horizontal along most of the coast, had been twisted here so that they pointed upwards, making the rocks and reefs around Todd's Neck particularly dangerous. The thought of Wayne gave Tirza a sudden cold chill. She had not thought about him for weeks. His face, pale and waxy, but still sprinkled with fox-coloured freckles, seemed to swim up towards her through the mottled water.

Soberly, she went on till she reached the highest point, where the ground jutted out to form the Spouter. It was here that the water was catapulted upwards, if the tide was right. Even before she reached the spot, she knew that today conditions were perfect because she could hear the crash, followed by a strange rushing sound, which died away in the pattering of the high-thrown spray falling down on to the rocks and trees. The only problem was to find a place where she could take her photograph without soaking her camera in spray. At last she found a spot upwind of the waterspout and partly sheltered by the spreading branches of a silver birch. Then she set herself to count the time between spouts, so she could click the shutter at just the right moment.

The breakers came rolling in with all the weight of the Atlantic behind them, threw themselves against the narrow gulf between the vertical rocks and burst upwards like the fireworks on Independence Day. Tirza became so absorbed in watching them, she almost forgot about her pictures, but then when she remembered she kept taking more and more shots until she had nearly finished her film.

With a groan she rolled over from her cramped position and looked around. The old summer cottage was just beyond her at the edge of the woods. If it was still standing. She took a few steps towards it, and then stopped. She could hear voices, and smothered laughter. Someone had broken into the summer house! Filled with indignation, she approached it at a diagonal, so she could not be seen from the big double veranda doors or the windows, most of which faced the sea. She heard a cry, as though someone was being hurt. She stopped, her heart beating fast and fear rising in her throat. There was an odd, grunting noise, like the noise Tobias's pig made when it settled down to a trough full of swill, a rhythmic snorting sound.

The doors of the summer house stood open on to the veranda. Whoever they were, they were making pretty free with the Libbys' property. She crept nearer, anger overcoming her apprehension, and looked in the door. At first all she could see was a naked back, a man's back. He was stretched out face down on the cane sofa and he was moving with that grunting rhythm she had heard. Then she saw a sheet of golden hair spreading down over the side of the sofa on to the dusty floor. Her cousin Martha was lying under the man, her naked right breast squeezed sideways under his armpit, and she was giving those animal squeals of pain. But her arms were clutched against the man's buttocks, pulling him down on top of her.

Tirza pressed her knuckles against her mouth, but some noise must have come out of it because the man turned his head and looked around with queer, unfocused eyes.

It was Sandy.

Tirza scrambled backwards and began to run down towards the beach. She missed the path and went crashing through the trees, bouncing from one to the other, bruised and bleeding. When she reached the main path she veered off again over the rocks. They were slippery with seaweed and she found herself falling, scraping her arms and legs on the barnacles. The camera flew out of her hand as she hurtled head first over the last of the rocks and landed, all the breath knocked out of her, on the beach. She wasn't sure how long she lay there, winded, her mouth full of sand. Then she rolled into the shelter of the rocks, clutching her knees against her chest, trying to make herself as small as possible. Dry, uncontrollable sobs broke from her in spasms, burning her throat and ribs. At last she pulled herself painfully to her feet. Her camera was lying on a patch of rock-weed. Automatically she picked it up, dusted off the sand, and put it in the case. There was no way of telling whether it was broken or not. Blindly she began to stumble back up the beach. She felt dirty, as if she had been flung into the filth of a bait tub. All she could think of was to wash herself clean again.

—◈—

Simon never knew afterwards why he had decided, that first Sunday evening after starting at high school, to blurt out his plans to his parents. Well, decided wasn't the right word. He'd blundered into it. They had been discussing the courses he was doing at high school and suddenly he found himself talking about how you could enlist as an officer if you graduated from high school... West Point...

'The army?' Tobias stared at him as if he had taken leave of his senses. Harriet's hands, occupied in mending a pair of Billy's trousers, fell to her lap.

'Ayuh,' said Simon defiantly. 'I'm going to join the regular army straight after high school.' He felt the air growing uncomfortable. 'And get out of this God-forsaken place.'

'Simon!' Harriet said.

'Well, it is, Mom. God-forsaken. What is there to do here but just plod along like a draft ox ploughing a furrow? I don't want to spend *my* life like you. Ploughing, planting, hoeing, milking, mucking out, harvesting, chopping wood, cutting ice. Year in, year out. Always the same old chores, round and round. Look at you! It's back-breaking work. The land is poor. It's all you can do to pay the taxes and keep the buildings together and barely eat and clothe yourselves. All those years you were saving for the tractor, neither one of you had any new clothes, excepting boots. One bad year and Dad is worrying about getting into debt. There's never a year good enough for you to put any money aside.'

'This is as good a farm as any in Maine,' said Tobias. His voice was dangerously quiet. 'As trim and well run as any you'll find.'

'Oh, Dad!' Simon sighed. 'I'm not saying you don't do your best. I know you do. That's what I'm saying. You work as hard as any slave, but the land isn't worth it. I might feel different if the land was better. Not full of stones and frozen for months on end and soaked with salty mists and rain. But I don't think I would. *I don't want to be a farmer.*'

He put his head between his hands and grabbed two fistfuls of hair, as if by doing this he could pull back his words out of the air.

'Now listen, boy,' said Tobias. He only ever called Simon 'boy' when he was really angry. 'This land has been in our family for three centuries, father to son. Ten generations. You're the only son to inherit, with Nathan having no boy. It's your duty to take on the land. And it's your duty to hand it on to your son in turn. And it's your duty to provide for your sister and her son.'

'My sister?' Simon shouted. 'My *sister*! Why should I provide for her? She couldn't wait to get out of here. You didn't try to stop *her* leaving. She's only here now because there isn't anywhere more convenient to go. As soon as she finds herself another man, she'll be off. You know that.'

'If that happens,' said Tobias between his teeth, 'then, no, you won't need to provide for her. But otherwise, when you are head of the family, it will be your responsibility.'

'Head of the family! This is the twentieth century, Dad. Martha doesn't feel any obligation towards me, and I don't feel any responsibility for her. She's nearly thirteen years older than me.' Shamefully, his voice broke. 'I *won't* be tied to this farm. It's not fair!' he shouted, aware that he sounded like Billy. 'If Martha can leave, so can I. And I will. Maybe I won't even stay to finish high school.'

He jumped to his feet. Tobias stood up more slowly. Harriet lowered her head and pulled a handkerchief out of her apron pocket.

'Are you defying me, boy?' Tobias's voice shook. 'Are you asking for the belt?' He was rarely angry, but Simon began to be afraid.

'Please, Dad. This is what I really want to do.' Simon scrambled for thoughts, trying to remember what he had said to Tirza. 'I wouldn't stay in the army for ever. I could come back later and take over. After all, you've got years to go yet. Twenty-five? Thirty?'

'In thirty years I'll be seventy-five. I reckon I'll still be working, but this farm will need a younger man as well.'

The air trembled between them. Simon wasn't sure if his father's anger was abating. He held his breath.

They all heard the slam of the kitchen screen door and the tap-tap of Martha's heels along the passage. She walked in the open door of the living room and glanced around at them with heavy-lidded eyes. She looked sleek, somehow, Simon thought, like one of the farm cats after it had eaten an oily mackerel and polished its fur till it shone. There was a gloss about her, although her hair was tumbled and her clothes had an appearance of disarray, as though she had just got up in the morning in a hurry. Yet, he recalled, when she had gone out earlier she had been as elegant as a fashion magazine. He wondered where she could have been.

He said the first thing that came into his head.

'Martha, you don't expect me to support you, *as head of the family*, do you?'

Her eyes swung round to him and she gave a little laugh. She chucked him under the chin in a way that had particularly annoyed him when he was younger. Now she had to reach up to do it.

'Support me, little brother? Of course not. Whatever gave you such a silly idea? There are plenty of *real* men ready to do that.'

She gave a little twirl of her skirts and went stepping lightly out of the room. Simon ought to have been able to give his father a look of triumph. Why was it, then, that he felt suddenly so heavy and sad?

On a morning in mid-September, Susanna Penhaligon woke just as dawn was colouring the sky over the ocean. She had slept deeply and well, and she lay still, feeling grateful. All her life she had slept in this room which, when they were small, had been the nursery, presided over by a fierce Scottish nanny clad in white linen so starched that – if it was dented by a child's hand or the edge of an ironing board – it would spring back into shape with a twang. When her sisters grew up and moved into other rooms, Susanna had taken sole possession of this one.

As children they had been obliged to have their beds lined up against the wall away from the window, with a screen around them. Their nanny believed in fresh air and an open window at night. Her only concession to the Maine winters, which could surpass in ferocity even those of her Aberdeenshire youth, was to erect a folding screen decorated with cut-out scraps between the three small beds and the Atlantic gales whooping through the window. When Susanna was a young woman, she moved her bed against the wall below the window. In deference to her upbringing, she still kept it open except on the wildest of nights. Captain Penhaligon had built the windows of his house deep and wide. The bottom of the window was level with the top of the mattress and it was as wide as the bed was long, so that

Susanna could look out without even raising her head from the pillow. Below the window the garden sloped away down to the road. Molly's roses were almost over, but there were two fine hydrangeas in full bloom, one a deep blue and the other the colour of ripe plums.

Beyond the garden the roofs of Flamboro tumbled down to the harbour, already busy even at this hour. With the days shortening the lobstermen and trawlermen moved at a faster pace in the mornings, anxious to be off so they could finish a day's work before darkness forced them home. Ben's boat was the first away, but Nathan was right behind him in *Louisa Mary*. Then a cluster of other boats followed. One of the Towson boys was having trouble with his engine. He climbed back on to the wharf and went off home to fetch something.

The church clock struck seven. Susanna twisted her head round to look up at the gilded weathervane. It was pointing south-west, but the trees stirred only a little in the breeze. A light wind. The boats would have a safe day's fishing. The morning bus clattered down Schoolhouse Lane and pulled up beside the wharf. It spent the night a few miles inland where the driver lived, and started its day's journeys to and from Portland with this trip from Flamboro at a quarter past seven. She could just see the heads of the high school children as they climbed the steps into the bus. Then it gave a toot of its horn and started back up the hill to the Portland road.

She leaned back against her pillows. The day before yesterday she had sat up later than she should, finishing the patchwork rug. She had worked the last of the border, and then sewed the binding round all the edges. It was a bit of an oddity. Not as beautiful as most of her rugs, designed on a whim really, but an interesting project. Molly had hung it over the footboard of the bed where she could look at it. Leaning forward now, she stroked the closely hooked pile of Wayne's picture. She sighed.

Yesterday, after the rug was finished and with no new project planned, she had felt suddenly tired. All day she had sat around with her hands loosely clasped in her lap, too weary even to read. Never in her life could she remember spending a day of such idleness. Her sisters, she knew, had been worried about her. But after her lazy day and a good night's sleep, she felt wonderful this morning. There was very little pain, nothing she couldn't will herself to ignore. For the first time in months she felt energetic.

There was a knock on the door and Molly came in with an early morning cup of tea for her. Molly and Kitty drank coffee in the morning, but Susanna had always preferred tea.

'Good morning,' said Molly. 'How are you feeling today?'

'Splendid! I'm going to have a bath after my tea and come down to the garden. I want to see what you've been doing with the pergola.'

'Arthur has repaired it for us quite well, and we just need to tie the clematis and wistaria back in place.' Molly put the tea down on the night stand and looked across her sister at the view from the window. 'It's going to be one of those glorious fall days – all bright colours and glitter. Give me a call if you'd like an arm along to the bathroom. I'll just be getting dressed in my room.'

'Thank you, dear,' Susanna said. 'I'll do that.'

Half an hour later, when Susanna still had not called her, Molly went back to her room. The tea was untouched. The rising sun spread a swathe of light across Susanna Penhaligon's pale face and her hands, resting lightly, palm upwards, on the patchwork quilt Molly had made for her twenty-first birthday.

'Oh, Susanna, my dear,' said Molly. She laid one hand on her sister's cold one. Her mother would have shut the curtains, but Molly left the sun brightening Susanna's room.

<hr>

Flamboro gave Miss Susanna a walking funeral.

It was not often done now, but the Penhaligons were one of the oldest and most respected families in the town, and they had always had walking funerals. There were eight men to carry the coffin, Ben and Charlie Flett, Nathan and Tobias Libby, Mr Wardour, the retired schoolteacher, Mr Foss, the Penhaligons' lawyer from Portland, and two distant cousins from Augusta. Not that it needed eight bearers, as Charlie Flett said when they started off down the steep path through the Penhaligons' garden. Miss Susanna had always been slightly built, and the last three years she had dwindled away to a mere wisp. Still, it showed the proper respect to have the full complement of bearers.

The Reverend Bridges led the procession, followed by the coffin. Then came Miss Molly and Miss Catherine, with the wives of the two cousins. They were followed by the church choir, who sang Miss Susanna's favourite hymns as they walked. Behind them came the rest of the mourners. It was difficult for the choir to keep together and stay in tune as they criss-crossed Flamboro, up one street and down the next. There was a strong cold wind blowing, which snatched their voices away and tossed them up to mingle with the desolate mewing of the gulls and the soughing of the trees in Christina's forest. Sometimes the last row of the choir was so far behind the first that their voices sounded like an echo repeated back and reverberating: 'Oh, Lord, our help... our help... help...'

When the minister reached the far end of the town beyond Nathan Libby's house, at the foot of the steep path leading up to the Tremayne estate, he brought the procession around in an arc and began to retrace his steps along the edge of the sea. As they walked along the harbour, the moored boats danced in the tossing waves and seemed to acknowledge their passing. The strong east wind was throwing the breakers halfway over Shore Road, and they were all soaked to the knees by the time they reached the steep steps up to the church.

The bearers, as always on these occasions, had some difficulty manoeuvring the coffin up the steps, which were almost too narrow for two people to walk abreast. Then they continued up the path and into the church itself. The church had never been so full of flowers, not even for a wedding. Love for Miss Susanna had stripped every garden in Flamboro of the last flowers of the season – chrysanthemums, late-flowering lupins, a few treasured roses and gladioli. Any gaps had been filled up with bright rowan berries and rose hips.

The service was short, as Miss Susanna had herself requested. A reading, two hymns, and a brief address from the minister. Then they all moved out to the burying-ground, presided over by the grotesque shape of the anti-aircraft gun with its sheepish gun crew. There was a small hard rain in the wind now, and the town shivered and huddled into its coats as the minister spoke the final words of the burial service.

'Earth to earth, ashes to ashes...'

A large herring gull, swooping in on a gust of wind, fluttered down shrieking and found a foothold on the church roof.

'In the sure and certain knowledge...'

The gull shrieked again, drowning the minister's words, and his cries were answered by a flock of gulls coasting out over the grey, thrashing ocean.

Chapter 18

Maine: Fall 1942

BY THE THIRD week in September, the last of the summer people were gone. The two houses in Flamboro which belonged to out-of-towners were shuttered and locked for the winter. The Mansion House extension had been closed until Memorial Day next year. Tirza no longer ran her crab lines. Mrs Larrabee had covered her stock with soft old sheets, arranged a few items in the bay window with a curtain behind them, and hung a narrow board, painted in black with the word CLOSED, from two hooks screwed into the bottom of her shop sign. Charlie Flett packed away the tin buckets and children's spades, the rubber rings, suntan lotion and cheap sneakers into cardboard boxes in his storeroom, and wrote SUMMER in thick red crayon on the outside of them.

Flamboro's ninth-graders, high school freshmen, fell into the rhythm of travelling to Portland each day with their older schoolfellows, and the lobstermen and trawlermen into the rhythm of a shorter, more intense working day. Fall was always an anxious time for them. The movements of the fish were more unpredictable than ever, the weather became more treacherous. Flamboro harbour froze over regularly each winter and an early onset of the cold weather meant a curtailment of the fishing season.

The farmers had finished the harvest and started the winter ploughing; their wives, exhausted with the long days of putting by all the produce for winter, surveyed their packed shelves with some complacency, and thought of quieter times ahead when they could catch up with their sewing and knitting. On Libby's

Farm, as on their neighbours', the pig was slaughtered for bacon and ham, and a few of the hens sold off to cut down on the winter feeding. Tobias had sent most of this year's heifers to market. He kept four. With the general shortage of food as the war continued, it would be worth his while to produce more milk and butter, and go back to commercial cheese making. They had not sold cheese since Martha was small, but Harriet had now hunted out her bulk equipment. She was prepared to make more cheese than they needed for themselves once the milk yield increased next spring.

Pierre Lamotte went off for his annual holiday to his home in Montreal, anxious as always about leaving his assistant Matthew in charge of the Mansion House kitchen. Although the dining room was much depleted at meal times, the permanent residents remained – a number of retired wealthy bankers and lawyers with their wives, many of whom resented the changes in the menu when Pierre was away. The British airman was the only younger guest, but Pierre was of the opinion that he too would be gone before his return from Canada.

At the beginning of the last week in September, a sudden snowstorm blew in from the north-east during the night, and the Libby farm lay under three inches of snow by the morning. Simon had to wear boots to walk to Flamboro to catch the bus. In the village there was less snow, soon trampled into slush around the harbour and up the road to the schoolhouse. As the bus wound its way inland, the passengers looked out on a wintry landscape, with here and there the red splash of a barn. The dark green of the pine forests stood up stark and sinister against the glitter of the snow, the shadows between the trees black as velvet.

Two days later the snow was gone, the temperature was back to normal, and black clouds were building out at sea. The cold snap had been enough, however, to start the deciduous trees turning colour. The birches were bright yellow, the maples a fiery red-gold, and the sumacs scarlet. Offshore Mustinegus Island burned on the surface of the waves, the crimson of the blueberry bushes lying at the feet of the taller blazing trees, threaded through with the green-blacks of the pines and spruces.

The thunderstorm, like the snowstorm, swept in at night.

Tirza was woken at one o'clock by a flash that lit up her room eerily, followed a few seconds later by a crack of thunder that rattled the windows in their frames. She climbed out of bed and went to the window. The ocean was hurling itself against the land furiously, smashing into the harbour walls and threatening the houses that stood along the front. Spray was thrown against their own front door with a smack like a slapping hand. The boats in the harbour leapt wildly at their moorings, as though they were struggling to break free. Tirza gripped the windowsill anxiously, straining to make out the shapes of *Stormy Petrel* and *Louisa Mary* against the heaving water. There was another flash of lightning and a crack of thunder from somewhere behind her, inland. Then the harbour lights went out.

Tirza padded over to the light switch beside the door and pressed it. Nothing happened. She opened her door and looked out. The landing had a window overlooking the sea and a faint greyish light was reflected in from the moon by fits and starts as the clouds raced across the sky. Nathan came out of his bedroom. He had put a pair of trousers on over his pyjamas, which stuck out in a frill round his ankles, and he was pulling on a heavy sweater.

'The electricity has gone,' said Tirza.

'I know. I'm just going to check on the boats.'

'I'll come too.'

'No need. You stay and keep dry.'

But she was already back in her room, thrusting her legs into jeans. She thudded down the stairs after him with a sweater in her hands.

'Put that sweater on,' he said, passing her oilskins, 'and oil up. It's going to be cold out there.'

They went out through the boat shed, where the dories had already been stored for the winter. At first the door seemed to be jammed. They had to thrust with their shoulders to open it, then it flung back wildly, hitting the clapboard wall with a crash. The wind was so strong they had to lean into it, and struggle to drag the door round on its hinges and hold it back so it would shut without smashing. Other figures were moving about in the driven spume and queer half-light, lit up every few seconds by the blue–white flashes of the lightning. Men were testing mooring warps and the fenders along the wharf. Arthur was struggling to roll a heavy drum of diesel against the bait shed door, which fitted badly and sagged on its hinges. If it blew open in the storm, the wind would be likely to lift the whole shed off the wharf and dump it in the sea like a load of driftwood.

Louisa Mary and *Stormy Petrel* strained at their moorings, but the warps were holding, and the heavy old tyres slung along the wooden sides of the wharf probably afforded better protection to the boats than the fancy red and white painted fenders round on the Mansion House pier. The hotel's motor runabout would have been laid up by now anyway, Tirza thought. A few windows in the town began to show light – the flickering of candles or the steadier glow of kerosene lamps. The electricity supply had only reached Flamboro ten years before, and many households had kept their lamps handy, doubting the reliability of the electric. Though Tirza could only remember one other time when it had failed.

'The line's down somewhere inland,' Charlie said to Nathan. 'Probably struck by lightning, or else a tree has fallen across it. The telephone has gone too.'

'As long as the boats are safe, I'm not worried about the electricity or the telephone,' said Nathan. 'We've done all we can here. Come on, Tirza.'

'Mary has just put some milk on to heat,' Charlie said. 'Come in and warm yourselves with hot chocolate before you go back to bed.'

They followed him along the street to Flett's Stores. The wind was easing a little as if, having brought down the supply lines, it had worn itself out. The rain too was slackening and Tirza took off her sou'wester and shook out her hair. The air smelled clean and sharp and charged, as though you could breathe in the crackling electricity which flickered under the great black clouds as they rolled away southwards.

On the store porch they pulled off their boots and followed Charlie across the shop. There was a pool of light spilling through from a lamp in the storeroom behind, but even so they bumped into sacks and boxes. Charlie picked up the lamp he had left at the bottom of the stairs and led them to the living quarters above.

'Tirza!' Mary cried. 'What are you doing out at this time of night?'

'Had to see my boat was safe, Mrs Flett.'

'Well, sit down there and get some hot chocolate inside you. And help yourself to my ginger and oatmeal cookies.'

The Fletts' kitchen seemed as cosy and safe as a cave in the dim light from the lamp, with the tail-end of the storm battering against the outside walls. Tirza hunched sleepily over her mug of chocolate, alternately sipping and nibbling as Charlie and Nathan talked about repairing the storm damage. She longed, suddenly, to be able to go back to the time when she was small, when this sense of safety had seemed real. Now she knew it was a trick life played on you, an illusion. Reality was the darkness outside, the storm and the danger. You could pretend. You could hide behind the curtain. But outside the darkness waited implacably.

<hr />

The storm damage was so bad that the school bus could not even reach Flamboro in the morning, so the older children of the town spent the day helping to clear up at home. There were shingles off roofs and debris flung by the sea all over the harbour front. Some of the boats had lost small items of gear, but considering the violence of the storm very little damage had been done to the boats themselves. What was worrying the lobstermen was the damage to their traps. Tirza went out with Nathan early in the afternoon, and they worked their way round his gang. Twelve traps had disappeared completely. They brought another twenty badly damaged ones back with them to repair at home, and mended several more aboard *Louisa Mary*.

Nathan was silent as they motored back to the harbour. The loss of twelve pots was serious. He would need to get to work at once cutting new laths and spruce hoops, and build replacements. As she jumped out on to the lobster car and took a turn around a post with a warp, Tirza saw Sandy standing beside the harbour, watching. She felt suddenly sickened, her throat tightened with pain, but would not look at him. Instead she took the nearly empty kegs as Nathan passed them up to her, and rolled them over to Marvin, the lobster buyer, for the catch to be weighed, then lifted the lobsters carefully into the right compartments in the car. When all the lobsters were unloaded – and there were very few of them – she untied *Louisa Mary*, dropped aboard, and Nathan motored round to his mooring place.

It took some time to unload the gear and the broken pots. Tirza felt that Sandy was watching her, but he made no move to approach. Eventually they had everything stored in the boat shed, and Tirza climbed into *Stormy Petrel*. There had been no time to bail her out before setting off to haul the traps. She was half full of rainwater and Tirza took her time, scooping it up and emptying it over the side, then soaking up the last puddles with the sponge she kept in the aft locker. When she had finished, she looked up and saw that Sandy was sitting on a bollard just above her head.

'Could we talk?' he said. His voice was quiet and strained.

Tirza wrung out the sponge and put it away. Then she pushed the hair out of her eyes with a damp hand and looked up at him. The sun was already beginning to sink behind the shoulder of Manenticus, and she could not read his expression against the dazzle. She shrugged, although her heart was pounding in her chest, making her feel breathless.

'I guess so.' She climbed up on to the wharf.

He took her by the elbow and began to walk rapidly away from her house, towards the north end of the harbour where the steep path led up to the church and the burying-ground. At the very base of the cliff a narrow path, sometimes covered at high water, led off from the end of the harbour walk. Clinging to the rocks like a ribbon of seaweed, it followed the headland round and then curved in along the shore of the cove where Tirza laid her crab lines. It was barely wide enough for them to walk abreast. On the right it crumbled away into the upper edges of the sea-washed ledges. On the left it was crowded by the fringes of Christina's forest, which flowed down beyond the headland, covering the rising ground. Although in summer the forest appeared from a distance to be entirely composed of spruce and pine, the fall shades of the dying leaves laced it through now with colour. Against the pine needles, blackening in the ebbing light, the patchwork of hues glowed like amber and rubies, gold and blood.

Sandy no longer carried even a single stick, and he forced

Tirza along at a fast pace until at last she began to resist the pressure on her arm. She was exhausted after her broken night and the heavy work of hauling all day. And she did not want this talk with Sandy. She was afraid of what she might blurt out. The scene she had witnessed in the summer house was burned on her mind, but the memory of her own part in it was confused. Had Sandy seen her? Or had he simply heard the sound of her faint cry? In the days since, she had tried with every ounce of her will-power to blot out the image of Sandy and Martha lying naked on the old threadbare seat, but it would not leave her. Sandy's animal grunts, Martha's cries of pain and frantic clutching movements came back to torment her, until she felt waves of revulsion rising in her stomach.

As she jerked her arm away from Sandy's hold, she stumbled on a projecting root in the path, and he reached out again to steady her. They were deep in the shadows at the edge of the wood here, hidden by the church headland from the town and by the trees from Christina's cabin which looked out from the other side of the slope over the sea.

'Where are we going?' Tirza asked, planting her feet firmly and standing still. 'This path peters out at the end of the cove, except for a branch which leads up to my grandmother's house.'

'This will do fine,' said Sandy. 'I just wanted somewhere away from prying eyes. Villages are the same everywhere – people always wanting to know your business. Here, let's sit on that fallen tree over there.'

He led her a few steps into the wood, where a birch tree had fallen a few years before. The festoons of bark were peeling off it in long silvery strips, but it was clean and dry. He put an arm round her shoulders, at which she stiffened, but then he said nothing for several minutes. As the silence continued, Tirza began to hear the evening murmur of the birds settling down for the night, and a squirrel, emboldened by their stillness, ran across the carpet of leaves and pine needles not a yard from their feet – Sandy's clad in highly polished tan shoes, Tirza's bare, brown and slender. She relaxed a little. In the silence the mournful cry of migrating wild geese floated down from the upper reaches of the sky.

At last Sandy sighed and stirred.

'I'm afraid I won't be able to celebrate our shared birthday with you tomorrow,' he said.

It was the last thing she had expected him to say. Birthdays were not much celebrated in her family, and she had certainly not expected to celebrate it with him. She did not know what to say.

'I've had my marching orders,' he went on. 'Got a cable today. I have to report to Boston tomorrow afternoon. They've arranged for me to travel over to England with some of your own boys from the Army Air Force who are going out. I'll have to catch the first train from Portland tomorrow morning. The hotel is running me over in the car.'

'You're going back to your... your squadron, is it called?' Tirza's throat was constricted and her mouth felt dry.

'I won't know till I get there. They might give me quite a different posting. They've made me a wing-commander, but I assume I'll still be flying missions. I hope they won't put me into training or desk work.'

He stared out glumly through the scattered trees at the ocean. It was turning a deep purple-blue, except where the sun, slipping down behind them, glanced off the waves and turned the curves of the breakers into green glass.

There was silence for a moment. Then Tirza said, with difficulty, 'I'm sorry you're leaving.'

He squeezed her shoulders lightly. 'I'm sorry to go, even though I've felt guilty, taking things easy all these weeks, while my friends are back there, risking their lives on every flight.'

'You couldn't help it. You had to get better.'

'Yes, well.' He sighed. 'I owe you a lot, Tirza. Looking after me, being a real friend.'

Her stomach turned over, and she clasped her hands tightly between her knees. 'I owe you a lot too. The camera...'

'Ah, now, promise me you'll work hard at your photography. I think you have a real talent for it. Look, I've had copies made of some of the other photographs I took here. There are some of your family I thought you might like.'

He pulled a yellow envelope out of his inside jacket pocket. 'Here, keep them safe.'

He tucked the envelope into the breast pocket of her shirt. It came to her warm from contact with him, and as he touched her she shivered.

'Are you cold? I'm a pig. I've dragged you off here, and you've nothing on but that thin shirt and shorts.'

He slipped his jacket off and wrapped it around her, then put his arm round her shoulders again.

She did not tell him that she was not cold. She wanted to ask, *Will you write to me?*, but did not have the courage.

'There's something I want you to do for me,' he said.

Suddenly, she was suspicious. *Something I want you to do for me*. Not, *Would you do something for me?* It sounded, somehow, like an order. An adult directing a child. Her chest grew tight, and now she did feel cold, even with his jacket wrapped around her. He pulled another envelope out of his pocket, one of the stiff cream envelopes the Mansion House provided for its guests, and sat toying with it.

'I've written a letter to Martha,' he said, and cleared his throat. 'Perhaps you've guessed that we... That is, we've been seeing each other quite a bit.'

He doesn't realise I saw them in the summer house, she thought. The sense of relief left her shaky.

'I've written her this letter, to try to explain. You see, back at home, I've got...' he broke off. There was silence again.

'Why don't you give it to her yourself?' Tirza asked in a tight voice. 'Go and see her. You could easily walk over there this evening.'

I don't want to touch your letter to her, she thought, with anger flaring up in her. *Why should I have to do this?*

'I don't think that would be a good idea. She isn't going to be very pleased. Got a bit of a temper, hasn't she, your cousin?'

Tirza glanced at him, then looked away. The moon was already rising, out there over the sea, although the very last of the sunset had not quite drained from the sky. Her thoughts were a tumbled confusion. *Is he afraid of her? But he isn't a coward. Why can't he mail the letter? I'm not going to take it. Why do men always think Martha is so special? She's stupid and selfish and cruel. Oh, please, don't let him go away.*

'I want you to give it to her after I leave tomorrow,' he said, holding out the envelope to her. There was nothing written on the outside. She kept her hands clasped together and her eyes fixed on the rhythmic pounding of the breakers on the ledges at their feet. The tide was rising and if they weren't careful, they would be cut off.

'Tirza?' he said anxiously. 'Please?'

Reluctantly, she took the envelope and held it with the very tips of her fingers, as though she thought it would burn her.

He tightened the arm round her shoulders.

'I'll never forget you, Tirza. Will you remember me, and try to think kindly of me?'

He took hold of her chin and turned her face towards him.

'Remember how I took you for a boy, when I first met you? Lord, what a mistake! But then, you've grown up a lot this summer, haven't you?' Gently he smoothed her hair back from her face. 'Pity you aren't just a little older.'

She tried to pull her head away.

'Tirza? You aren't crying, are you?'

He peered at her in the wavering light, then he kissed her eyelids, brushing away the unwilling drops that had gathered there. She sprang to her feet, dropping the letter, and his jacket slid from her shoulders on to the forest floor.

'Why, Tirza.' His voice was surprised, but gentle. He stood up and pulled her towards him and put his arms around her. She felt as though she was on fire, but she clung to him, putting her arms around his neck and digging her fingers into his thick brown hair. Dimly she was aware that she was almost as tall as he was. He had only to bend his head a little for his mouth to come down firmly on hers. They kissed fiercely, and a pain grew in Tirza's stomach and chest until she cried out.

'Did I hurt you?' he gasped. 'I didn't hurt you, did I?'

She shook her head, and pulled his mouth down to her again. His body was pressed hard against her, and his hands seemed to be trying to drive her into his very flesh, one gripping the back of her head, one cupped round the seat of her shorts so tightly that she could feel each fingertip through the thin cotton.

At last he released her, and they came slowly apart. Tirza drew in her breath in shuddering mouthfuls, and she saw in the slippery moonlight that his eyes had that peculiar, dazed look. He shook his head.

331

'No,' he said. 'No. Tirza, you're only twelve.'

'Thirteen tomorrow. My great-grandmother – Girna's mother – was married at fourteen.'

'Oh, Tirza.' He ran his finger tenderly down her cheek. 'I wish, I wish... But what's the good? I'm leaving tomorrow.'

'Don't go.'

'I have to. It's no use.' He stroked her hair. It hung to her shoulders now, and it had begun to lie in a sleek dark wave. He lifted a handful of it and kissed it. She put her arms around his neck again and clung to him, and he pulled her to him so hard that he lifted her feet from the ground, so that only her toes brushed against the dead leaves. This time when he released her, she felt blood on her lips, and as she ran her hands down his chest his heart pounded under her fingers like the beat of a storm tide.

'No,' he said again. 'No.'

He wrapped the jacket round her. Then he stooped to pick up the letter, which gleamed pallidly at their feet. He reached out to slip it into her pocket next to the photographs, but she recoiled. She did not want that thing *there*, so close to her skin, where her small breasts lifted the soft old cotton into firm points. She took the envelope from him and held it away from her, dangling from one corner, as though it was contaminated.

He put his arm around her again and they began to walk back along the narrow path towards Flamboro. The edge of the waves licked her bare feet and his polished shoes. Just before they rounded the shoulder of the cliff, he kissed her once more, and she clung to him, crying silently. At the beginning of the road, below the burying-ground, she handed him his jacket and turned away. When she looked back, he was gone.

<hr />

Tirza waited until late afternoon the next day before she went up to the farm. The bus was still unable to get through to Flamboro, so there had been no school, and she wondered wildly whether Sandy would be unable to reach Portland to catch his train, even if the driver took him round in a loop to the south to avoid the worst of the fallen trees. She tried to blot Sandy's image from her mind, but all day she felt as though a rope was wound tightly around her body. Her muscles shrieked with tension and she found herself mouthing soundlessly strings of disconnected words, willing him to stay.

To her surprise, most of the family had turned up to celebrate her birthday, and Abigail had cooked a special dinner at midday. Even Christina had been invited, and Billy, whose improved behaviour during the summer was standing him in good stead now he had started first grade, was allowed to come from the schoolhouse during the dinner recess. Martha did not appear, for which Tirza was grateful.

'Clarice has come over to give her a home permanent,' said Harriet apologetically.

'It doesn't matter,' said Tirza, her heart lifting slightly. She wanted to choose her own moment for confronting Martha.

They had all brought her presents, mostly clothes. But Christina gave her a copy of *The Rubáiyát of Omar Khayyám*, bound in white leather and tooled in gold with a complex Eastern pattern. Simon had bought her a large book of Audubon plates, which must have used up a good deal of the summer earnings he had been saving for a hunting rifle.

'This is really great,' Tirza told him. They were sitting on Nathan's narrow front porch while the others lingered over their coffee, talking about the progress of the war. Billy had gone back for afternoon school.

'Oh, well,' said Simon. 'I was thinking when we picked the cranberries in the marsh that you'd like a good bird book.'

'This is much more than that.' She stroked the maroon cover fondly. 'Some people even split them up and frame the pictures, but I wouldn't ever do a thing like that.'

'Glad you like it,' he said.

He had just told her of the quarrel with his father about the army. To Tirza, who knew his voice as well as she knew the feel of her own skin, it was clear that he could barely keep from crying, however fiercely he gouged at the edge of the porch rail with his pocket knife. She told him he should keep quiet about his plans until he finished high school, by which time Tobias might be persuaded to change his mind. Simon agreed gloomily.

Tirza wrapped her arms round her knees, trying to fold closely in on her own body. She saw herself as a tight bud on a rose bush, layer upon layer locked in. But a bud would open out and bloom, while she felt she had already opened, bursting outward last night in Sandy's arms, every layer and cell of her complex self laid open to him. Now she had shrunk back to this withered bud, blighted, never to open again. She wanted to tell Simon how desolate she felt. She needed to explore the sick, surging feeling inside her whenever she was near Sandy or even thought of him – part excitement, part anticipation, part fear. There was no one else she could confide in, not even, she felt, Christina. Yet somehow she could not find the words to tell Simon. She hugged her secret to herself, though she ached to talk about it. They fell into silence again.

As the short afternoon wore away, the birthday party broke up. Christina was the first to leave. She kissed Tirza and strode off home, cutting up the hill behind the schoolhouse. Then Harriet said that she and Tobias were meant to be calling on the Fletts for a cup of tea before going back to the evening milking, and Simon went with them. Nathan settled down in the boat shed to mend his broken lobster pots, and Tirza helped Abigail wash the dishes.

When she was free at last, she realised that if she went to the farm now, she would catch Martha alone. Clarice had walked past the kitchen window ten minutes ago, Billy was still at school for afternoon softball, and the rest of the family was over at Flett's Stores. She went up to her room to fetch Sandy's letter. It was lying on the top of her chest of drawers, beside the china-headed doll Mrs Larrabee had given her last spring, and the stack of painted Shaker boxes Sandy had bought for her. She had put them there more than a month ago, and Abigail had not questioned her about them, so perhaps she thought Tirza had bought them herself. She ran a finger over the smallest one, feeling the delicacy of the bent wood and the snugness of the joints. Then she opened it and took out Sandy's photograph. Tears welled up in her eyes and she rubbed at them angrily.

The sealed, unaddressed envelope was no longer a pure cream. She and Sandy must have trodden on it in the dark in the forest, leaving dirty smudges on the paper. One corner was bent where she had pushed it carelessly into the hip pocket of her shorts before she came in last night, for fear her father or grandmother might see it. She had not felt capable of any conversation, but had pleaded a headache and gone early to bed.

The envelope looked grubby and unprepossessing. Well, what did that matter? She didn't care. She thrust it once more into her shorts pocket and set out for the farm. To save time, she took her bicycle, even though the first part up to the Tremayne place was so steep she had to push it, and parts of the farm track had been so badly torn up by the army jeeps that it made cycling difficult.

When she reached the farm she knew at once that the rest of the family had not yet returned. The cows were clustered near the house end of the pasture, waiting to be milked. Sam, she had heard at dinnertime, was over ploughing a solitary Libby field on the other side of Swansons' farm and Patience had the day off. She opened the screen door of the kitchen and called. There was no answer. It occurred to her suddenly that Martha might have gone over to Todd's Neck. But the Ford pickup was standing in the yard, and Martha was not one to walk when she could borrow the truck.

Tirza went round to the porch. Patches was curled up in the sun and Martha was lying on the porch swing, with her elegant legs stretched out and crossed at the ankles. She was reading a magazine and her newly permed hair was tightly curled up around her head. Tirza thought it had looked better before, when it hung loose.

'Hi,' she said lamely.

Martha glanced over her shoulder.

'Oh, it's you. Uh, happy birthday.'

'Thanks.' Tirza sat down on the top step, with her back against one of the posts which supported the jutting upper storey. She did not know how to begin. She could just hand Martha the letter and walk away, but that felt wrong, so she sat, searching for something to say.

Martha tossed her magazine on to the wicker table. It slithered off the edge and fell to the floor. It was a glossy fashion magazine and the cover showed a woman with very red lipstick wearing a navy blue suit with square shoulders like an army officer's uniform and very high-heeled shoes. Tirza thought they looked ridiculous together. The woman had a navy hat like an upside-down flowerpot, trimmed with a frill of veil, and she was standing sideways with one hip hitched higher than the other and her breasts thrust forward. Tirza suddenly felt very tired. She locked her hands together between her knees.

'Did you want something?' Martha said.

How like her, Tirza thought. Why do I always have to justify myself to her?

Out of the corner of her eye she caught sight of the distant figure of Billy plodding up the farm track from the sea, dragging his schoolbag in the dust. She was running out of time. She did not stop to work out what she was going to say.

'Sandy's gone,' she said.

'What?'

'I said, Sandy's gone. Sandy Fraser. You know fine who I mean.'

Martha sat up suddenly and swung her feet off the seat. The swing rocked violently.

'What are you saying?'

'Sandy's gone,' Tirza said for the third time. 'He asked me to tell you.'

'Gone? Gone where?'

Martha sprang across the porch and seized Tirza by the shoulders. She jerked her to her feet. She pushed her face close to Tirza's. Her breath smelled of beer. The moment froze, and Tirza wondered where she had managed to get beer in the farmhouse. Perhaps she kept a supply in her room. Perhaps she spent her days drinking. Perhaps she was drunk now. But Martha's eyes were perfectly sharp, boring into her own.

'He's had his orders,' Tirza said. 'He has to go back to England. To the RAF. To fight.' Her voice cracked a little on that, but she held all her muscles tight. She wasn't going to give anything away to Martha.

'When?' Martha gave Tirza's shoulders a shake.

'First train to Boston this morning.'

Martha gave a cry. She shook Tirza again.

'Why didn't you come sooner? When did he tell you, you little bitch?'

Tirza held herself very still. 'He told me yesterday. And he asked me not to come until he was well away. He didn't want you to know.'

'I don't believe you.' Martha raised her hand and slapped Tirza hard on her left ear, so that her head was knocked sharply sideways and her ears rang. She jerked loose from Martha's other hand. Patches jumped up and ran away across the yard.

'It's true.' Tirza felt tears shamefully filling up her nose and throat. The realisation that he had really gone, which she had fought against all day, suddenly rolled over her.

Martha grabbed her and shook her again, so that her head snapped back and forth on her shoulders.

'You little trouble-maker, what have you been saying to him?'

'I don't know what you're talking about,' Tirza gasped.

'You tried to warn him off me, didn't you? I've seen you, hanging around him, trying to get noticed.'

'I've seen you too,' Tirza shouted, discretion tossed to the wind. 'I saw you in the summer cottage. How could you do that? Lying there naked? You're not married to him. You're filthy.'

Martha stared at her. Then she laughed. 'You don't know anything about it, you stupid child. What makes you think it was my idea?'

There was something about the defiant way she said it. And the way Sandy had been so reluctant to face her. Tirza suddenly knew with certainty.

'It *was* you. You're no better than a she-goat on heat.' It was a shameful thing to say. Tirza had overheard one of the soldiers use the phrase and was appalled to find the filthy words spilling out of her lips. Martha hit her again, hard, but she did not even try to defend herself. She hung her head. Martha pushed her aside.

'Gone?' she said. She looked round wildly. 'He can't be gone. He said, he *promised...*'

'Mo-om!' Billy was standing below them in the yard, his socks falling down, his schoolbag dropped in Harriet's flower border. 'What's going on? I'm hungry.'

Martha stared at him as though she had no idea who he was, then she swung round to face Tirza again. Her eyes had glazed over, the way they did, Tirza realised, when one of the planes flew low over the shore.

'He swore,' Martha whimpered, 'he *swore*.' She groped blindly in front of her, then she pushed past Tirza down the porch steps. Tirza watched her helplessly, unsure what to do. Martha stumbled across the yard towards the pickup. Then she stopped, turned back, and scooped up Billy. She began to run to the pickup, pushed Billy inside and climbed in after him.

Tirza ran down the porch steps and across to the truck. The engine fired. Tobias always left the keys in the ignition. Tirza struggled to pull the letter out of her shorts pocket, but it was bent and jammed in hard.

'Wait!' she shouted over the engine noise, and she banged on the door of the truck. As if that was a signal, it leapt away and she was thrown sideways, falling hard down into the packed earth of the yard and gashing her elbow on a stone. The truck roared away down the farm drive towards the road just as the envelope came free of her pocket.

Winded, Tirza got to her feet slowly, nursing her elbow in her other hand. The house and yard seemed small and far away, and sounds came to her thickly through the pain in her ear. She trudged across to the kitchen door and went through to the storeroom where Harriet kept her preserves and also the family medicines. There was a jar of Christina's healing cream here, Tirza knew. The same cream as she had given Sandy. Drearily she smeared it over her bruised and bleeding elbow, and in the process spread some on the envelope, which she was still clutching. No doubt Martha would fly at her about the state it was in when she finally managed to deliver it, but Tirza was past caring. She screwed the top on the jar, pushed the letter back into her pocket, and went out into the yard to pick up her bicycle.

As she bumped slowly down the farm track towards the sea, feeling shaken and sick, she wondered whether she ought to tell anyone about Martha going off in the truck. Before, when she had had one of her peculiar turns, she had simply run to hide somewhere. She might be a danger to other people behind the wheel of the truck. Harriet and Tobias should be coming back this way soon. It must be past milking time. It was odd she hadn't met them yet.

Over the smell of the sea and the freshly ploughed earth in the fields to her left, Tirza suddenly caught a whiff of something else, something bitter. She slid off the saddle and braced the bicycle between her legs. She sniffed again. It was a smell of burning, like a picnic campfire, but she didn't think that anyone would be having a campfire today, on the first of October, with all the summer people gone. A stab of fear ran through her. It might be a forest fire. There was nothing to be seen from the Libby woods to her right, but a small fire might have started somewhere at its heart, as yet unseen. If it was Christina's forest, then Christina's house and Christina herself were in danger. Tirza felt sick, suddenly overcome by a picture in her head of a wall of fire rushing towards the cabin. There was nowhere to go except to leap into the sea.

She shaded her eyes with her hand and searched the sky in the direction of Flamboro. There *was* something there. A thin wisp of rising smoke, which might be no more than someone burning rubbish. She climbed on to her bicycle again and began to ride as fast as the broken surface would allow down to the coast path and the way home.

As she turned on to the path, the smell grew stronger and she could hear voices shouting. She stood up on the pedals to force the bike up the slope and saw Simon running down the path towards her. He grabbed the handlebars to stop her.

'What's happening?' she asked.

'The Tremayne place,' he gasped, out of breath. 'It's on fire. Dad's gone back to the village to get help. I've got to get back to our house to call the fire brigade.'

'The telephone wire is down.'

'No, only in Flamboro now. Ours was fixed this morning. Give me your bike.'

She climbed off and handed it over.

'I don't see how it could catch on fire. The lightning was nearly two days ago. That can't have started it.'

He swung the bicycle round to face the opposite direction and threw her an agonised look over his shoulder.

'I told a couple of the soldiers how to get in there, and I guess they told others. I think they've been taking their girls there. If one of them left a cigarette burning...'

'Or lit a fire to keep warm,' said Tirza slowly, 'now that the weather's colder.'

'It's all my fault,' said Simon in a tight voice. He mounted her bike and rode off.

Tirza ran on up the hill, past the end of the Libby land, past the gully where the foxes lived, and stopped short where a group of women were standing by the stone wall looking across at the mansion. A thick column of smoke was rising now, and she could make out a flicker of flames in one of the upstairs windows, the one where she had read from the book of Robert Frost's poems.

'Can't we do something?' she demanded of Mary Flett.

'Not much we can do, Tirza dear. We're all bringing buckets up from the village till we have enough for a bucket chain. We can throw water from the well on to it, but it won't make any difference, try how we will.'

'By the time the fire engines get here from Portland,' said Marion Larrabee, 'it will be too late. And they'll have to cut through the chains on the gates before they can bring the engines in from the county road. I'm afraid it's finished.' She wiped her eyes on her apron. 'It's a sad sight. I remember how it used to be in the old days – a fine house and a fine family.'

There were one or two murmurs of agreement, but then a crowd arrived from the village with more buckets and everyone climbed over the stone wall and ran across the garden to see what could be done.

The people of Flamboro worked hard to try and save the house of the absent Boston owners. They formed four lines to pass the buckets from the well to the house. Ben had managed to rip off the old well-cover and found the water as good as ever inside, although the house had had piped water for fifty years. The buckets travelled back and forth in disciplined order, but the feeble splashes could do little against the blaze. One or two of the fishermen climbed up the walls and tried to dampen the roof, but the flames leaping out of the windows drove them back. Tirza thought of the bed curtains spangled over with sparks and shrivelling away into ashes, and the proud canvases of old Tremaynes curling at the edges and dropping from their frames. She was sorry about Everard Tremayne with his jaunty hat and merry eye.

By the time the fire engines arrived and broke down the gate, darkness had fallen and the fire seemed to burn all the more fiercely red against the black sky. The townsfolk were ordered brusquely back out of the way by the firemen, who unrolled great festoons of hose and ran about with their axes and helmets, but twenty minutes after they arrived the house gave a sigh like a hurt animal, and the whole roof collapsed inwards. Everyone stayed to watch, drawn by some strange fascination with the destruction. The firemen's hoses made no appreciable impact on the blaze, which roared up into the sky after the collapse of the roof, then settled down to a steady, determined devastation until the walls had fallen outwards, one by one.

It must have been ten or eleven o'clock before the fire subsided into sullen coals. There was nothing left of the two-hundred-year-old house but the cellars, the chimneys and the stone steps, and over all the rest a heap of ashes and charred timbers. One by one people shook themselves, gathered their families together, and talked about going home to bed. It was then that the big black Chrysler that belonged to the Mansion House nosed up the weed-grown driveway and parked behind the fire engines. The manager of the hotel came stepping carefully over the sprawling maze of hoses, looking for someone. Everyone turned round, surprised at this late arrival on the scene, because the Mansion House usually kept to itself. He sought out Tobias and drew him aside from the crowd.

Tobias's pickup had been found blocking the north path leading over Todd's Neck to the Mansion House. No one had been concerned at first, but when it had been there for a couple of hours, some of the staff had investigated. They had discovered Martha Libby. She had jumped from the cliff near the Libby summer cottage on to the sharp rocks below, with her son Billy in her arms.

Chapter 19

Coda
Maine: Fall 1980

I

TIRZA FOLLOWED ROUTE 1 out of Portland for a few miles before turning on to the side roads. Portland had aroused no emotions, it was so changed. It had grown upwards and its modern skyline gave her a sense of walking around an unknown town. She had not lingered. After her brief meeting with the lawyer, Gabriel Foss, she had done no more than visit the harbour. This was less altered than some other parts of the town, though the majority of the boats in the harbour – even at this late season of the year – were pleasure craft and not working boats. She wondered whether the pattern was repeated all over Maine, the native Mainers no longer independent farmers and fishermen, like the men on either side of the state crest, but vendors of hamburgers and skippers of pleasure cruisers.

She began to regret coming back.

She retrieved her rented car, which was parked near a modernistic building housing the state art collection, and worked her way on to the ubiquitous Route 1, which for so many years had threaded together the towns of the eastern seaboard. There were motels and fast food stops and 'genuine craft' outlets on both sides of the road, and she began to doubt whether she would recognise the Flamboro turn. Where were the children selling small cardboard cartons of laboriously picked blueberries laid out on their mother's borrowed card-table? Where were the pickups loaded with pumpkins, which used to flaunt signs saying, BIG AS YOU CAN LUG, ONLY 50¢ !!

The turn off to Flamboro was clear enough when she reached

it, although the county road at first looked quite unfamiliar, despite her daily bus journeys to and from the Portland high school. The late afternoon was warm with Indian summer weather, so she rolled down her window. The road began to climb a gentle hill, and suddenly its shape unrolling in front of her was familiar. She knew the exact moment when she would catch her first glimpse of the sea, from the top of the hill, glinting between two folds in the landscape. And at the same moment she smelled it, the rich seaweed and salt-water savour of it, stronger for some reason than it was in Scotland. Then the road dipped down and she lost the sight of it, though not the smell. Her heart had begun to beat unevenly.

She took a left turn marked Flamboro, then a right signposted for Todd's Neck. A few minutes later, and she was running along Libby land. As she neared the farm gate she slowed the car to a crawl and studied the left-hand side of the road. The gate was there, sagging and unpainted, and under a sprawl of bridal wreath vine there was something that might have been the remains of the farm sign. Fifty yards further, on the right, the drive to Swansons' farm was a neat tarred strip curving away between tidily pruned fruit trees. Beyond, she could see the end of the barn, though it no longer carried advertising for chewing tobacco. The house had always been hidden from the road, but a freshly painted white five-barred gate closed the drive. Beside it, on a post, hung a white sign with black letters, also newly painted: SWANSON. So they lived here yet. Tirza wondered whether Hector was still farming. He would be, oh, sixty-five or so. Too young for a Maine farmer to retire.

Then the road looped away to the right. On the Libby side of the road, farmland gave way to the woods which lay inland from the marsh. They looked totally unchanged, disconcertingly so. The Libby fields a little further on, lying on Swansons' side, where Tirza had made hay with Tobias that hot summer of '42, were turned over to grazing now. A fine herd of Jersey cattle was placidly cropping the grass or standing sleepily chewing the cud. The quality of the beasts seemed at odds with the unkempt air of the old Libby farm. Perhaps the Swansons owned these fields now.

A bend in the road took her to the left again, and as she came round it she saw a large black and gold sign, full of antique curlicues, which pointed to the Todd's Neck turn and the Mansion House Hotel.

The road through the Libby woods to Todd's Neck was shorter than she remembered, but then she had never driven it before, only walked it, walks which remained in her mind as always hot and plagued with mosquitoes from the marshy fringes of the wood. The meadow at the end of the woods, where the road started out over the Neck itself, also seemed diminished by time, unless the wood had crept over part of it. Alders would lead the way, quickly colonising the edges of a field when the farmer's back is turned. The larger, slower-growing trees would follow, until the land became unusable, and had to be hacked free of the forest again.

The meadow seemed too small now to accommodate the wagons of the Shakers. Tirza remembered suddenly the Shaker girl in the over-sized sunbonnet. Had she remained in the community? There were only a handful of Shakers left these days. Rich folk paid ridiculous prices for their simple and beautiful pieces of furniture, but people no longer wanted to follow their austere mode of life. The Shaker girl had been Tirza's own age. Probably she had turned her back on her people, deserted them as Tirza had done.

She drove on to the beginning of the Neck. The path down to Libby's Beach still led off on the left and looked well trodden, though the summer people would be gone by now. She wondered whether the out of season guests at the Mansion House were the same retired rich outlanders, come to be pampered at great cost here on the coast. Suddenly she marvelled what could have possessed her to book a room here. Was it just that she wanted to prove something? That she now belonged to the world which patronised the Mansion House?

The reception area in the hotel was unchanged from the day she had walked through it and up to Sandy's room with her arms scratched from picking cranberries and her bare feet covered with sand. There was the same mahogany panelling, the same dim, gilded lamps, the same vast old reception desk, the same bellhops in maroon uniforms with gold piping. The carpet must have been replaced, but it could have been the same. The heels of her shoes sank into it as her sandy toes had once done.

As the bellhop showed her to her room on the second floor, she felt a moment of panic. She hoped they had not given her Sandy's old room. No, this one was two doors away. As the door was unlocked, a young couple came out of Sandy's room and murmured a polite greeting to her as they passed. They were holding hands. A honeymoon couple, surely. Not able to afford the Mansion House in the ordinary course of things.

The bellhop handed her a card with meal times listed on it, and left her alone. She went to the window. The room had the same view as Sandy's. Mustinegus rode out there offshore, the cliffs tumbled away at the foot of the hotel, and when she flung open the window, which groaned as though it had not been unsealed for some time, the cries of the gulls washed up to her, and the pounding of the breakers ran through the movement of her blood. She pressed the heels of her hands against her eyes. She must not let herself give in to this, to the insidious way the place was working on her.

⸻◈⸻

Tirza got up next morning determined to take things at a slow pace, to allow herself time to think. As usual, she woke early, before breakfast was served in the hotel, so she went outside to explore the grounds. The garden layout was different, she thought, but she had not paid it much mind when she was younger. A shortcut still ran through it to the pier, though. This had been rebuilt and extended, and a breakwater constructed on the offshore side to provide shelter for the throng of boats now moored here. It almost amounted to a marina. On this side, the south side of the Neck, several small cottages had been built in traditional style along the shore, each with a small pier of its own. She remembered some people in reception last night talking about going over to the cottages. These must be an addition to the hotel facilities.

At breakfast, eating her waffles with maple syrup, she asked the waiter, a middle-aged man, whether Pierre Lamotte was still the chef. He was polite, but baffled. He had worked at the hotel for twenty-five years, he said, but had never heard of a Pierre Lamotte. So, Pierre, did you return to Montreal and marry your French Canadian girl and start your own restaurant? Pierre, with

345

his French accent and his worldly-wise ways, had always seemed immensely old to Tirza, but thinking back she supposed he must have been about the same age as Hector Swanson. Why had he not been drafted? Or perhaps he was, later. After that summer she had never again come here to sell crabs.

The first thing she would do after breakfast, she decided, was to walk along the beach to Flamboro and look things over anonymously. No one there, she was sure, would recognise her. She took the path down over the rocks to the beach, but kept well away from the place where the side turning had led off to the Libby summer house. It was not difficult, because there was no sign of the old path. Everywhere under the trees along the cliff was an unbroken undergrowth of ferns and sapling trees.

She had forgotten the bright silver of the sand on the beach. Accustomed for the last few years to the small pockets of coarse yellow sand round her part of the west Scottish coast, she had not remembered that this sand was so fine and silky. She ran handfuls of it through her fingers for the sheer pleasure of it. And like an omen, it seemed, she found a perfect sand dollar. She hid it carefully behind a distinctive rock to collect later, then she took off her socks and shoes and hung them round her neck by the laces. The tide was halfway out. She rolled up her jeans a few turns and waded into the edge of the water. And caught her breath. As a child she had learned to swim from this beach, but she hadn't swum often from choice. Three hundred and fifty days of the year the breakers struck the breath from your body with an icy slap. By comparison, the sea around Caillard was almost balmy.

Halfway along the beach she climbed up the ledges near the petrified trees. The marsh stretched away, unchanged, towards the woods, with its treacherous clumps of green, its cranberries, and over there a glimpse of Libby's Pond. She followed the thin path along the top of the ledges, and tried to make out where the foxholes had been, but there was no trace of them at all – no depressions in the ground, no fragment of burlap trailing from the encroaching sand, no abandoned piece of equipment. Christina had been right. This desecration by the army might never have been.

In fact from Todd's Neck to the end of the Libby farm track, she could see nothing to indicate that any time had passed while she had been away. It gave her a strange sensation, like a sort of Rip Van Winkle in reverse. She had grown older, but the place had stayed the same.

The last of the Libby fields, nearest the sea, had been used for a crop this year. Early potatoes. She could see a few ragged leaves left flapping under the lee of the stone wall. It needed ploughing, though. And parts of the old wall had tumbled over and not been rebuilt. She stopped at the far end to climb into the gully. The foxes' den was still there, but she could see no sign of life about it. Intentionally she had left her cameras behind in the hotel, fearing they might identify her, but she wished she had them now, just in case the great-great-great-great-grand-children of her foxes should come skipping out to play amongst the undergrowth.

On the far side of the gully she clambered cautiously out on to Tremayne land. It seemed likely that the property, in such a beautiful spot, with its wide view of the ocean, would have been sold and built over. But there was nothing here except the desolate ruin of the garden. Further on she found what must be the remains of the orchard. Many of the trees had died and fallen. Those that remained had grown into grotesque twisted shapes. There was something pathetic about them. If they had been wild trees, they would have grown to their natural shape from the start, but these trees had been shaped and pruned, and then abandoned, and they were as forlorn as a pet dog turned loose to fend for itself in the wild.

There was a gap in the orchard which had once been a path, and she followed it back towards the house. Or where she thought the house ought to be. She found it at last, a raised mound of rough grass and weeds growing over rubble. It was almost impossible to identify even the floor plan, but the marble front steps remained, with clumps of weeds spurting out of the cracks. On the side away from the sea she found the opening leading to the cellars. Leaning over the dank hole she could just make out a rubble of broken flowerpots, from which rose the same dank smell as she and Simon had smelled on that cold winter's day when they had first climbed in.

Why had no one built here? Clearly the Tremaynes had never

347

returned. Did they still own the land?

At the top of the steep stretch of the coast path leading down into Flamboro, Tirza paused, sitting on a rock and putting her shoes and socks back on. Well, she had expected changes, and here they were. There was just one lobsterboat in the harbour, and she could see only two more hauling offshore. There was no sign of any trawlers. The bait shed had been pulled down and replaced by a smart new building with a sign saying FLAMBORO YACHT CLUB. The lovely old road surfaces of broken oyster shells, which used to glint like a rainbow after showers, had gone. The roads were all utilitarian black now. The houses gleamed with new paint, and Tirza wondered whether it was still as difficult to maintain in the teeth of the salt-laden storms, or whether modern paints were impervious to this bane of the householders' lives. The town had grown very little, though she could see some new houses up where Schoolhouse Lane led inland. The church was unchanged, and the gilded weathervane was pointing south-west. With a curious mixture of reluctance and eagerness, she climbed down the last stretch of path and came out on the wharf side next to her own house.

She tried to look at it dispassionately, but that was impossible. The boat shed had been turned into a three-car garage. A single-storey extension had been built on to the opposite side of the house, with a big picture window overlooking the ocean, which seemed grotesquely out of character beside the sturdy shuttered windows of the old house. The porch, which had always been too narrow, had been widened too, and from an open window she could hear the shrieks and applause of a TV game show. Turning firmly away from the house, she walked on along the harbour front.

The working boats left might be few, but there were plenty of sailing boats, and her heart lifted a little at their lovely lines. She had not owned a sailboat since *Stormy Petrel*, and something like envy stirred in her as she saw a man slotting a mainsail on to a mast, ready for hoisting. She watched as he tidied his lines into neat coils and slipped the mooring ropes. He looked up and caught her eye.

'Like to come along?' he said. He smiled at her quizzically. 'Just going for a run along the coast. Back by this evening.'

She shook her head and smiled back. 'Thanks, but I can't. Have a good trip.'

Shore Road, behind the harbour-front houses, held a few more shops than in the past – gifts and crafts, boating supplies, sports clothes. But there was one familiar sight. Flett's General Stores and Post Office. The same porch with the rocking chairs. The same old men sitting there, watching the life of the village. No, not the same men, but some of them might recognise her. Tirza ducked her head a little as she went in.

The inside was changed. The pot-bellied stove was gone, and the sacks and barrels of loose goods. Probably food and health regulations had put a stop to that. There was modern shelving and a shining modern counter with electronic scales. But the post office section at the back of the shop looked exactly the same, with its glass-fronted mailboxes surrounding the grated wicket where you could buy stamps.

A grey-haired man behind the counter was leaning back against the shelves with his arms crossed and talking to two customers, a man and woman in hiking gear. When they had gone out, Tirza carried a few purchases over to the counter – some film, a packet of cookies and a pair of shoelaces. She needed none of these things, but wanted some excuse to linger here. It seemed the most familiar place in Flamboro, despite the changes in the décor. She scanned the shelves behind the man's shoulder.

'Do you have any anoraks? Size twelve? No, I mean ten in US size. I think.'

He lifted down three – one green, one sky blue, and one red and navy – and laid them out for her to see.

'Not many left at the end of the season,' he said. His voice made her hands tremble. He sounded exactly like Charlie.

She tried on the green one hastily, then took it off again.

'I'll have this one. Do you accept credit cards?'

'Sure.' He looked surprised that she should ask.

While he was filling in the slip, a woman came through from the back shop. Her hair was still brown, but it was threaded with grey, and she looked at Tirza intently. Tirza turned sideways to avoid her gaze.

'I guess you must be English,' the man said in the roundabout way Maine people have, avoiding the direct question.

Tirza flicked her eyes up to him, and then lowered them again as she signed the slip. 'No. I grew up in Maine. Over there they reckon I sound American. I guess I don't belong anywhere much any more.'

The woman came out from behind the counter and touched her arm.

'It's Tirza Libby, isn't it?'

'Yes, Miss Bennett,' said Tirza weakly. 'Hello, Pete.'

<hr>

Julia and Pete Flett would not allow her to leave until she promised to come to supper the day after next. Tirza walked out on to the porch of Flett's Stores unsure whether she had done a stupid thing, coming here. Or perhaps it was inevitable, from the time she had agreed to attend the opening of her exhibition in Boston, that she should fetch up here on the creaking boards of the old village store, where the retired fishermen and farmers studied her speculatively from their rocking chairs and the gulls whooped noisily around the back yard, looking for scraps. She had walked into Flamboro an hour ago an unknown outsider. Before the afternoon was over, village gossip would have spread the word that Tirza Libby, who had deserted her family the moment she was finished with school, had – as unaccountably – returned.

There was one more place she intended to visit before she walked back to Todd's Neck. She headed north along the harbour towards the church. The Penhaligon house, standing high above its sloping garden, seemed almost unchanged. Someone was continuing to care for the garden. The railings around the widow's walk, which thrust up from the roof, glinted in the sunlight where the arrow-shaped tips had been painted gold against the black of the posts. The steep narrow steps up to the church were the same and its clapboards had a fresh coat of paint, so that it stood out almost blindingly against the darkness of the forest behind. The first of the cold winds had begun turning the deciduous trees to their autumn colours.

Tirza did not go into the church. Instead she turned right to the burying-ground. The anti-aircraft gun was long gone. The concrete platform, erected so noisily on those spring days, remained. But it was changed. In the centre stood a war memorial, a bronze statue of a sailor with his hand shading his eyes as he looked out to sea. A plaque on the base listed the names of all the sons of Flamboro and the neighbouring farms who had perished in the war. Arthur Pelham was amongst them. Two metal seats had been set here, screwed down to the concrete to stop the gales from carrying them away. There were tubs of flowers, mostly past flowering now, but a few ivy-leafed geraniums trailed crimson and white blooms over their edges.

It was a curiously welcoming spot in what had once been the forlorn surroundings of the burying-ground. Tirza sat on one of the benches, with her hands laced together between her knees, and surveyed the prospect. The town was laid out below her like a model, and before her the view of the sea stretched well beyond Crab Island and Mustinegus. To the right she could see part of the Tremayne land. The nearer end of Libby's Beach was hidden by the intervening headland, but the far end was visible, and that end of the marsh, and a glint of water from Libby's Pond. On Todd's Neck she could see part of the roof of the Mansion House. She twisted round and looked inland. Behind the coastal fields she could make out the dull red barn and the grey-shingled farmhouse at Libby's Farm.

In the burying-ground itself, she found Wayne's small stone first, and beside it a memorial marker for Walter and Eli, whose bodies had never been recovered. Then the elaborate grave-stone, which he had brought back from Italy thirty years before his death, marking the grave of Captain Penhaligon. It was ten feet tall and visible to ships at sea. The hard white marble resisted the weather and it dominated the burying-ground with its carved ship cradled in the hands of an angel. People in Flamboro had disapproved of it at the time, Tirza had been told as a child, because it was so flamboyant and showy, but when she was small she had always liked the idea of the ship so tenderly protected. Next to Captain Penhaligon's grave (*And Also Margaret His Wife*), three identical stones stood in a row. Miss Molly and Miss Catherine had joined Miss Susanna here.

Just beyond the Penhaligons was the Libby plot. Tirza averted her eyes from Martha's stone, with its dates of a curtailed life, and knelt down beside Nathan's grave. It was more recent than

Miss Molly's and Miss Catherine's, but now after five years the ground had settled. Someone – perhaps Julia Flett – had recently planted it with winter pansies.

Tirza laid her hands flat on the earth amongst the pansies.

'I'm sorry, Dad,' she said. 'It's inadequate, I know. I don't really believe you can hear me, wherever you are, but I wish I could believe you would forgive me.'

She stayed there, the ground warm beneath her hands though a cold wind played around her shoulders, until her knees began to ache and her arms to tremble. Then she got up, and sighed, and brushed off her jeans, and began the long walk back to Todd's Neck.

—◆◆◆—

Tirza lunched on the closed porch of the hotel overlooking the steep drop to the sea. In summer the folding glass screens were removed and stored away, so that it became an ordinary open porch where the guests could sit during the day in comfortable cushioned wicker chairs or dine in the evenings al fresco. Now that the cold autumn winds whipped around the end of Todd's Neck, the glass screens had been fixed in place for the winter. Even so, it was still a pleasant place to eat, more spacious feeling than the formal dining room with its plush-covered chairs and maroon wallpaper. Apart from Tirza, only the honeymoon couple and one solitary elderly man were eating lunch out here today.

When the waiter brought her melon sorbet, Tirza detained him.

'I see there are a lot of boats moored round at the pier. Are any of them for hire?'

'Certainly, madam. There are several skiffs, and three motor boats of different sizes.'

'No sailboats?'

'Just some small catboats we hire out to children in the summer.'

'Are they still in the water? Could I hire one for the afternoon?'

'Why, yes, I suppose so.' He looked at her doubtfully. 'We ask for a certificate of sailing competence. Some sort of proof that you know how to handle a sailboat. The sea is very treacherous around here – currents and things.' He sounded vague, as though he had never set foot in a boat.

'I know all about these waters. I grew up in Flamboro. I don't have any kind of certificate, but I went out in my father's lobsterboat as soon as I could walk.'

She could see him readjusting his ideas. The Mansion House did not normally entertain the daughters of lobstermen.

'If you need reassurance that I can handle a boat, I'm sure Peter Flett from Flamboro would vouch for me.'

'I'll speak to the manager of our sports facilities, madam.'

Tirza ate her sorbet with quick impatient gestures and drank her coffee without tasting it. It had been a whim to ask about hiring a sailboat, but the thought that she might be barred from doing so made her determined. The waiter came back at last with a smile on his face.

'That will be quite all right, madam. If you would like to speak to Mr Olson at sports reception, he will arrange everything for you.'

Mr Olson proved sensible and efficient, and half an hour later Tirza was casting off from the pier. She paddled her way out from the close-ranked boats. No one else was on the water apart from two grey-haired women rowing a skiff with rather flashy expertise along the shore. The catboat was rigged much as *Stormy Petrel* had been, but in other ways was very different. The hull was fibreglass instead of wood, the mast a hollow tube of metal that twanged like a primitive musical instrument. The sails and ropes were nylon, and there were buoyancy bags strapped permanently under the narrow side decks. Tirza had been told she was required to wear a life jacket, but once she was well under way she took it off again. It made her feel as though she had grown an extra, bloated body.

The wind was still blowing steadily from the south-west, and took her easily and rapidly out to Mustinegus. As the little lightweight boat skimmed over the waves, dancing to the slapping movement of the water and rushing eagerly ahead, Tirza experienced a surge of exhilaration. She felt physically stronger and more energetic than she could remember feeling for years. She reached across the wind to come round to the side of the island where the cove lay, then headed close to the wind to bring the boat in to the sandy beach.

It looked exactly the same.

Well, perhaps some of the trees were taller. And the path through the woods had been kept cleared. She walked over to the first farmhouse, the one abandoned after the hurricane of '38. The house and barn were totally ruined now, but there was one outbuilding in good repair, with its doors hooked open. She saw why when she walked on a little further, to the old fields. Someone was keeping sheep on the island. It wasn't uncommon along the Maine coast, where the land for farming was scarce and poor, for a farmer to move a whole flock of sheep on to an island for most of the year. In the worst of the winter these sheep would be moved back to the farmyard until after lambing, but at the moment they roamed wild here. They ran away from Tirza at first, but then dropped their heads and began grazing again when they saw she meant to come no nearer.

The old Indian encampment, where she and Sandy had picnicked, was a little more overgrown. The mounds which covered the shell heaps were still there, but she did not search for arrowheads. Instead she retraced her steps to the north-east side of the island and found the blueberry thickets as flourishing as ever, though the crop was all but finished. She found half a dozen late berries and ate them, relishing the sweet wild flavour which had been such a part of her youth.

That evening she dined early and – escaping from a retired stockbroker and his wife, who were disposed to be friendly – she retreated to her room. She felt suddenly bone weary, and longed for bed.

She was already showered and changed into a nightgown when her bedside telephone rang, making her jump. She lifted the receiver.

'Hello?' she said cautiously.

'Tirza? It's Alex Wrycroft here. I wondered how you were. Has it been very difficult, going back?'

'Oh, Alex.'

She kicked off her slippers and climbed into bed, pulling the patchwork quilt up over her.

'Yes,' she said, 'it's been some difficult. But so far I've just been wandering around, getting my bearings.'

'Seen anyone you know?' he asked, choosing his words carefully.

'Only the Fletts at the store in Flamboro. Julia Flett used to be my teacher at the village school, Miss Bennett. She recognised me straight off. I didn't think anyone would know me. I thought I could walk around incognito, as if I were wearing a mask. I wasn't yet seventeen when I was last there.'

'I recognised you from the photograph taken when you were twelve.'

'It's odd, isn't it? We change so much inside as we grow older, it's difficult to believe we can possibly look like our younger selves.'

'Oh, I don't think we change all that much inside either. I think we still carry around that same childhood self. It's just that we build a tough carapace around it.'

She was silent.

You are still in love with him, aren't you? he had said.

'So you haven't been to the farm yet?' Alex went on, as though there had been no awkward pause.

'I might go tomorrow. I'm not sure.'

'I think you should go.' His voice was warm and strong, giving her confidence. 'I wish I could be there with you, to give you some moral support.'

'Oh, I wish you were too!' she cried, then remembered she had said the same thing in her letter. There was another pause, across the three thousand miles that separated them. Then she said, suddenly struck, 'What time is it there?'

'Half past three in the morning.'

'Alex, you loon, go to bed!'

'In Aberdeenshire,' he said mildly, 'loon means young man. And I am in bed. What about you?'

'Just going.'

'I'll ring you tomorrow, probably. To see how things have gone.'

'All right. Good-night, Alex.'

'Good-night. Take care.'

The telephoned clicked and went dead.

When Tirza met Alex by the crofts near Caillard, she invited him to come over to her island for lunch the next day. Although he said he wanted to talk to her about this supposed connection between their families, he seemed in no hurry to start, that day they first met. Instead they talked about the fishing on the loch, about her photography and his farm, where he reared pedigree Aberdeen Angus and kept a small herd of Highland cattle, a minor passion of his, he said. And then as they walked back to Caillard together, she asked him to lunch.

She had entertained no one since moving to the island, except Moira McIver who came over from the inn occasionally for coffee. But for some reason she felt in no way threatened by Alex Wrycroft. In a lifetime of dealing with potentially danger-ous men in threatening situations, in countries at war or amidst total breakdown of law and order, she had learned to rely on her instincts about who could be trusted and who could not.

Alex himself said gently, 'Perhaps you should check out that I am who I say I am?' But she shook her head and laughed.

What did give her pause for thought, after he went back to his room in the Prince Returning, was the food she was going to provide. Fending for herself, either in urban apartment or jungle camp, she had never learned more than the most basic cookery, and had existed for years on scratch meals out of tins, or sandwiches, or eggs. If she was going to appear even moder-ately welcoming, she would have to do better than that for Alex Wrycroft. In the end, Moira came to her rescue with a piece of cold poached salmon, some salads which she packed up in plas-tic ice-cream boxes, and half a cheesecake.

'Just let me know when I can do the same for you,' said Tirza, and Moira laughed.

They ate their excellent lunch in the kitchen with the door and window standing open to the warm summer breeze. Then they carried their mugs of coffee outside and sat together on the flat boulder by the back door, looking out over the bay, with the houses of Caillard away off to their right.

'Now,' said Tirza, putting down her empty mug on a cushion of moss. 'Don't you think it's time to tell me what this is all about?'

Alex wedged his own mug carefully amongst the pebbles and clasped his hands around his knees.

'There is no easy way to say this, so I won't insult you by skirting round it.'

He turned to face her.

'I am Sandy Fraser's son.'

She looked at him in astonishment. She had guessed that his story must in some way relate to Sandy. She had even noticed a resemblance, particularly when he smiled. But Alex must be much the same age as she was.

'I don't understand. How can you possibly be? You're much too old,' she said bluntly.

'He was only eighteen when I was born. My parents were childhood sweethearts. They married as soon as they left school, when they were sixteen. You do know...' he raised a quizzical eyebrow, 'that it's long been possible to marry younger in Scotland than in England?'

'Yes, I did know that.'

'Their parents were against it. My father's father was a doctor. He wanted his son to go to university and then follow him in his profession, join his own practice. My mother's father was factor for the local absentee laird. I don't suppose her parents minded so much about her finishing her education, but they thought she was too young to take on the responsibilities of marriage and children. Well, they didn't listen to their parents. You know what teenagers are.'

'I've never been a parent.'

'No. Sorry. It comes of just emerging from the parent-of-teenagers period myself – you think everybody else has been going through the same stresses. Anyway, they got married – that would have been in 1927, and I was born in the summer of '29. My sister Fiona was born in '31, and my sister Gillian in '34.'

'You mean he had *three* children?'

'Four, in fact, but I'll explain about that in a minute. Three before the war, certainly. They were twenty-three, they had three children, and my father could only get a job as a junior clerk in a solicitor's office in Inverness. We lived in a two-roomed flat and there was never quite enough money for us to eat properly. As far back as I can remember, they quarrelled endlessly.'

Tirza tried to reconcile this picture of Sandy with her memories, but it did not fit. He had seemed free of any constraints.

'So, what happened?'

'They split up. But they didn't divorce. There was a lot of shame attached to divorce, of course, in those days. My mother took us back to live with her parents in 1935, when I was six. There was plenty of room in the big factor's house, and only one of her brothers and sisters was still living at home – her youngest brother, who eventually took over as factor from my grandfather after the war. The laird gave my mother a job in the estate office.'

'And Sandy?'

'He moved to Edinburgh. One of his old schoolfriends had been to university and then became a master at one of the big public schools there. He found Dad a job teaching at a small prep school which wasn't too fussy about qualifications. Dad was a great reader and he was quite a success as an English teacher. I think he taught some history too. And of course, he was a very good rugby player, which was a great asset.'

'Of course,' said Tirza dryly.

'The moment war broke out, he joined the RAF. It seems he had always dreamed of flying. He came to see us just before he left for basic training. I was ten by then, and I remember his visit very clearly. My parents seemed to be happy to be together, and I longed for him to come home so we could all be a family again.'

'And did he?'

'Just a moment.' Alex paused, as if gathering the pieces of his story together. 'He spent, I think, two leaves with us before he was shot down in '42. He must have had other leaves, but perhaps they were too short for him to come all the way to Scotland, or perhaps he went somewhere else. Then we heard, in the early summer of '42, that he was missing, presumed killed.'

'Wait,' said Tirza, wanting to postpone this. 'I'm going to make us some more coffee.'

Leaving him sitting there in the sun, she went into the kitchen and put the kettle on, then she went into the bathroom and locked the door. She stared at herself in the mirror. Her hair was windblown, and her face looked back at her drawn and pale. She ran a basin of cold water and plunged her face in, then rubbed it roughly dry.

When she came out with the two mugs of coffee, he began again.

'We had a few bad weeks. My mother cried a lot. Then we got the cable saying he'd been picked up, injured, at sea, and was recovering in some hospital in the States. You can imagine how astonishing that was. My mother sat us all down, even little Gillian who was only eight, and said that when the war was over, she was going to make sure that Dad came back to live with us. He'd find some work on the estate and we'd all be together again.'

Alex took a long drink of his coffee, then rested his chin on his hands.

'After he got back to Britain he was allowed a short visit to us, before he went back to the RAF. But the autumn of '42 – that was a difficult period in the war, and they didn't allow him much time. He seemed strange to me – distant – though I couldn't have put into words at the time why I felt that. After the war he did come back, and lived with us for a year. And it was at the end of that year that my youngest sister was born, Heather. In '47. By then I was as old as he had been when I was born, and about to go off to university myself. The marriage didn't last. They began having rows again, and he moved out for good. This time they got a divorce.'

'But I don't understand,' said Tirza. 'Why is your name Wrycroft, not Fraser?'

'Oh, well, my mother married again, and I took my step-father's name.'

'Wasn't that a bit unusual? You must have been quite old.'

'Twenty-one.' He smiled at her. 'There was a reason. You remember I mentioned the old laird? There was a son about the same age as my parents. He was serving in Singapore when it was overrun by the Japanese. Altogether he had a bad war. Afterwards he came to Scotland to convalesce – he'd always spent his summers there as a boy, and he'd known my mother since they were children. Their love affair just grew from that. I think it probably started before my parents finally broke up. Perhaps it was one of the reasons for the final split. His name was Michael Wrycroft and he adopted all of us legally when he married our mother. And he decided to live permanently on the estate and farm it himself, with my uncle's help. He was a dear man, and he made me heir to the estate, as if I had been his own son. In fact he was much more of a father to me than Sandy ever was, though he started a bit late.'

Tirza turned all this over in her mind.

'But you didn't lose touch with Sandy, did you? What became of him? And how did you know about Maine?' She stared at a flock of black-headed gulls diving into the bay for fish, and began to bite the side of her thumb. 'I suppose Sandy could still be alive. He'd only be sixty-nine.'

'No,' said Alex, and he took her other hand gently. He began tracing patterns on her palm. 'No, I'm sorry, Tirza. He died just last year.'

'I always thought,' Tirza whispered, 'that he must have been killed in the war.'

They sat for a long while in silence, and Tirza felt a sense of darkness welling up inside her. *I have lost him again. And to have come so close...*

'I kept in touch with him,' Alex said. 'He went back to his teaching job in Edinburgh after the divorce. He was good with children, and he retired only three years before he died. It was kidney failure.'

He sighed heavily.

'I sat with him a good deal when he was dying, and it was then that he began to talk about that summer in Maine. He'd never spoken of it before. He talked a great deal about you, how you helped him recover, what good friends you were, as if you were the same age and had known each other for ever. About your Indian grandmother who lived in the forest. About sailing your boat to some island, and how you put your hand right on an Indian arrowhead — as if you could see it inside your mind, he said.'

After a moment's silence, Alex felt in the breast pocket of his jacket, then held out his hand, palm up. The small arrowhead glinted against the work-roughened skin.

'And he told me about his affair with your cousin Martha.' Alex cleared his throat. 'He said she was unstable after the death of her husband, and very demanding. In a way, I suppose he saw parallels with his own situation and my mother alone back in Scotland. He and Martha became lovers, and he didn't try to excuse his part in it, but he said she was haunted and hungry, that was his phrase, haunted and hungry. He said he left a letter with you because he was afraid of what she might do if he told her he was going back to Britain and to his wife and family.'

'But she did it anyway,' said Tirza.

'Yes. But he didn't know that until much later, some years after the war. He met one of the American officers who had been stationed near Flamboro, Tucker I think his name was. He was in Edinburgh for the Festival. That's when he heard about your cousin's suicide. Was that after she read his letter?'

Tirza twisted her hands together. She had never told anyone what had happened that day. When the police had come asking questions, no one had thought to speak to her, and she had kept silent.

'I never had a chance to give her Sandy's letter. I told her he had gone, and she just went crazy. She drove off in the pickup. I banged on the side and shouted to her, but she ignored me.'

'So what became of the letter?'

'There was this enormous fire. A big country house, standing empty. It caught fire that same evening. The soldiers had been using it – looting, drinking the wine, seducing local girls. There were three fatherless babies born to village girls later. The firemen reckoned one of the soldiers had left a cigarette burning and it had set alight the brittle old bed hangings. When I heard about Martha, I was still at the fire with the others. I didn't know what to do. I guess I went a bit crazy too. And I wanted to protect Sandy – I didn't want them to think that he had caused her to jump off that cliff. So I dropped the letter on part of the fire that was still smouldering, and watched it burn away.'

Alex put his arm around her shoulders. She was shaking, despite the warmth of the summer day.

'I don't know how you coped. You were only twelve,

weren't you?'

'It was my thirteenth birthday.'

'Of course. The same date as Dad's birthday.'

'Was that all he told you?'

'No. There was one last thing he said, the night before he died. He had been talking to me about my own marriage and saying that I should be grateful for what I had had, even though I had lost my wife, because our love was based on what he called "kinship of the spirit", not just sexual gratification. Then he started talking about Maine again. He was very tired and weak, and he would talk for a few minutes, then have to rest again. He said Martha satisfied his frustrated sexual needs, which had grown out of the failure of his marriage, but the recollection brought him nothing but shame.'

Alex tightened his arm around Tirza's shoulders, and cleared his throat.

'He said that it was in Maine he had found someone he really loved, despite the difference in age. He was in love with you, and wanted you, but persuaded himself it was in your best interests never to contact you again, because he was afraid he would ruin your life.' He drew a breath.

'I have to be honest with you, Tirza. When I learned that my father had been in love with a twelve-year old girl, I was appalled. A child the same age as his own son. But now that I've met you, I think I understand.'

Tirza covered her face with her hands, but tears trickled down between her fingers and fell into her lap.

'You're still in love with him, aren't you?' he said.

'It's much worse than that,' Tirza answered.

Tirza's second morning at the Mansion House dawned to a pale misty curtain of rain, opalescent and pearly as the inside of an oyster shell. She ate her early breakfast alone on the porch, watching the curtain waver and fade. The sun broke through hesitantly. The few scattered spruces along this side of the promontory sparkled as if each individual needle was threaded through a splinter of rock crystal. By the time she left the hotel, the ground was steaming gently, and wisps floated up through the woods along the northern cliff and blew away like smoke. It was the first day of October. Her birthday. The day the Tremayne house had burned down all those years ago and Martha had thrown herself from these cliffs.

Tirza was on her way to the Libby farm, but before taking the path over the rocks down to the beach, she turned aside where the narrow track had once led to the old Victorian summer cottage. It was difficult to find the traces of the path. Alders had encroached on it and brambles, heavy with fat blackberries, snagged at her hair and ankles. Eventually she emerged into a familiar flat area, the clearing where the summer house had stood. The fieldstone foundations were still here, enclosing a space which seemed not much larger than a sheep fold. But the timber frame and the shingled sides were long gone. A wild cherry tree had taken root within the space where older generations of Libbys had sat at their ease on wicker furniture, admiring the picturesque view and the remarkable water spouts.

The ocean still shot vertically into the air up the rock gullies. Tirza stood at the edge of the Spouter, looking over, and the spray spattered down on her, soaking her hair and the shoulders of her new anorak. The drop to the sea was not so great here as from the cliff by the Tremayne house, where the whale had been washed ashore, but the rocks were much more vicious. It was somewhere here that Martha had thrown herself on to the jagged outcrops below. Tirza had never known exactly where. She had never again come to this place after the day when she had seen Martha and Sandy in the summer cottage.

She had felt an inner compulsion driving her to this spot, as if by coming and standing at the top of the cliff it would be easier, or at least clearer, to come to an understanding of her own place in that confused web of events. Despite the sharp rocks below, there was nothing sinister about this stretch of cliff. There was the drip of moisture off the trees, the soft compost of pine needles and rotting leaves underfoot, and a clean, sea-smelling breeze flowing in from the north-east over the running tide. Fragments of mica in the granite rock glinted and beyond the headland the sands of the beach shone silver where they lay above high-water mark.

Tirza made her way back to the path and down to the beach. She walked briskly, keeping to the hard wet sand until she came to the end where the ledges jutted out into the sea, and the farm track met the coastal path. The rutted damage caused by the army jeeps had been repaired long ago, but she noticed as she walked up between the fields that the farm had a neglected air. The bottom field was not the only one in need of ploughing before winter. There was an empty pasture studded over with thistles and other pestilent weeds, and the gate to it hung open and broken from the gatepost.

There seemed to be no stock on the place, and no people. No living thing but the crows winging from the woods and a gull perched on the rusty remains of a harrow, oiling its feathers. The farmyard was deserted, except for a coon cat and a three-colour money cat lying in the sun where the half-wild farm cats had always basked, against the south-facing wall of the cow barn, sheltered from the wind. Did each generation learn from the one before? Or did they have to make the discovery of this haven afresh for themselves?

Her feet slowed to a stop. The buildings were all perfectly sound, although the white paint on the shutters and doors of the house was beginning to flake, and the red paint on the barn was dull and weathered. The grey-brown shingles were all in place. The yard and the farm drive down to the county road were no longer beaten earth. At some time they had been tarred, but not recently. Weeds were beginning to find a toehold in small cracks and in hollows where earth had collected.

A man was sitting in one of the rocking chairs on the porch, watching her. He got slowly to his feet and came to the top of the steps, and stood looking across at her. His resemblance to her uncle Tobias was strong, but his build was more bulky, and a heavy belly bulged over his belt, suggesting a heavy eater or a beer drinker. He walked with a pronounced limp.

Tirza crossed the yard to the bottom of the steps and tilted her head back to look up at him.

'Hello, Billy,' she said.

<hr/>

They sat facing each other on the porch. Billy had resumed his seat in the rocking chair, but Tirza had taken an upright chair with a worn rush seat. She had avoided the easy posture of a rocking chair — she wanted to remain in control of this conversation.

'Mr Foss in Portland contacted me,' she said. 'I saw him in his office two days ago, and he told me you were very anxious to speak to me, but he didn't say why.'

'Ayuh,' said Billy. 'I asked him to let me explain. But let's have some coffee first.' He turned and shouted through the screen door, 'Patience! Can you bring out some coffee?'

'No call to shout, I'm right here.'

The woman elbowed the door open and it snapped shut on its spring behind her. She was carrying a tray neatly covered with a green and white checked cloth, with coffee pot and cups, and a plate of English muffins.

'Well,' she said, eyeing Tirza curiously, 'you've taken long enough to come home.'

'You remember Patience Warren, don't you?' said Billy. 'Patience Potts, as she is now.'

'Of course. How d'ye do, Patience?'

'Not too bad.'

'Patience has been my housekeeper since she was widowed fifteen years back.'

'Seem to have spent more of my life living in this house than any other. Will that do you, Mr Billy?'

'Ayuh, that's fine.'

Billy waited to speak until she had left, pouring out the coffee and passing Tirza sugar and cream, which she refused.

'Aren't you married, then, Billy?'

'Never seemed to find anyone.'

'Me neither.'

'Except Simon,' he said.

'Well.' She took a sip of her coffee.

'That would have sorted things out just fine, I've often thought, as far as the land was concerned. You'd have had kids, no doubt, and we'd all be able to see the future.'

Tirza put down her cup and looked at him.

'Is that what this is all about? The land? The farm doesn't seem to be in very good heart to me.'

'No. Well, things have never been easy for me, with my injury. And after Grandpa died and I had a spell of ill health, it's got worse. We had sheep for a while, but I couldn't shear them myself. I was paying more out in feed and vet's bills and shearers' wages than I was making out of them.'

'Uncle Tobias always had cows. There's good pasture on this land.'

'Sure, but things aren't what they were when we were kids. Round about the sixties, the government started interfering more and more. They made you put in all this new equipment. Regulations a mile long. No hand-milking. No way. The milk had to go down a tube from the udder to the tank – no contact with the air, or the whole lot had to be thrown out. There was no way I could sustain a herd large enough to cover the cost of the machinery.'

'But I saw cows over on the fields by Swansons' farm.'

'I rent out all that land to Hector Swanson. He's the big noise in this part of Maine for dairy farming. One of the first to put in a milking machine, do you recall? He cuts the hay on some of our scattered fields too. I let him have the hay cheap, in return for him keeping the land clear.'

'So what do you grow, then? Vegetables?'

'Potatoes, mostly. Other things are too labour intensive. And the Maine potato is still a commercial crop. I hire in casual labour for the picking, but otherwise I get by with a hired man on half-time. He works the rest of the time for Hector.'

'It seems a shame,' said Tirza. 'This used to be such a varied farm, always something different to do – strawberries, the dairy herd, haying, the vegetable crops, the wild berries, chickens...'

'It might have been possible, if Simon had come back, as he said he would. Grandpa was counting on that. But afterwards I guess he kind of gave up, and I wasn't able to take on the work.'

Tirza hunched over in her chair, biting her thumb and trying to see Simon walking across the yard with his swinging stride, the sun glinting off his short fair hair.

That summer of '64 in Vietnam, Tirza was beginning to make a name for herself as a war photographer. And since her newspaper had no correspondent based nearer than Hong Kong, she had started to file her own reports on her observations of the war. Official war reporting she left to others – she avoided the Five o'clock Follies, when JUSPAO held their daily briefing for the press at the Rex Hotel. Instead, she wrote pieces in which she tried to make sense of the chaos around her by concentrating on scenes she had witnessed herself. In the early days, the helicopter pilots – who would sometimes give a lift to correspondents upcountry to one of the firebases – were unwilling to have a woman aboard, so she explored Saigon and the surrounding country. Her photographs showed the Vietnamese, not the American troops. Women wading through rice fields blown apart by bomb craters. Once-elegant streets of the city, lined by French colonial buildings, where gaunt street hawkers squatted surrounded by their wares – a handful of vegetables, some tattered copies of last year's *Le Monde*, three or four cooking pots hammered out from US army scrap. And the hordes of child beggars who swarmed everywhere. Slipping between the fashionable silks of aristocratic Vietnamese ladies. Tugging at the trousers of swaggering US Marines. Their claw-like hands extended. 'You Numbah One. You gimme money.'

After a time, she established contacts amongst the helicopter crews. The journeys upcountry in the lurching choppers, the rhythmic 'whump-whump' of the rotors, the scrambled landings, the enemy gunfire raking the side as they banked and circled, hanging precariously out to get her shots of the violated country below – all of this became a way of life.

One day early in May she was making her way wearily home after a mission of three days. She had passed the Opéra and was just turning into the side street where she rented a room of decayed grandeur, infested with cockroaches, when she heard running feet behind her.

'Tirza? Tirza? Wait!'

It was Simon.

'I see you're a lieutenant-colonel now, very impressive,' she said, as they sat drinking an *apéritif* at an open air café half an hour later. She had showered and changed out of her dun-coloured trousers and jacket into a wisp of thin cotton made up for her into a simple sheath by the Franco-Vietnamese dress-maker who lived on the ground floor of her building.

'Yes.' He made a face. 'But I'm stuck here at a desk in Saigon. Not like Korea, where I was in the thick of it. I'm mostly a pen-pusher at headquarters here.'

She studied him across the table as keenly as he was studying her. It was seventeen years since they had last seen each other, the summer they graduated from high school and Tirza left Maine for good. Simon had filled out since those gawky, ado-lescent days, but he was still slender, without the solid farmer's build of his father. The glaring Vietnamese sun glanced off his fair hair and he seemed unable to take his eyes off her.

He told her about his occasional visits by helicopter to the war zone, where the US army was sweating and thrashing about in the jungle, fighting an elusive, invisible enemy, and he was sur-prised to discover that she had spent more time there than he had.

'I managed to borrow a motorbike this time,' she said, sipping the long, ice-filled drink with gratitude. 'Rode it out with my interpreter to a village that had just been "liberated". It's hard to tell which is worse for the villagers – being overrun by the Vietcong or being liberated by Americans. At least this time the village wasn't burned to the ground and the women raped by our gallant boys.'

'You sound very bitter.'

'Have you any idea what kind of hell these people are going through? No, probably not. You're part of the war machine. They talk to me, you see. A woman. And a civilian. They tell me stories that would make your hair stand on end. And of course I can't send all of it back Stateside – it would be censored. I try to hint at it in the spaces between the lines, and let the pic-tures do the talking.'

'Hey, hey!' He reached across the table and took her hand gently in both of his. 'You don't need to get mad at me. Some of us feel just as helpless.'

<hr>

After that, they met whenever they could. For half their lives they had been separated, and Tirza found she could no longer think of Simon as a brother. Sometimes they were still linked by unspoken childhood memories, but they had grown distant. For the first time she saw him as a distinct person, with his own out-line, no longer part of her flesh and blood. There was a space between them which, oddly, they both felt compelled to bridge.

About a month later, Tirza hitched a lift on an army convoy which was moving up into an area near a short section of the Ho Chi Minh trail which had just been captured by South Vietnamese troops. From their temporary camp, she set off early in the evening to take some pictures of the trail before the rapid tropical twilight fell. The track wound through the jungle, sunk a little below ground level and roofed over with vines which had been woven together into a mat of dense vegetation. From a few yards away, nothing could be seen. Inside, on the trail itself, Tirza felt as though she was making her way along one of the under-ground tunnels the Vietcong were said to have dug deep into the heart of South Vietnam. The light was poor and green, and despite allowing long exposures she was doubtful whether her shots would show anything but a muddled darkness.

She kept on going forward, however, past a group of South Vietnamese soldiers who shook their heads at her and tried to turn her back, but she pointed to her camera and to the track ahead until they shrugged and turned away.

Round the next bend the darkness was deeper, but a sudden crawling sensation on her skin told her there were people breathing nearby. Before she could retreat, in the eye-blink between knowledge and escape, hands reached out and grabbed her. A dirty rag was stuffed into her mouth and a sack smelling of chickens pulled down over her head.

Her captors tied her hands behind her back, and took away her Nikon and her army boots. Blind and choking inside the chicken sack, she had no sense of the direction in which they forced her to march. She was aware only of the speed, the hushed urgency and the pain of her bare feet stumbling over sharp branches and lassoing coils of creeper. After what seemed like hours, they halted and she sank to the ground with her head between her knees. There was whispered conferring and the clank of rifles laid down. Later, they removed her gag but kept her blindfolded, untied her hands and thrust a bowl of rice into them. With fingers numbed from the cords she stuffed the congealed mess blindly into her mouth.

It was perhaps two days later when she was pushed to the ground and knocked sideways with the butt of a rifle. She lay unprotesting as her hands were again unbound, waiting for the bowl of rice. None came. Straining her ears, she could catch no movement close by, only – at a little distance – the sound of a cock crowing and women's voices. Cautiously she pulled off her blindfold, dazed and blinking in a bar of fierce sun that sliced through the jungle canopy. Her captors had melted away into the trees and a few hundred yards ahead was a wide stretch of open ground and paddies, and a small, unkempt village, like dozens of others she had seen.

Whether the communist guerrillas had lost interest in her, or found her a burden, she could not tell. Why they had taken her hostage, and then hadn't used her or put a bullet through her head, she would never know. The villagers were neither friendly nor hostile. They looked at her sideways, then passed her on from hand to hand until eventually she was dumped within walking distance of one of the South Vietnamese forward bases.

When she managed to reach Saigon at last, Simon was beside himself. He grabbed her by the shoulders and shook her.

'Are you crazy? It's a miracle you weren't killed! Can't you at least behave with basic caution, you stupid woman?'

Then he dragged her into his arms and kissed her painfully, crushing her ribs into his, his teeth driving violently into her lips.

That afternoon he booked a suite at the Continental Palace and managed somehow – Tirza never knew how – to secure two weeks' leave. Lying half awake in the wide, sagging bed under the foamy tent of the mosquito net, Tirza watched the fading sunlight falling through the green shutters in dusty bars across Simon's bare back as he poured out drinks for them. The elderly waiter, spruce and discreet in his white starched uniform, had brought them a light meal and laid it on a bamboo table beside the window. She wrapped the sheet around herself while he set out the tiny bowls with their fragrant and mysterious contents and polished the heavily chased silver on a cloth before arranging it with meticulous care, but he kept his eyes averted from her, merely bowing in silence as Simon slipped some rustling notes into his hand.

Their room was on the first floor, overlooking the garden, and as Simon sat beside her on the bed, feeding her fragments from the china bowls as if she were a convalescent child, she closed her eyes. The tastes – lemony, spicy, strange – on her tongue mingled with the scents of jasmine and frangipani stealing in on the evening air. Occasional sounds drifted in, the chink of glasses and the murmur of soft voices, the mechanical buzz of the cicadas, a footstep in the corridor outside.

Later, lying naked in Simon's arms, she rested her cheek against his gold hair, curling and faintly damp. His sleeping head was burrowed into the hollow between her shoulder and her breast, and his hand rested lightly against the small of her back. Overhead the ceiling fan revolved slowly, hypnotically, like an ironic echo of helicopter blades, while the sweat on her own skin dried slowly until she shivered. Simon stirred, kissed the curve of her breast and fell asleep again.

While his leave lasted, they wandered in the same dreamlike state through the older, unspoiled parts of colonial Saigon, dined in one of the French or Corsican restaurants, then by unspoken mutual urge, made their way back to the Continental Palace. Sometimes, as they threaded their way through the noisy crowds thronging the terrace along the street, one of Simon's fellow officers shouted out to them. The soldiers' tiny Asian girlfriends looked like children. But Tirza hardly noticed them, sleepwalking with Simon back to the bed with its bower of white net, which stirred and swayed constantly under the rotating fan.

Simon bought her silks from Thailand and draped them round her naked body. She felt shy of him then, until he took her back into the safe, hollowed-out bed. Then their lovemaking was fierce, frantic, as though the slithering hours could be held back by its intensity.

Two days before his leave was over, Simon asked her to marry him.

She lay back against the pillows looking up at him. The scent of the frangipani was very strong tonight, after rain during the afternoon.

'Oh, Simon,' she said, laying her hands on his chest, 'I'm very fond of you. You're probably the person who matters most to me in the world, but I'm not sure I'm in love with you.'

He ran his finger over her lips, tracing their shape in the half-light.

'I know. But I think I'm in love with you. It's been creeping up on me, without my noticing. And I think you might come to love me in the same way. We're not adolescents. Caring about each other is probably more important than sexual passion, don't you think?'

She laughed. 'We seem to have found our way to that.'

'Yes, we have.' And he pulled her towards him. 'What do you say? Will you marry me, or must I work my wicked will on you without benefit of clergy?'

Laughter bubbled up in her as she pressed her face into his shoulder. 'All right,' she said, giddy with a sense of being carried away on a running tide, rudderless. 'All right, I'll marry you.'

In the morning they bought an antique French ring – an emerald the colour of the deep cleft in the ocean shelf out beyond Mustinegus, where Nathan laid many of his traps. They sent telegrams off to their families, and spent the next two days as irresponsibly as two children on an unexpected holiday.

At the end of that week, Simon had to make one of his visits to the war zone. The uncertain position of the troops had moved once again. The helicopter pilot found himself over enemy territory and before he could regain a safe position, a Vietcong rocket brought the helicopter down to the roof of the jungle, where it hit the tops of the trees and burst into flame.

The next day Tirza left the Continental Palace for her old lodgings near the Opéra, sent a telegram to Maine, and went back into the jungle with her spare camera.

Tirza picked up her cold cup of coffee and looked across the rim at Billy.

'I do understand that it's been difficult for you to run the farm, but I don't know why you wanted to see me. I'm not sure it has much to do with me, since I walked out on the family all those years ago.'

Billy cleared his throat and leaned forward, setting his large hands squarely on his plump knees.

'This farm always belonged jointly to the two brothers – my grandfather, Tobias, and your father, Nathan. They made an agreement to share out the income, the bulk of it going, of course, to Tobias, as he was working the land, but some to Nathan because of his share in the ownership and because he always did some work on the farm. As you did, too, of course. Nathan also owned the house in Flamboro and all its contents, and *Louisa Mary*. The proceeds of their sale were put into a trust for you after Nathan's death, which Foss's firm administers.'

He cleared his throat again.

'You and I are the only ones left of all the Libby family, Tirza. You own half the land already, as well as all of Nathan's own money. I've made my will. I discussed it all with Nathan before he died. I'm leaving the remainder of the property to you.'

Tirza put down her cup with a crash, so that it fell over in the saucer.

'But I don't...'

'Wait a minute.' He held up his hand to silence her.

'I always liked you, Tirza.'

He laughed, and it turned into a cough which blocked his words for several minutes. When he recovered, he smiled ruefully.

'Oh, I know you despised me. I was an awful kid. Useless and whining. I know that. But I admired you so much, and I wanted to be like you. You were so independent and courageous.'

Tirza felt shamed. How often she and Simon had pushed Billy away, avoided him, refused to take him with them, even when he could have come too – picking crab apples or visiting the Boston ladies. She started to speak again, but he interrupted her.

'You probably think I'm morbid, talking about wills and all, when I'm only forty-three. But, well, they've diagnosed lung cancer. I've only got a few months. It would settle my mind if I could know that the land was in safe hands.'

'Oh, Billy.' Tirza leaned forward and placed her hands over his. 'What has happened to us all? First Martha, then Simon, now you. Are you sure? Can't they do something for you?'

He shook his head. 'Things have gone too far. And to tell you the truth, I shan't be sorry to go. I'm so tired these days, I'd just like to lie down and sleep, and not have to get up again. Say you'll take on the land, Tirza.'

He looked at her pleadingly, and Tirza felt as though she was trapped.

'I'll have to think, Billy. I have a career of my own, you know. I'm always travelling.'

'I know.' He slumped back, as though he had grown smaller. 'It isn't really fair of me. But you know what Christina always says about our responsibility to the land.'

It was a moment before Tirza took in his words.

'What did you say? You don't mean... Girna isn't still alive?'

'Ayuh. Still living in that cabin up to the woods. Won't listen to reason.' He smiled, half proud, half exasperated. 'She's part blind, but still as tough and resilient as an old Indian squaw.'

Tirza stood up.

'I'll go and talk to her.'

By the time she had walked down the farm track and over the headland into Flamboro, Tirza was exhausted. Back at home on her island, talking to Grace on the doorstep while they watched the gulls, or making short forays to photograph Highland buildings, she had thought she had at last recovered from the long-drawn-out effects of the malaria and dysentery which had first driven her to Scotland. Now she realised that she had not fully regained her strength. In her youth she had walked constantly about these paths and cliffs, but now the distance from Todd's Neck to the farm, and from the farm to Flamboro, had left her knees weak. She sat down on one of the old bollards on the wharf and rested her chin in her hands.

Billy's news of his illness had shaken her. In her long years of wandering she had assumed that he had married, that he had a growing family of sons preparing to assume the Libby inheritance. When she had pictured the farm, she imagined a wife for Billy not unlike Harriet, briskly feeding the hens, baking her own bread, helping with the milking and harvesting when she was needed. But, of course, she had been deluding herself. Times change. And though it had been pleasant to invent a happy ending to Billy's story, she had had a hand in destroying his life.

When men had finally been able to climb down the cliff where Martha had thrown herself, racing to beat the incoming tide, they had found, as they suspected, that she had been killed at once. Billy, still gripped in her arms, was alive but unconscious, cushioned by Martha's body from the worst of the rocks. His spine was damaged. He lay in a coma for three weeks, then at last began to live, and to breathe by himself, and – eventually – to walk. But his long period in hospital put him two years behind at school. His twisted leg and back debarred him from sports. And it was difficult for him to make friends. His screaming nightmares, his blackouts, his sudden panics, frightened the other children. No wonder, then, that he had never married.

No wonder, either, that he could not cope with the farm. No wonder it looked so shabby and unloved. But he did not deserve this final blow. Inwardly, Tirza raged. She wanted to hit something, to blame someone. When Simon had been killed in Vietnam, she kept demanding, *Why?* He had survived the Korean war, when he was constantly exposed to danger. Why did it have to be his helicopter, why that pilot who strayed over enemy territory? Did you have to believe that it was predestined? And that whatever we do, we are helpless? One of the things she had been fleeing all these years was this fear of an immutable fate. That long-ago summer she had become entangled with Sandy and Martha. By her own will – or not? In the years since, she had never been able to decide whether – if she had acted differently when she took Sandy's final letter to Martha – all their lives might have been changed. Or whether Sandy's departure and Martha's death had already lain there ahead of them all, when the first strands of that summer had begun to weave together.

She wanted to believe that she had some control over her own fate. But she was afraid.

At last she stood up, wincing as her knees snapped. The road to the schoolhouse seemed longer than it used to, when she went unwillingly to lessons. The building had been extended, and the old dusty playground covered with concrete. As she walked past it the children came streaming out for their lunch hour, some of them running home across the village, others opening Snoopy and Mickey Mouse lunch-boxes, to eat under the shade of the same old maple that had stood there in her schooldays.

She climbed up the field behind the school, her calf muscles protesting. It was a relief to find that it had not been built over, as she suspected it might have been. The path over the shoulder of the hill and through the forest was clear and well trodden. Either Christina herself made regular trips to the village, or people from the village walked this way to visit her. Looking down the glades under the trees, Tirza could see here and there the sudden burst of autumn glory – a birch dangling leaves like gold pennies, a maple so brightly scarlet it seemed to be on fire. And in the spaces between the trees, the ocean. Slate blue shot with glassy green, laced with foam as the breakers rolled in and threw themselves against the booming caves under the cliff. Ebb and flow, spring tides and neaps, balmy weather and hurricane. Always changing, yet for ever there. And away over this same sea, her own small cottage and her cat faced her grandmother across those three thousand miles with the running tide between.

She walked softly down to the cabin. Smoke was rising from the fieldstone chimney. The morning's rain had penetrated to the clearing, and damp leaves stuck to her shoes as she approached the door. It stood open, as it had always done except in the worst weather. Inside, she could see a figure bent over the stove, leaning short-sightedly close to the cookpot. A rich aroma of clam chowder – warm, sea-scented and nutty – filled the living room, which had grown smaller, surely, and even more cluttered with untidy piles of books and pieces of drift-wood, and sketches laid down to dry and forgotten about.

'So you're here at last, Tirza,' said Christina, without turning round.

Tirza drew in her breath sharply, and stepped over the threshold.

'How did you know?'

Christina turned and grinned at her roguishly.

'Oh, I haven't become a seer in my decrepitude. Pete Flett's youngest lad Paul brought me a quart of clams this morning and brought me the news too. And my hearing has grown sharper, to make up for my deficiencies of sight.'

She raised her face and Tirza kissed her, noticing that her right eye was filmed over and milky.

'I get by well enough,' said Christina, answering the unspoken question. 'Certain busybodies have tried to persuade me to go into a home, or move in with Billy – who, of course, is no kin of mine. Not that I hold that against him. The selectmen wanted to buy the land again, but I'm not likely to sell it to them now. What use would the money be to me, compared with the roots of my blood and being? Cut yourself some bread, child.'

Tirza did as she was told, accepted the bowl of chowder she was handed, and sat down opposite her grandmother at the table, where every scratch and dent was like the features on the face of an old friend. They ate in comfortable silence, mopping up the rich juice with their hunks of bread.

'Paul lays a crab line in your cove down yonder,' said Christina, 'whenever he's home from medical school.'

'What happened to *Stormy Petrel*?'

'Your father kept her until he died. Kept her in good trim too. She was sold with the rest of his property.'

Christina cut a piece of blueberry pie and pushed it across the table.

'You're still baking?' Tirza asked.

'Ayuh. But there's no cream to go with it, now there are no cows on the farm. I miss it, but no doubt it's better for me to do without.'

When they had eaten their pie and washed it down with glasses of the well water, which was as sweet as ever it had been, Christina got stiffly to her feet and went to a corner beside the bookcase. She began to tug a large cardboard box towards the table, and Tirza lifted it up and carried it across.

'When they were going to sell your father's things, Billy asked me if there was anything I wanted. I saved these things for you. Go on, child, open it. They're mostly your own belongings from your bedroom.'

A lemon scent rose from the box. A layer of southernwood was spread over the contents, just inside the lid. Southernwood, for its long-lasting properties. Southernwood, called by some, old maid's comfort. Southernwood, given as a pledge of love. Tirza lifted the objects out of the box one by one. There was the patchwork quilt from her bed that Miss Molly had made for her seventh birthday, and the china-headed doll from Germany that Mrs Larrabee had given her from the shop. Her pocket knife, which she had unaccountably left behind when she went off to her vacation job at the diner. The *Rubáiyát* and the book of Audubon bird paintings, richer and more stunningly beautiful than she had remembered. Simon must have spent a fortune on it. An oval Shaker box, decorated with a primitive picture of a red barn.

'They're all there,' said Christina.

Tirza unpacked the boxes and stacked them up. Inside the smallest was the picture of Sandy beside his Spitfire. It had faded to a soft brown.

In the bottom of the cardboard carton there was something bulky.

'Lift that carefully,' said Christina. 'There is something wrapped up inside.'

The soft lumpy object was Miss Susanna's last hooked rug, the patchwork rug for which they had drawn the pictures at that long-ago tea party.

'Miss Molly left it to you in her will, with the request that I should look after it until you came back.'

'I can't think why you should all have been so sure I would come back,' said Tirza a little resentfully.

The rug had been wrapped around a small leather casket.

'I don't recognise this.'

'It's your mother's jewellery. There isn't anything of great value, but a few things have been in the family a long time. There are some old Indian pieces of silver and turquoise that my mother left to me. Nathan was going to give them to you on your twenty-first birthday.'

Tirza looked at the treasures of her childhood spread out on the table, and she wanted to say, *But all these things are dead.*

'You can do with all this whatever you want,' said Christina. 'Throw them away, if you like. But I thought the choice should be yours.'

'That's what it's all about, isn't it?' Tirza said, fingering the rug. 'Do you know what I've been talking to Billy about this morning?'

'Of course. I knew what the provisions of the wills were. Nathan told me all the details before he died. *I* said he could never count on your coming back. But he wanted you to have the choice.'

'How long has Billy been ill? I mean, with cancer? I never asked him.'

'Five or six years. Not long before your father died. He has suffered a good deal, but I don't think he has put up a fight. From the start he was resigned. Too resigned.'

Tirza looked at her curiously.

'You sound as though you think he could have done something to resist it.'

Christina spread her hands and shrugged.

'The strength of the warrior lies in the mind more than in the body.'

Tirza opened the box containing her mother's jewellery and laid it out against the dark old wood of the table. It seemed to have no connection with her.

'So you didn't think I would come back.'

'Not as long as you blamed yourself for Martha's death.'

Tirza's head snapped up.

'What makes you think that I blamed myself?'

Christina laid her hands over Tirza's. 'Child, I saw you that last evening with Sandy on the path by the cove. I was gathering firewood in the forest just above, and I saw you together. You were like two lovers. Then I heard you had been seen coming from the farm when the Tremayne house was on fire. And then Martha jumped from the cliff. You hated her for her affair with Sandy, and you blamed yourself for her death.'

Tirza turned her hands over and gripped Christina's.

'For years I did. You're right.'

'But now?'

'I've met Sandy's son. He's about the same age as I am. Did you realise Sandy already had three children?'

'I suspected he was married.'

'Did you? From what Alex has told me – the things Sandy said about Martha – and what she said to me that evening... Perhaps it would have happened anyway, once she knew he was leaving.'

'She had become unbalanced, you know, after Will's death. And she had always been a difficult girl, who flew into rages if she couldn't have her way. I think she made demands on Sandy he didn't want to give in to. She had probably created a whole fantasy in her mind.'

Tirza gave a sharp sigh and stood up.

'Poor Martha. She was so beautiful, and I always wanted her to like me, but she never did.' She heard another voice echoed in her words. *Oh, I know you despised me... But I admired you so much, and I wanted to be like you.*

'Come on, let's clear this table, and then I'll fill your water tank from the well.'

When the dishes were washed and the water carried, Christina lit a kerosene lamp against the growing dusk and closed the door of the cabin.

'I've never wished you happy birthday, Tirza.'

'Oh, I'm too old to celebrate birthdays.'

'Nonsense. You aren't much more than half my age.'

'Remember that discussion we had once? I marvelled that you could have built this house when you were an old lady of forty?'

'Yes, and I said that when you were that age, it wouldn't seem so old.'

'I still think you were marvellous.'

'Thank you for the compliment.' Christina sat down in her old rocker and clasped her hands in her lap.

'And now have you made your choice about the farm and the land? Will you come home?'

Tirza linked her fingers together.

'I have a home, on the other side of the ocean. I bought an island in Scotland, with a cottage and a pier. I have a cat. And I have friends in the village on the mainland. I'm putting down roots.'

'Well, you already had roots there. My father came from the Highlands, remember.'

'So he did... I don't know... Is it possible to live both there and here? To have a foot on either side of the ocean?' She laughed wryly. 'To bestride the ocean like a colossus?'

For a long time they were silent, while the cliffs echoed to the running tide and the wind – rising with the onset of darkness – thrashed in the trees.

'In Vietnam...' said Tirza, 'Simon and I... we slept together. For two wonderful, strange weeks. In the middle of all that ugliness and pain and violence, we had this magical time of peace and extraordinary joy. I've never felt like that before or since... After he was killed, I found I was pregnant. It was the only thing that kept me going. It was as if, carrying his child, I had to go on living, survive the ambushes and shellfire, the crazy risks.'

She lifted her face to Christina, and tears ran thinly down her cheeks.

'I felt that the baby... somehow, it would mean that Simon hadn't died altogether. But I lost it at five months. I've never told anyone before. They patched me up – I had to go to one of the forward field hospitals. They told me to go home. But I didn't have any home. Less than ever.'

She held out her hands.

'Why is it that everything I touch is blighted? I sow death in my footsteps.'

'No!' said Christina, getting up and striding to the door. She threw it open and the wind and tide rushed in like a voice crying out.

'You can't live in the past. The past is a country of the mind – we wander there like dreamers in a shadowy landscape that hides its meaning from us.'

'I don't mean to live in the past,' said Tirza quietly. 'I've been running away for years to try to escape it, yet it was always there. At the same time I kept seeking out danger. It was as if...'

She stopped.

'As if... I had to keep testing my right to be alive. Martha died. Billy was terribly injured. Sandy – I thought – had been killed after he went back to the war. Then Simon was killed. By going constantly into danger, I was offering myself up to death. It was a kind of sickness. Only in the last year, living in Scotland, with the sea as my neighbour again, have I begun to feel... not healed, exactly, but as though something within me was turning.'

'There are seasons in our lives,' said Christina, 'a pattern, like the old Indian cross within a circle. Our lives move round the circle, but not always at the same pace. You have been caught too long in the north, which teaches strength and endurance through suffering, but you don't have to remain there. When you were young, you ran away. And losing Simon and his child must have seemed like an echo of what had happened with Sandy and Martha. But you also moved on. Do you think the work you have done since then has been worthless? You have focused the world's attention on poverty and suffering which would have gone unheeded. Was that worthless? You have inspired operations and campaigns to relieve hunger and igno-rance. Was that worthless?'

Christina drew a long breath.

'Once, you were courageous. Has that vanished? Are you going to remain fixed, speared for ever on past tragedies? Remember the other quadrants of the circle. The west gives rain, the south warmth, and the east peace and light. You have the rest of your life ahead of you. Live it. The only way to find joy is by creating it.'

Tirza came and stood beside her, and put her arm around her grandmother. Once, Christina had seemed so tall. Now she barely reached Tirza's shoulder, but the wiry back was as straight and springy as one of the trees in her own forest.

'I will try,' she said.

THE ANNIVERSARY

The most evocative and compelling family novel since Rosamunde Pilcher's *The Shellseekers*, *The Anniversary* sweeps the reader into the fabric of a family, a community and an era.

It is June 11th 1994 in the depths of Herefordshire and Natasha Devereux's family and two hundred guests gather together to celebrate the fiftieth anniversary of St. Martins. From the vision of one woman who fled Bolshevik Russia and opened her doors to artists, musicians, writers and refugees from war-torn Europe it has become a sanctuary for five generations of a family who – over the course of one day – face marital crisis, impending birth, teenage trauma, a father's roving eye into forbidden territory, momentous news from the past, communal financial crisis, and a lost love from the summer of '57.

As the evening shadows spread-eagle across the lawn to the rambling house and the great old copper beech, Natasha comes to the fruition of her life's work. The kaleidoscope of memory has been shaken, decisions have been taken. There has been a birth, and a death, but above all a celebration.

THE TRAVELLERS

Sofia Niklai, a reclusive exile, and Kate Milburn, locked in a stifling marriage, form a tentative friendship on a windswept beach in Northumbria. While Sofia forces herself to confront her father's diaries, Kate must face half-remembered shadows from her childhood. Together they make an impulsive journey to Hungary, Sofia's homeland. It is a journey from which neither can return unaltered.

Their meeting in Hungary with Istvan Rudnay, also marked by the dark experiences of his youth, leads them to a discovery of the warmth and love so lacking in their own lives, whilst he in turn comes to a reconciliation with the past and hope for the future.

Sharply observed and recounted with tenderness and wisdom, *The Travellers* delineates the intense joys and sorrows of individual lives upon a broad canvas of recent European history.

ONE TRUE THING

Anna Quindlen

A young woman is in jail accused of the mercy killing of her mother. She says she didn't do it.

Ellen Gulden is a young, successful New York journalist. When her mother gets cancer, her father, a university professor, insists she come home. As she looks after her mother their relationship – tender, awkward and revealing – deepens and Ellen is forced to confront painful truths about her adored father.

But as Kate lies dying, and in the weeks that follow her death, events take a shocking and unexpected turn. Family emotions are laid bare as a new drama is played out: between Ellen and her brothers, between Ellen and her father, and in court.

OBJECT LESSONS

Anna Quindlen

'Afterwards, all the rest of her life would seem to her a hereafter. Here and hereafter, and in between was that summer, the time of changes.'

Young Maggie Scanlan begins to sense that, beneath the calm, everyday surface of her peaceful life, everything is going strangely wrong. Her all-powerful grandfather is reduced to a shadow by a stroke, and to Maggie's astonishment this causes her usually unemotional father to burst into tears. Connie, her lushly beautiful mother, who Maggie could always be sure of finding at home, is now rarely there. And her cousin and her best friend start doing things that leave her confused and frightened about sex and sin.

WILD YOUNG BOHEMIANS

Kate Saunders

Melissa Lamb and her cousin Ernestine are at the centre of the Wild Young Bohemians, an exclusive dining club at Oxford for the beautiful and ambitious. Melissa is in the grip of an obsession. Ernestine however, mild and practical, does not see through Melissa's ruthless determination to restore her derelict family mansion – a Gothic legacy of lust, greed and death, with a spectacular secret that has slept for a hundred years.

Melissa will let nothing stand in her way – until a vengeful stranger enters their magic circle. But he is only a catalyst: the seed of evil is already sown.

LILY-JOSEPHINE

Kate Saunders

Lily-Josephine had a talent for love. Wilful, enchanting and passionate, she was the centre of a charmed universe – until her foolish, indulgent father married again. Like Snow-Drop in Grimms' fairy tale, Lily ran from her jealous stepmother one idyllic summer evening in 1941. She escaped to find sanctuary but, at Randalls, discovered a love far greater than any she had ever known . . .

A generation later the events set in train that night begin to unravel when Sophie Gently falls in love with Octavius Randall and the bizarre and tragic history linking their families is uncovered.

Praise for Kate Saunders:

'Hugely enjoyable, glossy, sexy and wittily turned' *The Times*

'Gripping and entertaining' *Sunday Telegraph*

'A marvellous read' Jilly Cooper

SEESAW

Deborah Moggach

Take an ordinary, well-off family like the Prices. Watch what happens when, one Sunday, seventeen-year-old Hannah disappears without a trace. See how the family rallies when a ransom note demands half a million pounds for Hannah's safe return.

But it's when Hannah comes home that the story really begins.

Now observe what happens to a family when they lose their house, their status, all their wealth. Note how they disintegrate under the pressures of guilt and poverty and are forced to confront their true selves.

And finally, wait to hear about Hannah, who has the most shocking surprise in store of all.

CLOSE RELATIONS

Deborah Moggach

Louise, Prudence and Maddy are three grown-up sisters happy to lead very different lives. But when their father leaves their mother, his wife of forty years, they find their own lives too are plunged into chaos. Passions run high as the different generations bicker, fall out, test their emotions and pick up the pieces in this rich and profound novel of generations and family.

Praise for Deborah Moggach:

'Moggach is a skilful narrator, deftly weaving together the threads of each family member's life, creating an instantly recognisable world' *Daily Telegraph*

A SIMPLE LIFE

Rosie Thomas

Hidden beneath the comfortable family life she shares with her successful husband Matthew and their two perfect sons lies a shameful secret that has haunted Dinah for fifteen years. She and Matt never speak of it or the impossible choice he forced her to make all those years ago; they think the cracks have been papered over.

But when a chance encounter brings the past into sharp focus once more, Dinah realises she can no longer deny the truth. She decides to risk everything – her husband, her sons, her perfect lifestyle – in order to claim what was always hers.

EVERY WOMAN KNOWS A SECRET

Rosie Thomas

What happens when you fall in love with the one person you shouldn't?

In the aftermath of a family tragedy Jess Arrowsmith is powerless to resist her attraction to Rob, twenty years her junior, and the person she has reason to hate most in the world. As their love affair threatens to blow her family apart, Jess finds herself in a desperate struggle to defuse a crisis that puts at risk all she holds dear.

Praise for Rosie Thomas:

'She tells her story with seductive skill' *The Times*

'Immensely sensitive, full of insight' *Woman's Journal*

'Honest and absorbing, Rosie Thomas mixes the bitter and the hopeful with the knowledge that the human heart is far more complicated than any rule suggests' *Mail on Sunday*

INTO THE FOREST

Jean Hegland

Nell and Eva live alone in the forest. Recently orphaned and completely isolated, they struggle for normality in a post-holocaust world in which the busy hum of society is slowly replaced by the silence of nature. From chaos comes strength however, and through this cataclysmic destruction the sisters discover their hidden power. As they blaze a path into the forest and into an unknown future, they become pioneers and pilgrims – not only creatures of the new world, but the creators of it.

At once a poignant and lyrical portrayal of the power of sisterly loyalty and a horrifying cautionary tale about the future of humanity, *Into the Forest* is a deeply moving account of human nature and our fragile existence on earth.

'A truly admirable addition to a genre defined by the very high standards of George Orwell's *1984* and Russell Hoban's *Riddley Walker*' *Publishers Weekly*

ELECTRICITY

Victoria Glendinning

Charlotte Mortimer, a spirited, sensual young woman, is testing the limits of her world. A world bounded by strict conventions, a world on the brink of change. And Charlotte is going too far . . .

Electricity is a tour de force, a fast-moving novel, both funny and moving, about connections, contacts and shocks – electrical, emotional, sexual, intellectual. Set in the 1880s, it is the story of one spirited, sensual young woman's adventure, recounted with wit, candour and an intimacy of closely observed domestic and technical detail.

OTHER BESTSELLING TITLES IN ARROW

☐	The Anniversary	Ann Swinfen	£5.99
☐	The Travellers	Ann Swinfen	£5.99
☐	One True Thing	Anna Quindlen	£5.99
☐	Object Lessons	Anna Quindlen	£5.99
☐	Wild Young Bohemians	Kate Saunders	£5.99
☐	Lily-Josephine	Kate Saunders	£5.99
☐	Seesaw	Deborah Moggach	£5.99
☐	Close Relations	Deborah Moggach	£5.99
☐	A Simple Life	Rosie Thomas	£5.99
☐	Every Woman Knows A Secret	Rosie Thomas	£5.99
☐	Into the Forest	Jean Hegland	£5.99
☐	Electricity	Victoria Glendinning	£5.99

ALL ARROW BOOKS ARE AVAILABLE THROUGH MAIL ORDER OR FROM YOUR LOCAL BOOKSHOP AND NEWSAGENT.

PLEASE SEND CHEQUE/EUROCHEQUE/POSTAL ORDER (STERLING ONLY) ACCESS, VISA, MASTERCARD, DINERS CARD, SWITCH OR AMEX.

EXPIRY DATE .... SIGNATURE...

PLEASE ALLOW 75 PENCE PER BOOK FOR POST AND PACKING U.K.

OVERSEAS CUSTOMERS PLEASE ALLOW £1.00 PER COPY FOR POST AND PACKING.

ALL ORDERS TO:

ARROW BOOKS, BOOKS BY POST, TBS LIMITED, THE BOOK SERVICE, COLCHESTER ROAD, FRATING GREEN, COLCHESTER, ESSEX CO7 7DW.

NAME...

ADDRESS ....

....

Please allow 28 days for delivery. Please tick box if you do not wish to receive any additional information ☐

Prices and availability subject to change without notice.